Praise for
The Secret Sisters

"Honesty, humor, and fearlessness. Illu
all women navigate."

"Believable. . . . Brilliant. . . . Beautifull

Armchairinterviews.com

"A page-turner, full of surprises, insight, and spine-tingling erotica."
—*Helena Independent Record*

"Penetrating. . . . Honest. . . . A rough gem of a narrative. Death, danger, sexual discovery, and resurrection." —*Missoula Independent*

"Not entertainment in the traditional sense . . . it's an emotional maelstrom worth getting wrapped up in." —*Easton Express-Times*

"A modern tragedy. . . . Rodgers wisely resists the temptation to whip up tidy endings, and her smart choices give *The Secret Sisters* the necessary measure of grit."
—*Texas Monthly*

"Rodgers's tale finds its full measure as a story of a woman who comes through the most painful losses with a renewed appreciation for life."
—*Booklist*

Praise for
Bald in the Land of Big Hair

"Ms. Rodgers's . . . book is impressive in its immediacy. With engaging honesty . . . she describes in ways others may find helpful how cancer has affected her sexuality, her faith, [and] her life with her family."
—*New York Times*

"A mix of Molly Ivins's blowsy wit and Anna Quindlen's suburban logic, [*Bald in the Land of Big Hair*] manages the rare literary feat of being painful and funny in one urgent breath." —*Entertainment Weekly*

Also by Joni Rodgers

Crazy for Trying

Sugar Land

Bald in the Land of Big Hair

The Secret Sisters

A NOVEL

Joni Rodgers

HARPER PERENNIAL

NEW YORK • LONDON • TORONTO • SYDNEY

HARPER PERENNIAL

A hardcover edition of this book was published in 2006 by Harper-Collins Publishers.

FIRST HARPER PERENNIAL EDITION PUBLISHED 2007.

Designed by Joseph Rutt

The Library of Congress has catalogued the hardcover as follows:
The secret sisters : a novel / Joni Rodgers.—1st ed.
p. cm.
ISBN-13: 978-0-06-083138-7
ISBN-10: 0-06-83138-3
1. Women—Texas—Fiction. 2. Houston (Texas)—Fiction. 3. Loss (Psychology)—Fiction. 4. Children—Death—Fiction. 5. Women prisoners—Fiction. 6. Sisters—Fiction. 7. Widows—Fiction. I. Title.

PS3568.O34816S43 2006
813'.54—dc22 2005050802

ISBN: 978-0-06-083139-4 (pbk.)
ISBN-10: 0-06-083139-1 (pbk.)

07 08 09 10 11 ❖/RRD 10 9 8 7 6 5 4 3 2 1

For Gary

I owe you.

This is the debt I pay
Just for one riotous day . . .
Slight was the thing I bought,
Small was the debt I thought,
Poor was the loan at best—
God! but the interest!

—Paul Laurence Dunbar, "The Debt"

Part I

A Little Sorrow, a Little Sin

Pia

Whatever happened later, Pia could always know that her eyes were even more green than *something* and that *something something* else. Edgar never finished the sentence, and Pia lacked his way with words, so she hadn't even a good guess as to what he was about to say.

"I love that color on you," he whispered just before the entire world collapsed inward. "It makes your eyes even more green than . . ." *something.*

He did that sometimes. Whispered in her ear. When he'd been drinking a little and watching her from across the room, thinking of later things and earlier things and all sorts of things that were possible between them. Sometimes he didn't even say anything that made sense. He just murmured "la la la" and jangled her earring with the tip of his tongue, and for some reason Pia found this more sensuously eloquent than any words. Edgar was ridiculously inventive with his tongue.

"I'm not a handsome man," he told Pia when they were first dating, "but I am blessed with moments of amazing dexterity." And those moments emerged as promised over the twenty years they were together.

"It makes your eyes even more green . . ."

She definitely heard that much. Keeping her gaze forward, her expression composed, Pia leaned slightly into the whisper. She smiled and tilted her head so that his mouth brushed close to her hair. She wasn't really listening for specific syllables, just allowing his breath against her neck.

It was New Year's Eve. They were at a party, surrounded by polite laughter and chamber music and expensive perfume. They were dressed up. Edgar wasn't usually a dressed-up sort of person, but he looked good in a tux and didn't mind wearing one in winter, when Houston isn't as hot. This was one of the museum's major annual fund-raising events. People with money to donate had to be finessed into forking it over, and every year Edgar did his tie-and-tails best to romance the big benefactors. He was decked out in what he called "Sunday-go-to-meetin'" clothes, even though this wasn't Sunday and "meetin'" had not been a part of their lives for a long time. Pia regretted that later. She wished she'd made an issue of it and dragged him to mass; wished they'd had the boys confirmed and Sunday-schooled, giving them some sort of faith to seize on to when loss yawned like a sinkhole, destabilizing and swallowing everything for miles.

something something

She didn't quite catch it. Pia was left with that unfinished edge unraveling between her ear and the part of her brain that would have collected the words carefully, kept them in a private time capsule. Edgar's Last Words. Part of his private obituary, along with so many other details of him no archaeologist could ever dig deep enough to discern. His sleeping sounds. How he pressed his knuckle under his nose when he was angry, trying not to say something cruel. The way he cracked the boys up by orating street signs in an officious announcer voice.

"Accurate Air Incorporated," he would read from the back of a truck, and then tag it with a fake slogan. "We incorporate air accurately!"

Edgar Wright Ramone, PhD, curator of Eastern European displays, husband of eighteen years, father of James and Jesse, Eagle Scout, cribbage shark, master of the Cajun barbecue, a man blessed with moments of amazing dexterity, whispered his last words to his wife.

something something

Then suddenly, soundlessly, he simply crumpled. And not gracefully or in slow motion. It was an abrupt, boneless descent. His champagne flute shattered on the museum's marble floor. His chin glanced off Pia's shoulder, leaving a small, blue bruise. There was no extending of the hands, no attempt to balance or catch himself. Pia felt in her feet the solid knock of his head against the mosaic tile circle, above which a huge pendulum swung, illustrating the rotation of planet Earth. It happened so fast, Pia didn't even drop her champagne. Someone took it from her hand as she knelt down, confused, calling Edgar's name.

"Edgar?" It was a question, not a scream or even an exclamation. "*Edgar?*"

The party guests tried not to look, looked, were embarrassed for the couple they assumed to be drunk, became curious, grew concerned, told an intern to call 911, watched a doctor in evening attire administer CPR, told the chamber musicians to stop, stood stunned, sat stunned, and finally left whispering, passing hushed voices back and forth. The sibilant consonants and breathy vowels made a shuffling sound, like paper unfolding behind their hands.

Shush sha . . . said maybe an aneurysm . . . sha sha . . . family . . . really makes you think about . . .

Edgar ended with the dying moments of the year. It turned midnight as they placed him on a gurney. Bells rang across the city. It was 2001. Pia got into the ambulance with Edgar's body. The sirens were silent, and the driver talked on his radio with the same rustling paper tone as the partygoers.

There was paperwork. Forms to sign. A required explanation of legalities before she could officially release his organs for donation. Pia did all that. Then she had to call home and tell the twins to come and get her because she'd left the car at the museum, and they came, and she had to tell them their father was dead. The sun rose on the new year a little while later, but instead of finding Pia the Wife where it had left her, it came up on an empty place, and in the shadows stood Pia the Widow.

Pia's brother, Sonny, and his wife, Beth, worked at a funeral home, so the business of family attrition and human disposal was something they knew from every angle. Beth was the office manager. Sonny's profession was a little less self-explanatory. His business card said "Death Event Coordinator." Pia didn't know if the death was the event or if the event was the whole production that had to be coordinated afterward, but whichever—this was his profession now. He had an appropriate vehicle in which to convey death, a price list, a planning guide, an embossed order of worship. There was a flowchart of steps to be taken, none of which led to despair or chaos—only loss. And Sonny saw loss as a fordable stream.

He sat with Pia at her kitchen table and led her through a workbook called *Coping with End of Life Issues*. Pia was grateful and amazed that she could feel so calmed, so cradled by compassion as he presented all this unthinkable information. It was the innate priest in him, she decided. He no longer wore the collar, but he was still a minister, a comforter.

"Beth suggested we plan the memorial service at our church," he said, showing her a little floor plan of the sanctuary and fellowship hall. "I'm not sure we'd have adequate seating at the funeral home."

"The church doesn't mind that we're not . . ." Pia wasn't sure what word she should use—noun, adjective, or verb.

"God doesn't read labels." Sonny set his arm around her shoulders in a brotherly one-armed hug and added a small, bracing squeeze. "The United Methodist policy is open hearts, open minds, open doors. We're pretty lax about who comes and goes."

After Sonny left, Pia called her sister, Lily, and Lily cried, her voice muffled and hoarse.

"*Oh, Pia! Oh, my God!*" Lily wept softly, the phone cupped close to her mouth for what little privacy was possible. "I'm so sorry I can't be there for you right now."

Lily's attorney tried to arrange for Lily to attend the funeral, but prison officials could not be persuaded, and this made Pia so sad. Lily and Edgar had always been great friends, and it would have meant a lot to Pia to have her sister beside her in the blowing rain at the cemetery. Usually, a family can depend on funerals to force some semblance of togetherness, but with such irreparably tangled circumstances and the wind whipping so, what was left of Pia's little family was effectively shredded to a few loose strands.

Sonny orchestrated everything from Edgar's body in the morgue to Edgar's ashes in the vase. No, the *urn*. They didn't call it a vase. Pia wondered if it would be incredibly crass to use it for one after the ashes were scattered over the Gulf of Mexico. It was ridiculously expensive. She wasn't about to just throw it away. Edgar wouldn't have liked that. (Not that it mattered much what Edgar would or wouldn't have liked. Edgar would have *liked* to be *alive*.) Pia leaned over to Sonny and asked him at the church. About the vase. About the appropriateness of using it and whether it would hold water.

Sonny listened carefully to her question, nodding and holding her hand. He suggested she wait and see how she felt about it later. Then he called someone on his cell phone and said it looked like rain, so they were going to want the canvas pavilion set up at the cemetery after all. But the canvas pavilion did little to keep back the bitterness of the day. Flapping in the wind, it struggled to define the ritual space, to form a firmament between the cold, soaked sky and Edgar's empty grave. Pia didn't understand why it was necessary to be there. Sonny told her something about dedicating the site, even though the actual remainder of Edgar's body was in a black plastic container in the trunk of Pia's car. Edgar's parents had had his name carved on the stone between their names, as if they hadn't expected him to forge granite-worthy bonds to anyone else in his life, and somehow, their dying wish overwhelmed Pia's living preference.

At the cemetery, Jesse and James stood like sentries on either side of their mother; pale gray eyes forward, dry and stubborn; square jaws set hard, lips bowed slightly, pulling back against the sorrow; broad shoulders forming a straight line with the brim of Pia's netted black hat. The twins were not quite eighteen. Over the past year, they had become unrecognizably tall. At some point their soft curly hair got cropped off and businesslike, and their voices descended in pitch from angels to men. They had men's complexions. No more baby-soft cheek and chin, no adolescent petulance or stubborn acne. Their faces were stippled with five o'clock shadow on the sides and above the mouth. Pia realized she should have told them to shave, but their shaving was something she'd never even thought about. Edgar paid attention to that sort of thing.

She kept noticing small fissures like this. Cracks in the wall. Edgar had been the mortar of their immediate family. The boys were exactly what Edgar raised them to be. Strong. Kind. Responsible. Pia was proud of them. When it was time to walk away from the grave, they each offered her an arm, and she tucked her hands into the warm crooks of their elbows. It felt good, but they smelled so much like Edgar, she had to pull away.

Beth was in her element, setting out dessert bars and bubbled brown casseroles back at the fellowship hall. She had the reception organized down to the last wedge of bundt cake, assisted by a group of stout, oldish women from her church. As the afternoon wound down, Beth stood beside Pia and kept the receiving line moving along; squeezing each person's hands tightly between her own, reminding them to sign the guest book, assuring them that the very hairs of our heads are numbered and that Edgar was now celebrating an eternity of joyful adoration in the presence of the Prince of Peace.

Pia stuck with a simple "Thank you so much for coming."

"Don't be so brave," said Jenna, whom Pia would have introduced as her boss, even though Jenna would have introduced herself as a friend. "You are absolutely entitled to fall apart, Pia. And I want you to take as much time as you need, okay? This is all about you and the boys getting through this. I don't want to see you back in the office for at least a month."

Pia nodded. She nodded a lot that day, without even hearing what she was agreeing to, or thanking someone for, or giving a general acknowledgment of.

Edgar was such a wonderful man.

Nod.

The boys look so much like Edgar.

Nod.

Now you be sure and call me if there's anything I can do.

Nod.

How are you holding up, hon?

Nod.

Edgar's family, friends, business associates—all the population of his life story—trailed off into the waning winter afternoon. Pia found herself leaning against the wall in the ladies' room of a church her soul didn't know. Through the air vent, she heard Sonny talking on his cell phone. Everything went pretty well, he was telling someone. Yeah, he was saying, things were pretty much wrapped up. In the church kitchen, Beth bent over the sink, the sleeves of her stodgy brown cardigan pushed up over the dishwater. She looked like a sparrow with stubby, worn wings.

As Pia walked out across the parking lot with James and Jesse, the sky lowered itself into a faded January sort of light that, even in a place where it's always warm, feels gray and gives out far too willingly. Too quietly. Too soon.

Beth

This is a good day for Beth.

She is happy and most at home when she is cradled by creed, instructed by ritual. Officially, she's the office manager for Olson & Sons Funeral Home, but because she helps people arrange financing, she often becomes involved with them and feels obliged to attend services. Today is a very big service. Three high school students have been killed in a car accident. Drag racing. Just like some tragic song from the 1950s. Only real. Permanent. They don't get to live again every time K-Classic Radio has an All-Nostalgia Weekend. Today is the funeral for the sophomore who was ejected from the backseat.

The grief of the parents is palpable. Pure and blinding as unfiltered sunlight. It is mercifully unimaginable for most people—the sense of amputation, the broken mirror that is the death of a child—but not for Beth. She is intimate with grief. Consecrated by it. Commissioned. Beth has been ordained by grief to serve the grieving. Grief is her mandate. It sanctifies and empowers her.

Everyone is given a candle on the way in to the sophomore's service, and during the closing prayer, hot wax dribbles down, burning a bit at first, then forming a warm wax glove over the tip of Beth's thumb. It quickly hardens to a protective armor but still feels smooth as margarine. Beth imagines this is what it feels like to be embalmed.

For some people, funerals are funerals. Dry mouths, wet eyes, seven-layer salad, all the protocol that provides a framework in which to begin a widowhood or acknowledge one's status as an adult orphan. But for Beth these are opportunities to minister. To be an example of faith. Beth knows that somewhere in the process there will be a moment when she will take the client's hand and say, "Sonny and I do understand what you're going through. My husband lost his mother to emphysema three years ago. And then his father died. A stroke. Very sudden. And then," Beth says, gently folding the client's hand between both of hers, "two years ago, our only child, our little daughter Easter, was killed by a drunk driver."

This has a startling effect on clients. If they are not there due to the loss of a child, they suddenly feel lucky. And if they are there due to the loss of a child, they feel a little less alone. They are generally more receptive to both the financial issues and Beth's gentle nudge toward a less secular service.

"One moment, she was our bright, beautiful little girl," she tells them. "The next moment, she was a lamb in the arms of Christ. And knowing that she is with her King, I am able to rejoice, even in my sorrow."

She doesn't tell the client that the drunk driver was Sonny's sister Lily, who is now rotting in prison. Beth refrains from mentioning that in public, because she would never hurt or embarrass Sonny by airing fetid little family details to strangers. She refrains from mentioning it in private, because it still tastes like sulfur. The syllables of that woman's name strike across Beth's tongue like a match. Having to speak it during the trial, the appeals, the sentencing hearing—having to say *I have, with the help of God, forgiven Lily* and *I pray for Lily* and *I believe Lily is a changed person since her drug and alcohol rehabilita-*

tion program—this has left Beth's mouth permanently scarred. Disfigured. She had to say those things. For Sonny. And to set a Christian example. She swallowed the truth and let the law of kindness bind her mouth. But the truth remains just under the surface like a latent cold sore.

That's not what the client needs to hear. That's not the message God has laid on Beth's heart to share. Clients often find a reason to call Beth after the funeral. Sometimes it's months later when the true mass and measure of bereavement begin to hang on them like a leaded vest, weighting their shoulders and compressing their chests. Beth is always ready for that call. She has a bookmark in her Bible at Isaiah 43:19.

> *I will make a way through the wilderness and*
> *streams in the dry land.*

"God will make a way for you in this wilderness," she assures the client. "If we dwell in the dry land of sorrow and anger, we deny ourselves the joy of living in Christ. We can't always understand God's plan," she tells them, "but we know it is wondrous and filled with love."

Beth has also gleaned a number of beautiful poems from the Internet.

> *There's a land called Understanding*
> *Far across Sorrow Sea.*
> *If I hope to walk its landing*
> *I must* da da da dee dee.

Beth doesn't know them all by heart, but she has them in file folders with several other uplifting printouts she's run across in her struggle to discover the benign purpose to God's mysterious plan. She is certain there is one. She often gets thank-you cards, and she sees these as proof that her suffering was designed to bless others. Yes, Easter's death feels like a vicious, violating miscarriage of everything just and holy, but to view it that way would be a betrayal of faith. So Beth clings to the scripture and soldiers on.

Unfortunately, Pia is not ready for Isaiah 43:19. She is not open to exploring God's purpose in taking Edgar home, and she's made it clear on more than one occasion that her heart is hardened to any spiritual gifts or lessons that might come out of it. Pia has taken a lengthy leave from her job, let her yard and garden go to weeds, and firmly entrenched herself in the dry land of sorrow. With her smart suits and smooth French knot of sleek honey-gold hair, she was always razor-stylish. Now she looks fragile, bloodless, dry as onion paper. She has faded from classically slender to sickly thin. A sleepless blue semicircle smudges the translucent skin beneath her overcast gray eyes. A backwash of dishwater-gray growth at her forehead and temple shows how long it's been since she had her roots done.

Half an inch a month. Six months since Edgar died. Three inches of sorrow.

After the sophomore's funeral, Beth goes home, warms up a lasagna she prepared earlier, and carefully covers it with Reynolds Wrap. At least once a week, she goes to Pia's house with a roast chicken or Hungarian casserole or Yankee pot roast. For the boys. Pia was never one for cooking, so Beth worries that they haven't been eating as well as they did when Edgar held down the fort. While many young widows are left to struggle with new and unfamiliar responsibilities having to do with money and career, Pia has found herself in the uncharted territory of her own home.

Here is the result of ignoring God's design for the family, Beth thinks, but of course she never says that out loud. *Judge not, lest ye be judged*, Jesus said.

Pia and Edgar were a couple of the new order. His job was inconstant, rising and falling at the pleasure of grant givers and fund-raisers. Between lengthy sabbaticals, he worked twenty or thirty hours a week, much of that in his office at home. Pia went back to work less than a month after the twins were born, leaving Edgar to care for them—to *mother* them—while she built her reputation as an authority on the environmental impact of the oil industry. They bought a house in the suburbs so the boys could go to school there, but Pia's commute into downtown Houston carved an additional eighty minutes of family time off each end of the day.

At first, Pia worked as a liaison between the oil industry and the EPA, which meant she made occasional trips to Washington. Then she started working for a Houston law firm whose primary focus was suing industrial polluters and playing on the sympathy of jurors, shaming them into awarding massive punitive damages to leukemia patients and women with vague autoimmune complaints. Pia's industry expertise was suddenly worth a great deal of money. Poor Edgar was her anchor, maintaining a place for her to come home to as she traveled here, there, and everywhere. She was in Sacramento the day of Easter's baptism. She listened to most of the boys' little school plays and soccer games over a cell phone from Baltimore or New York City or Detroit. And the one time Beth made a tiny little comment about it, Pia got ridiculously defensive and stomped off.

"C'mon, Beth," Edgar had said with a sigh that might have been long-suffering, or maybe just plain suffering. "Give it a rest. I know it's not the Cleaver way, but it makes perfect sense for us. Pia's doing important work, for which she gets handsomely paid, and that enables me to stay home and do what I love. I'm taking good care of the boys, so they're happy. I'm writing grant proposals, so the museum is happy. Pia's kicking butt and taking names. Everybody's happy! How is this not a good thing?"

Now he knows. You reap what you sow. Beth hopes he is looking down on them as Pia harvests the bitter fruit of her own ambition.

Lily

(102 days)

I had a little Sorrow,
Born of a little Sin,
I found a room all damp with gloom
And shut us all within.

Finally allowed to go to the missionary women's book mobile library thingy today. Checked out Complete Works of Edna St. Vincent Millay.

Letter from Pia. Hope to hear from King tomorrow.

(103 days)

Pia called. As soon as I heard her voice, I started bawling.

PIA: Lily, hush. Stop fussing. You don't want to draw attention to yourself.

ME: I'm sorry, I'm sorry, I'm sorry.

(104 days)

Reading Like Water for Chocolate, a book about yearning.

No Pia call.
No King.

(105 days)

King called. He got a new car. Traded in my Mustang. I'm OK with that, but he took my name off the insurance policy, which makes sense, but it also makes me feel one more step away from home.

KING: Lil, it makes no sense to pay the higher premium because of your DUIs when you aren't even here to drive the friggin' thing.

ME: I know! It just makes me feel bad. I can't help it.

KING: If you want me to go down there and—

ME: No. That would be stupid. Especially with all the money we owe for the lawyer and everything. And who knows what kind of job I'll be able to get after this.

KING: We can't think about that right now, Lil. We just gotta concentrate on getting you out. Schickler says he'll have an answer later this week. About the appeal. He's feeling pretty confident. He's going to get the sentence overturned, and you'll come home, and we'll get our life back, car insurance and all, OK, babe?

ME: Yeah. OK.

KING: It'll be OK.

ME: OK. Just keep telling me that.

(107 days)

Letter from Pia. Short but sweet. King called, all ecstatic about getting this huge contract to do landscaping for all the county library branches. This takes a lot of pressure off, though we might still lose the house. He was out celebrating with the crew and called me from Paddy's Ice House, sounding like the great big goofy good ol' boy, whom I love. Haven't heard him so happy in a long time.

So I go to sleep glad.

(108 days)

Reading The Hours, a book about letting go.

No Pia call.
No King.

(109 days)

No Pia call.
No King.

(110 days)

Library day. Returned E Abbey Desert Solitaire and checked out a Stephen King novel, which some friggin' criminal skank promptly ripped off. King called and was totally unsympathetic.

KING: Lily, it's a lousy paperback novel. Who gives a crap?

ME: I do! I have to pay for that out of my work account, and I don't dare say a word for fear some friggin' criminal skank will beat me up in the laundry room. And now I have no book to read for at least three days. That's what really burns my ass.

KING: Hey, Lil, you know what really burns my ass? A flame about this high.

ME: Ha ha. I vaguely remember when that joke was funny. Sadly, you've told it about ten thousand times since then. And it doesn't work on the phone.

KING: Geezes, you're in a lousy mood today.

ME: Oh, ya think? I can't imagine why I would be.

KING: Look, I'll send you a friggin' book, OK? I'll send it today.

ME: Don't yell at me!

KING: (escalating up like a friggin' up escalator) I'm doing my damnedest to help you get through this, Lil. What the hell else do you want from me!

ME: Don't hang up! King? King, are you still there?

KING: Shh, baby, stop. I'm here. I wouldn't hang up on you. Geezes. Calm down. Christ.

ME: King, you gotta call Schickler. Tell him he's gotta get me out of here. I can't do this.

KING: Lily, he's on it. Hang in there, babe.

ME: I can't do it, King. I can't.

(111 days)

Numerical symmetry. And it's worth remarking upon. That's how pathetic my life is.

Pia letter.
No King.

(112 days)

No Pia call.
No King.

(114 days)

Pia called. Finally!

PIA: I know. I'm sorry I haven't called. I can't seem to keep the days straight.

ME: Don't apologize. I'm the one who's sorry for putting everyone through this. I've been worried is all. I know it's hard for you these days, and it kills me that I can't be there for you.

PIA: Did you hear about the sentence appeal?

ME: We don't have to talk about that right now. Let's talk about something happy. King visits next week! This girl is going to braid my hair really cool.

(Big silence.)

PIA: Lily, just tell me about the appeal. Don't make me work for it.

ME: It's dead, Pia. They threw it out.

PIA: All right. We knew that was a possibility. Let's not spend time falling apart over it. Forward, right? Next box on the flowchart. That's how you solve problems. You get the information, you take the next step. So now we . . . what? What happens now?

ME: Now I accept the fact that I've been found guilty and sentenced to seven years in prison.

PIA: No. That's inconceivable. There has to be something else we can do.

ME: According to Sharp-Dressed Schickler, that's all there is.

PIA: Then we'll get you another attorney.

ME: No, Pia. King and I are borrowed up to our necks. We're going to have to sell our house. And I'm not taking any more money from you. It's over. And Schickler says with time off for good behavior, I'll be up for parole less than a year from now. I'm just going to lay low and accrue that good time and aim for that parole hearing.

PIA: A year? That's the best we can hope for?

ME: Hey, right now, it doesn't sound so bad. I mean, compared to seven? I'm 33 years old, Pia. If I don't get paroled, I'll be your age when I get out. I'll be 40 years old. And I'm not saying you're old or anything, but I'd never get to have children. No family, no career, no life! Pia, there's no way. I won't survive. I will friggin' kill myself.

PIA: Lily, don't say that. Don't even think that. You will always have a family. And there's no reason why you can't have children. Lots of women choose to wait these days.

ME: Yeah, but King's not gonna choose that. I wanted to try for a baby before, and he went along with it because we thought if I was pregnant, they might go easier on me. My last night home, we got smashed and, oh my gosh, we did every perverted thing we could think of. And then we sat on the porch drinking coffee until the sun came up. Discussed the possibility of running away. Cried a lot. I know it's selfish, but . . . oh, I was hoping there was a baby inside me, Pia. I didn't want to be in this place all alone. But whatever. I got my period after a while. King was relieved. He didn't even try to pretend.

PIA: Well, under the circumstances, I'm relieved, too, Lily. Think about it.

ME: I know. It's not right for me to have a kid after I killed somebody else's.

PIA: That's not what I meant!

ME: It's not right for me to stand up, drink water, breathe air. I wish they'd sent me to the friggin' gas chamber, because I will never take another step without feeling like I stole it. Seven years doesn't begin to cover it.

PIA: Lily, I know you're remorseful, and that—that's valid. But you've got to be careful saying things like that at these hearings. It's a ridiculously harsh sentence for what you're charged with.

ME: Manslaughter, Pia. Just say it.

PIA: It's not easy to say.

ME: I know. That "slaughter" part. That's difficult. When you see it on paper, it's just one letter off of "laughter," but when you say it out loud, it sounds so bloody, doesn't it? Like horror movies or meat-packing plants or a big bloody stump of—

PIA: Lily! Please. For God's sake.

ME: I'm just saying, it doesn't sound like an accident. And it was an accident, Pia.

PIA: I know, Lily.

ME: (all weepy again) It was my fault. I don't deny that. But you have to know I never in a million years meant to hurt her.

PIA: I know.

ME: There was hardly any blood, Pia. Hardly any at all.

(119 days)

King came. Thought I had finished crying, but while he was here I kept misting up. It was just so good to see somebody whose face isn't as hard as a cinder block.

ME: What's going on in the world today?

KING: Same old, same old.

ME: Ah! How exquisitely wonderful that must be.

KING: Lily, geezes. Don't start bawling again. I can't take it anymore.

ME: I'm so sorry, baby. I'm so sorry for putting you through this. I'll make it all up to you. I promise.

KING: You know what really burns my ass?

ME: Um, a flame about—

KING: I keep reading in the paper. Some guy robs a convenience store and gets 18 months. Some drug dealer gets probation. And you get seven years for a lousy goddamn accident? It's a bunch of friggin' Mothers Against Drunk Driving political lobbyist bullshit.

ME: That doesn't mean I don't deserve it.

Pia

something something

And then nothing.

Pia stepped off the edge of that moment and fell into widowhood as if it were a well. It was the beginning, the end, the center of what felt like a storm-circled eye in the middle of her life. She'd lost loved ones before: grandparents, parents, her little niece. And there were disconnects less dramatic but more complicated than death: a tight-lipped cold war with her sister-in-law, the mangled circumstances that led to Lily being sent to prison. These events did not prepare Pia for her husband's death, but they did teach her the unstable nature of the phrase *worst that could happen*. She was no longer surprised when the definition shifted. She'd learned there is no such thing as *why*. What caught her off guard was *how*. And *when*.

As painful as it was when Pia lost her parents, that at least made sense. It was the natural order of things. Her mother, a classic beauty well into her seventies, was a lady who knew when to make her exit. Mother lingered just long enough to leave an indelible impression and spent her last days drumming her flawlessly manicured fingertips on her oxygen tank with the gracefully contained impatience of someone waiting for a train. The last time Pia saw her, she was sitting in an Adirondack chair out on the front porch, a chinchilla wrap tucked around her shoulders. Lily placed a Virginia Slim between her own lips and lit it, then carefully balanced it in her mother's hand. Stylish tendrils of smoke curled out from Mother's fabulous face, necklacing her, literally taking her breath away.

After she died, the smell of smoke hung in the drapes and permeated the front room, where Pia's father sat in his recliner, absently stroking the empty oxygen tank, which he refused to return to the medical supply store. He would be next. That was the assumption, and it held true. Lily stopped by like she did every day, to make his coffee, sliced banana, and cinnamon toast on her way to work, and she found him, feet up in his favorite chair, a little dog named General Patton sound asleep on his cold, rubbery lap. Sonny and Beth made all the funeral arrangements, but Edgar stepped up to shoulder the unpleasant task of putting down General Patton, who was far too flatulent, runted, and stiff to learn a new home. Edgar took him to the vet, then brought the tiny body back to the funeral home, where Sonny and one of the morticians made it presentable and tucked it in the crook of Daddy's arm on a blue sateen pillow.

Edgar loved that. It reminded him of the mummified cats and fish found in the tombs of the pharaohs. A historian by trade and an optimist by nature, Edgar had a forgiving vision of the past and a hopeful vision of posterity. Having spent so much time combing through debris of days gone by, he was conscious of the messages he personally projected into the future. *Look how we loved our ugly little dogs*, he wanted to tell the unborn archaeologists looking back on us from beyond history's horizon. *Look how we loved our lonely old men.*

Pia kept Edgar's ashes on a night table next to the bed where she lay, staring at the ceiling for the first several weeks. At first her entire body was taut and trembling. Her mind spun and skipped like a scratched CD. She couldn't quiet it enough to sleep. Then she experienced a slowing, a profound powering-down like the engines of an airplane after it lands. When Pia tried to describe it to her therapist years later, she compared it to the settling of branches after the felling of a tall tree. Edgar crumpled to the floor and, as if he were the bridge they were crossing, she and the boys tumbled down with him. They wore the sustained, numbing sadness like body casts. Pia woke up every morning feeling the loss and longing in her stiffened limbs, along with a dull headache she couldn't shake off but learned, after a while, to live with.

She tried to focus her ebbing energy on the boys, but they went back to school a few weeks after Edgar died. (Everything immediately fell into that chronology for Pia: Before or After Edgar Died.) As long as school was in session, they ran like cable cars within a routine Edgar had established when they were first-graders. A routine that didn't include Pia.

"Maybe you should cut back on the travel for a while," Edgar had gently suggested a month or so before he died. "Since this is our last year together."

He meant it was the last year before the twins went away to college. His chronology was still charted in the living befores and afters of fatherhood.

Pia didn't know how to respond. This was the closest Edgar had ever come to complaining about the way things were. It had never been an issue. Every day of their school career, Edgar had rousted the boys out of bed, fed them something hot, and kissed them on the forehead as they headed for the bus stop. Any day that wasn't an everyday day was a holiday, and holiday rituals were in place. Sleep in, pancakes for breakfast, coffee and newspaper on the patio, dinner and a movie downtown. Pia was always home on weekends, so she was part of that holiday routine. It wasn't an effective daily schedule they could adopt for the long run, but it worked well through the summer.

When school started again in late August, what little time James and Jesse spent at home between school, soccer, and socializing was consumed with homework and college application essays. Pia doled out money and collected quick hugs as they dashed out the door to soccer tournaments, double dates, study groups, and other mysterious pursuits, connected to Pia only through text messages they hastily thumbed into their cell phones.

WE B @ ROBINS. LOVE U :) J/J

Pia spent most of her time watching television. News mostly. Murders, robberies, carjackings, aggravated assaults, bilking of the elderly, Marvin Zindler's rat and roach report, storm warnings, sports. An apartment complex burned down. A senator was arrested with a prostitute. An elderly couple died of asphyxiation, having locked themselves in their garage with the motor running, strapped into the little Chevy they shared till death do us part. Only they defied death and departed together. Pia felt like she was watching all this from inside a waterfall, but that didn't stop the stock quotes from scrolling by between advertisements for spring fashions, cell phone services, and a product that was supposed to enhance male performance. Late at night, there were infomercials for fitness machines, real estate courses, and knife sets. Pia actually went online and ordered the knife set. She didn't really need a knife set, but the transaction made her feel engaged with the world in some small way.

In September, of course, came the destruction of the World Trade Center buildings. Pia stared at the live coverage, experiencing the gradual descent from curiosity, to concern, to disbelief, to heartsickening realization, just like the horrified New Year's Eve party guests at the Natural History Museum. She experienced a breathless sort of understanding when the first of the Twin Towers disintegrated into itself, a kinship with all those people taken by absolute surprise, caught with a fading smile on their lips, half focused on some unraveling conversation about *something*. They looked up, took in a sharp, startled breath.

something something

Then nothing.

Pia knew what it meant to feel the floor disappear beneath your feet. She was living in the same oblivion they tumbled into.

CNN's endless coverage of the great falling quickly became an addiction. Entranced by the mangled steel, blurred faces, and shattered glass, the endless parade of motherless children and orphaned mommies, Pia let the battered voices and bulldozer noises play all night on a portable set at the foot of her bed. It became a performance-art piece that captured the way her own steel-smooth existence had become erratic, dangerous, fatally confused.

Her headache took on the hissing character of a coolant leak. Pia felt a vital sort of energy—her soul perhaps—passing upward through a slow breach in her skull. She pulled her hair back into a tight French braid, and that seemed to help form a retaining wall around the details and memories the headache tried to push out. Everything Pia was trying to keep straight. The terror warning color spectrum as opposed to the storm warning color spectrum. Edgar's social security number. Which days she was supposed to call Lily.

Lily was allowed three ten-minute phone calls per week, as long as she stayed out of trouble and worked a certain number of hours in the prison laundry facility. The all-encompassing *unsaid* cast shadows across every conversation, but the connection was important to both of them.

"Thank God for you, Pia." Lily always said this at least once during the conversation. "I don't know what I'll do if I lose you."

"You won't lose me," Pia said. "I'm here."

"Are you all right?" asked Lily.

"I'm fine."

"You don't sound fine."

"Well, telling me that doesn't help."

"I'm sorry. I don't know what to say." Lily breathed a sigh, and the sound of it made Pia worry that Lily might have started smoking again. "I don't even know the stock remarks."

"Lily," Pia began carefully, "I was going through Edgar's books, and there were several that I thought you might want. And Edgar would want you to have them."

"I'd like that. Thank you."

"So I was thinking maybe I could drive up there next week—"

"No," Lily said sharply. "I told you fifty times. I don't want you coming here."

"But the boys—"

"Absolutely not! You promised, Pia. The last thing I want is for them to see me like this. And I don't want to spend my call minutes arguing about it, okay? So let's just drop it."

Pia dropped it but didn't say anything in its place.

"C'mon, Pi. I don't want to waste my call time on dead air, either. Talk to me. Tell me about the Double Js. Are they managing all right?"

"They're fine," said Pia. "Busy with all the senior-year stuff. Sonny is taking them camping next weekend. And Beth has been . . . well-intentioned. She keeps bringing food and praying over us."

"Yark," Lily said. Then she coughed, and it definitely sounded like cigarettes.

"It doesn't do any harm," said Pia.

"Here's my prayer: 'Dear God, if you in fact exist, *you suck!* Amen.' I don't understand, Pia. Why do the wrong people keep getting dead?" Lily started to sound choked up and tearful, the way she often did when her phone minutes were almost exhausted for the week. "I wish it was me, Pia. I wish I was dead instead of Edgar. I should have been killed instead of—"

"Lily, spare me the melodrama. Reality is about all we can handle right now."

"I'm sorry," she said meekly.

"It's okay," Pia told her, softening her tone, but not too

much. “Everything’s going to be all right. We just have to work through it.”

“Pia, you remember how Mother used to yell at us for bickering when we were kids? She’d quote that proverb about the law of kindness on your tongue.”

“Yes.” Pia smiled, remembering.

“And she would shame us into being nice by saying that when we got old and gray, two of us would go to the first one’s funeral. And then one of those would go to the other’s funeral. She said only the last one standing would truly know how precious it is to have a family.”

“I remember.”

“More than anything, Pia, I didn’t want to be that one.”

Lily

(122 days)

Library day. Checked out Selected Poetry and Prose of Wordsworth.

> Hermits are contented with their cells;
> And students with their pensive citadels.

Can't stop thinking about that. I get it, but I'm not sure it's possible.

No letters or calls.

(125 days)

Pia called. Told her about Wordsworth "Nuns Fret Not at Their Convent's Narrow Room" thing.

PIA: Hm. I'm not familiar with that.

ME: "In truth the prison unto which we doom ourselves, no prison is." And there's this other part about "souls who have felt the weight of too much liberty." That's so me, isn't it? "The weight of too much liberty." God, that's so exactly true! I've been all over the map since grad school. That nothing office job at the performing arts center, the community theater stuff, all the partying—I've been going nowhere at 90 miles per hour. But now I have this chance to ditch my whole bullshit life and totally reinvent myself. The first three months I was in here, I was bawling every night. Literally shaking and bawling my head off all night and then trudging through the day with this incredible headache.

PIA: Really? Was it like a sort of constant, dull ache or more of a sharp—

ME: Doesn't matter! That's over. From now on, I'm making this place my involuntary ashram. I'm going to do yoga, meditate, read. Hey! I'm going to read the Bible. Cover to cover. Really use this time for spiritual and intellectual growth. Observe everything around me and be totally open to the teachings of the universe. I'm going to do a better job keeping my journal, too. Write every day. Journaling is very therapeutic, you know?

PIA: Sure. Absolutely. That's a healthy way to approach it. Positive attitude. The most important thing is to just get through it and get home.

ME: Oh, yeah. Hell, yes.

PIA: Please, Lily, be careful. Be inconspicuous and stay away from . . . bad people.

ME: Well, duh.

PIA: Don't be scared. And if you get scared, try not to look scared. If somebody tries to mess with you, just cover your face and scrunch down into a little ball. Just go like scrunch!

ME: (laughing my head off) Yes, that will impress them with how not scared I look.

PIA: I'm serious! And don't start smoking again, because you worked so hard to quit.

ME: OK already!

PIA: And don't cry, Lily. Don't let those people see you crying anymore. You show them that you're strong enough for this. Because you are, Lily. You are strong enough for this.

ME: Friggin' A! Dang right. Oh. Shoot. My time's up, Pia.

PIA: OK.

ME: Tell the boys hi and I love them and I'll catch 'em on the flip-flop. And Pia? Will you tell Sonny what I said? About reading the Bible? I mean, don't tell him that I told you to tell him, just . . . you know. If it happens to come up in conversation.

PIA: Sure. I'll tell him.

ME: So . . . OK. Well. Take care of you, big sister. And when in doubt, SCRUNCH!

And we actually parted laughing.

(126 days)

Thought Jesus Chick was going to burst a blood vessel in her head when I asked if I could check out a Bible. I guess this is the moment missionaries live for. Homecoming of the prodigal.

Halfway through Genesis and it's a lot more interesting than I remember from Catholic school.

(127 days)

Halfway through Exodus, and the story, which was moving along pretty well, has devolved into a load of stuff like "Anyone who has sexual relations with an animal must be put to death!" (Sadly, this covers several guys I knew before I met King.) And "If a man beats his slave and the slave dies, he must be punished. But he is not to be punished if the slave gets up after a day or two." And "If a man seduces a virgin, she shall be his wife, and he must still pay the bride-price for virgins."

Exodus 21:23—"You are to take a life for a life, eye for eye, tooth for tooth, hand for hand, foot for foot, burn for burn, wound for wound."

Translation: Payback is a bitch.

(131 days)

Library day. Tried to return Bible to Jesus Chick, but she wasn't having any of that.

JESUS CHICK: (all disappointed) But sister, why? You're allowed to keep it and still check out other books. It's yours! It's a gift! What happened to your ambition to read it cover to cover?

ME: That pretty much fizzled somewhere between the counting of the Gershonites and the tent pegs of the Merarites.

JC: Oh, you were almost through the Pentateuch! Keep reading, sister. Or skip ahead to Joshua, why don't you? Things really start to pep up with Joshua!

So I had to slink away without Erica Jong's Fear of Flying. What was I supposed to do? I'm not in a great frame of mind to read on about how friggin' Abijab begat Aminadab who begat Yabba-dabba-doo-dad, but these women work for God. You don't want to piss them off.

(137 days)

King came. Brought a whole stack of paperbacks from the used bookstore. Gloriously trashy escapist fiction that will allow me to avoid the Jesus Chicks for a few weeks.

ME: See, this is why I love you, King. You don't give a damn if I better myself.

KING: (laughing) Hey, it's our mutually low standards that keep us together.

ME: (laughing, and then not laughing) Thank God for you, King. Because no matter how you slice it, this place is nothing like an ashram. For some insanely screwed-up reason, they get us out of bed at 3:00 AM. Breakfast at 3:30. Then we wait in line for a clean towel and clothes for the day. Then we're all shuffling around in our baggy, bluish-white, cadaver-colored scrubs like it's a haunted nuthouse or something.

KING: Yeah. Somehow I thought it would be—you know. Edgier.

ME: Yes! I know exactly what you mean. I was so scared about coming here, it never occurred to me how friggin' boring it was going to be. Pia thinks I'm surrounded by scary, arch-criminal offenders. In reality, it's a lot of pathetic idiot girls, whose sociopathic lovers got them all druggy and used them as mules or God-knows-what and then turned around and testified against them. There's a few edgy types, but mostly, women here are just sad. Everybody who killed somebody has an excellent excuse, of course. Except this one poor nightshade of a lady who drowned her kid in his little plastic swimming pool. She creeps me out, but she's mostly in the infirmary.

KING: Geezes, Lil. I don't know what to say. I don't know how to help. That's what kills me.

ME: Oh, babe, you help. You love me. You make me feel human. If it wasn't for you, the only thing I'd have to look forward to is standing in line for clean sheets once a week.

(140 days)

I liked Psalms and Proverbs and the sexy Song of Solomon. Skimmed Ecclesiastes (snore). Halfway through Isaiah, the bipolar prophet.

(144 days)

Dreamed about Easter. Woke up screaming, so everyone's been on my case all day.

No Pia call.
No King.

(152 days)

King called. He bought new boots. I don't know why that makes me feel sad, but it does.

No Pia call.

(153 days)

Two friggin' idiot girls fighting over if you had three wishes, is it allowed to wish for additional wishes.

IGNORANT HO #1: Uh-huh. 'Cuz I can wish for anything I want, and I want more wishes, and if I don't get more wishes, then I didn't even get one wish, and that's BS!

IGNORANT HO #2: Huh-uh. 'Cuz you only got three wishes, so if you had more wishes, you wouldn't have three, and the question is if you had three, so if you had more, that's a whole different situation.

My Three Wishes

I wish I was dead.

I wish I was dead.

I wish I was dead.

(171 days)

That did not hurt me.
I did not feel it.
That did not hurt me.
I did not feel it.
That did not hurt me.
I did not feel it.
That did not hurt me.
I did not feel it.
That did not hurt me.
I did not feel it.
That did not hurt me.
I did not feel it.
That did not hurt me.
I did not feel it.
That did not hurt me.
I did not feel it.

(181 days)

Wish they could give me something to help me sleep. Like the electric chair.

(188 days)

This is not very therapeutic.

(200 days)

Two-zero day. Don't know why, but days with two zeroes are hard. Spent most of my cubicle time reading Lamentations.

> From on high he sent fire,
> sent it down into my bones.
> My sins have been bound into a yoke.
> They have come upon my neck.
> He has handed me over to those I cannot
>   withstand.
> In his winepress the Lord has trampled the Virgin
>   Daughter of Judah.

Translation: Days with two zeroes seriously suck.

Beth

This is not a good day for Beth.

The car won't start, and that's just the sort of small thing that puts her past the edge of what she can endure.

"Oh, God damn it!" she cries out loud. She strikes the heel of her hand against the steering wheel. "Start! Start, you stupid beast!"

This does nothing but hurt her hand. Beth swears again, then covers her face and whispers a small prayer, asking forgiveness.

"Heavenly Father," she adds, "You gave Abraham's concubine water from a stone. I know you will start this stupid car for me."

When it still doesn't start, she calls Sonny on the cell phone, and he comes right away. He opens the hood and peers in without cursing. In fact, he smiles, because he thinks all that technology is such a wonder, even when it fails to perform its intended function. This attitude is beyond Beth's comprehension. She finds it extremely annoying.

But that's Sonny.

After tinkering a while, he does get Beth's car going. He insists on driving it, however. Insists that she take the company car provided to him by the funeral home. He says he'll take Beth's car to the shop.

"Why don't I take it to the shop, Bethy?" he says so easy and kind that, well, what the hell is she supposed to say?

Beth slides into the driver's seat of the funeral home car. It's a new Lexus. Luxurious and dependable. Comforting. Maybe that's the point. It's a car for someone who can't stand one more gram of trouble at the moment, someone for whom comfort is a necessity. When Sonny drives clients to view caskets and monuments and burial plots, they sink into the plush seats and hide behind the tinted windows. It's designed to cradle them. Bereaved people are entitled to at least that moment to feel cradled.

But the Lexus is low on gas, and when Beth pulls up to the pump, she accidentally gets too close and grazes a cement retaining wall that separates the lanes. She thinks she needs to back up, but when she does, the side mirror snaps off.

Not a good day. This is not a good day.

She calls Sonny again, and he is so unflappable, it makes her want to scream and shake him. He tells her not to worry about it. Insurance will cover it.

"No harm done," Sonny says, even though harm obviously has been done. It *has*. Why refuse to acknowledge that?

He insists that it's a small thing. He tries to make her feel better, and she knows she's wrong and ungracious for not feeling better, but sometimes Beth doesn't want to feel better. Sometimes Beth wants to feel worse. She wants to feel entitled to curl up in the backseat of the car and cry like the clients sometimes do. Beth is amazed the seats aren't tearstained. Then she remembers that Sonny keeps a box of Kleenex back there. He thinks of everything.

Beth drives the Lexus back to the funeral home and endures her boss's formulaic woman-driver jokes on her way to her office. She sits in her chair. She places her hands flat on the desktop for a moment, then opens a manila folder and begins adding up columns of numbers. The rhythm and the motion quickly take her in. This is her music, her heartbeat, her pulse. She feels herself falling down the columns, tapping the numbers in with her fingers and hitting the plus key with her thumb. There are no accidents, no variables. Orderliness envelops her.

Pia

The talking heads went on through the winter. A growing ambience of fear layered the nation like pollen dust; sifting through the television, infiltrating Pia's dreams, seeping into her heart like a virus. When Rumsfeld told everyone to go out and buy plastic and duct tape, Beth rushed to WalMart with her official Homeland Security shopping list. She generously assembled an extra home safety kit for Pia and the boys, presenting it to them along with Ready.gov guides for surviving biological, chemical, and radiation threats.

Pia knew she should be enraged or at the very least amused by the way it was all being played, but she couldn't quite locate that discerning part of her head that used to be savvy to propaganda and passionate about politics. What troubled Pia terribly is that this was the part of her that had made her good at her job. After several months of excuses and halfhearted promises, Pia finally typed up a letter of resignation. It sat on her desk for another month or so, and then one gray morning at the end of a sleepless night, she got up and FedExed it Priority Overnight. Jenna was on the phone within fifteen minutes of receiving it the next day.

"You are not quitting," she said firmly. "I'm treating this like a leave of absence."

"Treat it however you need to, Jenna, but I won't be back."

"Pia, how can you say that? Do you have any idea what's going on in the world?"

Jenna had been calling once a month since Edgar died, trying to reignite Pia's interest in one case or another. Apparently, it was easier for her to talk about impending invasions and incursions in the Middle East than to address what was going on in Pia's personal life. The invasion of tragedy, the incursion of fear. Jenna deftly skirted every conversation in a wide arc around the issue of bereavement.

"It's all about the oil industry, Pia. We are up to our eyeballs. Last week, I turned down a major consulting fee, because without you—well, suffice it to say that we would *really* like to have you back. We're willing to work around whatever you need. We'll cut back your travel. This time we really will! I personally guarantee it. No more than ten days a month."

"No, Jenna."

"*Eight* days. Hey, I get it. I'm a single mother, too. But for God's sake, Pia, James and Jesse are legal adults."

"They still need me to be home."

"Not 24/7, they don't."

"Okay, then maybe *I* need to be home." Pia sat up straight and tried to make that posture apparent in her voice. "I'm sorry. The bottom line is, I'm done. Thank you for understanding."

"I do *not* understand! For one thing, how can you afford this?"

"I'm working it out," Pia answered sharply.

Pia had always been comfortable in her role as primary breadwinner for the family. Edgar had always hoped the boys would go to Harvard, his alma mater, so they'd carefully saved for that and for their retirement. There was life insurance. They'd had all the pen-and-paper conversations about where they wanted to be in ten years and how they would get there.

But this torn parachute of financial planning failed to address the possibility that Pia would find herself alone in her early forties, trying to find her way through a world where people and things—families, tall buildings, a way of life—could simply disappear without warning.

"I'll freelance if I need to," she said. "Research. Editing. Stuff I can do from home."

"Well, leaving aside the fact that you are monumentally overqualified for *stuff you can do from home*, Pia, this is not you talking. You are a proactive, do-what-has-to-be-done person. Hon, it's been over a year."

"Has it?" Pia said vaguely. It didn't seem possible.

"Well, wasn't it New Year's . . ." Jenna trailed off, and Pia could hear her clicking something. "Pia, are you on some kind of medication?"

"Excuse me?"

"Maybe you need to cut back a little."

"I'm not on any medication, Jenna."

"Well . . . maybe you should be."

Pia didn't say anything. That wasn't something she was willing to discuss.

"At least let me take you to lunch," said Jenna. "I'm in Philly for another week. Fly in for the day. There's a great new Thai place around the corner. Come on, Pia. Come Tuesday."

"Tuesday doesn't work for me."

"Thursday, then."

"Jenna, please don't make me manufacture excuses. I can't right now, okay?"

There was no way Pia could explain the fragility that had overtaken her. A hypersensitivity to the vibrating velocity of life. Daylight slashed through her sunglasses. The sound of a car alarm placed a vise on the back of her neck. At times she was so acutely aware of the Earth's rotation beneath her car, she had a hard time centering herself in the correct lane. A trip to the supermarket left her feeling dismembered. The idea of getting on an airplane was paralyzing. She had nightmares about looking down from the sky and watching the world spinning itself smaller and smaller. Apprehension crept over her and colored even the smallest decisions. Walk out to the mailbox or wait for the boys to pick up the mail on their way in? Pick up the phone or let the machine take a message? Pia couldn't explain it to Jenna, but it simply wasn't in her anymore to leave the boys and face what felt like death in order to spend her days doing things she no longer cared about; spend her eyes on other people's faces; spend her voice raising alarms when there was no hope for change.

"You know what scares me," said Jenna. "I haven't heard you laugh since Edgar died."

"I guess you're right," Pia admitted. "But what's to laugh about these days?"

"Politics, men, media, teenagers—what's *not* to laugh about?"

Pia wished with all her heart she could see it that way.

"I bet I could make you laugh right now," Jenna said. "If I make you laugh, will you come back to work?"

"Jenna . . ."

"Okay. Here it is. Office romances are a minefield. We know this, right? But Pia, I have been seeing Fakar Kandim."

"Fakar . . . from biochemical research? You're kidding."

"I know! Believe me, everything you're trying not to say right now, I've already said it to myself. He's an office subordinate. He's eleven years younger than me, with all the baggage that entails. He's *Muslim*, for Christ's sake, or Mohammed's sake or whoever! But he is so—oh, Pia, he is so damn *lovely*. He's the first person I've wanted to be with since the divorce. And the last person I could have imagined myself marrying! But we are. We're getting married."

"Wow," Pia said. "That's, um . . . it's complicated. But if he makes you happy, I think it's great. I'm not laughing, Jenna. Why would I laugh?"

"Oh, that's not the funny part. It gets better! You know his last name is pronounced 'can-*deem*,' but everybody sees the way it's spelled and says 'condom,' which drives him absolutely up a tree. Now, when Elliot and I got married, we both hyphenated and became Fullier-Lee. So I ask Fakar if he's willing to do the same." Jenna started giggling like a girl at a slumber party. "And he points out to me that his name would be Fakar Fullier-Kandim. Which is not that bad on paper, but when they try to call his name in court . . . well, you see the dilemma."

"Oh, dear." Pia had almost forgotten what it feels like when laughter originates in the rib cage and ripples up across the forehead. "Oh! How sophomoric are we to think that's funny?"

"I know! Fakar sees absolutely no humor in it, but I'm sorry, it's hilarious."

"It reminds me of that woman in accounts receivable. Remember?"

"*Yvonna Stiffe-Johnson!*" Jenna was practically in tears now.

"Yes! Oh my gosh. How could she not see that?" Pia laughed until her lungs felt flushed and open, her whole body warm and inhabited. "Thanks, Jenna," she said when they'd both finally caught their breath. "I needed that."

"You need to come back to work, girlfriend. That's what you need," Jenna said.

There was silence. And more clicking.

"Pia, I'm sorry for your loss. My God, I am so very sorry this happened to you. This on top of everything else. It's so wrong. But it happened. That's reality. *Death happens*. But life goes on. Pia, it's been a year. Common sense and a dozen different world cultures say that's enough. It's time to rejoin the living. I'm telling you as a friend. Get yourself some goddamn Zoloft and get back in the game."

Pia stood quietly by the window, feeling the hard corners of truth as Jenna spoke it. She thought about how it might feel to sit laughing in a booth at the Thai restaurant. But immediately in the wake of that thought came the unsettling idea that she might get lost on her way there. What if her phone didn't work? What if the ladies' room was occupied?

"Pia, seriously, are you all right?"

Jenna's question seemed to come from far away, and Pia had no answer.

Lily

(278 days)

This week blows. For whatever reason, Pia's not writing, and King called to say he couldn't come next week. Got shifted to the ironing machine and burned the bu-fu-ing crap out of my hand. Fight broke out in the library. I wasn't there, thank God, but the place got trashed, so I'm stuck with the Bible and whatever King decides to send me until they reopen.

(281 days)

Started the New Testament. Having been crucified four gospels in a row, Jesus is now roundly and soundly dead. I have this theory about the whole salvation thing. It's not that he had to balance out some cosmic eye-for-eye, tooth-for-tooth payback equation. It's that he had something to tell people, and death is the only thing that makes us pay attention.

(284 days)

Played cards with some girls.

No Pia call.
No King.

(289 days)

Library open! As God is my witness, I'll never be hungry again! Checked out A Man in Full by T Wolfe.

Pia called and also Pia letter, but not much to say either way.

(292 days)

Library day. Returned A Man in Full. Checked out Saint Burl's Obituary by D Akst. Is it me, or do all the books in the Jesus Chick collection center on some form of prison?

(307 days)

Letter from Pia. Pictures of the Double Js. Also library day. Returned The River King by A Hoffman. Checked out R L Ozeki My Year of Meats, a friggin' awesome book, telling the kind of truth that gets people crucified.

King called, but we didn't even use up our minutes.

(316 days)

King came. Brought me D Gabaldon book Outlander.

KING: (just sitting there with big face on)

ME: What are you looking so morose about?

KING: Hello? It's my friggin' birthday.

ME: Oh, geez! Oh, King! Honey, happy birthday. I'm sorry I forgot. (getting all gulpy and weepy) Oh, King, you remember last year on your birthday?

KING: I try not to think about stuff like that.

ME: King, this is probably stupid, but lately I just get this weird feeling that . . . King, if I ask you a question, will you promise not to lie to me? Because if we're totally honest with each other, we might make it through this. But if we can't be totally, totally honest—

KING: Yes! I am! Okay? There you go. There's some honesty for ya.

ME: (getting kind of high-pitched) What?

KING: What you were gonna ask me. I am. And I'm sorry. I don't mean it to hurt you. I don't want to make this any tougher on you than it already is, and I hate myself for not being the kind of man who could step up and do the honorable thing, but I never signed up for this, Lily. That's just not what I'm made of. I mean, c'mon! Did you seriously expect me to live like a friggin' monk for seven years?

ME: It's only been ten months. And I'm getting parole in 90 days! Don't even make me think about being stuck here beyond that! It's not happening.

KING: Okay! I'm sorry. Like I said.

ME: So . . . is this someone I know? Are you using condoms? Do you love this person?

KING: No, she's just— Yes, of course! Hell no, I don't love her. I'm not even pretending.

ME: Does she know that?

KING: Yes! And she's fine with it.

ME: How could anyone possibly be fine with that, King?

KING: Her husband is in prison. OK? That's how. They have an understanding. Desperate minds call for desperate measures. I guess we should have talked about this. We should've agreed on some kind of arrangement.

(Big silence.)

ME: Desperate times.

KING: They sure as hell are.

ME: (wishing I had something to throw against the glass) The saying, dumb-ass! It goes "Desperate times call for desperate measures."

KING: OK, well, same difference.

ME: Yeah. Whatthefuckever! Guess I'm in no position to be a purist about anything.

KING: C'mon, Lil, don't do this. I love you. You know I could never love anyone but my shenanigan girl. And we are gonna make it through this. You know that, right?

ME: Right.

Desperate minds call for desperate measures. Give me a fucking break. And now that I think of it, I already read Outlander.

(317 days)

Traded Outlander for J Picoult Keeping Faith. I find this ironic.

No Pia call.

(322 days)

Didn't read much today. Headache. Cried a lot last night.

(325 days)

There is such a thing as kindness.

I will not forget that.

(336 days)

No phone calls today. Somebody ripped the cord out. We were all on lockdown until they found it. Hope they fix it soon. King is probably going nuts. I just want to hear his voice.

(Day 365)

I have been in this place one year.

Happy Incarceversary to me.

(367 days)

King came! We talked and talked. Just like the first night we met, and the next day we could hardly talk anymore, our voices were so raw from talking over the loud music and the traffic noise. I never met anyone whose mind works the way his mind works. No abstracts. Just blocks of things that fit together and make his life. Golden opportunities, slob idiots, beautiful girls, unfair labor laws, too damn many birds, inconveniently narrow alleys, rotten deals he don't have to put up with, big fat juicy steaks, family dinners, family arguments, not speaking to family, making up with family, big tires, fastidiously groomed facial hair. In the mind of King Vincent, King Vincent is hung like a wildebeest, there's no reason to wear pants at home, and being 30 pounds overweight is a sign of prosperity. In the mind of King Vincent, there's nothing more beautiful than a pregnant woman. I remember, I really loved that he said that. I'm going to remind him of that when I get out of here. After my parole hearing, we should try for a baby. He'll get me pregnant, and I'll pick out new curtains and keep him company. I am going to love him and cook for him and do our laundry and no one else's and never leave him alone again.

(389 days)

King came! He told me last week he'd try to come more often, and here he was. Love him, love him, love him. I knew I could count on him. He brought me a dress and shoes for parole hearing next week so I don't look like a scarecrow when I go in there. And when I come out.

ME: I'm gonna walk out that gate and wrap myself around you and never let go.

KING: I'm good with that, Lil.

ME: I'm a changed person, King. I never appreciated what I had before. I always thought I could be doing something better. Now I know. There is nothing better. I just want everything back the way it was before.

KING: Lily, if things don't go our way next week—

ME: Don't say that! We've got to stay positive, honey. Schickler told me exactly what to say, and exactly how to say it. Finally, that degree in theatre arts is gonna be worth something, huh? I plan to give the performance of my life. So you just stay positive with me, OK? Just a few more days. We gotta keep that positive vibe.

(392 days)

Huge fight in the laundry room today. I managed to stay clear. Hated to see Molly take a beating, but she just would not keep her mouth shut, and I am not sacrificing one flat minute of good time for anyone. Parole hearing in three days.

(395 days)

Parole hearing tomorrow. Went to library and returned Stone Diaries, but didn't check anything out. Won't be needing it! Jesus Chicks having "Taking Pride in My Appearance" workshop and salon day. Endured their endless yakking so I could get my hair done. Want to look my best for King when I walk out of here tomorrow.

Trying to hold my positive vibe.
POSITIVE
POSITIVE
POSITIVE

Beth

This is not a good day for Beth.

She hates this long drive. If Sonny were driving, she'd be asleep right now. She'd retreat to that drifting, half-aware state where you're not really living the same time line as everyone else but you're still present enough to hold your mouth closed. They would stop to fill the gas tank and eat lunch at a Waffle House in one of the little towns along the way. But Sonny won't go with her. He says he's not ready to see Lily and feels no need to participate in this process. But the truth is he'd rather stay in a house full of dead people than spend the day in the car with Beth. He feels no need to participate in a lot of processes that involve her, it seems.

Beth thinks people are looking at her as she turns down Ransom Road. She thinks they must be wondering why she's headed in the direction of the women's prison. Is her best friend a forger? Is her mother a felon? Maybe they think she's a missionary. Beth hopes they do.

As she pulls into the Ransom facility, she remembers how much she hates this place. Hates the idea of it, the fact of it in her life, the process of entering and exiting. She hates its reason for being and her own reason for being in it. And more than anything, she hates Lily. She hates the pretty pink dress Lily wears. It's a Kool-Aid–colored stain on the gray floor, something Lily never would have worn if she weren't trying to costume herself as a decent person. Beth hates seeing them take the shackles off Lily's hands, because Beth feels shackled without any hope of release. Her hands, mouth, and heart are chained forever to grief and obligation.

"It'll be like at the trial," Lily's attorney tells Beth in the hallway. "We just need to hear you say that you know this was a tragic accident. That alcoholism is a disease. Lily has a disease, and you don't hold that against her. You forgive her."

Beth nods. She will say that. But the truth is Lily is not an alcoholic. She's just someone who likes to drink. She's not powerless in the face of it, not gripped by inner demons. She could have resisted drinking that day. She probably did. She really hadn't had that much. Only enough to impair her sensibilities just slightly, just enough to cause one small miscalculation. She was what you might call a party girl, but that was a weekend thing. It never interfered with her job or her ridiculous community-theater productions. It was a Saturday-night sort of thing. She just started a little earlier than usual on that particular Saturday. She could have waited if she'd wanted to. Did she intend for Easter to die? Of course not. Is she devastated over it? Yes, certainly. But does that change anything for Beth? No. It doesn't.

She sits through the hearing, wondering which sin is greater: the sin of perjuring herself and saying she has forgiven Lily or the sin of hating Lily forever. World without end. Without possibility of forgiveness or reconciliation. A stumbling block. A stumbling block. A wound on the body of Christ. Anyone who sees that will suffer a diminishing of faith. If she forgives, she becomes a living testament, proof of God's grace in the world, evidence of the Holy Spirit's power to heal wounds, divisions, piercings, devastations. Beth wants very much to be that, so when her time comes, after all Lily's simpering and remorseful tears and professions of rehabilitation, she will go to the wooden chair and give her wooden testimony. Tragic accident. Insidious disease. Unfettered forgiveness.

Lily weeps as she describes her nightmares, depression, and guilt. She mentions Pia's trouble, how Pia lost her husband and needs her family now, completely disregarding the fact that Beth and Sonny call her every Sunday afternoon and have almost convinced her to come to church with them. Lily makes it sound as if she is Pia's only hope for recovery. Then Lily gushes about how much she loved Easter, her sweet, sweet baby niece. She talks about Easter's first communion the week before the accident. How precious dear little Easter looked in her frilly white dress, all chiffon and giggles.

Beth feels a hot pressure in her throat. Not tears. Bitterness. Rage. She can't stand for Lily to speak of that dress with her tacky pink lipstick mouth. It smears the memory of Easter's perfect white crinolines with all the blood and mud and vomit and sexual filth Lily's foul mouth has been party to.

"I guess I always felt kind of special about her because—well, she's kind of named after me. You know? Easter and Lily, you know? Like Easter lily? I kind of thought that was a cool sort of connection between Easter and me."

Beth looks back on the carefully charted list of baby names, a Lotus spreadsheet she made on the computer in the student library, before she even found the courage to go to Father Sonny and tell him he was going to be the other kind of father. Beth had mapped out boys' names and girls' names, cross-referenced with literary origins, celebrities, and other connections, along with columns of pros and cons for each selection. She doesn't remember listing the Easter-Lily connection. If any such thing had crossed her mind, it would have been listed as a con. Lily under the "Cons" heading. That play on words makes Beth want to laugh out loud. She pushes her fist against her lower lip to stifle it and notices Lily's attorney giving her a little smile-nod. He probably thinks she's remembering Easter in her pristine white dress.

He gives her another little smile-nod at the end, after she's done what she came to do. Good girl, says that little smile nod. He tells her later what an inspiration she is. But the parole board is not inspired to let Lily go. And Beth is not inspired to so much as look at Lily as Lily shuffles from the room.

Pia

Before the Bolivar Ferry left the dock, Pia knew she was making a terrible mistake. It was overcast and cool, which was unusual for a late summer day in Galveston. She and the boys were taking Edgar's vase—no, no, his *urn*, it was an *urn*—out to scatter his ashes in the Gulf of Mexico. But this was wrong, Pia decided. This was very horribly wrong.

To begin with, it wasn't legal, nor should it be. Human remains—*cremains,* rather—being dumped willy-nilly unregulated into the environment? These weren't ashes in the sense of . . . well, *ashes*. They were the pelletized rendering of a human body with all the biohazards that entailed. Sanitized certainly. The extreme heat. Whatever sort of fire burns so hot as to consume every earthly trace of a man and his skeleton. But still.

Pia saw a dolphin leaping and for some reason became convinced that this was an omen or Edgar reincarnated or something, even though she never thought about stupid things like that. She wasn't stupid. She wasn't like that. She wasn't envisioning Edgar floating above the clouds with angels and harps or writhing in fire with demons and scythes. She wasn't waiting to find pennies on the floor or the ambient crackle of other-worldly white noise on her answering machine. She hadn't felt his presence at the hospital or the funeral or in their empty house at any time in the year since he died. She'd felt the opposite of his presence. The *gone*ness of his presence was what she'd felt.

Hugging the vase to her chest, she sheepishly told the boys she wasn't ready to do it. They just stood for a moment, looking at her with Edgar's eyes, forming words with his mouth, his voice times two. They looked so much like him, she couldn't even hear what they were saying. They were each other's twin, and someday they would be his twin, because he was frozen in time and memory now. He would never grow old to provide a shadow of things to come for them, a slowing in contrast to their energy. He would have made a good old man. Pia felt a stab of hope that, if she lived long enough to see her sons become that, she would see what Edgar would have been, and then she had to look away.

The dolphin disappeared into the murky waves. The skin on its back looked greasy and tough, tar-colored and slick in an unclean way. Pia wasn't about to pour the last of Edgar into that clammy, polluted depth. America's third coast was smudged with unchecked industry, littered with the shocking disregard of the very people who professed to love it, those who blustered the loudest with their "Don't mess with Texas!" bravado. She'd sat in on enough subcommittee meetings to know what unnatural elements teemed in those waters. If she dumped Edgar into that stew, he'd probably come back as a toxic zombie to haunt the rusty tide pools.

This was the first appearance of the sharks, Pia would tell her therapist a year later.

"And it wasn't in my head, Dr. Ackerman, it was an unmistakably physical experience."

She felt them lurking. It was a vague but undeniably real stirring just above her diaphragm, a vague swish that made her entire body tense.

"Mom?" James cupped his hand under her elbow. "Are you okay?"

"Yes."

"Are you going to, um . . ." He cocked an eyebrow toward the water.

"No. Not here. Not now," Pia told him. "I'm sorry I dragged you boys all the way down here. It just doesn't feel right."

"*Mom*," Jesse groaned. "Oh my friggin' God."

"Shut up!" James stepped between them. "It's her decision. She doesn't have to do it if she doesn't want to."

"Fine." Jesse folded his arms across his chest. "Whatever. So what *do* you want to do?"

"What if we take him to Key West?" said Pia. "We could meet there during spring break. Just like we used to. That might be fun."

"Fun?" Jesse echoed blankly, and this time Pia had no trouble reading the expression in his eyes. "Sure. Yeah. We could take him parasailing before we dump his chicken-fried ass in the ocean. There's some really big fun!"

"*Dude!* I told you to shut up!" James barked. He put one arm around Pia's shoulders. "I think that's a great idea, Mom. And when my brother is done being a big A-hole, he will think so, too. *Won't you, brother*?"

"Whatthefuckever," Jesse muttered, turning away from them toward the sooty waves.

Pia felt a sudden stab of certainty she would never see Jesse again. She was positive that if she let him leave for Harvard in a few days, he would never look back, never wonder what happened to her, never shed a tear or feel a clutch at his throat when someone spoke her name. She would die alone in the house and remain undiscovered for months. And a year later, Jesse would pour her rendered remains into whatever dank tarn was at hand and move on with his life.

But of course that didn't happen.

When school started in the fall, Pia forced herself to fly with them to Boston. She helped them settle their things in their dorm room, took them to Sears and bought a tiny refrigerator, popcorn popper, and Mr. Coffee. They parted on Orientation Day with a warm embrace, just like all the other mothers and sons. And just like all the other mothers and sons, they spoke on the phone as often as he was willing but not nearly as much as she would have liked. It was healthy, Pia recognized, for the boys to create their own lives away from her. And she phrased it that way to avoid admitting to herself the simple truth that they were better off without her. She firmly resolved to be calm and pleasant on Orientation Day, and she *was* calm and pleasant, until she arrived at the airport for the return flight to Houston.

The sharks had been lurking just below the surface of Pia's diaphragm for quite some time, but this was the first time they attacked.

Waiting her turn to be searched, Pia was actually grateful for the long line that zigzagged between metal posts and nylon divider straps, because it slowed the airport terminal traffic to a crawl and gave her a chance to focus. The sharks swished past the back of her heart when she saw the National Guardsman posted near the coffee bar. He was excruciatingly young and pretty-faced, even with his purposefully grim expression. He grasped his automatic rifle with a sort of nervous anticipation. The way a Little Leaguer grasps a baseball bat.

When Pia stepped through the metal detector, an alarm shrilled and a young man with blue streaks in his hair escorted her off to the side.

"Remove your shoes and set your feet on the orange footprints, please."

As she stood with outstretched arms, the sharks began thrashing with a vengeance, feeding on the haze of suspicion and hostility, the chemical imbalance that pervaded the concourse and Pia's own nervous system. The young man passed a wand over her body and between her legs, finally homing in on a pen she'd forgotten was in the pocket of her blazer. He pawed through her bag, his hands sheathed in latex gloves. He took each item out of her makeup kit, tested the mascara on a napkin, rolled the lipstick in and out. By the time he'd forced the zipper around the jumbled contents and shoved the bag back into Pia's arms, she was barely breathing. She tried to step around another passenger who'd been pulled aside.

"Random, my ass!" he barked. "I've been *randomly* jerked out of line seven flights in a row."

At first, Pia thought she was having some sort of cardiac episode. She made her way to the slidewalk and leaned on the rail in a cold sweat, checking a list of symptoms tucked away in her brain from a long-ago CPR class. Her heart writhed and clattered against her breastbone. Her throat narrowed, then closed altogether. The sharks sank their teeth into her intestines and shredded her lungs. She thought about picking up the white courtesy phone and requesting an ambulance, but she couldn't speak, couldn't even cough. Instead, she stumbled to a chair in the corner near her gate, swallowed some Dramamine with a soft drink, and comforted herself with the only mantra that came to her in that moment. *I am not afraid to fly. I am not afraid to fly. I have been on a thousand flights, and I am not afraid.*

Her flight was called a few minutes later. Pia managed to find her seat and fumble the two halves of the seat belt together while the flight attendant stowed her carry-on.

"Are you all right, ma'am?" asked the flight attendant.

"I think so," Pia managed to whisper.

"Do you have a fear of flying?"

"No. I'm fine."

"A lot of people are experiencing some apprehension with the whole 9/11 thing. For someone who's already nervous about flying, it can be pretty intense."

"I'm sure it can, but I'm fine. Thank you."

"Would you like a pillow and blanket?"

Pia's eyes were already closed, but she must have nodded, because she felt the flimsy blue blanket being tucked around her shoulders.

"There's nothing to be concerned about," said the flight attendant. "Security is very tight. There's a sky marshal right up front, and the crew is trained to deal with any emergency."

Pia nodded and closed her eyes. For some reason, hearing all that constricted the blood vessels in her forehead. The whine of the engine went through her like a slice of sheet metal. A little while later, she felt the lurch of the pullback, the shuddering taxi ride, the lift and bank of the takeoff, and just before she lost track of herself, she felt the flight attendant pass by and squeeze her hand.

Beth

This is a good day for Beth.

She doesn't wake up until almost six, and when she does, it's only with her eyes. Not the full body wrenching awake. Just an opening of the eyes, and that is such a relief, she doesn't care what time it is.

In the shower, she doesn't have to cry, because the cold water gives her that same gasping in her midsection. The streaming over her face keeps her from needing tears there. She emerges shivering, which isn't pleasure but is an acceptable substitute, because she can feel it permeating her body in the same way pleasure would if she could feel it. Sensation is something she has come to cherish in all its forms, having learned the slow torture of numbness.

She moves the blow dryer over herself until her body and short-cropped hair are dry and warm, then she lets her fingertips drift over the rough spot on her chest. It's just below her clavicle, on the left, about three inches in from the ball and socket of her shoulder, slightly above her heart. She caresses it until she feels a dry papery edge, then lets herself scratch slight downward strokes until her nail catches enough of a purchase to raise the edge a bit. She works along the perimeter, lifting and loosening until there's enough to get hold of. Then she pulls at what she thinks of as a circle of armadillo skin, which is dry but still thickened and soft from the water. She fancies she hears, but really only feels the sound of fabric tearing as it comes away. Blood pools into the divot underneath. Beth dabs it with a square of toilet tissue, which snags on a crescent of white scar tissue struggling to form around the small, warm crater. This is easier to take hold of and comes away with the jagged sensation of zipping a canvas bag.

There's a bit more blood than she expected. It takes her breath from her in a low, hummingbird sound. She dabs, keeps dabbing, leaning in toward the mirror to see if she can glimpse the raw pink of her inner self laced with the frailest, most delicate capillaries, but the viscous blood pools in again. She dabs, keeps dabbing. Leaning. Peering inside herself. Finally, there's just a small trickle of red that stays in the newly torn crescent.

Beth takes another square of tissue, folds it into quarters, and holds it against the top of a bottle of rubbing alcohol. She tips the opaque plastic bottle forward and back quickly, not wanting to waste any by spilling or drenching the tissue with more than it can absorb. When she blots it against the divot near her shoulder, she closes her eyes to savor the cauterizing sear. The pain is mouthwatering, but shame pools in beneath it. She's going to leave this one alone now, she promises. If it gets any bigger Sonny might notice.

She holds the alcohol tissue there for another moment, then opens a drawer and takes out a Band-Aid. Folding open the waxy paper backing, she squeezes a small dot of Neosporin on the sterile white pad, thinking of the magazine ad that promises quicker healing if you do that. The ad shows side-by-side photos of a slashed finger that's been bandaged with Neosporin and a slashed finger that's been left to find its own way. It shows you the difference in their ability to heal.

Beth is fascinated by this ad. Who would slash their finger

for a magazine ad? What did that feel like? Did they use a razor blade? A surgical instrument? Did they really keep the Band-Aid on for days or did they peel it off at night and let their fingertips find that crackle-dry edge? Perhaps the person with the unhealing finger slash was not ready to be whole again. Perhaps that tiny fissure was a small secret doorway whereby her soul escaped in and out of her body. Like the slashed opening on the front of a tent.

Zip it open to leave. Zip it shut to keep it clean.

Zip it open to go back in. Zip it shut to hide.

Pia

When Pia awoke, she was experiencing some turbulence. As she looked out the window beside her cramped seat, the airplane wing seemed to be bobbing and wobbling.

Sometimes Edgar would take a pencil between his thumb and index finger and wobble it up and down until it looked like it was bending and flexing. "Wet noodle," he'd say in a silly wobbled voice. This was what he did when he was helping the boys with their homework and they made a silly mistake or complained too much or got whiny.

"Forty lashes with a wet noodle," he'd tease.

The airplane wing wobbled like a wet noodle. Pia wondered if it was going to fall off. That ought to frighten her, she thought, but it didn't. The boys were safely installed in their dorm rooms. They'd get a call. From Sonny probably. That was comforting. Sonny would see to everything, from Pia's body in a drawer to Pia's ashes in the ocean.

"Excuse me, ma'am? Are you Pia Beaulieu?"

Pia startled at the flight attendant's touch to her arm.

"Oh." Pia glanced around the cabin nervously. Was she being

searched again? Did they find something terrible in her checked bags? "It's Beaulieu-Ramone, actually, but yes, I'm Pia."

"Would you like to join us in first class?" the flight attendant asked, setting her hand on Pia's forearm.

Pia was acutely aware of even a small touch like that now, and she knew it was because she was touched so little. She'd hardly seen the boys all summer, and they never hugged for more than a moment anyway. She could tell they wanted to be let go. She was like an old person in a home now, like a baby in an incubator, starving for that fleeting pleasure, that light pressure of human on human.

"First class?"

"Yes, there's a gentleman who'd like you to join him." Pia's face must have betrayed her misgivings about that, because the flight attendant smiled and patted her hand. "Don't worry. He says he's a colleague. Barret Mayor." The flight attendant's voice inflected upward, questioning, as if Pia should either verify this information or dispute it. She held a business card toward Pia with one hand, steadying herself with her other hand on the back of someone's seat.

Turbulence.

Pia took the card and stared at it, trying to put the name into some kind of context. Barret Mayor. She wouldn't have known who he was if she hadn't seen his name adjacent to the name of a law firm with which she was familiar. They'd represented a company that wanted to continue manufacturing a pesticide that had been banned in the United States because it was proven to cause lymphoma. (They could still sell it overseas, Your Honor. Africa, India, South America. They had no such regulations. If it could still be sold, why destroy the livelihood of an entire Indiana town?) Pia had been contracted to do research and speak on behalf of the Institute for Planetary Conscience. After a year of wrangling negotiations and six weeks of intense pretrial preparation, she'd presented two days of unfathomable science compressed to laymen's terms. When it came time for them to cross-examine her, their lawyer had stood, smooth as a river stone, and said, "No questions." But that was almost three years ago, and they'd had a seemingly endless parade of attorneys. At the moment, Pia couldn't conjure the face of a single one of them.

"Ma'am?"

The flight attendant was being purposefully patient, but her smile stretched a little too bright to ring true. She rocked to the left a little with a sudden dip of the airplane. Someone was ringing her from first class. The teenage boy behind Pia pushed his knees against the back of her seat. A baby cried across the aisle. The plane rocked to the right, dipped, came back up. Pia nodded, stood unsteadily, and pulled her purse from beneath the seat in front of her.

"I'll get the rest of your things later," the flight attendant said, leading the way to the forward cabin, while Pia kept her eyes away from everyone left behind in coach. There wasn't any need for the smiling attendant to indicate the empty seat. It was the only empty seat on the other side of that curtain that comforts the better half by shielding their cloth napkins and glass glasses and fresh-baked cookies from envious view. The flight attendant took Pia's bag and stood smiling. Bright smiling. Bright as a knife blade.

Pia thanked her and sat next to river stone–smooth Barret Mayor of the unscrupulous law firm, of the unapologetic first class. He was very much the way she remembered all the attorneys from all those meetings. Smooth-faced, shaven so clean he was expressionless, white shirt with just a hint of pale blue line in it. Even in the heat, their suits were sharper or starchier or fresher or maybe just more expensive than Edgar's Sunday-go-to-meetin' clothes. Barret Mayor was not young, but he was unquestionably handsome in a tailored, bookshelf way. His comeliness was something dry and substantive, something he wore.

"Ms. Beaulieu-Ramone," he smiled. "What a pleasure to see you again."

Pia nodded. Usually someone with his southern gentlefolk way of speaking would say "*B*-loo," with the accent on the first syllable, or "Ba-*loo*," like the bear in the *Jungle Book* movie. But Barret Mayor smoothly said it with only slightly more texture in the middle than the color. "B'lue," he said, pronouncing it the way Pia would have said it herself if she'd needed to correct him, the way her father used to say it when he told his customers to whom they should make the check payable, the way Edgar had formally spoken it when he proposed.

She took the outstretched hand and again felt that acute awareness of touch, more so this time because his hand felt like *man*. The musculature was pronounced and sure, his grip firm, purposefully friendly, the practiced connection of a politician or a mercenary or a priest as you escape on Sunday morning.

"Mr. Mayor. How nice to see you again."

"Oh, please," he said warmly, "call me Barret. I'm sure I've been called worse around your office lately."

He took her hand between both of his and laughed out loud. Pia tried to smile.

"I haven't been around my office lately," she said.

"How very fortunate for me."

Pia realized with a sudden blush of discomfort that this must be why he'd invited her to join him in first class. He thought she was still consulting for the Institute. The plane rocked to the left, to the right; the tail section seemed to be swinging behind them like an eel. On the other side of the curtain, the baby was in full scream now.

"Sounds miserable back there," he said, gesturing toward the curtain. "I guess your altruistic organization has higher purposes for their money than to treat you to first class?"

"Well, this is a personal trip, but yes. They do."

Pia didn't like volunteering information to this stranger but felt obligated to make conversation now that she'd accepted the seat.

"Luckily, I always book two seats," Barret Mayor was saying. "So I can spread out with my work. Or just in case."

"You book two first-class seats? For yourself?" Pia didn't mean to sound disapproving, but he rushed to justify himself.

"Not exactly for myself. It's really not as extravagant as it sounds. It's not uncommon for me to see associates, opponents, people with whom I need to network. Airplanes are a good venue for less formal conversation, and you never know who you might run into. Life is full of wonderful surprises, isn't it?"

Pia smiled and nodded because she had no idea what he meant by that.

"So you're on vacation, then?"

"No." Pia tried to avoid his frankly expectant look by meticulously adjusting her seat belt, but after a long moment she grudgingly said, "I was visiting my sons at school." He didn't press for any details beyond that, just smiled in a way that allowed Pia to add, "They're at Harvard," without feeling she was bragging.

"Harvard boys! You must be very proud."

"Yes."

"My daughter's at Stanford," he told her, and it made him a little more human when he deftly whipped out a small photo in an acrylic frame. "Sarah," he said, the way a human father would.

"She's lovely," Pia said, handing the photo back to him, and he nodded, proudly agreed as he tucked it back in his breast pocket. Pia felt a moment of horror that she'd never carried a little acrylic frame like that when she traveled. And up to this moment, she would have thought herself a thousand times more motherly than any sharp-pressed corporate mattock.

"Yeah, she'll finish in the spring. You can bet her mother and I, oh, we are just about as proud as a coupla peacocks."

"That's wonderful." Pia searched for something else to say. "What is she studying?"

"Her undergraduate degree was in French and French literature," he said, the way you'd tell another parent about some charming but silly thing a child has said. "And her master's . . . I believe it's foreign studies or something in that area. I'm not sure what she's planning to do with all that. I don't think she's too sure herself. Keeps talking about the Peace Corps. We're hoping she'll grow out of that."

"My husband was in the Peace Corps," Pia said. "It was a wonderful experience."

"Oh, I don't mean anything against it, Pia—may I call you Pia?—but it's not what we'd hoped she'd do with her life. Truthfully, I had hoped she might study law and someday, maybe she and I might even go into practice together." He set his hands flat on top of the briefcase that lay in his lap. "Mayor and Mayor. I suppose it sounds silly, but it's been my daydream. I don't mind admitting it. We don't see each other as much as I'd like. Her mother and I divorced two years ago. They moved to Boston, and of course, I'm based here."

Pia knew he meant "here" to mean home in Houston, but it could have meant here on the other side of the first-class curtain, or here in a pleasantly lit hotel room, or here inside a palm-sized computer. Here between things. That was where Pia used to live, so she understood.

The flight attendant came back to ask if they wanted a glass of wine before dinner, and Pia did. She wanted her shoulders to feel something other than nagging stiff. She wanted the conversation to be something other than painfully obligatory. She wondered why his name might have been mentioned in her old office lately, wondered if it had something to do with the dark oiliness of the water off Bolivar.

"I was terribly sorry to hear your husband had passed away," he said suddenly. When Pia glanced up, surprised, he added, "It only makes sense for us to keep track of these things."

"Of course."

"And I am sorry."

"Thank you."

"This must have been a difficult year for you."

"Yes. It's actually almost two years now," said Pia. "It doesn't seem possible."

"I know how it feels. Being separated from my wife. It's a difficult adjustment. But they say the first year is the worst."

Pia hated it when people drew comparisons between divorce and widowhood, between widowhood and cancer, between widowhood and being stuck in traffic. The tacit message in that seemed to be, "People get over things all the time. You should get out more."

"Well, I um, I guess you'd like to get back to your work, so I think I'll go on back."

She unbuckled her seat belt, started to get up, but he took hold of her hand.

"Please! Don't be silly. She'll just be another minute with the wine, and then there'll be dinner. Look, I certainly understand why you might feel uncomfortable talking with me. That's fine, Pia. Really. We can just sit quietly. This isn't a deposition, Pia, I promise."

"Oh, it's not that! I just—I don't want to distract you from—"

"I'm serious. You can ignore me. Just pretend you're seated next to some devastatingly charming stranger."

"Mr. Mayor—"

"Barret. Please call me Barret."

Sitting forward on the front edge of her seat, Pia pressed her palms together in a gesture Edgar used to tease her was a cross between a Catholic schoolgirl and the *Thinker* statue.

"Barret. I don't know what you want from me. You must know I'm not involved in anything anymore. I haven't even spoken to Jenna or anyone at the firm for several months."

"Yes, I know." His tone was easy and soft in a drowsy southern way. "Please, Pia. Don't go. The fact is I'm planning to run for Congress, so I'm actively steering my caseload toward homeland security issues. The matter I'm currently litigating isn't remotely related to environmental concerns. I promise you, I have no agenda here." He held his hands open as if to show her they were clean and empty. "And believe me, I don't book this other seat expecting to pick up some beautiful woman or other to put in it. Fate's never been that kind to me." He smiled a broadly impeccable smile. "At least not until today."

The plane tipped a little, and Pia felt it in her stomach. She hadn't even thought of that angle, hadn't thought of herself as "some beautiful woman or other" that someone would want to pick up in order to fill an empty chair.

"That's probably the lamest pickup line I've ever used," Barret said. "I'm sorry. I'm a little nervous."

"Don't worry," Pia said. "It's not the lamest pickup line I've ever heard."

"Is it working for me?"

"A little." She felt herself smile, relaxing a bit.

"You know, I saw you being searched back at the gate, and I was racking my brains, trying to recall where I knew you from, and then sitting here—it just hit me. Of course! That whole thing in Boston. I remembered you as a calming presence in all that animosity," he said. "You weren't self-righteous and militant like so many of your former associates. You're one of the few people I know who understands what it is to travel all the time. And I'm guessing you've learned in the last two years what it is to be lonely."

Pia nodded, and Barret took her hand.

"I can't think of one earthly reason why we shouldn't share a glass of wine and a nice dinner. As nice a dinner as you're going to get on an airplane, anyway. And then—look here. We can swing these fancy TV screens around and watch whatever we want. Look at this thing they've got for your laptop now. You could engineer a hostile takeover of the damn airline from here. It's more complicated than the cockpit."

He did this thing that could be called a chuckle, if chuckling were infinitely more sophisticated. Pia remembered now. This folksy, friendly style he had. This winning patter that made any dissenting view silly and overwrought. It made Jenna rant and curse in the elevator, but at this moment it felt like a down comforter, and Pia wanted to sink into it.

Barret squeezed her hand and again that rush of need coursed across her spirit.

"I wish you'd stay," he said.

Pia didn't mean to nod, but the plane dipped and nodded her head for her, and then the flight attendant was there, doing her best to balance the wineglasses on a tray.

Lily

(400 days)

Two zeroes. Spent the day with my face against the wall. Promised Pia and King I wouldn't let anyone see me fall apart crying, but I miss them both so bad. I miss the twins, I miss my life, I miss my walls. These walls here—that's what's going to kill me. These walls feel like they're a thousand feet thick.

(412 days)

Library day. Complete Works of C Rossetti. Used to love her stuff when I was in high school. Rossetti, Neruda, Rilke. Like taking a milk bath in words.

> I wish I were a little bird
> That out of sight doth soar . . .

(415 days)

Letter and care package from Pia today. Huge gladness about that on several levels.

1. I hate it when I don't hear from her.
2. Tampons! Real Tampax in a variety of sizes. Thank you, Pia! The kind they supply here are so cheap and nasty. There is much to be said for small niceties. Smooth glide applicator. Never never never to be taken for granted.

Also stamps, vitamins, pens, and pictures of the Double J Boys at college. She sent a notebook, but they confiscated it. We're not allowed to have spiral-bound. I hate to ask her for the expensive perforated kind, but I'll die if I don't have paper.

(421 days)

Checked out Madame Bovary for the third time. Little old Jesus Chick grabs the book and gives it a big kiss before she stamps it.

JC: Oh, Flaubert! Good for you, sister. Good for you.

ME: Um . . . yeah. Thanks.

JC: (flipping through the pages) Where is it, where is it? Ah! Here. "Love, she thought, must come suddenly, with great outbursts and lightnings—a hurricane of the skies, which falls upon life, revolutionizes it, roots up the will like a leaf, and sweeps the whole heart into the abyss."

ME: (just trying to get my book out of her grippy little mitts) Yeah. Cool. That's great.

JC: It's amazing to me that words like that can live in a place like this. But they do, don't they? Oh yes, they live and thrive and find their best possible purpose!

ME: (desperately trying to work my way to the door) Yup. OK, then. See you next week. Say hi to Jesus for me.

(424 days)

Returned Madame Bovary. Checked out The Agony and the Ecstasy.

No Pia call.
No King.

(427 days)

Jesus sisters did "Self-Esteem" and "Admitting My Mistakes" workshops today. Does anyone else find that combination sort of ironic?

(434 days)

Memo to the Ass Clown guard in the purple sunglasses: You do not scare me.

ASS CLOWN: There's no smoking in the laundry.

ME: Blow it out your colon, Gomer.

AC: Put it out or I'll put it out for you.

ME: And yet they say chivalry is dead.

AC: Prisoner, you've got a count of three to put that thing out! (Only he says it in his big ol' "Why don't I pretend like I'm black so I can be cool in my gay little sunglasses" dialect. Like "Prez-nuh, yew gotta cownah threetah put that thang ah-oot!")

ME: Count of three? Wow! Somebody's been workin' on his flash cards.

And the ass clown sprays me. Whips a spray gun out of the laundry sink and sprays me in the face and then just laughs like it's the funniest thing since Laurel and Hardy. If I wasn't so afraid of losing good time, I would have kicked his ass clown ass.

(437 days)

Pia called, but Ass Clown wouldn't let me go up.

Rossetti's To Do List:

> Today, while it is called today,
> Kneel, wrestle, knock, do violence, pray.

(441 days)

Embraced spirit of Rossetti and got Ass Clown good.

ME: (flinging a tampon—whoop-ta-SMACK! Side of the head!) Have a nice day, Ass Clown!

AC: (acting like it was soaked in rendered plutonium) What the—AAAGH! Mother of God! What the hell is wrong with you? You think that's civilized? You think that's funny?

ME: (laughing myself sick) Oh yeah. It's funny. Moira, you think that's funny? See, Moira thinks it's funny, too.

AC: Well it's not! There's gonna be consequences for that, prisoner! You're gonna see some serious-by-God consequences! That's an assault charge, prisoner! That's 60 days good time!

ME: (not laughing quite so much) Sixty? No way. You can't do that.

AC: Oh, I can do it, prisoner. Consider it done. Sixty days. SIXTY! Count 'em down! That's right. Go ahead and pick a fight with me, prisoner. You're not gonna win.

ME: Well, that gives you something to brag about down at the gay bar, doesn't it, Ass Clown?

AC: (goes mumbling off down the corridor through this all-out hurricane of everybody in the place laughing all our asses off) Freaking uncivilized insalubrious witch.

ME: (cracking up again) "Insalubrious"? Oo, them's fightin' words—for a GAY WAD!

Holy crap, that was hilarious. "Insalubrious"? Oh my friggin' God. Can't stop laughing. Ribs hurt so bad I'm crying. Take that, Ass Clown. On the other hand, there's the 60 days. With total good time lost, I am now 16 months from my next parole hearing. Crap. That hurts.

(450 days)

Went to sleep reading Rossetti and dreamed about Easter.

Thus am I mine own prison.

Pia

Pia lay beside Barret Mayor in the big sleigh bed she and Edgar had bought before the boys were born. Drifting her hand along the length of Barret's body, she felt serene, satisfied, and deeply grateful.

When Barret was there, she always slept easily and woke early. She liked lying there in the half-dawn, watching the lines of his face become more deeply defined as the day came on. She loved lying there thinking about how utterly, wonderfully indecent Barret Mayor could be. When he awoke, he would dress in his expensive suit and be a corporate attorney again. As long as he was sleeping, Pia could keep his salacious whispers, skillful fingers, rapacious mouth—all the tenderness and attention to detail that led into long, gusty plateaus of something that felt like horsemanship. Everything that took place between them in the dark was intensely embarrassing to Barret by the light of day, when he was all conservative views and crisply dry-cleaned demeanor. Pia quickly learned not to mention it.

When Barret wasn't there—which was often, because his job kept him traveling a great deal—he called every night at eleven to "tuck her in," and she fell asleep with his voice in her ear. When he was there, Pia felt less afraid and more alive than she had since Edgar died. She went out into the world and did things when Barret was with her, something she seldom did by herself anymore. His charm was contagious. When Barret was with her, Pia was intelligent and witty and conversational. She was adventurous and relaxed all day and fell asleep beside him each night, feeling deliciously comforted on a profoundly private level.

But when the weekend was over and Barret went on his way to the airport, Pia was left with a vague sense of shame and a not-so-vague fear that someone was going to find out what she was doing. The effort of hiding Barret—from the boys, from Sonny, from Beth's scrutinizing eye, and worst of all from Lily—was getting to be inconvenient. Pia didn't like being the sort of woman who had things to hide. She didn't like the distance her secret created between herself and the boys, who anyway seemed to be growing more distant by the day through the natural progression of life. She didn't like the yawning gaps in her conversations with Lily, who was never shy about pointing out a conversational void and filling it with questions. Pia didn't want to be interrogated about what Barret looked like and what they did with their time together. She didn't want to answer her own questions about how she could start an affair like this when she was so *not strong*. She didn't want to ask herself if it was really fair to Barret to let this thing go forward without telling him about the sharks.

Pia knew she wasn't dying of a cardiopulmonary irregularity. Research was, of course, her first response to everything, and her initial research pointed toward something far more frightening than a failing heart. Pia's initial research indicated that she was going crazy. Simple fact-finding forays into medical resources gave rise to phrases like *panic disorder* and *post-traumatic* and *anticipatory anxiety*, which dominated her notes as she followed the inevitable path into the psychiatric sector.

According to the American Psychiatric Association Web

site, 75 to 90 percent of patients afflicted with panic disorders were helped by medication and cognitive behavioral therapy, which included the five key elements of Learning, Monitoring, Breathing, Rethinking, and Exposing. This was the opposite of Pia's early technique, which included the five key elements of Denying, Hiding, Avoiding, Gasping for Air, and Focusing on Impending Death.

Pia wasn't quite ready to pathologize what was happening to her, but she did stock her purse with over-the-counter medications for motion sickness and sleeplessness. She practiced breathing while she was in the bathtub and forced herself to mentally recast those people and places that seemed to draw the sharks more than others. She forced herself to drive, to enter a new supermarket that opened in her area, to walk through the park just before sunrise. She felt certain she was making progress. But still. It didn't feel right to become involved with this man and not tell him that she was struggling against the slow losing of her mind.

For several months, Pia put Barret off with bland excuses, but Barret was wise enough to wait for her. That was what ultimately made her love him. The way he waited. He adjusted his schedule, extending almost every weekend to three and sometimes even four days, and he rarely went to his own house in Chicago. From the moment Pia picked him up at the airport, to the moment she dropped him off again, he seemed to be biding his time. While others kept asking her when she was going to go back to work, he said he saw no reason why she should be in a rush. While Jenna left messages about case studies and pending bills, Barret talked to her about the time his junior high softball team won the state championship, about a play he wanted to see, about a book he'd picked up for her in the airport gift shop. And when he sensed that Pia was finally ready, he mentioned his daughter being in town, that she would like to meet Pia, have dinner with them, that the boys should join them if they were coming home for Christmas break.

"Actually," Pia said, "we're going to meet in Key West."

"Ah, that sounds wonderful! You know, maybe Sarah and I could—"

"*No.*" She realized how sharp it sounded and tried to take the edge off. "This just isn't the time, Barret. I'm sorry."

"Don't be. I didn't mean to intrude. It might actually be better if we did this next month, anyway. I'm speaking at this conference in San Francisco, and Sarah's going to stop down to hear me. Why don't you come with me. We could have dinner with her. Maybe take an extra day or two. Drive up the coast."

As he was talking, Pia was doing the mental math. How many hours to fly to San Francisco? Would she be able to suppress the sharks for that long? They were getting more and more aggressive. If she could have canceled the Key West trip without it being inhumanly hurtful to James and Jesse, she would have.

"That does sound nice," she said as warmly as she could. "Let's get through the holidays before we make any solid commitment, though."

"Sure. Of course."

He was an astonishingly patient man. It made Pia think of the way her mother used to check on angel food cake. Open the door, press very gently, see what the relative resistance or lightness is, close the door, come back again after a little bit.

James ended up doing it. Pia and Jesse ended up arguing about it—if you're supposed to just dump the ashes or scoop them or what. James asked the helicopter pilot, who said most people hold it out the square portal and dump, which James did, and before Pia could say anything, he tossed the vase—the *urn!*—the stupid expensive receptacle thing—out the open door into the wild helicopter noise and blowing water. Watching it disappear into the waves, Pia felt a momentary impulse to jump in after it, but the other helicopter man slid the door shut and they skimmed back over the ocean toward the sandy edge of the island.

Pia rested her forehead against the window. She wished she had decided on embalming and a grand procession to a mausoleum. Edgar would have made a wonderful mummy. She put her hand over her mouth because that thought made her want to laugh. A mummy in a great, gilded sarcophagus. He would have loved that. Not this. This all seemed so anticlimactic. It was Edgar, living in his skin for all those years, and then . . . whisper, shatter, dump, splash. The last fragments of his body disappeared from Pia's life, and as they did, the thought of his body didn't pass across her mind, wistful or fond. It pooled in a dark place between her tailbone and tightly crossed legs, then fanned upward to her nipples, which suddenly felt hypersensitive. The most genteel word Pia could put to the feeling was *longing*. She was acutely aware of her own void places, and that made her wish she'd let Barret come along after all.

Guilt grated against the back of her heart. Edgar was completely gone now, and she was seeing someone else—*sleeping with someone else*. Jesse was sitting there looking and acting like a stranger. James was the only one crying. Maybe it was the wind in his eyes, the way he'd leaned out the helicopter's sliding side door and then dumped—no, he didn't just dump it. He *poured* it out the way Edgar had poured out his whole life on the three of them, without hesitation or hurry, without reservation. It was his reason, this family. He brought it into being and it brought him into being, and together they made a kind of sense that was now completely lacking in Pia's life.

She thought about the ceramic receptacle bobbing on the water below. Perhaps it would wash ashore and someone would find it. Maybe it would wash up right outside their hotel and she would find it herself!

Don't be stupid, she told herself harshly.

What would be the odds of that? If it washed up anywhere, it wouldn't be anytime soon or anyplace Pia would ever see it again. And that was for the best. It would have been silly to hang on to something like that, anyway. It was a little strange to have it sitting there on the nightstand while she and Barret—

Pia quickly checked that thought. Home in bed with him again the following week, she was grateful it had never occurred to her before.

"What are you thinking about?" Barret asked. "You're a million miles away."

Even in the quiet after time, he kept moving in such a way that Pia had to set her hands against the wall over her head to keep from forgetting her dignity and becoming completely undone again.

"Hmm?" he murmured against her neck. "What could be more distracting than this?"

"Nothing," Pia said truthfully. "I'm here."

"We are going to have a wonderful time in San Francisco next week," Barret said. "The weather's supposed to be beautiful. You can spend your days on the waterfront, spend your nights with me. And your mornings with me. And maybe a few carefully planned lunch-hour assignations?"

"Actually, Barret, about that . . ."

"What is it, my pretty Pia?"

"I can't go. I'm sorry I said I would. I want to go, but I can't."

"Why not?"

"Of course, I'll reimburse you for the ticket."

"You didn't answer my question."

"Barret," Pia said, with a conscious effort to breathe, monitor, rethink. "I know this sounds like an excuse or like I'm being a wimp, but the truth is . . . I'm afraid of flying."

"What?" Barret raised up on his elbows. His expression was a mixture of curiosity, amusement, and irritation. "Since when?"

"Since the last few months. I don't know how or why. I just am. And I need you to understand."

Pia regretted saying anything. She wanted to be honest, but her timing was ill-chosen, to say the least. Barret had completely pulled away from her now and was propped up on pillows, staring at the ceiling.

"Well, Pia, that's ridiculous. You spent your entire career flying all over kingdom come. The first time I kissed you, we were on an airplane. How can you be afraid of flying?"

"I don't understand it myself, Barret. All I can tell you is that it is very real and very intense, and I don't want to subject myself to it unless it's absolutely necessary."

"What about your little jaunt to Key West? I suppose that was a matter of life and death?"

"Yes." Pia sat up and edged away from him, pulling the sheet up over her breasts. "I promised my sons we would scatter their father's ashes. On New Year's Eve. It was two years since he died. And if it makes you feel any better, I had a miserable time."

"Oh. God . . . I'm—*aagh!*" Barret dropped his chin to his chest. "I'm a jackass. I'm a knucklehead. Pia, I am so sorry I said that."

"It's all right."

"No, it's not all right. It was incredibly callous. I apologize."

"Barret, stop! I'm the one who should apologize. I should have been honest with you about this from the start."

"The thing is, Pia, it's very important to me that you come to San Francisco this week. A lot of politics go on at this conference. I wanted very much for you to be there."

"Barret, I can't imagine your political retinue will have much use for me. We're not exactly on the same page."

"But that's the beauty of it! My political retinue is in line. It's *your* political retinue I'm trying to reach. If I'm going to make a successful run for Congress in three years, I've got to do some serious fence-mending with certain people who may have misinterpreted where I stand on certain issues. You could be a tremendous help to me, Pia, and besides all that—oh, hell, I might as well tell you. I've spent a bloody fortune. I booked the Presidential Suite at the Lexington. I had this whole ridiculous thing planned out with a limo and flowers."

Pia didn't realize she was still clutching the sheet at her collarbone until Barret reached out and took her hands between his own.

"Monday evening at ten-thirty, room service will be delivering champagne and a chocolate-raspberry torte topped with a dollop of whipped cream and an obnoxiously resplendent diamond ring. It's my stupid, overblown, politically incorrect way of asking if you would please do me the honor of becoming my wife. And the effect will be greatly diminished if you're not there."

"Oh, Barret . . ." Pia tried to pull her hands away, but he held fast. "Barret, that is so very sweet of you. That's all amazingly sweet. I don't know what to say."

"This can't be coming as a huge surprise to you," he said. "Not after some of the conversations we've had lately."

"No, but candidly, Barret, I try to avoid those conversations."

"Why?"

"I'm not sure it's such a great idea."

"In what way?"

"In several ways."

"Such as?"

"Barret!" Pia folded her arms in front of her body, feeling vulnerable and naked. "Do you hear what you're doing? See, this is what you do. You cross-examine. It's your way of boxing another person into your point of view."

"No," he said sharply, "it's my way of cutting through the crap and the obfuscation and getting the real issues on the table. I mean, for God's sake, Pia, what are we waiting for? We're not dewy-eyed freshmen. We've both been around the block, and sadly, we've gotten our butts kicked. Some terribly unfortunate things have occurred. But where we go from there is entirely up to us."

"Yes, but—"

"Number one." Barret framed each point with his hands. "Let's clarify the primary relevant fact here: *I love you.* That is what this is about. But on a secondary level, frankly, I hate being single. Trying to meet people, trying to make conversation with someone who doesn't know or care anything about my work, trying to weed out the crazies and the gold-diggers. I've lost my taste for the disposable lay-date, which requires more alcohol than is prudent and leaves me with the urge to take a very hot shower, if not rush out for a complete round of medical tests. That's not what I want in my bed. That's not what I want to be in someone else's bed. Call me old-fashioned or stodgy or whatever, but I like being anchored to a home, where shared values and common interests provide a framework for plain old everyday *comfort*. I like being married. And you, Pia—you, I love. I won't say I loved you that first day on the airplane, but I was fairly certain I was going to. I was never in this to waste your time. Or mine. If you don't love me, Pia, you should tell me now."

"Barret, I do love you," she said, with her heart and her eyes wide open. "But what if—"

"What if what?"

"What if I turn out to be one of the crazies?"

Barret's warm, rolling laughter made her laugh, too. As if she'd been joking.

"Come with me to California," he told her. "We'll go off the deep end together."

Pia cupped his face with her hands, stroking his gray temples and resolute jaw, bordering on words but not quite finding them. Barret turned his face into her palm, kissing her wrist.

"This could be a whole new life for both of us," he said. "Please say yes."

She didn't want to base this decision on the fact that after Edgar died, her life was utterly bleak until the day Barret Mayor invited her to bump up to something better. But she wasn't sure anything else was relevant. What are the odds, she wondered, of finding two good loves in one lifetime? About as likely as a crematorium jar washing up in your bathtub.

"Okay," Pia said unsteadily. "Yes."

"*Thank you*," he breathed. "My beautiful Pia. My beautiful wife. Let's not put it off. Let's get married while we're in California. I don't want to leave room for any doubts or naysayers."

"What about Jesse and James? And Sarah?"

"They'll be happy for us," Barret said, joyfully surrounding her, hugging her to him. "Hey, what's this? Are you trembling at the idea of being a congressman's wife or the idea of getting on the airplane?"

"A little of both," said Pia, and they laughed together.

"You're making way too much of this fear of flying thing, Pia. You're not crazy. This is some interim anxiety thing. Look at what you've been through. Understandably, you're a bit shaken. But the Pia I know and love and respect—this woman is no wimp."

Pia smiled, hoping with all her heart that he was right.

"Maybe you need a little something to take the edge off. You know, Gabriella had some trouble after we split up. She saw a very good doctor. He was extremely helpful."

"You're sending me to your ex-wife's therapist?" Pia teased. "How romantic."

"His name is Heller, and he's an internist, not a therapist. But he's a good guy," Barret said seriously. "I trust him to be discreet. Maybe he could prescribe something, just to get you to California and home again."

Pia knew she should tell Barret about the sharks. Now. Before this went any further. But she wanted so much to be drawn into his unshakable belief, the invulnerability of his embrace.

She did tell Dr. Heller.

"We'll do an EKG," he said, "but it sounds like a panic attack."

She mentioned the attrition of her family over the last few years and asked if there was a connection. Perhaps the sharks were attracted by all that death like blood in the water.

"Possibly," Dr. Heller said. That was something he said a lot. "Perhaps you should talk to someone about that when you get back."

He gave her a booklet with a misty pink cover, tore a yellow sheet off his pad, and wrote out the prescription.

Lily

(730 days)

I have been in this place two years.
That oughta learn me.

(732 days)

In the infirmary. My nose is broken. That pig Moira friggin' broke it. All I've been trying to do since I got here is have as little contact with anyone as I possibly can. She's throwing a laundry bin at someone else, ends up smashing me in the face, and since I'm the one bleeding all over the floor, I get busted for fighting. Thirty days good time lost.

On the upside, I like the infirmary. Clean and quiet. Wish I could stay here until parole hearing.

(734 days)

Reading Wuthering Heights. A book about love that turns cruel.

No Pia call.
No King.

(764 days)

Reading The Heart Is a Lonely Hunter, a book about clean laundry. Pia called. Said all the stuff for my hearing is notarized and FedExed over there. Good to go.

ME: I don't want to jinx myself, but I think I'm getting out of here, Pia. I feel good about it. I'm thinking positive.

PIA: Me, too.

ME: Are you okay, Pia? You sound funny.

PIA: I'm fine. I'm on this medication and it's sort of . . . groggy-making-ish.

ME: Groggy-making-ish? I love that. It sounds like something Edgar would have said.

PIA: It does, doesn't it?

ME: Medication for what?

(And suddenly Ass Clown comes and plugs his pudgy little thumb right on the thing and disconnects us.)

ME: Hey! That was an important phone call!

AC: I'm supposed to escort you to your hearing at 3:15. C'mon. Chop chop.

What an ASS. He stared at me during the entire hearing, which was like eight shades of agony to begin with. Beth sat there like she did at the trial, the appeals, release hearings, etc. I wish the stupid lawyer would stop asking her to come. Ostensibly, she's there to speak on my behalf, but her sitting there being all tragic/forgiving just makes them hate me worse. How could it not? It makes me friggin' hate MYSELF! As long as every hearing is about her, I will never get out of here.

So all Pia's searching/applications/paperwork about the halfway house etc. was for nothing. But I love that she did it. She really did try for me. King and I racked up another two grand in legal fees, but they turned down my application to be moved to the med/min security facility, too. Because of tampon incident, etc. The worst part is how King didn't even look at me during the hearing. The whole time, he just sat there with this completely shattered expression on his face.

And all this with good old Ass Clown as my escort. Didn't that just put a cherry on top.

(775 days)

King hasn't called or visited since the hearing. I guess that pretty well says it all.

PIA: Maybe he's tied up with things.

ME: Well, I guess I'm being selfish, but I want him to be tied up with me.

(778 days)

King finally called. He filed for divorce. I guess I shouldn't be surprised, but it hurts so bad I can't friggin' breathe.

On the good side, he has to bring the papers here for me to sign, so he's coming (he's coming!) as soon as he gets the papers together. More than I've ever wanted anything, I just want to see him. And I think maybe when he sees me he'll change his mind. My nose actually looks better since it was broken. I actually like the added character. I've lost weight, my hair is longer. I do push-ups and crunches every day, so my stomach is almost perfectly flat, and I have this nice rack and firm arms. King loves a nice, firm upper body on a woman.

He got rid of a lot of stuff when he moved to the apartment. He says he's bringing me a big box of books. He was very businesslike about everything, but he sounded choked up at the end of the conversation. Tried to tell me he was eating a sandwich. I call BS on that. King loves me. No way can that man sit across the glass from me, looking at this upper body, and tell me he doesn't love me anymore. I call BS on that.

(782 days)

King coming today! Washed my hair in the sink last night and tore up a towel to make rag-rollers. I'll probably get nailed for that, but it was worth it. I look dee-vine, all things considered. No hairspray, though, so I hope he doesn't get here too late. Not sure how well I'll hold up.

Later—no King today. I must have got the day wrong. Hair held up OK. Trying to sleep sitting up so I don't wreck it, just in case he comes tomorrow.

(788 days)

Schickler came with divorce papers today. That King is such a chickenshit.

ME: You go tell King I'll sign the papers when he personally brings them here himself.

SCHICKLER: (all whoop-de-doo look at me I'm a lawyer) blah blah blah

ME: (all pathetic stupid criminal skank) Oh yeah? Well, blee blee blee!

SCHICKLER: blah blah blah

What did he even say? Now that I think of it, I don't even know how he argued me down, but he went off on all this legal stuff and how he could make trouble when I come up for parole again and made me feel like a murderer and a stupid bimbo and just argued me down with lawyer crap until I signed. Hate hate HATE friggin' lawyers! So that's that. And I don't even get my books. All my stuff is in storage, and Pia is paying for the storage unit, which is just one more thing that's another part of the whole friggin' thing.

(789 days)

Pia called, thank God. I was losing it.

ME: (all sobbing) Pia, thank God for you. I'm losing it. King is divorcing me. Three thousand one hundred twenty-two days we were together. And it took him less than 800 to stop loving me.

PIA: Maybe he hasn't stopped loving you, Lily. Maybe he just couldn't handle all this. It's difficult for people. Surely you must recognize that.

ME: Oh, gosh! How selfish of me! I am so friggin' sorry to have inconvenienced you all.

PIA: All I meant to say is—

ME: I know. You don't have to say it. I know it's my own fault. And that friggin' Schickler. Hate hate HATE friggin' attorneys. All attorneys are shit.

PIA: Lily, you can hardly blame the attorney. You certainly can't blame attorneys in general.

ME: The money we spent on that jack-wipe! First, he says if I go to rehab, I'll be not guilty. So I go through that whole rehab farce. Then he tells us I'll be out and getting on with our lives within 13 months. TWO YEARS LATER, he shows up and shoves divorce papers in my face. And I'm sure that just sucked up another chunk of money. HATE friggin' attorneys!

PIA: Fine. I didn't mean to upset you. I shouldn't have said anything. It'll be okay, Lily. Just keep thinking about how Mom used to say "Weeping endureth but a night." Remember?

(Moment of silence for Mom.)

ME: Maybe it was inevitable. Do you think we'd have lasted if all this hadn't happened?

PIA: If this hadn't happened, something else would have. Some marriages can stand the refining fires, some can't. It doesn't mean there's no love. It just means people are human. They get beaten down.

ME: I guess.

PIA: Barret told me that his ex-wife left him when he was going through this drawn-out, difficult case. Really struggling, traveling a lot, having stress-related health issues. She loved him, but she couldn't live with it. So she left him. And Barret takes full responsibility for his role in that.

ME: Who's Barret?

(Big silence.)

PIA: He's my husband. We got married a few weeks ago.

(Even bigger silence.)

ME: (my mind absolutely H-bomb blown) Oh, my God!

PIA: You'll like him, Lily. He's funny, thoughtful, extremely intelligent. (She does this weird little giggle.) Hopefully you can overlook the fact that he's an attorney.

ME: OH, my GOD!

PIA: Lily, I've been trying for weeks to find the right time to tell you, but after King told me about the divorce—

ME: OH—MY—FRIGGIN'—GOD!

PIA: No, no! Wait! Let me explain!

ME: Yeah, Pia! Please explain why you didn't tell me I was about to get dumped on my ass! Explain how you went off with some guy you just met and—

PIA: I'm trying to tell you! Will you listen?

ME: OK. One man at a time. First, when did King tell you about our divorce?

PIA: He told me a while ago. Because of the storage thing, Lily. Which is fine, by the way. It's no problem. Barret took care of it. King asked me not to say anything. I assumed he wanted to come there and talk to you himself.

ME: All right. That's valid. I get that. But this other thing—Pia! How well do you know this man? How long have you been seeing him? And how could you send me five dozen letters a week, yakking about your stupid azaleas and never mention . . . (getting kind of tearful) Pia, how could you fall in love and not tell me?

PIA: I wasn't ready to talk about it. I wanted to tell you, Lily, but when King told me about the divorce, I was afraid it would make you feel bad.

ME: You got a second chance to be happy, Pia. Why would I feel bad about that? That's so unbelievably precious. I'm so, so happy for you.

PIA: Thank you.

ME: It just kills me that you didn't share it with me.

PIA: I'm sorry, Lily. So much has happened. Sometimes I feel like I don't know you anymore. I don't know my own sons anymore. I don't know myself anymore.

ME: So tell me that! Promise me, Pia, if there's something going on with you, I'll hear about it.

PIA: OK.

ME: Promise!

PIA: I promise.

ME: Whatever happens.

PIA: You're the first to know.

Beth

This is a good day for Beth. She is digging in the garden.

This morning she woke from a dream of killing Lily, and it comforts Beth to dream of killing Lily. Not in the way someone might think. Not to burst into the visitor block like an avenging angel, whip out a gun, and blow her head off. Beth is not like that. Beth doesn't even go to movies like that.

In her dream, Beth kills Lily with her bare hands. Her own thin naked fingers, tight around Lily's neck. It's the skin. The sharing of sensation that creates an intimacy of tragedy, of death, of the exit of spirit that they share. In Beth's dream, she grabs hold of Lily's neck and the hold tightens until Lily is on the floor, blue cheeks turning ashen, begging eyes bulging white. Beth shifts her thumbs together directly over Lily's larynx, pushing down against the pulse as the pulse quickens, flutters, fades.

Then Beth stretches out her hand. A ray of light erupts from her palm. Lily's spirit, hovering just above her body, tears open the flesh and muscles of her chest and reenters between her first two ribs. And Beth says to herself, I must be a saint. I have forgiven Lily, raised her from the dead, and given her back her life.

But because two nights later she dreams of killing Lily again, Beth knows she is not a saint. In fact, Beth believes it is a dark sin to even think that. She has not forgiven anyone anything in a very long time, and the fact of that unforgiveness has mummified her in a way she recognizes but cannot remedy.

Lily used to say she didn't believe in sin. Lily is one of those New Agey people who says "spirituality" instead of "religion" and thinks spirituality comes from books in the Spirituality section of the independent bookstore in the groovy neighborhood near the artsy import shops and the funky furniture place and the Healthmasters School of Massage, where Lily was a student before she went to prison. Long before Easter, Lily was openly scornful of the Catholic Church, and now she has condemned Beth to a lasting purgatory outside it. She and Pia blamed Beth for Sonny's leaving the devoted life. It didn't seem to matter that Beth had also left a cloistered place—her childhood—and had become utterly alienated from her own sisters and parents. Lily and Pia assumed that it was a case of the Catholic schoolgirl and the priest who wanted each other more than they wanted God. But in truth, Sonny and Beth were both under the impression God no longer wanted them, and this was what brought them together.

They tried, while Sonny's mother was still alive, to be an extended family. But Beth couldn't stand Lily from the start. She was crude. "Earthy," Lily called it proudly. "Pardon my French," she'd say, but she was unpardonable, fouling her mouth with every obscenity in the book, calling herself a "recovering Catholic" and mocking the sacraments she was raised on. Beth serving tea was an invitation to a whole communion send-up. Sonny coming in the door caused her to pantomime the swinging of a censer.

These things left Beth burning with annoyance and a vague

shame that moldered in the small part of her that almost agreed with Lily. There were moments when all that ceremony did strike Beth as a little bit ridiculous. Like the changing of the guard. Standing in front of Buckingham Palace with her Advanced World History class, Beth had laughed. All that ceremony and pretense and pointless tradition. Were they actually guarding anyone? All that marching back and forth and bearskin hats and bagpipes. Who was it for? Did the queen watch from her window or was she perched on her throne, indifferent? Was she even alive up there? And even if she was, why should all the world worship this withering dominatrix and her unmercifully ill-behaved son? Beth has come to feel the same way about the church, and the thought that she might be becoming like Lily makes her hate Lily even more.

And so Beth dreams of killing Lily, and she wakes up feeling satisfied but unsettled. She uses the nervous energy to dig in the yard. She has decided to plant a tree. Someone gave her a card at Easter's funeral. "A tree has been planted in memory of" and then Easter's name was written in the blank space provided. Beth liked that card better than all the others. What good was all that "in sympathy" and "sharing your sorrow" and "in your time of grief"? All those gilded card-stock flowers and scrolling poems about God's kindness and the sender's concern. What earthly good were they? Plant a tree. Yes. Something real, some evidence of the sentiment. Something you can see. Only Beth couldn't see that tree—it was in Colorado or Saskatchewan or something—so she has decided to plant one of her own, by which she can measure the growth of its unknowable brother.

Digging always makes her feel better. Stronger. More human. She likes to feel acquainted with her own deep muscle and bone, and she knows she'll feel that later, when she wakes up aching.

She digs. Reliving. Digging. Reliving. All these months later, she still can't stand it that Lily mentioned the dress at her parole hearing. She had no right to fawn over it now, thinking

Beth might not have seen the exchanged glances between Lily and King when Easter wore it at her birthday party.

"Well, la-de-da!" Lily had said. "Don't you look like the princess of the universe!"

"I *am* the princess," Easter declared. "You better do as I say!"

And there was another glance exchanged.

"Hey, Easter Bunny," Sonny called, "come see what Aunt Pia brought for you."

"Presents!" she squealed. "Presents for me!"

Only now does it occur to Beth that she should perhaps return the music box to Pia. It was probably expensive. Pia might want it back. She could probably sell it. Or keep it on a shelf in her own house, instead of having it loom over the toys and animals on the shelf in Easter's room, just one more thing for Beth to dust every week. It looks expensive, which is only one of the ways in which it was an entirely inappropriate gift for a five-year-old. Beth had to set it up high to keep Easter from pulling the fairies' delicate wings off. Easter kept wanting to play with them. She wanted to force open the little windows in the trees rather than wait for the music to play all the way through to the part where they opened by themselves, allowing happy children to peek out for a moment before they closed again.

"Come back! Don't go!" Easter shrieked when the children disappeared. She clawed at the dragonflies as they twirled by. She broke a leaf off the umbrella tree, trying to make it turn again after the works had wound down.

"No, no. Here. See this little key? Turn the key like this," Pia stiffly demonstrated. "Turn the key, counting to twenty. Can you count to twenty?"

Easter nodded enthusiastically, though it wasn't true. Beth and Sonny had been working with her, but . . . oh well, Beth doubted she had the small motor skills to turn the key, anyway. Within five minutes she was screaming, and Pia was apologizing, and Lily and King were looking at each other and rolling their eyes.

"Isn't that special?" Lily said, and King laughed his loud, uncouth laugh, as Lily sat on his lap right in front of everyone. Draped herself all over him right in the middle of Easter's first communion reception. And now Lily sits there in her prison chair, saying how adorable Easter was that day. How sweet and pretty. Beth drives the shovel into the dirt and turns over another clump of grass.

Easter was not pretty, and it doesn't bother Beth one bit to acknowledge that. People would look at her with a vague curiosity, sensing something was not quite right about her but unable to define exactly what it was. She had a huskiness about her, a soft hirsute quality, a heaviness about the brow; like a bear cub almost, but paler, moister, more kinetic. Her lips were full and overly red, and when she spoke, some people assumed she was deaf, because she had that same inability to match the shape of her mouth to the words in the air around her, even though the impulses behind the words and the mouthing of them were the same as they were for anyone else. Her head seemed to sit too close to her wide shoulders, as if she were shrugging always, as if she lived in a perpetual state of frustrated incertitude. She ambled. She was slow. She was often angry.

"No fair!" she would explode, and it wasn't. So Beth worked hard to restore some sort of balance. She enrolled Easter in a special preschool as soon as they would accept her. She and Sonny observed through a two-way mirror as the teacher worked with her. They took notes. They read books. They enrolled her in private school the following year, and before school started, they met with the kindergarten teacher and explained Easter's special needs.

"She's not retarded," Beth emphasized. "She has learning disabilities, but she *can* learn."

By the time she celebrated her first communion, she was

starting to read. She could work all the way through *Hop on Pop* if someone sat patiently with her. Beth and Sonny were patient, but sometimes it seemed that was too much to ask of anyone else in the world. It was impossible to find someone to babysit in the summer. Pia was always out of town. Edgar always had some excuse. Beth didn't even bother asking the boys. Why Sonny insisted they ask Lily that morning—that's something Beth does not understand to this day.

Turning another clump of sod, Beth feels the heat of the day on her back. She'll be sunburned, she thinks, and the thought is pleasing. She envisions herself peeling, molting like a dragon, leaving her dry skin behind, dead as paper, and emerging new.

Beth lives for these little deaths and resurrections.

Lily

(1095 days)

I have been in this place three years.
Father, Son, and Holy Ghost.

(1100 days)

Another double zero. Got through okay.

Jesus sisters did a little poetry contest in the library this week. Write a poem with a religious theme, best one wins a dozen of those evangelically luscious oatmeal cookies with currents and walnuts—and I WON the sucker! HA!

> Father, Son, and Holy Ghost
> Tied me to the whipping post.
> Know what burns my ass the most?
> Jesus saves, but he lets me roast.

Christina Rossetti it ain't, but I tried to give it a little zing of "cry for help." They love that kind of thing. I was in it for the cookies, babe, and I was in it to win. I made it known that I would beat the ass of anyone who tried to take one. Purely in the spirit of Christ's love, of course.

(1102 days)

Pia called. She's been pretty good about calling three times a week, since I don't have to save up my phone calls for King anymore. Talked about her new car, which she doesn't even want to drive, because she's all uptight about possibly wrecking it. Maybe that's a Barret thing. She never used to be so materialistic.

She never talks about Edgar anymore. And do not mention him in conversation if you would like conversation to continue! Maybe Barret doesn't like her talking about him because he's a corporate hyena and Edgar was this principled Kermit the Frog–type historian, and now everybody has him all deified because he's dead. You can never compete with a dead person for affection. This is something I know.

It's the rule: Don't speak ill of the dead. Feel free, of course, to treat the living like crap.

(1111 days)

Nothing to say about today. Just wanted to write down that number.

(1114 days)

Pia called. Talking to her anymore is pretty strained. We have these little plastic Barbie doll conversations about nothing. And if I do try to say anything about anything she bites my head off and spits it out like a crab apple. I was telling her how it pissed me off that they're not letting the Jesus Chicks bring their salon stuff anymore. So now I can't get my hair cut, and I had just decided to be bold and get it super short for the first time ever.

ME: I've been feeling like it would be a relief to unload all that weight and mass and years of damage and just start from fresh. So I was going to get a little layered pixie kind of thing, you know? Like Winona Ryder in that movie Girl Interrupted. Remember her adorable little haircut in that movie? Oh, God, I miss movies!

PIA: I don't think I ever saw that one.

ME: Yes, you did. It's that one where she's in the nuthouse, remember? So anyway, they're telling us it's some kind of security issue. They can't bring scissors here, because the country is on orange terror alert level. Like terrorists are going to break into the women's prison, posing as missionary beauticians, for Christ sake. That whole orange-red-yellow thing is such a bunch of crap. They just can't stand to let me feel good about myself for five seconds.

PIA: That's right, Lily. It's all about you. An entire government policy has been orchestrated to prevent you from getting your hair cut like Winona Ryder's.

ME: Wow. That was harsh.

PIA: Was it? It wasn't intended to be harsh. But I suppose it's never our intentions that hurt other people. It's usually our negligence, isn't it?

ME: (feeling like I just got punched in the face) Yes, Pia. I know that. I was negligent, and I hurt a lot of people. Are you concerned that I might not feel adequately ashamed and rotten about that? Am I not paying an adequate price? Do you feel like I'm getting some kind of terrific bargain here, since all it's cost me is my marriage, my freedom, and my opportunity to have children of my own? Is that not enough for you?

PIA: It's not about you, Lily! I'm not even talking about that!

ME: Then just what the fuck are you talking about?

PIA: Don't use that language with me! I will not sit here and listen to that foul language!

ME: Okay! I'm sorry! Pia, don't hang up!

But of course (CLICK) she friggin' hangs up. She tried to call back about a half hour later, but I only earned two phone calls this week, so I couldn't go up.

Whatthefuckever.

(1123 days)

Haven't heard from Pia, but I got some books in the mail. Apparently she signed me up for this Literary Classics book club thingy, which was a pretty cool thing for her to do. I've about exhausted the library here.

First selection is James Joyce's A Portrait of the Artist as a Young Man, a book devoid of quotation marks.

—Old father, old artificer, stand me now and ever
in good stead.—

A good prayer.

(1143 days)

Pia called. Sounded very wired. Weird. She and Barret are moving to Chicago. Don't know why this makes me feel bad, but it does. We're not the moving kind. We grew up in one house. Then Pia and I shared an apartment in the city. Then she and Edgar got their house, King and I got ours, and that's where I assumed we'd be living when our grandchildren came to visit.

PIA: Not to put too fine a point on it, Lily, but you're not living there either, are you?

ME: Geez. Do you have to be so mean all the time? When did you get so mean, Pia?

PIA: Well, I don't understand why you're making a fuss. I'm not moving to Bombay.

ME: I know. But still. I don't know if I can stand any more space between you and me.

PIA: Lily, don't make this any harder for me. I'm already incredibly stressed, trying to sell the house and clear out the boys' rooms. They're not being very helpful. Barret is gone all the time. I'm hating every minute of this whole thing. So I don't need you making it worse by piling on some tripe about me "not being the moving kind," whatever that means.

ME: OK. Calm down. You're right. I'm sorry.

PIA: You think I want to move to Chicago? Like that's my lifelong dream or something? I don't know anyone. I don't know where anything is. I don't know where to go to get library books or have my hair done or drop off the dry cleaning or send packages. I mean, how am I supposed to send packages to you and the boys, if I don't even know where to go?

ME: Pia, it'll work out. Just calm down. Geez.

PIA: The thing is, Barret is planning to run for Congress, and he needs to live in that district. It's where he's lived most of his career. Or at least, he's been based there. The powers that be are basically going to gerrymander it specifically so he can win. This move is very important to him. It's part of the whole plan.

ME: And what about you, Pi? Are you part of the plan?

PIA: What's that supposed to mean?

ME: Nothing. Tell me about your new house.

PIA: Well, I haven't actually seen it. But it's exactly what Barret wanted. A very upscale, gated community with a 24-hour security guard. Barret wanted to make sure I felt safe. Anyway, it sounds very nice. I'm sure I'll love it.

ME: Yeah, I love my gated community. 24-hour guards. Very upscale.

PIA: Ha-ha.

ME: So what are you doing about . . . you know. Edgar's stuff.

PIA: I'm putting most of it in storage until the boys have a chance to go through and take what they want. The interior decorator is using a few items in the new house. A few antiques. The rest really doesn't fit in, because the design concept is all pale wood, white walls, cream-colored furniture. Monochromatic, you know? He has this whole concept of shades of white.

ME: (singing) "And although my eyes were open, they might just as well been closed . . ."

PIA: What?

ME: You know. "Whiter Shade of Pale?" It was a little joke.

PIA: OK. Whatever.

(1171 days)

Big mail day. Letter from Pia. Just stuff about the boys. She didn't say anything about what's going on with her. Also got my Lit Classic book for this month. Collected Stories of Anton Chekhov. This from "Gooseberries":

> Everything is quiet and peaceful, and nothing protests but mute statistics. . . . And this order of things is evidently necessary; evidently the happy man only feels at ease because the unhappy bear their burdens in silence. It is a case of general hypnotism.

Just another day in the upscale gated community.

(1177 days)

A nice symmetrical number today. Got a little zing of pleasure from that, which is a comment on my pathetic life.

Pia called. Barret in Tokyo. Boys visiting her for weekend. I'm glad, because she sounds so strange.

(1186 days)

Pia called. Every time I talk to her lately she's either chattering like a crack monkey or mumbling like a zombie. I told her what the Jesus Chick was telling me about her mom's anxiety disorder thing. Pia got all bitch-pissed about my "thinly veiled attempts to psychoanalyze" her.

PIA: Maybe you'd better do some housekeeping in your own head before you start on mine.

ME: (being cool) I'm just saying maybe you should talk to somebody.

PIA: (with huge "Why are you so stupid?" sigh) I'm talking to you, aren't I?

ME: I mean somebody who knows about this kind of thing.

PIA: Who knows more than you do about throwing away one's life on human frailties?

ME: OK, that was uncalled for! How can you even say something so rotten to me?

(Big-time silencio.)

ME: Pia, are you OK? (Silence.) Pia, are you crying? Pia?

PIA: Fine! I'm fine!

ME: Pia, come on. Talk to me here. I'm getting very scared. You promised I would be the first to know if something is going on with you, and it obviously is!

(And she just falls to pieces, bawling her head off about how miserable she is and these meds she's on and I can't understand half of what she's saying, because she's just babbling.)

ME: Pia, stop. Take a deep breath. Pia? We're just going to breathe together. Like mom used to do when we were little, remember? Inhale . . . let it out. Inhale . . . breathe it out. Now tell me about the meds. What's up with that?

PIA: I don't know. The doctor changed it, because my stomach . . . I was losing a lot of weight. But this new thing—I hate the way I feel wooden and thick and when Barret—it used to be so good with us. Together. But now I'm just wooden, Lily. I don't feel anything, and I'd rather feel horrible than feel nothing at all. I'm so humiliated, Lily. Barret is so disappointed in me.

ME: Oh, my God. I had no idea, Pia. I'm so sorry. But we can solve this. We'll solve it together. You always said next box on the flowchart, right? So we're going to, um—well, obviously the first thing is to go back to this doctor and tell him what you just told me.

PIA: I did. He told me to give it some time and get through the move and then find a doctor in Chicago who deals with . . . with this sort of thing. He's referred me to a Dr. Ackerman, and I spoke to him, and he said I should keep taking the meds until I see him there next month.

ME: Well, I hope he's a shrink and not just another guy to write more prescriptions.

PIA: (sounding extremely small) He is.

ME: So do you think—oh shit! Pia, my time is up. I have 30 seconds.

PIA: Oh . . . good-bye, Lily.

ME: No, wait! Are you still there? Pia!

PIA: Yes.

ME: You need to go back and tell that dude to help you. And call me tomorrow. I have one phone call left this week. Promise to call me tomorrow, and we'll figure this out together. OK?

PIA: I don't know. I don't know. I have all these boxes and somebody's coming for them.

ME: Pia, you call me, do you understand? Promise!

PIA: I promise.

(1187 days)

No Pia call.

Shit.
Shit shit SHIT!
Fuckinggoddamnfuckingshitfuckinghell!

I feel like my heart is coming out of my chest.

(1189 days)

She promised.
She promised.
She promised.
She promised.

She promised.
She promised.
She promised.
She promised.
She promised.
She promised.
She promised.
She promised.
She promised.
She promised.
She promised.
She promised.

Beth

This is not a good day for Beth. And it is about to get worse.

She feels it sliding downhill, a ping of intuition nagging at the outer edge of her carefully organized mind, like a phone conversation of which she can hear only one side. She doesn't know what's wrong, but she has become increasingly certain that something is. The traffic is impossible, even though it's almost seven in the evening. A bitter winter rain comes and goes. Not enough of a hazard to provide Beth with an excuse to stay home, but enough to make the road a little skatey.

Sonny is slated to be on call all weekend, which he has been the last seven weekends, and people seem to be waiting until Friday afternoon to drop like flies. He is exhausted; silent at breakfast, absent from dinner, impatient with everyone at the office. He isn't sleeping well, which means Beth isn't sleeping well, either. He is concerned about the power supply to the old storage facility, about the seasonal lack of certain flowers, about some people's inability to pay for services, which Sonny simply doesn't have it in him to withhold. He is concerned about hard frost on the hibiscus trees in the front yard, concerned about rumors of prisoners being tortured in Iraq, concerned about his sister Pia, who has been answering her phone less and less over the last few months and not at all for almost a week.

It's extremely inconsiderate. Pia may be moving off to the la-de-da Chicago suburbs, where the beautiful people dwell, but that's no excuse to treat her brother with such a dismissive air, considering all they did for her and the boys after Edgar died. Beth is planning to speak to her about that when she returns the umbrella tree music box, and she is on her way to Pia's to do that right now.

"Return it?" Sonny had said when he found her packing it into a large box that morning. "Why would you return it?"

"Because I'm sick of dusting it," Beth answered more abruptly than she'd intended.

"Well, you should have said something. I would gladly—"

"I know, Sonny, but she's leaving next week. She might as well take it with her. Or sell it. I don't care. If we're going to buy a smaller house next year, I'm going to have to empty this room when we move. It'll be easier if I start now." Beth hacked off a slab of bubble wrap with large, orange-handled scissors. "Luckily I have plenty of time to myself every weekend."

"Beth, what do you expect me to do? Tell people to pile their loved ones out on the stoop till Monday and then go down the street with a wheelbarrow? *Bring out'cher dead! Bring out'cher dead!*" He mimicked a Monty Python movie, which Beth found flat unfunny. "I refuse to feel guilty. I'm just doing what needs to be done."

"So am I," Beth said, not unkindly, but not kindly either.

Sonny looked abashed. He left the room without saying anything. A little while later, he left the house without kissing her. Beth finished packing the music box and put it in the car.

She feels uncomfortable dropping in on Pia without calling. She tries Pia's number again on the way, but Pia still doesn't pick up. Pia is always home, however. It would be unusual for her to be out this late in the evening. And if she is, there's the key under a potted cactus, a sadly hopeful gesture Pia has made toward her boys, who have never taken advantage of it, as far as Beth knows. It would probably be a relief for both of them, Beth thinks, if she's able to leave the package in the entry and slip away without having to make small talk.

"Hi, Pia!" Beth says after the beep. She hates how fake and cheery she sounds. She hates feeling obligated to be cheery. "This is your sister-in-law. Beth. And I just had a little something I needed to drop off for you before you leave. Um . . . so I'm on my way over and . . . I'll be ringing your doorbell in just a few minutes. Bye!"

Pia doesn't come to the door, even after three or four persistent nudges to the bell. Beth locates the key, opens the door a crack.

"Pia?" she calls softly. "Anybody home?"

When there's no answer, Beth goes back to the car, hefts the bulky box into her arms, and carts it up the sidewalk to the entry. She starts to set it down on a bench just inside the door, but the bench is upholstered in a soft rose-colored satin, and the box is a bit damp from the rain. She looks around the foyer, but everything including the antique oriental rug seems pristinely clean and probably expensive, which makes Beth feel even more like a trespasser.

Beth steps quietly across the rug and deposits the box on the wooden floor of the hallway near some other boxes that have already been packed and labeled for the movers. But just as she sets it down, there's a faint tinkle of broken glass. At first, Beth thinks it's coming from inside the box, but then she realizes it's something upstairs. That ping of intuition. Beth tries to muffle it with plausible explanations, but if Pia is directly overhead being attacked by some sort of felon, Sonny would never understand why Beth didn't stick around to figure that out. Beth opens her cell phone and starts up the stairs.

"Pia?" she calls again, and then does her best to assemble as large a voice as possible. "Okay, whoever is up there—I have a gun!"

Beth hopes her cell phone might pass for a gun in the dimly lit hallway. The only light comes from a door, which stands ajar at the top of the stairs.

"Pia?"

Beth uses her thumb to press a 9 and a 1, then pauses, poised to hit the second 1. She pushes the door open and steps inside Pia's beautifully appointed bathroom. Across from the door is a large beveled mirror above a black pedestal sink, and on the floor beneath it lies a pile of something that looks like corn silk. Beth realizes it is Pia's hair.

"What on earth . . ."

A burst of short snippets in the bowl of the sink seems to indicate that Pia must have started with the intention of simply trimming a little, but the ragged tresses on the floor are ten and twelve inches long. Pia must have shorn herself like a yearling. No wonder she's too embarrassed to come to the door, Beth thinks. She must look ridiculous! Beth stops short of laughing out loud. She doesn't want to make Pia feel any worse about it than she probably already does.

Candlelight flickers around the corner from the raised bathtub area, and Beth hears the water trickling.

"Pia, are you okay?" Beth calls. "May I come in? Are you decent?"

She's not sure if the sound she hears is a yes or a no, so she steps around the glass brick divider.

"*Pia!*"

Beth's cell phone hits the floor with a staccato crack. The battery skitters across the tile and collides with a broken wine bottle.

"Pia . . . what . . . what are you doing?"

Pia is slumped in the bathtub. Her legs are naked, but she is wearing a man's dress shirt, tie, and sport coat. The tub is filled to its rim, and the water is red with blood. Pia rolls her head to the side and looks up at Beth, expressionless. She closes her eyes and starts to slide down into the water.

"No. You will not do this." Beth seizes the lapels of the sport coat. "*No, Pia!* You will not do this to him. You will not take the only family he has left!" She shakes Pia's limp shoulders. "Do you hear me, you stupid, spoiled bitch? *You will not!*"

She slaps Pia hard across the face, and Pia opens her eyes.

"*What did you do, Pia?*" Beth's voice shrills somewhere between panic and fury. "*You show me right now! Show me what you did!*"

Pia slowly raises one hand out of the water, and blood dribbles down from her wrist. Catching the wet, pink sleeve before it drops back into the water, Beth presses her thumb across it. There is an amber plastic prescription bottle floating between Pia's knees. Beth fishes it out with her free hand. Valium.

"How many?" Beth demands.

When Pia doesn't answer, Beth slaps her again.

"*How many?* More than ten?"

Pia shakes her head, but Beth doesn't know if this is a denial or wordless assurance that it doesn't matter anymore. Struggling to hold Pia upright, Beth fishes into the red water again, finds a slender chain, and wrenches the stopper from the drain. As the water level drops, she lets Pia slump back. She scrambles among the broken glass to find her phone. Replaces the battery with wet, trembling hands. Calls 911.

Pia's carefully washed lingerie items are hanging over a little drying rack. Awkwardly wedging the slippery cell phone between her chin and shoulder, Beth grabs a pair of panty hose and uses the long, filmy legs to tie tourniquets around Pia's wrists. She does this quickly, efficiently, without waiting for instruction from the emergency operator or pausing to second-guess herself.

Beth is good in an emergency. She'd taken a first-aid certification class at church when Easter was still alive.

"The Lord laid it on my heart to take it," she'd told Sonny at the time. "I just have a feeling He has a purpose."

In this moment, Beth is enraged to discover that His divine purpose was to save the life of this stupid, spoiled bitch. And in the next moment, Beth's belief in the divinity of purpose dies.

Part II

Dalphine

Pia

The little import shop was next to the entrance of Dr. Ackerman's office. If it hadn't been, Pia would never have seen it. Her life shuttled back and forth like a cable car these days. To Dr. Ackerman's office and back to her house in the gated community. Along this well-worn path, she had everything she needed. Grocery store, pharmacy, office supplies. Beyond that narrow corridor, lay the city of Chicago, but Pia could step out into it no more than a goldfish could step outside her bowl. Even within the narrow confines of her new world, she had strict rules that had to be followed. She could not come and go, except through her front door. She could not shop for groceries unless she did so in a very specific order every time. When she left Dr. Ackerman's office, she had to stand beneath the awning until her cab arrived, then step directly from the sidewalk into the taxi. She could not exit the pharmacy without seeing the taxi waiting for her. She could not step off the curb into the street.

This was not uncommon, Dr. Ackerman told her. He said agoraphobics often create a rigid routine in a network of safe places with a narrow corridor between them. Thus they are able to function at varying levels of normalcy. Pia wasn't so terribly bad off, he assured her. He'd seen patients whose entire universe shrank from a normal world to a town, to a block, to a house, to a room, and, in one sad case, to a chair. Pia should be grateful, he said, that after just six weeks in the hospital and seven months of therapy, she was "essentially real-life functional." But as Pia stood in the drizzle outside his office building, she could hardly remember what her real life was.

What triggered Pia's interest in the little shop was the fact that she *noticed* it. She *wanted* to go in because she was *curious*. This feeling was so close to forgotten, it startled her. Thrilled her. But the thought of actually leaving the sidewalk to push through the painted glass door made Pia feel like she was choking. She knew what would happen. Her feet would feel numb. A sickening vertigo would well up inside her. Her pulse would hammer against the inside of her head. Nothing was worth that.

She didn't tell Barret about the little shop. Details like this upset him. He was just getting comfortable with the idea of Pia being home alone again. He'd put off as much travel as he possibly could over the last several months, but now he was working on an important case that required him to divide his time among Washington, Europe, and India. Pia wasn't about to make it any more difficult for him. He'd been through enough.

When she first woke up in the hospital, he was there, sitting in the corner of the room, speaking softly into his cell phone. First he spoke with his secretary. Then Sonny, apparently, but that conversation was brief. Then Pia heard him dial another number and ask for Lily Vincent. And then there was a long silence, because it always took a while for them to go get her for a phone call. Barret drummed his fingers on the arm of the chair while he waited.

"Ms. Vincent, this is Barret Mayor . . . Yes, but I'm . . . No, she isn't. That's why I'm calling. She's had an accident . . . No, nothing like that. Apparently, she slipped in the bathtub. She lost a bit of blood and required some stitches on um, on her forearms . . . No! Certainly not. It was nothing like that. She slipped in the bathtub. A wine bottle broke. It was an accident. And I don't want you suggesting anything different to James and Jesse. You'd only be embarrassing Pia and needlessly upsetting things."

Lily was a loud talker. Even across the room, Pia could hear the thin edge of her voice on Barret's cell. She lay perfectly still, trying to catch what Lily was saying, but the words unraveled just out of reach.

"Well, you're entitled to your point of view, Ms. Vincent, but that doesn't change the facts . . . Look, I don't intend to sit here and listen to that kind of language," Barret said curtly. "Your brother asked me to inform you of the situation as a courtesy to Pia, and that's been done, so I believe our conversation is over."

If Barret believed it, it was so. This is something Pia had learned.

Now, almost a year later, Barret believed Pia was getting better. So each week she stood in the shelter of the awning, on the familiar sidewalk, at the familiar time, exactly where she'd stood every Monday and Thursday afternoon since leaving the hospital, waiting for the cab Dr. Ackerman's receptionist had already called.

It was a week or so after Dr. Ackerman readjusted her medication ("tweaked the meds," as he called it, and Pia liked him for that, among other things) that she suddenly found herself several yards down the sidewalk, browsing the display window of the street-level emporium with the words *human comforts* scripted in the center of the glass. Pia pushed her hands deep down in her coat pockets and allowed herself to feel the meaning of that phrase. Then she caught her breath, realizing the monumental step she'd taken, actively experiencing the *notic-*

ing and the *curiosity*. The feeling was a luxury. An awakening.

Framed inside the window display were candelabras, a fainting couch, an ornate birdcage, silk scarves tied to hooks on a tiger oak hall tree. Beyond all this, set back a bit, an ottoman squatted like a tent dweller on broad wooden legs. Pia leaned in toward the glass, bending her neck to get a better view of the piece. It was all leafy carved legs and fat upholstered belly, festooned with a wild splay of color and pattern. The cushion was covered in silk, brocaded with birds and lotus blossoms. The piece was too flamboyant, too foreign for someone who had originated in this country and retained a particular frugality of senses that originated with her Puritan forebears. Pia never even considered buying it. It wasn't that. It was the small victory she celebrated. This was the proudest moment she'd had in a long while, and seeing that extraordinary object was her private reward.

The following Monday, the ottoman had been moved closer to the window. There it was, this wonder of thread and wood, so close she could have touched it if not for the glass. And on Thursday, it was still there. And every Monday and Thursday thereafter. Every time she walked by, her eyes came up from the pavement, her head turned against her will. Pia wanted to go in, and the wanting quickly evolved from a luxury to an ache, but knowing what would happen if she stepped off her established path, she stood quietly at the window, pushing and pulling breath in and out of her chest, looking and longing on a chemical level for the colors and textures inside.

She'd been on the new meds almost three months before she went in. And then only because rain was pouring down. A young man dodged under the awning, his head bent over the boxes he was carrying. The collision left her unbalanced, and she was swept through the door the way a dusty hem is swept across a dance floor.

Apologies. Flustering. Tangle of umbrellas. Shaking off of raindrops.

"Are you all right?" he asked.

"Yes, fine. Fine," Pia told him, and she realized she was.

Elation surged up from the back of her knees to the top of her skull. The corridor, the inflexible space in which she was allowed to live, expanded ever so slightly. But even that small moment made her know it was possible. Maybe it was thresholds, then. Not the *places* so much as the *entering* that brought on the gripping headache. Maybe she could try the library someday, or the Museum of Fine Arts.

Pia tested her theory, carefully stepping off the doormat and onto the wooden floor, advancing just far enough to get a look at those silken lotus blossoms. Only to look for a moment, she promised herself, but the bell at the door brought a woman from behind a curtain of glass beads at the back of the store.

Looking tall and infragile as the Lady of the Lake, the shopkeeper strode toward the young man, took his face in her hands, and kissed him on both cheeks and then the mouth. She said something to him in French. He laughed and took the boxes back to whatever room or hallway lay behind the beads.

The lady's skin was darker than white, but lighter than dark; not really olive-colored, but rich and humid in the way the flesh of an olive is. Her thick accent placed her outside American, but she seemed too tall for Middle Eastern, too swarthy for European. Her hair was pulled back from her face, twisted into a black knot. Narrow white rivulets trickled through it the same way gray rain streaked down the wide shop windows. Her dress was moss-colored linen, delicately laced and beaded along the neckline. She was beautiful, but this was not the day Pia noticed it.

"Welcome!" the woman called, holding a cordless phone against the side of her breast. She wasn't wearing a bra, but she was small and firm enough that Pia didn't find it as distasteful as when Lily went without.

"May I help you, dear?"

"No, thank you," said Pia. "Just looking."

"Ah. Well, then. You won't mind if I just—hmm?" She indicated the phone.

"No, please. Go ahead."

Relieved to be left alone, Pia looked from the door to the ottoman, gauging the distance, calculating how long it would take to cross quickly, touch it just enough to know what the lotus felt like, and be out the door before the woman came back. Pia could hear her talking on the phone in the back room, speaking in an animated French, loudly, perhaps to someone overseas. A poor connection, perhaps. Or maybe she was angry. There was no escaping the sound and expression in her voice. Pia had taken six years of French in high school and college and couldn't help it that her mind searched out forgotten vocabulary quizzes and translated the words. The dispute had something to do with seven boxes, a ship, a red book, yellow paper. And Friday. Very important. No, Friday tomorrow, you imbecile, not Friday a week.

The shop was bigger than it looked from the street, but despite the depth of its sprawl and the height of the ceiling, the place had the private feel of an apartment. The merchandise seemed more like the personal effects of a worldly inhabitant than a seller's professionally acquired wares. Couches and chairs formed conversation areas here and there. A clawfoot tub was heaped with tassled pillows in the corner under an arch of willow branches. A high sleigh bed was made up with an eiderdown comforter and embroidered pillow shams. A breakfast table was set with china, crystal, fruit in bowls, and fresh croissants under a glass pyramid. It made Pia feel like an intruder, a voyeur.

She walked the perimeter of the room, staying close to the wall, focusing on the straight lines of the framed prints, the smooth sheen of the gilded sconces, keeping her distance from the more personal items in the soft inner confines. She stood for a few minutes at a glass case, looking closely at a display of vintage bracelets. Pia always wore bracelets now. Wide silver cuffs or a stack of thin, silver bangles. She'd searched the Internet and ordered several items that worked for her taste but adequately covered the scarred expanse between the sleeve of her blouse and the heel of her hand.

The woman was still chattering, and the words translated themselves at the edge of Pia's awareness.

"Yellow paper. No, *yellow*, you idiot!"

Pia wasn't sure how much time had passed, but she was fairly certain her taxi would have given up and left Dr. Ackerman's awning by now. She felt the sharks stir slightly at that thought. She felt them circling quietly as she crept to the center of the store and sat on the edge of a low burl coffee table, close enough to touch the flowered fabric of the ottoman. The texture was a paradox: the lotus blossoms embroidered with silk thread, liquid smooth, and everything that surrounded and grounded them rough, knotted with nubs of uncultured floss. She stroked her hand across the whole top from one corner to the other, then furtively moved over to sit. The moment she felt the knotted buds against the back of her legs, she knew she should not be there.

"Lovely, isn't it?"

Pia stood quickly, straightened her skirt, embarrassed and burning in the face, as if she'd been caught trespassing or conducting herself in some vaguely inappropriate way.

"Lovely, yes?" the woman repeated. "The ottoman?"

"Yes." Pia tried to place the florid dialect somewhere in her known world, but she wasn't curious enough to risk drawing the woman into conversation.

"I'd have to say it's one of my favorite things here in my little shop of delights."

Pia forced a polite smile.

"It's antique, as you can see. Probably 1920s. Perhaps early thirties," the woman said. "Pristine condition. *Pristine!* I purchased it from a dear friend. A customer. She traveled a great deal when she was younger. But she's alone now. Elderly. She's moving to an assisted-living facility. If not for that—well, you can be sure she wouldn't have parted with such a treasure." The shopkeeper bent down and tipped the ottoman backward. She supported it with her hand so the upholstery wasn't touching the floor but the underside was exposed. "Have you ever seen such perfect finish work? And it's just gently frayed—here, you see, and here at the edges—just enough to speak for its age."

When Pia didn't lean down to look at it, the shopkeeper let it settle back on all four feet. She went to a table nearby and repositioned a lamp with an ornate shade. Neither of them said anything for a long moment. Pia was trying to find some way to politely end the encounter, but just as she opened her mouth to excuse herself, the woman went on in her odd, lush accent.

"It was given to her by a man she met in Turkey. I believe she said this was in 1963. Yes, I'm certain that's what it was, because she said Kennedy was assassinated while she was out of the country." She stroked her hand over the patterned silk, then turned to straighten the shade on a floor lamp nearby. "He was a dealer in antiques and art. She was a photographer." The woman paused, combing through the lampshade's long fringes with her fingers. "She loved him, but she knew her family would never accept a man of color."

Pia kept her eyes on the lotus and leaves and tendrils.

"So of course, she never told them who gave her this extravagant gift. She never even told her husband or her children over the years. She kept her own apartment in the city for, shall we say, *personal use*, and it stayed there. She took immaculate care of the piece. You can see it's been cared for as it might not have been had it been in daily use with children and cats and dogs and whatnot. Now she's old. She's closing the apartment. Selling her pretty things and sending them off into the world. She said she wanted this piece in particular to find a good home. Someone who would appreciate its very special, private character. This is why she was willing to part with it for an amount that allows me to resell it at such a ridiculously low price."

Pia nodded, and then, only because an awkward silence followed, asked, "How much?"

"Sixty-seven hundred."

"Oh," said Pia. "All right. Well, thank you."

"Well, you are so welcome, sweet. You are so very welcome."

"I really should be going." Pia stepped back and glanced toward the door.

"I'm Dalphine," the woman said, offering her hand.

Pia nodded again, uncomfortably aware that she was expected to respond with her own name. She touched Dalphine's hand in the slightest possible way and murmured, "Nice to meet you."

"So very nice indeed! Yes. Can you sit for a while?" Dalphine asked.

"Oh, no. Thank you."

"I took the liberty of preparing a cup for you."

"Actually, I really should be going."

"Yes, of course! You'll sit!" She clapped her hands together, delighted, as if Pia hadn't even spoken. "I'm so glad."

Dalphine had already settled a tray on the coffee table. Gesturing toward the sofa, she seated herself directly across from it in a red leather side chair. Pia sat, not really wanting to, but certain it would be rude to do otherwise. Dalphine draped a linen napkin across her lap, and Pia thanked her, trying to remain at a distance without seeming impolite.

"That is the most adorable haircut," Dalphine said, ticking the edge of her cup with a spoon.

"Thank you." Pia's hand went automatically, self-consciously to the nape of her neck, and she fiddled with her single strand of pearls to cover the gesture.

"Not very many women are brave enough to wear it that short."

Pia tried to smile.

"Have you always worn it short?"

"No."

"I've always kept this wild mess, this lion's mane. I don't know why. I thought about cutting it short when it started going gray, but I've just always had it. I didn't know if I'd recognize myself without it."

Pia nodded. The unfamiliar feeling Dalphine spoke of so lightly had been haunting her since she'd cut her hair. Even so, she couldn't wean herself from the monkish feeling the razor-cropped style gave her. The low-price haircutter was one of the few stops along the corridor, and Pia went there every third week, on the same day, at the same time, to make sure the same young woman was there in her black T-shirt and jeans.

"My friend always tells me to keep it long," Dalphine went on, pouring coffee into the china cups. "He says all men love long hair on a woman. Isn't that ridiculous?"

"No. I think it's true," Pia said. Suddenly she felt hopeful that this might be the reason for the way Barret looked at her now in contrast with the way he did before. Perhaps that profoundly private connection they'd lost would grow back, just like her damaged hair was growing back now. Slowly but surely.

"Do you really? You think that's true?"

"Yes."

"Then you're doubly brave to cut it, aren't you?"

They sipped their coffee. It was frothed with steamed milk and sweetened with some sort of almond flavoring. Pia looked toward the window, watching the traffic as Dalphine watched her.

"Do you live in the city?" she asked.

"No."

"Ah. North, then? Or south?"

"Artevita."

"Ah! Lovely!" Dalphine clapped her hands together again. Delighted, Pia was sure, to know that her customer must have money. She wished she hadn't mentioned it. "How very nice for you. So quiet. Not like here. In the city you can hardly sleep at night for all the goings-on. Especially in this neighborhood."

"You live . . . here?" Pia heard surprise in her own voice and hoped it didn't sound rude.

"Back there, yes," Dalphine said, motioning toward the beaded curtain and whatever lay beyond it. "Well, I *sleep* here. I don't actually *live* here. I'm between lives right now." She raised her cup and smiled wryly. "Rule number one for the infatuated woman: Keep the apartment."

Pia didn't know if she was expected to laugh or express condolences, so she just smiled, hoping it looked at least a little less wooden than it felt.

"Well. So. Tell me," said Dalphine, "what is the color scheme in your house?"

"It's white. Shades of white." And of course, the stupid song flashed across Pia's brain and made her feel self-conscious.

"Interesting. White on white. Interesting choice."

"The designer said—well, it's this modern, monochromatic . . . thing."

"Monochromatic," Dalphine repeated. "Mono . . . chromatic."

When she dissected the words that way, Pia realized how stupid the idea actually was.

"The decorator had this whole austerity concept," she said. "My husband likes it."

"And you, sweet? You like this austerity?"

Pia wasn't sure how to answer. She'd loved it when it was first done. Everything was so perfect, so pristine. It seemed very safe, very calm. But later, it came to feel unforgiving. The whiteness provided a backdrop against which every imperfection, every spill and fraying, was highlighted like the negative images of an X-ray. Pia lingered long enough over the answer that Dalphine drew her own conclusion.

"Well, this must be remedied," Dalphine declared. "This

must be amended. Thank God you've found me, sweet! I am certain I shall prove to be your salvation."

Again Pia forced an uncomfortable smile, and they sat with their coffee cups. The rain beat down outside. The awning dripped with a sodden, heavy hang outside the window. While Pia grew increasingly uncomfortable, the lapse in conversation didn't seem to bother Dalphine. She leaned back in the side chair and took her cup, holding it between her hands as if to warm them. She closed her eyes and smiled.

"I love this music," she said. "Rodrigo. *Concierto de Aranjuez.*"

The symphony swooped and mantled. Violins and cellos caped and swirled around a Spanish guitar. Dalphine raised her hand and caressed the pensive strings and aching oboe that hung in the air beside them.

"If you listen," she said so quietly that Pia had to lean forward to hear, "you can almost hear his blood thickening. You can feel it . . . here." She lay her hand against her throat. "He's telling a whole life story. Or perhaps the story of that one moment that feels like a lifetime." The enveloping arrangement journeyed on, the guitar quickened, crescendoed, lost its rhythm, became erratic. Then it lay back against the body of the symphony, came away from itself, regained its composure, laughed a little, and finally let itself sleep. Pia felt an ache at the base of her throat. She closed her eyes, too, not wanting the music to end. But of course it did, and then there was another uncomfortable silence.

Dalphine opened her eyes and smiled, and Pia realized she was still leaning toward her, listening for what she might say.

"Such decadence," said Dalphine. "So lovely. Have you heard it before?"

"No," said Pia. "It was beautiful."

"I'd be happy to order it for you," Dalphine offered. "The guitarist is Zoltan Tokos. My favorite."

"Oh." Pia had forgotten for a moment where she was. "No, please don't go to any trouble."

"It's not a bit of trouble! And I want you to have it. I'm sending the order today, anyway. Several of my regular customers have heard it this week and absolutely insisted they had to have it. So you *must* have it. In fact, you'd be doing me a favor. I should be able to get a discount if I order a full dozen. Oh, I know! Purchase the ottoman, and I'll give you the Rodrigo, yes? As a gift."

"Really, I can't."

"Oh, dear. *Can't* is such a categorical negative. So absolute. Why not leave just a little room for the possibility of transformation?" Dalphine raised one eyebrow and waited for a response. "No? Oh well. Then I insist you take the Rodrigo at cost. A thirty percent discount."

Pia made herself nod and smile as she'd learned to do in any situation where she didn't know how to respond.

"The guitar. It's a riddle," Dalpine said. "A joke. Or a parable, maybe. How can the same instrument that twangs out some horrendous ditty about trucks and rural ice house imbroglios be used to create such a masterpiece? Honestly, it's the difference between Renoir and Elvis on velvet. I have no explanation to offer."

Pia nodded and smiled again, a bit more genuinely this time.

Dalphine straightened her skirt over her knees.

"You aren't one for chatting, are you?"

"No," Pia said self-consciously. "I'm sorry."

"Not at all! This is so refreshing! To sit with a friend and listen to the music. Most of my *clienti dolci* . . . most of them are so eager to talk talk talk. They can't keep still. They won't sit and listen to music with me. They would find that too . . . oh . . . *non so*. I don't know. Exhausting. Impossible. Why is that, do you suppose?"

"Perhaps they feel awkward, so they need to make conversation."

"Ah," Dalphine nodded. "But you don't?"

"Feel awkward or need to make conversation?"

"Either one," Dalphine laughed. "Take your choice."

"I suppose I—yes, I do feel a little awkward."

"Because strangers don't sit together? Share a coffee and a concerto?"

"No."

"Aha! Then we must be friends already, you and I."

Pia searched for another semigenuine smile.

"Well," she said, pulling her purse into her lap. "Thank you for the coffee and . . . um . . ."

"Oh, already?" Dalphine cried with an exaggerated frown. "But you'll come back, won't you? You have to come back. For the Rodrigo. Don't forget!"

Pia nodded and accepted Dalphine's outstretched hand, relieved to know she wasn't actually obligated to come back for the Rodrigo. She hadn't signed anything. She hadn't actually committed anything to paper. She'd taken Dalphine's hand, though, and there was something in the soft, dry grasp of it, the smooth, perfect parallel of her fingers, the warm cove of her palm that made Pia hurry out onto the familiar street.

The train was crowded, so Pia had to sit next to the window, and the rushing images intensified the feeling of disorder, disconnection, chaos. She wouldn't go back there again, she resolved, but as soon as that resolution settled into place, desolation settled over the top of it. The elation she'd felt at that slight expansion of her carefully constructed corridor turned on her like a tide and swamped back in its antithesis. The antithesis of elation. The opposite of expansion.

She closed and locked the front door when she came in, then went to her bedroom and closed and locked the door, then went into the bathroom, closed and locked the door, and turned on the water in the bathtub. She sat on the edge of a wooden chair while the water poured a constant ambient noise that filled the room with sound and steam.

"And you didn't go back for a month?" Lily said.

"No."

Pia lay in bed, cradling the sound of her sister's voice between the hard shell of the cell phone and the tender place just in front of her eardrum.

"Why not?"

"I don't know. I just didn't." Pia was uncomfortable with the tone of the question. "I've been caught up with work."

"You're working? Pia, that's great! What are you doing?"

"Copyediting. Fact checking. Things I can do from home."

"How much are they paying?" Lily had no qualms about asking people this question. "Hey, maybe that's something I could do from here, you know? From my *home office*." She followed the euphemism with a twist of coarse laughter. Her laugh had gotten that throaty texture it gets from smoking.

"Maybe," Pia said, without holding forth any real encouragement. "Look, I'm sorry I haven't called more often. I keep thinking I will, and then . . . time just goes by."

"Doesn't it though," said Lily drily.

"Sometimes." Pia glanced down at her watch, willing it to move things along.

"Anyway," Lily sighed. "Finish telling me about your ottoman thingy."

"It's old. It's beautiful in a really strange way. It's expensive."

"Well, it's not like you can't afford it, Pia. You should buy it."

"It's not the money," Pia tried to explain. "It's . . . I don't know. The *noise*."

"It's a noisy ottoman?"

"Yes! You know—*loud*. There'd be no peace with all that chaotic blossoming."

"Okay," said Lily. "But you should know, Pia, that sounds a little nutty."

"The woman at the store—she said she bought it from a customer who'd traveled a great deal when she was younger," said Pia. "But she's alone now. Elderly. Her husband is dead. And her children—they're off living their own lives. Maybe they weren't as close as she wishes they might have been. And she's . . . she's afraid to go out of her house for some reason. She doesn't know why. She hasn't always been that way. In fact, she used to have a wonderful job and a family and friends in the world. But she moved to a new house in an unfamiliar area, and somehow . . . I suppose she didn't know her way around and it was just . . . too much. There was too much out there. Outside. And she wasn't just being lazy or silly. It was physically sickening. Nauseating, I mean. She physically became ill if she left the path she was familiar with. Eventually, she was able to make her way to the train, and then sit very still on the train until it came to the station near her doctor's office, and on the way from the train to her house, she would stop at the pharmacy. Sometimes the market, if it wasn't too crowded. Otherwise she had them deliver. Absolutely anything can be delivered these days, you know. These days, you don't have to go anywhere if you don't want to. There's really no reason."

"There's a reason, Pia," Lily said quietly. "There's a million reasons. Believe me, I can think of several new ones every day I have to sit in here."

There was silence. Pia could hear cold hallway sounds beyond Lily's soft breathing.

"I've been thinking, Pia—and believe me, I have had *plenty* of time for thinking lately . . ." She let the word roll down her tongue in three syllables, *puh-len-ty,* and followed it with another ashy laugh. "Maybe you and I could start some kind of business when I get home. When I get out, you know. If I have a place to go, something to do. And if I accrue enough good time. They'll let me out sooner. I mean, I could conceivably be out of here in seven months."

"What sort of business?"

"I was thinking about like a bookstore, maybe? And we'd have a coffee shop right there. You know, as an alternative to those soulless corporate stores. A little shop, where we would have only good books. No self-help books or macho escapist thrillers or romance novels or any of that crap."

"Maybe," said Pia. She didn't feel obligated to validate or invalidate Lily's idea, because she knew Lily would have a new and completely different idea next time they spoke.

"So what sort of books are you copyediting?" asked Lily.

"Romance novels. It's a Christian romance series, actually."

"Oh," said Lily. "Oops. Sorry."

"It's all right."

"I didn't mean—"

"Really, it's fine. People get the wrong idea about—"

"Crap. They're telling me it's time, Pia. I have thirty seconds."

"Okay. Take care of yourself."

"Okay. You, too."

"I'll call you."

"I'll be here."

"Me, too."

"Bye, Pia."

"Bye, Lily."

They kept each other as long as they could, exchanging smaller and smaller words until the connection was severed.

"*Avanti, farfalla!*" Dalphine called when she saw her, as if Pia had only just walked out the door yesterday. "Come in, sweet!"

Pia had practiced saying what she thought she should say

about the Rodrigo, but Dalphine had been traveling and seemed to be under the impression that Pia had been in while she was away. She took Pia's arm and led her toward the back of the store, talking about her recent trip to Istanbul, Morocco, and the southern coast of Spain. It took Pia a moment to catch up to what Dalphine was saying about the windmills outside Tarifa. She was scanning nervously for the ottoman and not seeing it.

"You have to see all my treasures," Dalphine said, seizing Pia's hand. "I'm very proud. It's my African safari, you know, and these are my trophies. It's treacherous, you can guess, searching through the mountains of trash they have out for the tourists. But I've cultivated my friendships there. Dealers who—truly, they're my guides through this amazing labyrinth of shops and bazaars. They know the culture, the history, the streets. They know *i soldi*," she added, frisking her thumb back and forth across her fingertips. "They know the *money*."

There were dishes, small iron pots, copperware. There were antique fabrics, which Dalphine shook out and refolded, while giving an animated explanation of the florid ornamentation on a colored glass oil lamp hanging nearby.

"All hand painted. So lovely. They were once used in the Ottoman mosques. You see? See how they suspend it from the porcelain globe? The globes were originally intended to protect the lamp oil from mice, but the effect of them hanging in the mosque—they actually created an acoustic environment that enhanced the sound of the imam's voice as he spoke. And these—oh, I'm so pleased with these." She led Pia to a high shelf of ceramic plates, bowls, and vases embellished with leaves, flowers, and geometric designs. "Reproductions, of course. But very faithful to the Iznik designs of the sixteenth century. Very lovely—and not so expensive as you might think. You could incorporate these into your dining room decor or use them to serve dinner every day and not think twice about it."

Pia tried to take it all in, to respond with some kind of polite and coherent response, but the turbulent colors and the motion of the patterns made her feel like she was on a Ferris wheel. They were sitting with a tray of coffee between them before she could pull together even a few generic comments.

"So tell me, sweet. What brings you by today?" Dalphine asked, pouring coffee and dropping several sugar cubes in each cup without asking Pia how she took hers. "Did you make a special trip to see me? Or do you work in the city?"

"No."

"Just venturing in for a day of abandon and adventure, then?"

"No. Nothing like that."

Pia had never been the sort of person who did anything akin to adventure or abandon, and this certainly was the antithesis of that. Her weekly therapy sessions had become a droning precaution. The exam included a brief interview, the taking of blood, a probing of her lymph nodes. Basically, Dr. Ackerman wanted to make sure she was taking her medication and that she wasn't thinking of doing anything . . . crazy.

"She doesn't come for work or for play," Dalphine mused. "Then it must be *un affare di trar*. A romantic assignation."

Pia laughed at that. Dr. Ackerman was a fiftyish, flaccid man in thick glasses. She didn't even know his first name, but he seemed to know a lot about the meds. And he was Barret's friend, who could be counted on to be discreet. Pia would have liked to follow up with the kindly young man she'd seen in the emergency room, but Barret had been more than patient with her over the last several months. Discretion was the very least she owed him.

"So it *is* a dangerous liaison," Dalphine prodded.

"No, not dangerous," Pia said. "I hope not."

"Then you must have come back for the ottoman you admired."

Dalphine crossed her legs and took a deep draw from her cup. Pia sipped hers tentatively, as if it were still hot.

"It's Turkish," Dalphine said, and it took Pia a moment to realize she meant the ottoman, not the coffee.

"Is it still here?" she asked.

"Oh, yes. I have no intention of selling it to anyone but you."

Pia stared at her. "I'm sorry?"

"It's already yours."

"What?" Pia smiled uncomfortably. "No, it isn't."

"Oh, yes, sweet. It's yours alone. You just don't know it yet."

"Well, I haven't—I mean, it's beautiful, yes. But the price is a little out of my range, and the style really doesn't fit my home, which is more—I guess you'd call it modern, maybe. Austere. Less is more."

"Oh, don't be silly, sweet dear. *More* is more. By definition!"

"Nonetheless. It really isn't something I see blending in with that sort of decor."

"Blending in?" Dalphine smiled and pressed her hand against her heart. "Why should it blend in? The fabric is a perfect copy of an eighteenth-century Turkish *catma*. Handwoven in Bursa. Silk and embossed velvet. The legs are hand carved. And did you notice?" She leaned toward Pia and whispered, "It's specifically made to the perfect height."

"For what?" Pia was beginning to feel constricted and tense across her forehead.

"Oh . . . a variety of purposes," Dalphine shrugged with a mock innocence. "Use your imagination. In any case, it's very versatile. And so lovely. It's exotic. And you, sweet—you're absolutely crying out for something exotic in your life. Why do you think you're so drawn to it?"

Pia pretended to finish her coffee and set the cup on the tray.

"Now what do you suppose your husband would say," Dalphine said in a stage-whisper way, "if he came home this evening to discover you served up like a lavish feast on this lovely buffet?"

"I think," Pia whispered back, "he would say, 'How could you spend six thousand dollars on an ottoman?'"

Dalphine leaned back and laughed.

"Six thousand two hundred fifty!" she corrected, pouring more coffee. "And of course, you would tell him that a piece like this is an investment. Like investing in art. You wouldn't blink an eye over that price for a sculpture by—oh, name someone—Timothy Holmes, for example. One would gladly pay ten times that for a Holmes."

"My husband's investments tend to be more in the area of pharmaceuticals and fast-growth corporations, I'm afraid."

"*Assurdita.*" Dalphine waved her hand, brushing Pia's objections away. "It all depends on how you introduce the idea. It's like fine cuisine. Presentation is everything. With the right sort of presentation, you might discover he's more open than you think."

"I don't know what you mean." Pia kept her eyes carefully lowered to her cup and saucer and spoon.

"Well." Dalphine's tone was patient, unhurried. "Only that . . . if you were to surprise him, *fertito,* he might surprise you."

"Well, he would certainly surprise me this evening," Pia said. "He's out of the country. I'm not expecting him home until next week."

"He's a very worldly man, then! Someone who'd value a fine antique from abroad."

"Actually, he's a very practical man."

"Then he can well afford it!"

Pia laughed again. There was something about this sort of exchange that reminded her of who she used to be. She stared at the ottoman's garden of lotus blossoms and tried not to want them.

"Hmm," Dalphine mused after a quiet moment. "A suburban wife whose husband travels. Perhaps I do have something a little more practical for you." She rose and walked toward the beaded curtain again, beckoning Pia. "Do your tastes run toward antique or contemporary? I'm guessing antique. But you don't strike me as being too fussy for reproductions."

She held the beads aside for Pia, then stepped behind a display case filled with delicate earrings and heavy silver necklaces. She bent down, unlocked the sliding back panel, and brought out a large velvet-covered tray from a bottom drawer. Eight long objects lay side by side, like brothers in a bed. White as whole milk, contoured and smooth as poured marble, they were arranged by size: slender, less slender, not so slender, thick. In the muted light of the back room, it took Pia a moment to realize what they were, and when she did, she covered her mouth with her hand to suppress a giggle that sounded sadly like the Catholic schoolgirl she used to be.

"Oh! Um . . . goodness. No. I don't think so."

"For heaven's sake, *pattampoochi*." Dalphine smiled patiently. "What is there to be embarrassed about? You are a grown woman. I'm a merchant who sells items that provide comfort to grown women. Items for the home, items for the body. Items for the woman living inside the home. Living inside the body."

Leaving the tray on the counter, she stepped aside and rearranged a few bracelets on a little pewter tree. She came back and turned a few of the items to show their rippled underside.

"The history of sexual appliances is quite fascinating," said Dalphine. "Of course, we have phallic objects of varying types and sizes dating back thousands of years. The Romans were highly evolved, though not as debauched as they are often portrayed. The men went away at war. The women blossomed in their absence. Educated each other. Became skilled craftspersons. Thus, the dildo—from the word *dilettarsi*—which means 'to delight.' Eastern cultures were the most inventive in terms of design and aesthetics. These are Persian inspired. Western culture fell under more repressive influences, as you know, so we tend to see a more utilitarian approach."

Pia still hadn't moved a muscle or shifted her gaze from the tray.

"In Victorian times, women began to be diagnosed with a

rather vague malady called 'hysteria' whose symptoms included anxiety, impure thoughts, inordinate vaginal lubrication, et cetera, and amazingly enough, it was discovered that the most effective treatment was manipulation of the vulva until an emotional and physical release was achieved. Well! My sweet dear, what do you suppose? As word of this amazing curative therapy began to circulate, a great many women suddenly developed symptoms of hysteria and rushed to their doctors, desperate for relief. The more adroit practitioners were in such great demand, they began to experience pain and cramping in their hands. And as everyone knows, as soon as something becomes a man's problem, a solution is quickly found. Thus was born . . ." Dalphine waved her hand in a sweeping gesture over the shallow tray. "The vibrator, whereby we poor delicate females are freed from the scourge of hysteria."

"Is that true?" Pia asked, intrigued despite herself.

"Oh, it's well documented," said Dalphine. "They were sold as 'massagers' or 'lady's helpers.' The Sears and Roebuck catalogs featured a multipurpose model with a separate attachment for buffing one's high-button shoes."

Pia felt relieved to laugh out loud. Dalphine smiled, went out through the beaded curtain, and came back with some satin pillows, which she placed with a yellow invoice in a box on the shelf behind the counter.

"Now *this*," Dalphine said, gently lifting the first and fattest of the brothers and weighing it in her hands, "this is so lovely. The genuine article. Late seventeenth century. Definitely not for sale. It's ivory, so to sell it would be quite illegal now, of course. And anyway, as you can see, the size is—well, I think many women might find it distasteful, if not problematic. However"—she replaced the ivory dildo and picked up the one next to it—"modern technology has provided for us an amazing likeness. Truly, unless you were an elephant, you'd never know it's not ivory. But the feel is a bit mellower. Warmer. With the added advantage of—*molto pratico!*—batteries."

She twisted a brass ring at the base, and it began to emit a soft humming. When Dalphine pressed the subtle vibration against Pia's forearm, Pia flinched away as if it were a hot iron. Dalphine lay the seventh brother back in his place, quiet again.

"I think any one of these might make the week pass a bit more quickly," she said.

Pia was vaguely aware that her lips were very dry and slightly parted.

"These are individually poured and handcrafted in India, of course. I'll have nothing to do with selling some cheap factory-made toy. Believe me, not all are created equal. The superior quality of these is readily discernible. Much more *upscale*, you know, than something you'd purchase through mail order, for example. Online, you know. Another customer, a dear friend—she was just leaving when you came in, as a matter of fact—she's told me about some of the accessories she purchased by catalog. Such a disappointment! The crudeness of design, shabbiness of construction. And what will you do in this case? Return such a thing? It's appalling to think that would even be possible! And then there's the indelicate matter of giving one's shipping information to an organization of that nature. No. I don't believe in shame." Dalphine retreated to her stage whisper again. "But certain areas require discretion."

"Yes," Pia said. "Definitely."

"But what is she to do? Her husband travels in his work, and so does she. Something like this is an absolute necessity to her. You can imagine how pleased she was to be introduced to an item similar to this."

Pia couldn't drag her eyes away from the slender object in Dalphine's hand.

"I think you'd be pleased with the next size up, perhaps."

Pia nodded so slightly she wasn't sure she'd moved at all.

"This one, for example?"

Pia hesitated, then nodded again.

"Yes? Very nice. It's just two hundred ninety-five dollars."

Dalphine smiled and brought out a tortoiseshell box. "And this I give you as a gift." She opened the lid and laid the intimate object on a pink satin lining that made it seem even more intimate, as if the satin were the soft lining of Pia's private self.

"Very nice," Dalphine said again. Smoothing her hand over the closed box, she slid it across the counter. "And may I have the ottoman delivered, too?"

No, Pia meant to say, but she heard herself speak the words *Not today.*

"I'll wrap this, then." Dalphine smiled, measuring out rose-patterned tissue paper from a mounted roll. "I'll gift wrap it so you can make a present to yourself, and—oh yes! The Rodrigo! I won't even ring it up. Take it on approval. So you'll feel obligated to come back again."

Pia opened her purse, hoping she would find enough cash to pay for the purchase. For some reason, it felt unseemly to use a check or credit card. She usually kept four fifties zipped into one of the neatly organized compartments, but on occasion, when Barret was in a hurry, he would take one or all of them. It irritated Pia. Not because it was an invasion of her personal things, but because it left her feeling disorganized, unprepared, and unpleasantly surprised when she discovered them missing, as she did now.

"*Pia*. What a lovely name," Dalphine exclaimed before she slid Pia's credit card through a device mounted beside the cash register. "Not one we hear so often. Is it a family name?"

"Yes."

"And do all your friends tell you how lovely and unusual it is?"

As Dalphine unfolded a shopping bag with red ribbon handles, Pia tried to think of someone in her life she'd call a friend as opposed to an acquaintance or colleague.

"My husband likes it."

The brown linen-paper bag was thickly grown with Victorian lace and roses. It made Pia think of the castle in the fairy tale, grown over by roses and thorns while everyone inside slept for a hundred years.

"Pia. My dear. I'm so glad to know you." Dalphine smiled and shook out a sheet of white tissue and tucked it into the bag, flaring the corners just so. Then she placed the tortoiseshell box and the Rodrigo CD inside and offered it to Pia, presented it to her, holding it high by its bright red ribbons, making a gracious gesture. "Please, please do come back very soon."

Pia thanked her and hurried, flushed and self-conscious, from the shop out into the sunlight, where she paused on the sidewalk long enough to take the tortoiseshell box from the shopping bag and push it deep inside her large leather purse. She took out the CD, folded the shopping bag flat, and slipped them both into the pocket of her overcoat.

She waved to a cab at the corner, and all the way to the train station, the purse lay in her lap. At the station, she pushed through the door of the ladies' room and waited for a stall. Inside, she locked the door and took the box from her purse. She held it in her hands, measuring it the way Dalphine had weighed the old ivory. It was heavy and cool and the tissue paper smelled faintly of Dalphine's perfume. She heard the announcement for her train, but before she went out, Pia put the CD and the shopping bag into her purse and slid the tortoiseshell box into her coat pocket.

On the way home, she crossed her arms in front of herself to keep from reaching in and touching it. When she leaned toward the window, the package pressed against her leg and radiated a rushing sensation outward from the point at which it pressed through the fabric of the coat and lining. She repeated to herself that it was not possible for her to feel the pulse of the person sitting next to her, that it was only the rhythm of the train below. She watched people come and go from the lavatory, wanting to go in herself, thinking about standing, swaying in front of the mirror. Opening her coat. Sitting down on the commode. Opening her legs.

With that thought came the vertigo, and close behind it, the headache came pounding on dull Clydesdale hooves. As Pia walked quickly home from the station, the rose-wrapped package hung heavily in her coat. She finally allowed herself to put her hand inside her pocket and kept it there until she leaned against the inside of her own front door. She stood for a long time, trying to know what to do, reeling with the force of the headache, nauseous with shame and anger at herself.

When the phone rang, it so startled her that she made an involuntary sound, fluttered like a pigeon unsettled from the sidewalk, and when her hand flew from her coat pocket, the box clattered on the wooden floor beside the entryway rug.

The phone rang again, and Pia stepped into the hall, taking a deep breath before she answered.

"Hello."

"Pia, thank God." Barret sounded more angry than concerned. "I've been calling all afternoon."

"Oh. Yes. I'm sorry."

"Did you forget your cell phone?"

"No, but I . . . I decided to see a movie, so I turned off the cell phone, and then I forgot to turn it on again and I missed my first train, and I . . . I'm sorry."

"You know I always call. You know I worry."

"Yes, I know, Barret. I'm sorry," said Pia, and she truly was. She hated to hear that anguished tone in his voice. This was so very much not what he'd thought he was getting into when he asked her to marry him. And she really should have remembered. She'd been seeing Dr. Ackerman for nine months now, and every week on days she saw Dr. Ackerman, Barret always called right after the appointment instead of at eight, which was their appointed time to talk at night whenever he was away. He never actually asked or mentioned anything about the appointment and Pia never volunteered anything. It was as if it had all transpired in French, and he felt that Pia would provide subtitles as needed.

"Well. Anyway." Barret cleared his throat. Pia heard him clicking the keyboard of his computer in the background. "How are you? How was your day?"

"Fine. It was good."

"Are you sure? You sound a little tired."

"Just a little headache is all. Everything's fine. And Barret, Dr. Ackerman said—"

"It's all right, Pia. You don't have to tell me anything you don't want to."

"No, I do want to tell you. Barret, he said that with the new medication—with the lesser dosage—he said I was stable. He used the word *stable*."

"Well. That's good. That's excellent, Pia. You can just put it all behind you now. All that unpleasantness." That was one of the euphemisms he used in order to avoid saying words that made them both uncomfortable. They'd learned to phrase things evasively, keeping them in peripheral vision, and there was no question of ownership in Barret's semantics. It was Pia's unfortunate experience. Her health trouble. Her accident. Her unpleasantness, which she could now put behind her.

"So how was your day?" Pia asked, doing her best to do that. "How's Washington?"

"Still here."

"Is the case going well."

"It's fine."

"That's good. So . . . you'll call tomorrow, then?"

"Yes, of course."

"Barret," Pia started, but at the same time, Barret started to say something else. Then they both apologized.

"Go ahead," Barret told her.

"No, that's all right. What were you going to say?"

He didn't say anything for a long moment.

"What were you going to say?" Pia repeated. "Please don't leave it like that."

"I was just going to ask . . . what movie did you see?" Barret said.

"What?"

"What movie? You said you were at the movies."

"Oh. Right. It was . . ." Pia searched her mind for something she'd seen advertised recently, something he hopefully hadn't seen on the plane. "It was a foreign film. Something you would have hated. Really, it wasn't very good. I didn't even stay for the whole thing."

"What was it about?"

Pia couldn't tell if he was asking because he wanted to stay with her or because he felt obligated to make small talk.

"It was about this woman," said Pia. "And because there was a lot of death in her life, or maybe just because of . . . wrong thoughts . . . she thought that her skin was becoming like a doll's skin. Plastic and hard with air inside instead of organs and blood and et cetera. And more than anything, she wanted . . . she wanted to be able to feel something again. And so one night she decided . . . well, she didn't decide, but without really deciding, she um . . ."

Trying to think of what came next, Pia allowed enough of a pause for Barret to break in with a foreshortened burst of laughter.

"You're right. That does sound like something I would have hated."

They spoke for a few more minutes. Pia asked him about the brief he'd been up late preparing. Barret asked her about the progress of the manuscript she was polishing.

"Well," he said finally. "I'll let you get back to work, then. Don't stay up too late."

"No. You either."

They said good-byes, and Pia clicked the phone off with her thumb.

Returning to the entryway, she picked up the tissue-papered package from the floor, suddenly feeling enormously silly.

What a ridiculous waste of money. And time. Sitting there with some stranger when she had work to do. Her office upstairs. Her garden outside. Now that Dr. Ackerman had reduced her meds and she wasn't sleeping so much, she'd been planning to reorganize her photo albums this week. Cross-reference them according to date, holiday, and subject, box them by decade.

She held the package in her hands, not sure what to do with it now. She certainly wasn't going to return it. Good Lord. But to throw it away after spending almost three hundred dollars? Pia went upstairs, stripped the tissue paper off the tortoiseshell box, and buried it in a drawer of secret lace underthings. It was a drawer she rarely opened anymore, a good place to hide things from herself.

She decided to call Lily that night. It had been a long time since they spoke. Sometimes when Pia called, Lily was in the infirmary or solitary confinement. The first two years she was in prison, she'd managed to stay out of trouble, but things had seriously gone downhill since King divorced her.

"I wish he would have at least called me," Lily said. "For closure, if nothing else. It's a bummer to have it end like this. Anticlimactic, you know? Not with a bang but a whimper. Although the bang was pretty good while it lasted."

Pia cringed a little but didn't say anything.

"I hate to think what sort of men will be interested in me after this. Losers." Lily coughed a deep, coarse cough. "Losers with toupees. Shag carpeting, water beds. Men who like those women-in-prison movies from the seventies. *Women in Chains*. And I'll probably be grateful. Because I can't bear the idea of doing the self-serve pump for the rest of my life."

"*Lily,*" Pia said sharply. "You don't have to be so crude."

"*Pia,*" Lily mimicked. "You don't have to be so prissy."

"Do you want me to hang up? Do you want to continue this conversation?"

"No! Yes! Don't go, Pia! And don't threaten that. You don't know what that means. Pia? Are you still there?"

"Yes, I'm still here."

"Maybe I'd like to be prissy, too. Maybe I'd like to be fragile and civilized and polite. But around here a person can't afford to be. I'm serious. You wouldn't last five minutes."

Then I'll make sure I don't kill anyone, Pia thought.

"I'm sorry," she said out loud, more for the ugly thought than the sharp words.

Pia lay in bed that night, trying not to think about it.

The foreign object.

The rippled contour of it. It repelled and fascinated her at the same time, filled her with a strange admixture of revulsion and hunger. She couldn't even guess what Barret would think if he knew she had any such thing hidden away. Presentation is everything, she reminded herself. He might surprise me. Pia imagined him coming home to find her lying across the ottoman, imagined moving and being moved back and forth across it, feeling the knotted nubs catch across her nipples, her palms on the floor, his belly at her back.

She got out of bed and crept across the dark room, and by the light she always left on in the stairwell she found her way to the stereo in the hall. She'd laid the Rodrigo CD on top of it earlier, just after she'd hidden away the tortoiseshell box. She pushed a button on the front of the stereo, and the way it opened, slid a little shelf out for the disc, then swallowed it without a sound—it reminded her of the way she set the small white pill on her tongue and took it in every morning and again at night.

As the music draped behind her like a mantilla and the classical guitar came and stood beside her in the dark, she imagined Edgar sitting in the red side chair watching her straddle the brocade ottoman, silk on silk on silk, her knees drawn up to the perfect height.

She used to watch Edgar indulge himself. When they first

bought the house the boys were born in, she'd discovered there was a certain angle at which she could situate the easy chair in their room so as to see a reflection of the glass shower door in the bathroom mirror. Even through the steam, she could see him, fiercely concentrating, moving the taut skin with great precision up and back, up and back, bringing one finger across and over the cleft, not on every stroke, but in a sort of iambic pentameter. She wondered if Barret might like to watch her the same way. Pleasuring herself with the faux ivory artifact.

Pia returned to her bed and lay there, imagining her skin against the Turkish embroidery, how the stitches would feel like a thousand tiny tongues if she were to sit there, reduced to the perfect height from which to kiss his hand away from himself, replacing it with her open mouth. Barret loved that, and whenever Pia pleased him that way, she thought of Edgar. Edgar was her mentor. He'd taught her how to bring on the maximum degree of yearning without pushing past the precipice too soon. She'd practice-perfected the technique, because she was a virgin when they met and was determined to hold on to that treasure until they were married, but she loved Edgar and wanted to pleasure and please him. And to please him like that—it wasn't sex. She and her sorority sisters had debated this many times and come to a consensus. It didn't count.

Pia sank a little deeper into the bedding. She let herself imagine Edgar moaning, moving, crushing her into the silk and velvet. The image became so real, she rested her hand over her pelvis and let her hips roll slightly upward and back. She wanted to say his name, but she knew she was in the earliest part of sleeping, and the sound of her voice would splinter this perfect state of nonconsciousness. Then suddenly Dalphine was there within the dream, her mouth like black velvet, her tongue cool as ivory.

The dream-Pia held the hard milky object in her hands. It looked as large as an elephant's tusk as she coaxed it into herself and caused it to all but disappear.

Lily

(1252 days)

Library day. Returned The Optimist's Daughter. Didn't see anything I wanted to check out and got shanghaied by the Jesus Chick on my way out. The one who always wears the "IF IT IS TO BE, IT IS UP TO ME!" T-shirt. Yark.

JC: Leaving without a book today, sister?

ME: Yeah, nothing really blew my hair back today.

JC: Oh, let me pick something for you. It's three days till we see you again. You don't want to sit with an idle mind. That's just a breeding ground for negativity!

ME: Oh, that's okay . . .

(But she's already digging and flipping and ransacking through stuff.)

JC: Ah! Perfect. Omar Khayyam. And let me find . . . here. I marked a passage for you to meditate on. We can discuss it when you bring it back.

ME: (trying to contain my utter lack of enthusiasm) Terrific. Thanks.

Yeah. Maybe later. After I lobotomize myself with a knitting needle.

(1253 days)

Were you indeed not blinded by the Curse
Of Self-exile, that still grows worse and worse,
Yourselves would not know that, though you see him not,
He is with you this Moment, on this Spot,
Your Lord through all Forgetfulness and Crime,
Here, There, and Everywhere, and through all Time.

Okay. So I meditated on it. Wouldn't want to be sitting here idly breeding negativity.

(1261 days)

Pia called. Barret actually home for a change so she couldn't talk long. Told her about the Omar thing, but she didn't really seem to get it. She was all bugged out about a water main that broke on her street and messed up her sidewalk. Get a friggin' grip, Pia. You've got a sidewalk. You've got a street.

This month's Lit Classic came in the mail. Beowulf.

(1264 days)

So today that stupid Ass Clown walks up all mosey-on-over-and-strike-up-a-conversation.

AC: (oozing lameness) You sure do read a lot.

ME: Bite me, Ass Clown.

AC: So what are you reading there?

ME: It's called The Little Ass Clown Who Bit Me.

AC: (auger-nosing at my book) Beowulf? Cool! Awesome. Awesomely inspiring story.

ME: Yeah. Makes me want to rip your arm off and nail it to the wall.

AC: (all hur-yuckety-yuck-yuck) Ha. Like the monster in the book. Yeah, I get it.

ME: I wasn't joking.

AC: There's this book by John Gardner—I donated a copy to the library, in fact—it's called Grendel. The same story, only from the monster's point of view, and it really makes you think about the perspectives of right and wrong, you know? How there's always a flip side to—

ME: Yeah, well, that's fascinating, but don't you have a monkey that needs spanking?

AC: Wow. You um . . . you're really good at that, aren't you? The vulgar remark thing.

ME: Sets your little wobbly bits a-tingle, does it?

AC: No. It just makes me feel sorry for you. Because I think it's theater.

ME: Go fuck your mother, Freud.

AC: (turning all red in the face) I'm not letting you get to me anymore.

ME: (laughing my butt off) You're blushing, dude. Sheesh! You blush like a little flower girl.

AC: (stomping off) You're not getting to me. It's theater.

(1277 days)

Ass Clown is seriously getting on my nerves.

AC: So I, um, I see you're reading Grendel. What do you think of it so far?

ME: Could somebody please pass the pinhead repellent?

AC: Um, I don't know if you already know this, but they have this thing with the library. You can get your GED. General Equivalency Degree? It's just like a high school diploma. I could help you do that if you want.

ME: Wow. You'd really do that for me? Help me get a GED?

AC: Yeah. Sure. Happy to.

ME: Oh, that'd be awesome! 'Cause I'm just a little jerk-wad prisoner, Mr. Super Intelligent Guard Man. I'm too stupid to have really-o-truly-o graduated from high school.

AC: Well, it's not—I'm not saying that. I just thought—

ME: You just thought I'd give you a blow job if you taught me my multiplication tables.

AC: No!

ME: Maybe I don't need a general equivalency degree, Ass Clown. Maybe I've got a college degree. Maybe I've got my MFA. Maybe I've got a goddamn PhD in comparative lit.

AC: (all excited) You do?

ME: No, Ass Clown. God, you're an ass.

AC: Fine! Whatever! I was just trying to be nice.

ME: Well, go be nice to somebody else.

AC: Would you be surprised to know that I've got a master's degree in comp lit?

ME: Yes.

AC: Why?

ME: Because you're a dumb-ass.

AC: Well, I do. From SMU. I was #17 in my class.

ME: Whatever, pal. I see you're putting it to good use.

AC: It's a sad comment, but fewer than 30 percent of liberal arts graduates at the master's level are actually employed in their field of study.

ME: And only a lucky few work as slaves in a prison laundry. But I was only #19 in my class.

AC: Seriously, do you have your MFA?

ME: Yes, I seriously do.

AC: In what?

ME: Theatre arts.

AC: Oh. Then you really are lucky to be working in a prison laundry.

ME: (actually laughing) Oh, that was cold!

AC: (all excited again) Gotcha, didn't I! I finally got you!

ME: Yeah, how about that? Ass Clown made a funny.

AC: I have a name, you know. My name is—

ME: (not laughing) Hey! I don't give a crap what your name is. Keep it to yourself.

AC: Fine. Pardon the heck outta me. (looking all smug) Yup. I knew it was all theater.

ME: Yeah. Like when you lube your doorknob and pretend it's Mr. T.

AC: GEEZ! Do you have to be so raunchy all the time? Gah!

And he stomps off, blushing like a little cartoon piglet.

(1341 days)

Thank God that Ass Clown is off the floor. He was starting to get problematic.

MOIRA: Here comes your boyfriend.

ME: That garden tool? He's no friend of mine.

MOIRA: Baby boy's got a butt like a rudder. Yummy.

ME: Whatever, hon.

MOIRA: I hear he's leaving. Said he was moving out of state somewhere.

ME: Good.

MOIRA: Why, are your knees getting sore?

So now I'm in solitary for hitting her in the face with a tray, 45 days good time down the tubes. But I'm okay with that. Ultimately, I'd be worse off if I let shit like that get said about me.

(*1362 days*)

I have gotten very thin.

Beth

This is not a good day for Beth.

She has her period, and she hates that. It makes her feel sticky and unclean. She would like to get a hysterectomy. Or get that ablation procedure that burns the lining away and leaves an empty tomb. She wouldn't mind thinking of herself that way. Like the empty tomb where the angels were.

It was Easter Sunday, appropriately enough, when Beth and Sonny took their daughter to church for the first time. A Methodist church. It seemed like a middle ground. Easter was five years old, and they didn't want her to grow up unchurched, but Sonny was afraid they might see someone they knew at a Catholic church. And that might be a stumbling block in the faith of that person. Sonny carried a lot of guilt. Not so much because of the scandal or Beth's humiliation. More over the disillusionment of the fragile young minds at Saint Thomas Aquinas College. Having been a student there, Beth had a different perspective on how delicate and virginal the girls were about their faith and morality, but she honored Sonny's wishes. It was her duty as his wife to obey him, according to God's instruction through Saint Paul, so she made the best of it. Even the loosey-goosey nondogma of the Methodist church was better than nothing.

It was Easter Sunday, so the United Methodist Youth Fellowship gave a little program. While most of the children acted the story out in bathrobe-ish Bible folk costumes, a beautiful Hispanic girl stood in her white Easter dress and read from the Gospel of Saint Luke.

"On the first day of the week," she enunciated, "very early in the morning, the women took the spices they had prepared and went to the tomb. They found the stone rolled away from the tomb, but when they entered, they did not find the body of the Lord Jesus. While they were wondering about this, suddenly two men in clothes that gleamed like lightning stood beside them. In their fright the women bowed down with their faces to the ground, but the men said to them, 'Why do you look for the living among the dead? He is not here; he has risen! Remember how he told you, while he was still with you in Galilee: the Son of Man must be delivered into the hands of sinful men, be crucified and on the third day be raised again.' Then they remembered his words. When they came back from the tomb, they told all these things to the Eleven and to all the others. It was Mary Magdalene, Joanna, Mary the mother of James, and the others with them who told this to the apostles."

Mary and Joanna and Mary. Beth wished with her whole heart that she could have been one of them. The women who knew before the rest of the world. The secret sisters. It caused her to cry, sitting there that day, hearing the story of the resurrection but having so little to do with it. She missed the dedicated life. She missed singing the carefully ordered liturgy, wearing the carefully ironed uniform, performing her carefully cloistered rituals. But then she looked at Easter. For the first time, she was understanding the meaning of her name. Resurrection. Rebirth. Joy emerging out of sorrow. Beth imagined Easter reading from the Gospel of Saint Luke in front of the whole congregation someday, her voice clear and sweet as wisteria. Or maybe she would be in costume and play the Blessed Virgin Mary.

After the service, Beth enrolled Easter in Sunday school. The kindergarten class was small, the teacher petite and pretty in her denim jumper. Her name was Kari Harris. She cried and cried at Easter's funeral the following year, though she really didn't seem particularly fond of Easter and often complained about her behavior in class. Beth didn't mind that. She didn't feel like her private grief was being usurped or anything. She knew it was the idea of it that made Kari Harris cry. She probably cried at movies the same way. A six-year-old dies. That's a crying matter from any perspective. Beth knew from professional and personal experience that children's funerals are the worst.

"What could possibly be more horrific than having to bury your child?" Beth has heard this more than once since she started working at the funeral home, and before today, she would have said, "Nothing. There couldn't possibly be anything worse."

But today, Beth knows there is. Actually, she has known it for a few days. Sonny has tried to explain it to her, sitting her down on the couch, holding both her hands in his, talking to her with a practiced brand of eye contact she is very familiar with. This is how he guides people through the unthinkable. Beth prefers not to think about the unthinkable. The flood. The mud. The toppled trees. She's able to place these things in the background. While Sonny and the cemetery manager go over the particulars of the exhumation, Beth retreats to the dry ground of memory and denial.

"I know this isn't easy, but there's nothing else we could do," the cemetery manager says. "It was an act of God."

Beth laughs out loud, but it sounds like a cough with a sort of half-snort at the end of it, and she's embarrassed. Act of God. Beth used to wonder why that phrase was only applied to disasters. Now she understands. She thinks of Easter as an act of God. Like a long-prayed-for rain that refreshes, blesses, then soaks, saturates, overflows, floods, devastates. Too much blessing for the puny earth to absorb.

"Of course," Sonny says. "We're not blaming you. We're just—well, you can understand why my wife and I would be upset. It's very upsetting."

"Yes, yes, of course. Terribly upsetting." The man nods in sympathy, as Beth wonders why Sonny does not sound upset.

They continue talking, Sonny and . . . this man. Whatever his name is. Beth doesn't remember what was said when he offered his hand and guided her to this chair she's sitting in. He and Sonny speak the same language. The logistics of grief. The disposal of the dead. Beth would like to think Sonny is so at ease with it because of his faith in an eternal, assured, and infinitely better life to come.

"We'll be relocating your daughter's grave along with six others to area D-7, well above the newly designated flood plane," the manager continues, pointing to D with one index finger and 7 with the other, and then bringing the fingers toward each other till they meet at the final resting place. "Of course, we'll cover the costs of landscaping, flowers, et cetera. We'll replace any personal items that were lost or damaged and have the tombstone moved. And I think you'll find this is a real lovely area. This new area. It's real lovely."

"What's our time frame on this thing?" Sonny asks. Beth hears the word *thing* and turns it over in her mind for a moment. *This thing. This thing?*

"We're looking at about four days before we get the exhumations accomplished and the actual relocation taken care of," the man says. "Then there's the sod and the termite inspection. We'll have to get the county out here to certify that we're code compliant on everything. So I'd say . . . let's call it eight or nine days before you can come back in and do your thing and rededicate the site."

Beth wonders if they really have to do that. Their *thing*. The man shifts his practiced eye contact over to Beth, and his tone becomes conciliatory, slightly condescending. "I'd just like to say again how very sad I am for your loss, ma'am, and how very very unfortunate this whole thing is."

There it is again, Beth muses. *This thing*. But then she accepts that it's just a blanket term for whatever is unspeakable.

"Oh, of course," Sonny says. "And of course we understand this is no fault of yours. As far as the class-action suit and so forth—I just want to reassure you that we're not participating in that. Never even considered it."

Sonny is speaking for himself here. Beth will remind him of that later. She places a little bookmark in her head. Sonny stands up and offers his hand.

"Thanks for your time, Carlos," he says. Apparently the man's name is Carlos.

Beth stands and follows them to the door. They stand beside the car in the parking lot, talking about how this flooding has gotten worse every year and those new subdivisions upstream are not being planned with proper drainage and there's going to have to be some involvement by the county and maybe even the EPA.

Beth walks back along the brick wall until she reaches the iron gate. Across the cemetery, backhoes, winches, and orange cones are scattered among the slanted monuments and tilting stone angels, some of whom stand ankle-deep in swampy muck. A huge pecan tree is tipped sideways over the place where they buried Easter four years ago, its roots naked above the ground, its very nature torn inside out. More than anything in the world, Beth fears being so exposed.

Beth thinks about how empty the grave will feel once the workers have removed the damaged coffin, leaving nothing but an ablated hole in the ground. Like her vacant uterus. Like the rusted swing set in the yard. Like Lily's mangled car. A painfully empty and unsacred place where Easter's body was for a while before it wasn't.

Pushing through the iron gate, Beth walks down a cement path to the edge of the muddy water.

Why do you seek the living among the dead? the tilting angels whisper. *She is not here. She is risen.*

Pia

Dalphine was standing at the wall when the door chimes rang Pia in. She raised her hand and waved brightly, but never paused in her enthusiastic explanation of the investment value of a large tapestry she was showing to two customers.

Pia wandered toward the center of the store, pretending to look at a display of Buddhas arranged in rows on an elaborate sideboard. She edged toward the table where she and Dalphine had sat with their coffee, but a young man sat sleeping in the red side chair, a large case, one that might contain a musical instrument of some kind, on the floor at his side. His legs were stretched in front of him, propped on the Turkish ottoman.

Pia glanced toward Dalphine, wishing she would come over and tell him to take his feet down, but Dalphine continued romancing the young couple without taking her eyes from theirs. Pia stood behind the red chair and cleared her throat, hoping he'd wake up and take his feet down, but he only shifted slightly and continued his deep, steady breathing. She felt herself getting angry, though she wasn't sure why or at whom. She wanted to prod him on the shoulder. She wanted Dalphine to come over and tell him to leave. She wanted to shake his shoulder and slap his feet aside, as if he'd broken into her house and mud-died her carpets and rummaged her secret drawer.

Nervously, she took a few steps toward Dalphine, but Dal-phine's back was to her now, and she was extolling the virtues of the brightly colored batiks she'd bought from a craftsman in Jakarta. She unfolded one, wrapped herself in it, then threw it around the shoulders of the woman. She said something that made the young couple laugh.

Pia moved closer, pointedly examining the stained-glass shade of an iron floor lamp. She made her way back toward the young man, cleared her throat again. He didn't stir. She reached into her coat pocket and purposely dropped her keys on the floor.

Dalphine turned from her customers and waved again.

"Oh, Pia! Don't go yet, *farfalla*! I'll be right with you."

The young man stirred at the sound of Dalphine's voice. He stretched his legs and took his feet away from the ottoman. Pia would have bent to brush the upholstery with her hand if she could have done so without leaning her face so near to his lap. He scratched his face with both hands. His cheeks and chin were shaded with a half-growth of beard.

The door chimes crinkled above the soft music, and Dal-phine's customers departed with the rolled-up tapestry under their arms, linking them together like a bolt in a lock.

"One minute, Pia! Stay right there, sweet!"

She disappeared behind the beaded curtain and the young man followed her. Pia tried not to hear the intimate tone of their conversation, the sensual bending of Dalphine's laughter. She couldn't understand the hard lump of pure jealousy that formed in her stomach, and it made her uncomfortable enough that she started toward the door, wondering why she'd even bothered to come back.

"Pia!" Dalphine called again. She was edging sideways through the beaded doorway with the coffee tray. "You're not leaving without your coffee. Come sit."

"Actually, I'm not sure I have time today," Pia said. She didn't want her to think she'd come all the way into the city just to see her again.

"Oh, *tsh*! There's always time for friends." Dalphine set the tray down and leaned across the table to drape a napkin on Pia's lap. "What brings you in from Artevita today?"

"I had a manuscript to deliver."

"Ah." She set the tray on the burl coffee table. On either side of an ornate silver samovar, small iced cakes were piled on the blue-and-white Iznik plates. "You're a writer, then?"

"No. It's for my husband. He was asked to contribute a foreword for a legal principles textbook."

"Good God!" She laughed. "Sounds very dry. Have you read it?"

"Yes."

"Was it as dry as the pyramids?"

"Well, mostly it's, um—yes," Pia couldn't help laughing a little, and it felt good.

"I suppose it's a difficult topic to sex up," said Dalphine, and this time they laughed together, which was even more pleasant. "He's a lawyer, then?"

"A corporate attorney."

"Excellent! How lovely!" Dalphine exclaimed in a way that seemed inordinately enthusiastic until Pia connected the dots. "And what about you? What do you do?"

She served the coffee in delicate china cups while Pia considered it.

"Nothing important. I took some time off. But there's always . . . things . . . the garden, correspondence, you know. Keeping things in order. There's always that."

"Ah. Yes. Always that," Dalphine agreed earnestly.

They sat with their cups on their saucers.

"I do have a job, though." Pia wanted to tell her that, though she wasn't sure why it seemed important.

"Oh?"

"I work at home."

"Doing . . ."

"Copy editing."

"Ah, so I was right the first time. You are a writer, then."

"No. No, I only go over the manuscripts. Correct mistakes. Spelling, punctuation. Fact checking. Things like that. And continuity. I make sure the characters and situations and things are placed in the proper sequence. I make sure the author keeps her facts in order and follows the formula."

"A formula?" Dalphine's quizzical look created a small furrow above her slender nose. "There's a formula for writing a book?"

"Well, this kind of book. It's a Christian romance series," Pia explained. "Women join the club and receive a little romance novel every month. I guess they like to know they'll get what they're expecting."

"Ah." Dalphine took one of the small cakes and studied it. "Then you essentially edit the same book every month?"

"No, it's not like that at all. And anyway, I'm only doing five or six in the series. I don't like to work at it all the time."

"I think you should be a writer," Dalphine announced. "You talk like a writer."

Pia didn't know how to answer. She suddenly felt very foolish. Surely Dalphine had guessed that she really had come all this way to sit and talk about nothing. She must have guessed from Pia's description of her monotone days that in truth, she had nowhere else to be, nothing to contribute.

"Your skin is so perfect," Dalphine said after they'd sat quietly for a bit. "How old are you?"

"Both my sons are at Harvard now." Pia hoped Dalphine understood that she wasn't being coquettish about her age or bragging about the boys; this was simply the legend whereby the map of her life could be read. All her distances and longitudes were measured against Edgar and their sons. When she was young, her sons were in elementary school. Now he was dead, and they were away at college, and she was not so young.

"So this is the time of your reawakening," Dalphine said. "This is the time you come into yourself again."

"I used to think it would be that. Things didn't turn out quite the way I expected."

Pia lowered her eyes to the gilded rim of the delicate cup, not knowing what was being expected of her when Dalphine didn't say anything in response. Dalphine offered a plate of scones and small cakes shaped like half-moons.

"So tell me, sweet," she said after a while. "Did you enjoy your purchase?"

Pia's cup froze halfway between the florid saucer and her lips. When she looked up, she was conscious of an amusement in Dalphine's light, arched brows.

"The Rodrigo," Dalphine said. "Did you enjoy it?"

"Oh . . . the Rod—Rodrigo! Yes. Of course. It's lovely. Yes. I did enjoy that."

Dalphine poured another cup of coffee for each of them, then leaned outward and smoothed her hand across the embroidered ottoman as if she were stroking an Alsatian.

"Have you given any more thought to this lovely piece?"

"Yes," Pia confessed, but she was afraid to bring her eyes up to Dalphine's, afraid Dalphine might read something there.

"I knew it was a perfect match! Someone offered me forty-five hundred for it yesterday, but I said, 'No, it's taken. This lovely piece already has a home.'"

"Oh, no!" Pia cried. "I wish you hadn't done that."

"*Tshh*, sweet. It was no trouble at all."

"But I never said—I mean, I didn't mean to give the impression that—"

"Oh, I know." Dalphine never paused to allow Pia's objection. "But I have a very strong intuition about these things. And so lovely this piece is. So perfect for you. Yes. I think you really must have it."

Pia sat there, nonplussed and intensely uncomfortable, not knowing what to say.

"Now, tell me about your husband," Dalphine solicited. "Is he tall? Is he very tall and distinguished?"

"He's—yes. He's tall."

"With dark hair?"

"No," Pia said more sharply than she intended, but if Dalphine found the tone off-putting, she didn't show it. She ate another small cake, breaking it open, dabbing at the crumbs of icing with the tip of her tongue.

"It's, um . . . it's silver," Pia said.

"Hmm?"

"It was dark. At least it was in pictures I've seen. But it's mostly silver now."

"Ah." Dalphine shrugged and smiled, still perfectly at ease.

Another moment went by, and Pia gave a nervous little laugh.

"It's actually gray, I suppose. But he likes to say silver."

"Men are that way." Dalphine nodded and put her fingers to her lips one at a time, sucking the tip of each one with less sound than a kiss. "They have their vanity. Sometimes more so than women."

"Sometimes," Pia said.

"How long have you been together?"

"Two years."

"Newlyweds! This is your second marriage, then?"

"Yes," Pia said, and though she didn't say the words *I'm a widow*, something in her face must have said it as plainly as words.

"He died? Your first husband?"

"Yes."

"Sweet dear! I'm so sad for you, butterfly." Dalphine made a small fist over her heart. "Tragedy leaves one so fragile. It's important, I think, to surround oneself with gentleness and small pleasures. Do you like this music?"

"Yes. What is it?"

"South African jazz. Anatole Anzar. I have the CD for sale at the front."

"Oh?"

"Yes. He's the friend of a friend. He asked me to carry it as a favor, but I actually ended up liking it."

Laughter rippled through the word *friend*, and the image of the young man in the red side chair came back to Pia, uncomfortably confused with the dream images of Dalphine and the ivory dildo.

"He's from South Africa, Anzar is," she was saying. "He grew up there, listening to the musicians in the streets. He wanted so much to be like them. My friend told me Anzar hates that he's white. He feels guilty and ugly because of it. His wife is black. She has to tell him over and over that he's beautiful and not repulsive. He's like a little boy, the way he needs to be told over and over. He likes her to take his clothes off and tell him how beautiful his skin is. Each part. First, she has to kiss his cheekbones and eyelids and tell him how handsome his face is. Then she opens his shirt and tells him how magnificent his chest is, admires his arms, his elbows, his hands, even his wrists—she tells him how well formed and defined they are. Guitar players have beautiful wrists, you know."

"Do they?" Pia said.

"Oh, yes." Dalphine nodded.

"That must be annoying for her. To have to go to such lengths."

"But it's for her own benefit. She has to take a great deal of time, exclaiming over his hard stomach, his narrow hips, his red-gold hair, and of course there has to be a great production over his pride and joy. If she exposes it before it's well engorged, he gets very frustrated, and all is lost. He can only go on if it makes a proper showing. Oh, there's an entire ridiculous ritual." Dalphine laughed. "But I suppose all married couples institute their little rituals."

"Little rituals?" Pia said with genuine curiosity, but even as the words took shape in her mouth, she saw the thousand small ways in which it had been true for her and Edgar.

"Well, certainly, sweet. To replace the frenzy of first love."

"Of course," Pia nodded, wondering if this was perhaps the essential element that seemed to have gone missing for her and Barret. They had as yet no rituals to replace what they lost when Pia went through her Unpleasantness.

"I know of another gentleman, a staunch conservative," Dalphine went on. "After years of impotence, he suddenly achieved an assiduously firm erection every time he heard Ashcroft sing that little song about 'Let the eagle soar.' Somehow, it made his poor little member feel mighty again. I assisted his wife in burning a copy of the song from the Internet, outfitted her with some silk bedding of excellent quality, and they were reborn as lovers. It might seem silly to anyone else, but why shouldn't a woman want to take whatever steps are necessary to ensure her own happiness? Let the eagle soar, I say!" She laughed again, a drawn-out, easy laugh that sounded like wine pouring. "Truly, just when I think I've seen a little of everything, someone comes along and makes me say, Aha! Now there's something I wouldn't have expected."

Pia set her cup on the table. Her hands felt unsteady. She tried folding them in her lap.

"Do you have many lovers?" Dalphine asked. "With your husband gone so often?"

"*No!* Of course not."

"Well, don't be offended, sweet. It's not so uncommon, you know. People make arrangements between themselves. To accommodate each other in special circumstances."

"Well, we don't." Pia dabbed self-consciously at her lips with her linen napkin. It came away stained red, and she felt even more uncomfortable. "We're not like that."

Dalphine reached down and took her shoes off, and for a terrible moment Pia thought she meant to put her feet on the ottoman, but she tucked them underneath her on the red side chair.

"Then you must be very lonely."

"Sometimes."

"Do you ever travel with him?"

"No."

"Why not?"

"I prefer to stay home."

Pia didn't even try to explain. There was no way to make Dalphine understand that for her to be sitting here right now this moment was a supreme act of courage.

"How often do you see him?" Dalphine asked.

"He comes home for three days every other weekend. And we talk on the phone every night. And I've always written to him every day."

"Ah! You see? I knew you were a writer. I knew this!" She leaned forward and whispered, "What do you write? Is it wonderfully erotic and torrid and sensual?"

"No," Pia said primly. "I don't think he would like that."

"Oh, I think you're mistaken."

"You don't know him."

"Do you?"

"Of course!" Pia said defensively. "He's my husband."

"Last October, I went to an auction in Paris," Dalphine began, settling back in the chair. "One of the dealers who brings me the loveliest things from Paris—antique fabrics mostly, but interesting items of all sorts—she told me she was looking out the window of her hotel room one night. Her room was on the tenth or twelfth floor. I don't know—up, up high anyway. And she saw a man in the room across the courtyard from her. One floor below, just a little to the side. From her window, she could see him quite plainly, sitting in an easy chair. She said he was reading a letter and rubbing his hand across his trousers. Well, smart girl, she happened to remember she had a pair of opera glasses in her bag, and by the time she got back to the window with them, he'd undone himself and was feverishly working his hand up and down and clutching the letter in front of his face. He had to pause at one moment in order to go to the next page, and honestly, she had to laugh because of the way he fumbled and ransacked the pages to get to the next one—but then he was right back to it, driving himself unto the inevitable. And then, very carefully . . ." Dalphine set down her cup and used her linen napkin to demonstrate. "He laid the letter very carefully to the side, took out a handkerchief and mopped his brow and his hands, and then he folded the letter. Gently, gently, he arranged the pages and folded them. And before he put the letter back in its envelope, what do you think he did?"

Dalphine's voice had grown quiet, and Pia found herself leaning closer to hear.

"What?"

"He pressed it to his lips," said Dalphine. "He kissed it. It was such a sweet, sweet gesture. Honestly, she told me she cried when she saw it."

Pia thought of mentioning Barret's recent trip to Paris, but she wasn't sure she was supposed to participate in the making of such unconventional small talk. Was she supposed to interject some kind of response in the midst of Dalphine's humid stories or listen without any particular feeling? Pia had no idea why Dalphine wanted to tell her these things. And she couldn't imagine why she wanted to hear them.

"I know. You're thinking she ought to have had her curtains drawn," Dalphine concluded when Pia didn't respond.

"No, *he* should have!" said Pia.

When Dalphine laughed, the sound rang against the high ceiling and stained-glass panels.

"Ah, clever girl! Aren't you quick? Yes! Yes, perhaps he should have."

"Unless—"

"Unless what?"

"Nothing."

"Oh, don't be coy."

"Unless he wanted to be seen," said Pia impatiently. "I mean, doesn't that strike you as an odd thing to do in front of a window if you're not some kind of exhibitionist?"

"Exhibitionist," Dalphine echoed. "Hmm. You know, you're probably right."

"She should have called the police. Or at least notified the hotel manager."

"Perhaps. But I'm certain that didn't even occur to her."

"What . . . what did she do?" Pia asked hesitantly.

"My friend—you know, she brought me this lovely little chest right here, this beautiful tea chest—she pulled the desk chair over to the window and sat with her legs wide apart. She twisted her skirt around her waist. She had no underthings on, of course, because—well, whoever wears panties in Paris, you know?"

Pia nodded, though she didn't know. She was keenly aware of not knowing any such thing.

"She wanted him to look up and see her. She rubbed herself till she felt swollen and scorched. But—no. Not a thing! She couldn't feel anything unless he looked at her. And he never did. She *willed* him to look at her. Willed it with all her power. But no."

Dalphine shifted sideways in the chair.

"Did you ever feel that?" she asked. "That you were willing someone with all your power to look at you, but they didn't?"

"Yes." But it's even more painful, Pia wanted to tell her, when someone does look and you've disappeared.

"Has he always traveled so much?" Dalphine asked. "Your husband?"

"Yes."

"Why do you stay married to someone who's not there?"

"Because he's my husband."

"I thought you'd say because you love him."

"Yes, well." Pia set her cup on the tray and stood. "I really can't miss my train."

"Certainly not. What about the ottoman, then?"

Pia stood between the ottoman and the door, feeling torn.

"It's no difficulty at all," Dalphine said. "I could have my friend deliver it to you this afternoon. And I'll make you an excellent bargain. Fifty-three hundred plus delivery. If your husband says a cross word, you can tell him how you ravaged me on the price."

Pia knew Barret would say more than a cross word, and she knew she wouldn't be able to explain it to him. But for reasons she couldn't explain even to herself, she didn't want anyone else touching the ottoman again. She couldn't bear to have people putting their feet on it. It was as if it actually had belonged to her all along, and the fifty-three hundred dollars was just a pale acknowledgment of that. A formality.

"All right," Pia nodded.

"Yes? You'd like it delivered today?"

"Yes," Pia said, and when she said it, she felt something break through the mask she struggled to keep in place. Suddenly she felt lighter. Happier. She inhaled deeply and breathed out a smile that made her whole face feel relaxed and warm. "*Yes!* Yes, I'll take it!"

"*Aha!* Wonderful!" Dalphine clapped her hands together, then cupped Pia's face between them. "And you'll tell him what a wonderful investment it is."

"Yes, I'll tell him."

"And you'll tell him how it made you think of him." Dalphine linked her arm through Pia's on the way to the cash register. "How crazy in love with him you are and what a wonderful man he is to provide you with such fine things."

"Well, that might be laying it on a little thick," Pia said.

"He won't notice," Dalphine assured her. "Because you'll be naked, of course. You'll be magnificently, perfectly naked except for . . . this! This lovely batik! Oh, this is perfect! Did you see these lovely batiks?" she asked as they approached the display in the window. "Imagine presenting yourself to him naked but for these glorious, bountiful colors, hmm? Feel. Have you ever felt a texture like this? And for this price! You must. Take this one for one eighty-nine, and take this one as my gift. Yes! I insist."

Down the block from Dalphine's shop, Pia asked a hotel doorman to hail a taxi for her. As he opened the door, he set his hand on her elbow, and Pia hoped he couldn't feel that the place where Dalphine had placed her hand was still radiating an unexplainable vibrance. The cab was fragrant and festive as a temple. Glowing with large-bellied statuettes and tiny shimmering bells. Pia pressed the batik against her chest, feeling the colors even through layers of lavender-scented paper. On the train, she laid it across her lap and folded her hands on top of it.

She always sat on the aisle. It was less disturbing to her than the swiftly passing images at the window, and if the aisle seat was taken, other passengers were less likely to squeeze past and sit next to her. But as the train filled with commuters, a man stopped next to her and stood expectantly in the aisle. Pia crushed her knees to the side as he passed, but there was still a moment when their legs and raincoats tangled and pressed.

He sat down, laid his briefcase across his legs, and opened a laptop computer. His hands flew and tapped over the keys with the light dexterity of second nature. Pia laid her hands, palms flat, on top of the wrapped batiks, holding the package tight against her lap.

The ottoman came shortly after she arrived home from the train station, delivered by the young musician in a boxy black car. Pia stood in the entryway, holding the door for him, then followed him upstairs and stood in the hall while he hefted the ottoman upstairs to the bedroom, thumped it awkwardly on the floor, and stripped away the layers of heavy paper and bubble wrap in which Dalphine had carefully swathed it. Pia thanked him and held out a folded twenty-dollar bill. He thanked her and went away, leaving the silky Turkish scent of Dalphine's store.

Growing out of the plain Berber rug like a poisonous mushroom, the ottoman looked garish and psychotic and ludicrously out of place in Pia's white room. The colors splayed in a heap like the mangled body of some exotic bird, and Pia stood beside her trophy like a guilty feline. She pushed it closer to the wall, farther from the wall, over to the bed, next to the side chair. She tried it under the window, next to the armoire, behind the door, between the dressers, and finally heaved it into the walk-in dressing closet. There it looked twice as bad, because the back wall of the closet was a wall-size mirror, which slid aside and opened into the bathroom.

Pia pushed the ottoman back to the middle of the bedroom floor. With the double doors still open, the mirror became another white room on the other side of the dark dressing closet. Pia's white linen suit was lost in the starkness of that other room, but her skin had taken on a rich, translucent glow. Her cheeks were red and her forehead was warm and glistening from hefting the bulky piece back and forth. She looked as out of place as the ottoman.

Pia slid the mirrored door open, went into the bathroom, and turned on the shower. She took off her jacket and skirt and hung them in the closet, stepped out of her shoes, then stood for a while, still breathing deeply from exertion. She didn't generally like to look at herself when she was undressed, so she turned her back to the mirror as she removed her underthings. Just briefly, she imagined herself in Paris, walking without them, sitting in a sidewalk cafe, her bare legs crossed at the ankles and slightly parted at the knees.

When Pia reached out to open the hamper, she deliberately kept her eyes away from her forearms. The raised red scars marked her wrists like flags of an invading country, claiming the smooth, white territory in the name of . . . what? Pia tried to tell herself it was no more true than when Cortez or Coronado tried it, but she still felt usurped by the marks, claimed in the name of suicide. Conquered by a mind that was not indigenous to her.

She stepped into her shoes again and felt less afraid, less naked. The solid shaft of the heel, the cut of the curve gave her a little added height and strength, almost like Dalphine's, and the solid blue of the patent leather drew her eyes away from the soft white-on-white stretch marks on her abdomen. Pia pulled a robe around her shoulders and stood in the bathroom doorway, breathing the steam, feeling the shoes on her bare feet, and waiting to see what the ottoman would do next. She turned off the shower, went to the drawer of secrets, and drew out the ivory-colored dildo.

Beyond the open doors, the closet mirror was a faraway window, and Pia observed herself from a distance. She sat down on the ottoman and opened her legs. All the silken colors—the lotus, leaves, and birds—they suddenly made sense when she saw them alongside the private hues of herself. Shades of plum, mauve, and intimate rose, amber curls, even the raised ribbon of red beside the blue-tinted veins on her wrists. Maybe if Barret could see it like this, it would make sense to him, too. She wouldn't have to cover the marks with her sleeves. Perhaps someday, he might even kiss her wrists again, the way he had on the airplane that day, just before he kissed her mouth, not imagining what that meant to her, not knowing what a simple kiss means to the mouth of a woman who's been widowed.

Pia laid the tip of the ivory against her thigh and held it there until the cool surface warmed slightly. She thought about Barret and about the young musician. Shifting her hips forward against the nubby stitching of the ottoman, she locked her feet behind the curved legs. She thought about Edgar and his little rituals. His sounds, his movements. She watched the ivory disappear into herself, whiteness within and around her. Then she closed her eyes.

When the telephone warbled in the hallway, Pia inhaled sharply and closed her legs. It would be Barret on the phone. He would be worried if she didn't pick up. The light seemed harsh now, the object between her legs obscene. The hard plastic felt nothing like ivory; the rippled head was abrasive and blunt. Pia withdrew it abruptly and dropped it on the floor. He would be worried. She should answer. If she didn't answer he would think . . . whatever he was always thinking.

The phone warbled twice more before the machine picked up.

"Hey there. It's me," he said. "Pick up. Pia? Helloooo, beautiful." He kept pausing, waiting for her. "I'm back from the Peabody thing a little early so I thought I'd call. Pia? Okay. Well, I'll try back in fifteen or twenty minutes."

When Barret called back, Pia pretended she'd been sleeping, knowing he'd tell her they should hang up before she was too fully awake. He was always very concerned about Pia getting her proper rest without taking too many of the yellow capsules.

"You don't mind?" she said. "You're sure?"

"No, it's fine. Go back to sleep. We'll talk tomorrow."

"Barret?"

"Yes?"

"What's your room like?"

"My room? It's like a hotel room."

"What floor is it on?"

"Twenty-four, I guess."

"Is there a window?"

"Yes. Why?"

"Are the curtains open or closed?"

"Closed, of course. I don't need some deviant across the street peering at me in my bathrobe." Barret cleared his throat impatiently. "What's with the twenty questions?"

Pia lay in bed, wanting to tell him, willing him to see her, even for a moment.

"Nothing," she said. "I'm just sleepy."

Lily

(1400 days)

If I was going to kill myself, I would jump off a cliff. Or better yet, a glacier or something where no one would find the body. Whichever. I guess you have to go with what's available. Just so long as at the very last moment, I'd be flying.

(1402 days)

Let's all go to lame-ass anger management class today! As if the missionaries aren't bad enough. But the facilitator comes in and she has—oh, God, you really are there!—oatmeal cookies. OATMEAL COOKIES. Oatmeal cookies! With walnuts and raisins and tiny little currants. So a bit of anger management indoctrination was worth it. Hell, for these cookies, lesbian-white-supremacist-knitting indoctrination would have been worth it. I smuggled one back to my cubicle in my shirt. It's kind of messed up, but I'm having it right now.

Next week: "Expressing Emotion Through Haiku."

Whatever. As long as there's cookies.

(1405 days)

singing girl stumbles
songbird rattling grumpily
noisily, strongly

(1408 days)

what is your problem
pompous impatient lady
why should I tell her

(1410 days)

reading till my eyes
drop black ink from the corners
story has no end

(1431 days)

Pia calls today.
Barret always out of town.
what where why is home?

(1434 days)

shut that slack-jawed bitch
up, said big chick, and you can
believe I shut up

(1435 days)

Jesus preached freedom
shut up shut down shut
in is what I am

(1436 days)

weep not, Karla Fay
Tucker, in a day or two
you are out of here

(1439 days)

jealous jealous rage
goddamn parole board says
that girl's free to walk

(1452 days)

bla bla bla ba da
da da ya ba da ba da
whatthefuckever

Beth

This is not a good day for Beth. She has been on hold for seventeen of the last twenty-four minutes. The other seven minutes were spent in a vain attempt to explain to the button-headed idiots at the collection agency that they are threatening the wrong person. And not just because Beth got up this morning in no mood to be threatened. She knows for a fact this charge is in error.

"Ma'am?"

"Yes! I'd like to—"

"Continue to hold, please."

They are doing this on purpose. Beth isn't stupid. She knows how these boiler-room operations work. The person on the phone is not an accountant or a supervisor or anyone who can do anything other than answer phones and steadfastly repeat whatever is in the letter mailed out by the collection agency until you bleed out the money and die.

"Ma'am?"

"Do not put me on hold again," Beth says icily. "Don't do it. Do you understand me?"

"Okay, my name is Bart, and I do need to advise you that

this is an attempt to collect a debt, and any information obtained may be used for the legal purpose of—"

"No, this is not an attempt to collect a debt," Beth cuts in. "This is an attempt to extort money from someone who never incurred this charge. This is an error, as I've already explained to three other people."

"Well, can you provide some proof of that?"

"How am I supposed to prove that something didn't happen? I should think it would be incumbent on you to prove that it did!"

"Okay, you need to calm down, ma'am."

"Fine. I am calm. I am calmly telling you that This. Is. An. Error. The pediatrician's office apparently put in the wrong account number."

"No, that's not possible."

"What? What do you mean?"

"They don't get that wrong. That doesn't happen."

"Doesn't happen?" Beth feels her voice tightening to an upper register. "Don't even try to tell me that, young man. I happen to be an accountant. Errors happen. It's a fact of life."

"Well, this is all done through computers. What was the account number again?"

Beth reads it off for the seventh time, biting each digit in half, pressing her hand against the side of her head.

"Okay, ma'am, I'm seeing a charge for $64.83 for a well-child checkup and immunizations on April seventeenth of last year. Now, you've had ample time to arrange for payment through the office, but you've neglected to do so. So we're going to need that amount in full within ten days or it will appear as an open collection on your credit history. Now, I can accept any major credit card or we offer the convenience of check by phone."

Beth is seething, clenching, her jaws locked hard on the words she doesn't want to say.

"Ma'am? Did you want to give me a credit card?"

"No," Beth says quietly. "I did not. Because my daughter

was not at the pediatrician's office last April. My daughter . . ." Beth is so deeply hating the person on the other end of the phone for making her say these words in this context. But this needs to be settled, so she forces the syllables out of her mouth. "My daughter passed away several years ago."

"Oh. Well . . . I guess this was from before then. They must have got the date wrong."

"*The date?*" Beth hears herself shrieking, and she doesn't care. "The account number is an infallible papal writ, but the date can be wrong as easy at that? Are you an idiot? Is your stupid little head made of wood? Are you walking around with a croquet ball on your neck?"

"Hey, lady, I don't have to listen to that. It's not my job to sit here and catch crap from people who don't pay their bills."

"Oh, no, that is exactly your job, *Bart*. You are the crap catcher. When you pick up this phone, you know very well that the person on the other end is going to be unhappy, and if you are going to insist on extorting sixty-four dollars and eighty-three cents from me despite incontrovertible proof that you are full of it, then you are going to listen to sixty-four dollars and eighty-three cents worth of *my crap!*"

Beth bangs the handset on her desk several times, leaning forward so her mouth is close to the receiver when she lets loose a long, throaty, primal scream.

"There!" she hisses. "Your check is in the mail."

She hangs up hard, as Sonny dodges into her office, dragging the door shut behind him.

"Beth! What on earth? I have clients next door!"

"Well, why don't you go back in there and tell them the truth, *Father Sonny*?" Beth understands the meaning of Sonny's frantic hand gestures, but she makes no attempt to lower her voice. "Tell them death is about to take a sledgehammer to their pathetic, brittle, little world, and the rest of their living days will be haunted by it. Tell them it's expensive and grueling and torturous, and they will never, *never* recover. Tell them there is no way through this wilderness, so they may as well hang a wreath around their necks and lie down in their own graves. Why should they be brave? Why should they be quiet? Why shouldn't they tear themselves open and cry until they can't breathe? Death is a vicious, violating bastard, and God doesn't care!"

"*Beth!*" Sonny bounds around the desk, seizes hold of her, and clamps his hand tight across her mouth, hugging her against his body with one big arm around both her narrow shoulders. "Breathe, Beth," he whispers. "Take a deep breath in with me. Now breathe out. That's right. It's okay, it's okay, it's okay."

Beth shakes her head, though she can't speak. *It's not. It's not okay.* She doesn't understand how Sonny can not know that. Sonny strokes her back, kissing her hair and her eyelids and her flushed, wet cheeks.

"He cares, Bethy. He does. That's the only thing I'm sure of anymore. The only thing I still understand with any clarity. I promise, Beth—*I swear to you*—whatever this is, it is not about us being abandoned by God."

She nods after a moment, and Sonny releases his hold on her. They stand there, close, but not able to meet each other's eyes.

"Are you going to be all right if I go back in there?" Sonny asks.

Beth nods again.

"Honey, maybe you should take the afternoon off."

Again, she nods without speaking.

"Okay. All right. All right?" Sonny tips her chin up and kisses her mouth. "Okay?"

Nod, nod. What else is she supposed to do?

Out in the parking lot, Beth fumbles for her car keys. Drops them on the ground. She feels a swear word, raspy and bitter in her throat, but she swallows it. She slumps into the driver's seat, but when she tries to swing the door shut, a hand reaches out to catch it, and Beth lets out a startled cry.

There is a large black woman standing there. Her huge breasts hang heavily in a strained floral blouse. Her short, scrappy hair is pulled back with tortoiseshell combs and shot with gray. Her eyes are red and swollen. Her wide mouth trembles. Only a little sound comes out when she forms the words, *Thank you*.

Beth nods.

She is still nodding a few minutes later as she drives away. Something is filling up her lungs, permeating her skin, stinging her eyes, searing into her heart.

Beth is not certain, but she thinks it may be grace.

Pia

"Fifty-three hundred," Barret said a third time. "*Dollars?*"

Standing at the bedroom door, he was still holding his briefcase and coat. It was impossible to tell by looking at him whether he was coming or going.

"Well . . . it's Turkish," said Pia, but she immediately saw in Barret's face how foolish that sounded. "It's actually an investment. Really. That's what fine furniture is. It's investing. Like investing in art, for example."

"Pia, this isn't art. It's . . . it's . . . what would you even call that thing? I don't even know what its function might be. And I can't begin to describe what color it is, for God's sake. What color *isn't* it?"

"It's an ottoman," Pia said, but as to its function—she tried to remember Dalphine's exact words, but then decided this was not the right moment to go into it. She thought about telling him the color was the same as the inside of her, but that didn't seem right either. And he was right, anyway. Fifty-three hundred was far too much. This Pia would have been willing to concede. She knew when she bought it that Barret was going to choke on the cost, but it was only money. Sweat, yes, as Barret always said; their work, their efforts. And time. It was time, and that meant something. But it wasn't human flesh. It wasn't like having a part of your body cut off. And it wasn't love.

"Pia, I had no idea you were even considering a purchase like this."

"I wasn't considering it," Pia said. "I just saw it, and I wanted it, and I thought you might understand that. Not just that I wanted it, but that some things . . . some things already belong to you. You just don't know it yet."

"What?" Barret laughed gruffly. "That makes absolutely no sense."

Pia wanted to explain to him the way she'd explained it to herself, but now she couldn't quite remember how it all worked out. Something about what had happened to her over the past few years. Something she wished she'd told him about a long time ago. Before they were married. Because she hadn't meant to misrepresent herself as a whole person, a person capable of being the wife he wanted. But then she found herself in this unfamiliar house, not knowing where anything was anymore. She thought to say something about wanting to be with him in a way that was the antithesis of cross-examination, an exchange of something other than tense questions and answers.

"Pia, I don't know how you're expecting me to react to this." Barret set his briefcase on the dresser and hung his jacket in the armoire. "It's just not like you to be so . . ."

There were a hundred hopeful ways he might finish that sentence, and Pia waited without breathing to hear one of them.

". . . impulsive."

She let that sink in, examined the word from a copy editor's dispassionate perspective. Impulsive. Not quite what she'd hoped for, but it wasn't terrible. Impulsive could mean *brave* in a way, and there was that tinge of *freedom* in it.

So he was right. It wasn't like her.

* * *

Dalphine was curled in the red chair reading a book, but as soon as Pia came through the door, she called out and came to meet her.

"*Farfalla bella!* I was hoping to see you today. I want to hear all about how much you love your beautiful ottoman and want to decorate the entire room around it. I told you, didn't I? That you would want to build a whole new color scheme around it? And I have several things to show you. Perfect companion pieces."

She took Pia's coat and hung it on a brass coat tree to the side of the long display case.

"Tell me everything. Where did you put it? In your bedroom or the den? Tell me how much you love it. Give me a testimonial."

"I'm sorry," Pia said uncomfortably. "I actually came in because . . . well, I'm afraid I'm going to have to return it. Is that possible?"

"Of course it's possible, sweet." Dalphine smiled tightly. "We guarantee customer satisfaction. Did the piece not arrive in good condition?"

"Oh no, it was fine. It was nothing to do with your . . . the delivery."

"Then why? Why would you deny yourself a thing I know very well you are very much wanting?"

"Well, once I got it home it just . . . it really didn't fit in with the rest of my home. I don't know. I just . . . I changed my mind."

"Pia?" Dalphine stepped toward her and took her face between her slender hands. "I think you're lying to me."

Pia stepped back, still feeling Dalphine's handprints across her heated cheeks in cool, straight lines. She held her purse tightly in front of her waist.

"I'm sorry for the inconvenience," Pia said. "Of course, I'll be glad to pay for delivery and if there's a restocking fee or anything."

"Oh, *tsh*! What do I care about that?" Dalphine waved it aside. She seemed disappointed, hurt even. "Nothing! That's nothing to me. I only care about your happiness."

"I'm sorry," Pia repeated. "It really is a lovely piece, but to be honest, my husband didn't care for it. And it is an expensive item. I should have brought him in to look at it first."

"To get Daddy's permission?" Dalphine said, raising one eyebrow.

"No," Pia said sharply. "I wouldn't want him to make a major purchase without discussing it with me. I should have shown him that same consideration."

"Hmm." Dalphine frowned. "Perhaps you might have presented it to him differently?"

"Perhaps. Probably. Yes."

"Did you display it to him as I told you?" Dalphine asked, crooking her arm through Pia's and leading her toward the center of the store. "Did you serve it to him like a luscious dessert? With yourself as the cherry? Hmm? Did you suggest how accommodating the item might be in certain circumstances? Certain *positions*, if you will? Honestly, sweet dear, could I have spelled it out for you any more meticulously? I did everything but stage a demonstration for you!" Dalphine laughed and brushed the back of her hand along the side of Pia's neck. "Maybe *that* he would have liked, hmm?"

She left Pia standing, mouth slightly open, beside some rolled fabric. Pia heard her humming as she disappeared behind the beaded curtain and returned a moment later with the silver coffee service on a gaily painted tray.

"Here we are, sweet." She smiled, settling the tray on the table and herself on her red chair. "Now. Pia, Pia, Pia. What shall we do with you?" She took a resolute breath and positioned her hands flat on her thighs. "Why don't you keep the ottoman for a week or two and see if it doesn't, mmm . . . settle in?"

"I don't know," Pia hedged. "I don't think he'll change his mind."

"Oh, come now!" Dalphine teased a large ring around her finger. "Not even under the influence of your considerable charms?"

"He's not like your troubadour," Pia said. "He's not so easily led."

"Too bad."

They took their coffee between their hands and sat back.

"He's no longer my troubadour, anyway," Dalphine said over the rim of her cup.

"I'm sorry."

"Oh, and so am I! Well, to the extent that I needed him to make deliveries. Oh, now there's a euphemism. We needed him to make deliveries. Deliver us from boredom! Deliver us from joylessness and burning and masturbation. Deliver us from loneliness." Dalphine sat sideways in the red chair, her long legs crossed over the arm. "Honestly, with your husband traveling so much, do you get horrendously lonely?"

Pia avoided the question by asking, "Do you?"

"Everyone gets lonely, I suppose," Dalphine sighed. "When they can't sleep. Do you have trouble sleeping?"

Pia nodded. That was all right. Not so bad as to say it out loud.

"I sold a lovely oak headboard to a lady yesterday," said Dalphine. "She said it was her fourth new bed this year, but she's desperate to sleep, and it seems nothing can make her comfortable. She says she's been an insomniac all her life, but especially when she's lonely, and she gets so desperate, she can't even pleasure herself. Trying only makes it worse. Oh, she has her little toys and techniques, and all that's fine for when she's alone, but not when she's truly *lonely*. Then sleep refuses to come. And so does she!"

When Pia didn't laugh with her, Dalphine drummed her fingers against the arm of the chair. She stirred her coffee and took a sip. They both sipped and stirred.

"Well, since you're being not so forthcoming and forcing me

to pry, how is the other item working out for you? Did the week pass a bit easier?"

Pia didn't answer, but whatever Dalphine saw in her face made her lean forward and rest her hand on Pia's knee.

"Oh, *sweet dear*! This is a complete disaster, then, isn't it!"

"No, it's fine. Really."

"Is it the curve? Or is it too slender? We can do better. Customer satisfaction is paramount in my business. I pride myself."

Pia straightened her skirt and tried not to look unnerved.

"Perhaps you need to try it in combination with aromatherapy," Dalphine persisted. "Erotica. I have a lovely selection of candles and oils, and I just recently got in some very good books. Nothing ugly. Only beautifully written novellas. All women authors. Very literate, very floral. Some vintage. Beautifully illustrated, leather-bound. First editions, of course. And a special price for my especially dear friend."

"No. Really. No, thank you."

"Perhaps something handcrafted. I know an ocularist. She manufactures the most exquisite prosthetic eyes, but of course, people aren't popping an eye out every day of the week, and medical science being what it is, well, obviously, economics demanded that she develop a tandem *specialty*. She's an extremely skilled artisan. And very discreet."

Pia shook her head, which seemed to send a rush of blood to the back of her skull.

"It is an investment," said Dalphine, "but one well worth making. Personally, I think one's health insurance should pay for it. Think of the pharmaceuticals that could be avoided! Sleep aids, antidepressants, and what not."

Pia set her cup on its saucer, tracing the edge with her fingertip.

"Could we please change the subject?"

"Pia? Butterfly, what is it?" Dalphine asked with great concern. "You know you can confide in me."

"Actually, Dalphine, I really don't feel comfortable discussing this."

"Ah, of course not. It's a sensitive subject," said Dalphine. "It is an area, however, in which I happen to be—shall we say *fluent*. For whatever reason, people often feel free to confide in me, and I find that all those stories—the private stories we feel some inexplicable need to share—they become a sort of collective cartography. We each contribute our tiny snippet of the map, thereby showing each other the way."

"I suppose," said Pia. "It just seems . . . unseemly."

"Oh, yes, doesn't it? And yet"—Dalphine leaned close to Pia's ear—"we feel compelled to listen, don't we?"

"Yes," Pia answered, barely above a whisper.

"For example," Dalphine said quietly and in the most matter-of-fact tone of voice, "this woman—the insomniac?—yes, well, she's become terribly depressed. She told me she can only sleep when she reaches a profound level of climax, and she can only reach this climax when she is fiercely intent on one particular image. The white canopy bed she slept in at her sorority house. She's on a quest to find a bed that feels like this one particular bed. She has to imagine all the sorority sisters standing around her as she lies on this white canopy bed. It's their rite of initiation, you see."

Pia focused her eyes on a display of pottery dishes, gazing intently at a blue-and-white bowl, following the fragile lines with her eyes.

"The oldest girl is beautiful and dark and strong. This girl tells each sister what to do. 'Touch and kiss her legs,' and they do. Not like a man would, barely grazing a thigh on his way to the target, but softly. With great care. Ankle, calf, knee, hip bone. And the dark sister says, 'Now her neck, her arms, her breasts.' So they nibble at her palms and her wrists, her arms, and so on and so on, paying particular attention to those little details of the human body—the web between her thumb and index finger, the place where her collarbones meet. Their tongues make her think of mother cats when they dab at her nipples. And then the wise sister draws the labia majora apart and the insomniac feels a clever, perfect nose to her clitoris, nudging it side to side. It's such an unusual sensation, she feels she's about to climax, but she knows it's just the first kind that feels lovely but doesn't go too deep. She knows this is not enough to make her sleep. She needs her ivory treasures."

A tall clock ticked in the corner. Pia felt the pulse of it, though she couldn't feel herself breathing.

"She takes them out and thinks about the dark-haired girl telling the others to draw her knees to her chest and place a pillow under her bottom. They hold the two round halves apart, and it frightens her to feel so open, but 'Don't be afraid, sweetheart,' they all say, 'it's only little Isolde. She's very slender, and we'll be gentle.' The little friend—remember, I showed you?—it's as slim as a finger and slides quite easily into the rosebud opening. *The garden gate*, she likes to call it. She likes to be penetrated there, because it requires such exceptional patience and tenderness. She thinks of the sisters cooing like doves as she breathes it into that shadowy part of herself. And when they turn the little vibrator on—oh, it's obscene! She's pulled between shame and pleasure, mortified to hear herself whimpering and moaning, astonished she could be so easily transformed. 'And now for mighty Tristan,' the dark-haired girl says, and the insomniac opens her legs like a swallow spreading her wings. She takes the thickest of the ivory treasures—oh, it's not for everyone, but she's an adventurer. She thinks of the sisters passing it around the circle, sees the weight of it in their hands. They nudge it against her, discover how pliant she is. But the sisters tease the insomniac by withdrawing the item and rubbing the round head against her belly. They keep tantalizing her with it until she's in an unspeakable state, clutching at the other girls, grasping at their hands, pulling their breasts to her mouth, and they laugh when they see how she tries to attack the objet d'art, thrusting her hips forward. She pleads for the item and begs them to go deeper until they decide she's ready to receive all of it. She's taken over by bold, sure strokes in harmony with the slender shimmering. Mighty Tristan and sweet Isolde. Tenor and soprano. They transport her to that elusive plane of sensation, and she climaxes with such depth, her lips are numb, the muscles in her feet spasm. She feels her heartbeat in her neck and forehead, senses a sudden bright pulse, and she spurts musk—she ejaculates just like a man. And she's overwhelmed with gratitude, because she knows now she'll sleep."

Dalphine's dark eyes suddenly settled directly on Pia's.

"Did you know a woman can do that? Ejaculate? Just like a man?"

"Oh . . . God . . . no," Pia stammered, hardly expecting there would be a quiz at the end. "I mean, yes, I . . . I think I read something about that."

"Oh, yes." Dalphine nodded emphatically. "They can and do. Have you ever?"

"I don't think so."

"Oh, you'd know it. You would definitely notice."

Pia raised her coffee to her lips, but it was cold and bitter. She realized her legs were stiff from sitting motionless for so long. She tried to shift her weight, straighten her skirt, change her position in the chair without disturbing the swollen feeling between her legs.

"Well. Goodness." She tried to sound casual, to laugh a little. "Do all your customers tell you such personal details?"

"Sooner or later."

The way she said it made Pia feel unnerved and short of breath. As if her diaphragm and lungs had fallen out of rhythm for a moment.

"Well." She searched for some kind of response. "It's wonderful that she's so . . . open. I mean *comfortable*. With herself, I mean. In the sense of . . . of being able to share something like that. Because you know, there are things you don't just openly talk about with—"

"Strangers?"

"Yes."

"But Pia! I thought we were becoming such good friends!"

Dalphine pushed her bottom lip forward in a mock pout and gestured toward the coffee service, as if that had sealed a pact between them. Suddenly, the delicacy of the saucer in Pia's hand, the lipstick on the edge of her cup—it did seem very personal.

"Sometimes I say too much," said Dalphine. "Forgive me, sweet, if I've embarrassed you."

"No, it's . . . it's just that I really can't understand how something like that—I mean, in the course of casual conversation, how does something like that just come up? As it were."

"She came to me for advice," Dalphine said. "She was worried it might mean she was a lesbian."

"Ah." Pia nodded as if that explained everything. "Well . . . isn't she?"

"Heavens no. It's perfectly natural. All people are homosexual on some level. Men because they're narcissists, women because they're needy. Only another woman understands exactly *how* needy. The time my friend spent in the sorority was a sheltered, affirming period of her life. Of course, what this dear lady wants is to feel that sheltered and affirmed in the life she now shares with her husband. Her secret circle of sisters—they merely represent the tender attention lacking in her life."

"That does make sense," said Pia.

"And so this begs the question, sweet, what is lacking in your life?"

"I should go." Pia stood abruptly.

"Oh. Should you? So soon?"

"My husband is coming home tonight. I was going to order in some dinner." Pia tried not to sound small. "But there's the issue of, um . . . about the ottoman? Would it be possible to have it picked up today? Before my husband comes home?"

"Oh. Back to that," Dalphine said curtly. She unfolded her

legs from beneath her and sighed heavily. "I thought we agreed you were going to keep it for a few days. Because as I explained, I'm without my delivery help."

"Oh. Yes. Right. But are you certain there isn't any way I could—"

"I have the perfect solution!" declared Dalphine. "Keep the damn thing just for another week. Two at most. We'll look around the store and find some wonderful elements to act as companion pieces, just to make sure it doesn't look too out of place while you're waiting for it to be picked up. And then, while it will break my heart to see you sacrifice something you obviously love, if you must do it to keep the peace, I suppose you must. We'll return all the items for a full refund."

"Well, I suppose there couldn't be any harm in that," Pia said. "And like I said, I'd be happy to pay the restocking fee."

"Oh, *tsh*! I won't hear of that!" Dalphine said emphatically. "Your absolute satisfaction is my only concern."

Pia apologized again, angling toward the door, and on the way to the front, Dalphine picked out some pillows and a silk throw she decided were perfect matches for the ottoman.

"Good-bye, sweet!" Dalphine waved as Pia was leaving. "Oh! But not without the aromatherapy! Come back! Come back! I simply will not let you leave without a little something for yourself. Since you're giving up your treasure."

She pulled Pia back to the counter, selected gardenia and sandalwood candles and bath oil, and held them up together for Pia to inhale. The unexpected combination of aromas blended with a lingering unsettled feeling, which made Pia feel light and open across her forehead.

"And these! Yes!" Dalphine showed her two heavy brass and mirror candle sconces. "For above the bath. Take the pair. You must or the effect will be ruined. Here. Take one for seventy-five, the other as my gift."

"Oh, no. Thank you. But no. Really. I shouldn't."

"But I insist! I see how dearly you want them. If you won't

accept it as a gift, then you must take them at cost. Sixty-five each—and don't even try to argue. I won't accept a penny more."

She set the sconces heavily in Pia's hands, and Pia found herself nodding. She hadn't even looked at them when she came in, but at this moment she did want them. She wanted them more than she'd ever wanted anything. Or maybe she just wanted something more than nothing, and these things happened to be right here in her hands. The sound of the transaction ringing up sang through the store, along with her voice and Dalphine's as they laughed together about something Pia said.

"Enjoy your conjugal visit, sweet." Dalphine smiled, holding out the large Victorian rose shopping bags. "I'll be thinking of you with great envy."

Long after Pia had given up and cleared away the dinner and gone to bed, Barret called, saying something about a client flying in from Tokyo. A meeting. The need to be polite, to go to dinner. The service slow. The flight missed.

Pia was almost relieved, having realized on the train that not only had she failed to make arrangements for the return of the ottoman, she'd spent an additional six hundred dollars on pillow shams, oils, essences, and the sconces.

I'm sorry, Barret said again, and next week, he promised, and I'm sorry again, and Pia said it was all right and she understood.

"Are you angry?" he asked.

"No, of course not. It couldn't be avoided." She knew her lines.

"I was thinking," Barret said, "maybe you could come here for a weekend."

Pia searched her jumbled memory for where exactly "here" meant.

"For a week even. I'm staying in a hotel that's right in the center of the city," Barret told her. "There's plays, concerts, galleries. The opera is just three blocks away. They're doing *La Sylphide*."

"We just saw *La Sylphide* here. Last season. Don't you remember?"

"Oh, that's right. I always confuse that one with *Tristan and Isolde*," Barret said.

Pia's breath caught in her throat.

"What's so funny?" Barret asked, wanting to laugh with her.

"Nothing. I'm drinking a glass of wine and it went down the wrong way."

"Should you be drinking wine with your medication?"

"No. Of course not. You're right. I'll pour it out."

He didn't say anything, so she walked to the sink and turned on the tap for a moment.

"Pia, come and see *La Sylphide*. You said you'd love to see it again. This would be a second chance for us. To see it."

"There's a sale at the library on Saturday. I promised Lily I'd send her a box of books."

"She'll understand."

"And Irene called yesterday with another manuscript."

"You could work on it here. Use your laptop on the plane."

"Stop it!" Pia said angrily. "You know it's impossible. You know I can't do it. And you know it humiliates me to say so. I don't believe you really want me to come at all! It's just pretense. You know you're safe making an invitation, since I'm never going to accept."

"You *are* angry about this weekend. Admit it. You're angry."

She couldn't bear to be cross-examined by him. It broadened, deepened, hardened the distance between them.

"I'm trying to understand all this, Pia. I am," Barret started, then backed off and started again. "If I did something to bring on this . . . this situation—"

"No! Barret, of course, you didn't. It's my fault. Completely." She waited, but Barret didn't say anything to confirm or deny. "I'm sorry. It's late is all. I'm tired. Let's not go to sleep angry."

"Right. Right. Of course," Barret agreed quickly. "And Pia, I've been thinking. About that Turkish monstrosity. Look, I'm the first to admit I'm no connoisseur of fine antiques, and if you think it's really worth the money—if it makes you happy—I think we should keep it."

"Thank you, Barret. But no. That's all right." Pia cleared her throat and glanced at the sconces on the sideboard. "I would like to keep it. But I know you hate it."

"I'm sure I'll learn to love it. Or at least get used to seeing it glowering at me from the corner. I'm sure the Turk and I will become best of friends."

"You just might," Pia said. She wanted to say more, but the longer they stayed quiet, the more difficult it was to think how Dalphine had told her to phrase it. *A variety of purposes.*

"Or maybe," Barret suggested, "we could go pick something out together next weekend. Something we both like. We could go together and settle on something more appropriate."

"Yes. All right," said Pia. "We'll do that."

They spoke for a little while about practical things, made their peace, and said their good-byes, but not without Barret reminding her to "take care of herself," which sounded solicitous in a simple and friendly way but carried a load of unarticulated baggage.

Pia lay on her back, looking up into the space where the soft white of the walls disappeared into the recess of the vaulted ceiling, remembering the way she and Edgar used to talk on the phone each night when she was the faraway one. Now that she knew what it was like to be left at home, she felt guilty and selfish for the way they'd lived. If Edgar had hated it, he never told her. But he may have been unwilling to take up their brief time together with arguing over something he thought would never change. Pia wondered what he would think of this different person she was now and how he would fit into the narrowing corridor of her life.

Pia tried to stroke herself, tried to hear Edgar in memory and use his voice the way he used to use hers. She opened her legs slightly, quickened the strokes, tried to remember what it was she used to say as she talked him through it. The words were mixed up now with Dalphine's stories and Barret's solicitude. A climax of sorts finally came, but it was joltish and unsatisfying.

Dragging the comforter off the bed, gathering it around herself, Pia went to her desk, bare feet soundless on the thick white rug. She reached out of her shroud just enough to hold the pen in her hand.

Dear Barret,
Having another busy week. The garden is going well, though the iris bulbs were late arriving from

When she crumpled the paper into her hand, the dry scent of it breathed upward, along with the scent of herself still on her fingers.

Dear Barret,
I miss you. And yes, I'm angry. Why do you always have to be the

This one Pia tore in two halves, crumpled separately on the sterile desktop. The comforter fell from her shoulder, and she shivered a little.

Dear Barret,
I decided not to return the ottoman. I'm keeping it. It's mine. Dalphine says it always was, I just didn't know it.

Pia was conscious of the feeling of the ink flowing onto the paper, the slender line of the pen in her hand, its cylindrical profile against the curve of her palm.

Dalphine is an insomniac. She can only come when she concentrates on a particular fantasy about a particular day on the train. She was carrying a wrapped package in her lap. Fabric from Jakarta. It smelled like sandalwood, even through the brown paper. A man sat down next to her and took out his laptop. As the train swayed along, their shoulders brushed, parted, brushed, parted again. It annoyed her at first, but after a while, she realized she was waiting for each sway so she would feel that brief touch. Without speaking or looking at him, she reached under the laptop and cupped her hand between his legs. He never paused in his work. His fingers flew faster over the keys as she stroked him through his trousers. She moved her other hand beneath her package and inched her skirt up inside her raincoat.

Barret never mentioned the letter on the phone, but he did rearrange his schedule so he could be home a day earlier than planned. He never mentioned the letter during dinner, but he sat next to Pia, instead of facing her from the far side of the table. And later, he made love to her the way he used to. Before the hospital. Before the shark-infested ocean came between them and engulfed Pia's ability to be loved.

"Tell me about Dalphine," Barret whispered. "The way you told me in your letter."

"Dalphine lives in an apartment in the back of the shop," said Pia. "She has many lovely things in her bedroom. She has a beautiful . . . Turkish . . . ottoman. Very much like this one. She says she can't do without it, because it's exactly the right height."

"For what," Barret breathed in Pia's ear.

"Oh, a variety of purposes. When she's alone, she stretches her body over it. She loves to feel the coarse fabric on her nipples."

"And when she's not alone?" Barret shifted his weight and slowed the pace, raising Pia's knee in the crook of his arm.

"Then her lover . . . he stands over her with—"

"Show me." Barret's voice was hoarse and urgent.

"Like this." Pia took his hand and led him across the room.

The ottoman was precisely the correct height. She was able to brace her hands and heels, which gave her the needed leverage to match Barret's pace and intensity and undoing, until he collapsed, pressed his forehead against her neck, kissed her back and shoulder blades, dragged her onto the floor, embraced her with both arms and both legs, whispering, "Oh, Pia, my beautiful wife. Lord God, I've missed you."

Customer satisfaction. That thought made Pia laugh, and suddenly her heart was opened so wide, she started crying.

"Shh, shh, shh," Barret said. "What's this now?"

But Pia didn't want to ruin what she was feeling by binding it in words. She just smiled and wrapped her arms around her lover, and they cradled each other until they got cold and Pia reached up and pulled the duvet off the bed to cover them.

"Good golly, Miss Molly." Barret raised himself on his elbows and grinned. "I don't know where this is coming from all of a sudden, but I am not about to complain."

He stroked her hair and nuzzled her neck. They kissed for a while before they let the moment go, and then they lay together, talking about iris bulbs and terra-cotta tiles. About the upcoming local elections and how the outcome would affect Barret's future run for Congress. About the possibility of purchasing a new car for Pia, because Barret was certain she would soon be ready to start driving again, and Pia felt such happiness, she let him think that all weekend and almost believed it herself.

As she made breakfast Sunday morning, Pia glanced up and found him looking past his newspaper at her, watching her as she moved back and forth in the kitchen.

"You're looking smug," said Pia.

"I'm feeling smug," said Barret, stretching his legs, clasping his hands behind his head. "I haven't felt this unwound in a long time, Pia. I feel well loved and well laid and ready to conquer the world."

"Ah." She smiled. "Then deposing a few environmentalists ought to be a piece of cake."

Barret laughed his old easygoing laugh, which made Pia kiss him, which made him pull her onto his lap and kiss her back.

"Pia," he said gently, "at the risk of starting an argument . . . After Boston, I'll be in Paris for the summer. You said you've always wanted to see Paris. Maybe this new medication—"

"Oh, it's really not that." Pia stood up abruptly, avoiding his eyes by busying herself with a small stack of cards on the counter. "I just don't see how I could right now. I've got catching up to do—from before, you know. And then the boys will be here for spring break. That guest room really needs to be redone before they get here. And this manuscript I'm working on—it's a nightmare. Honestly." She laughed a fidgety soprano laugh. "This person's high school English teacher should be flogged."

Barret didn't say anything more until they were at the door. He held his suitcase in one hand and cupped his other hand against the side of Pia's face, looking like he desperately wanted to say something or hear something or know something about what would be there when he came home again.

"Don't worry." Pia took his hand and held it hard. "I won't do anything."

Lily

(1460 days)

I have been in this place four years.

North, South, East, West.
Fire, water, air, earth.

Four is all there is. Four is sufficient. Parole hearing in two weeks. I don't know what to tell them other than that.

(1472 days)

Reading R of Omar K again.

> I sent my Soul through the Invisible,
> Some letter of that After-life to spell:
> And by and by my Soul returned to me,
> And answered, 'I Myself am Heaven and Hell.'

(1474 days)

Pia called to find out about the parole hearing.

ME: I tried not to get my hopes up, but it still kills me.

PIA: Oh, Lily. I'm so sorry.

ME: Anyhoo. I'll probably get moved to minimum security later this year.

PIA: Well, that's something.

ME: Yeah, that's something.

(1497 days)

King called. I didn't even recognize his voice at first, then I just wanted to crawl inside the phone and grab hold of him and not let go.

KING: Are you doing OK?

ME: Me? Sure. Doing dandy. How about you? How's business.

KING: Business is good. Yeah. Everything's going good. The thing is . . . I wanted to tell you, Lil. So you don't hear it from Pia. Brynn and me are getting married.

ME: Brynn, huh? She sounds . . . trendy.

KING: I moved in with her and her kids about a year ago, and we just found out we're gonna have a baby.

ME: Then you should definitely get married. It's the right thing to do.

KING: Well, yeah. And we're really happy, so . . . there's that.

ME: That's wonderful, King.

KING: Lily, I want you to know I'll always—

ME: Well! Wow. Look at the time. I gotta get going. So thanks for calling, and I hope you two are really, really . . . you know. Et cetera et cetera. Seriously. I wish you the best, King.

I guess I should feel gut-shot, because I sort of thought we might get back together someday. But it's actually a relief. The worst thing about being in here is knowing I ruined so many people's lives. There's one off my conscience, I guess. And baby makes three.

(1499 days)

Two-zero day coming up tomorrow, but I think I can handle it.

(1500 days)

Fuck you if you are reading this.
Even if you are me.

Beth

This is a good day for Beth.

She begins by quitting her job. She knows Sonny is going to be stunned, because they've worked at the funeral home together for almost fifteen years. He's spoken of actually acquiring the business from their boss someday, and their boss, having no children who might inherit it, is receptive to that idea. He thinks Sonny and Beth would be like him and his wife and like his parents were before them; working side by side, building the family business. He would like to see them keep the place going for another generation.

But Beth has decided she no longer wants to surround herself with death every day. Unbeknownst to Sonny, she has been going to a support group called Good Grief, and when she mentioned that she worked at a funeral home, Jimmy-Jill Roman, the Good Grief group facilitator, crinkled a little about the eyes. Suddenly, Beth realized how unhealthy that must seem—how unhealthy it in fact *was*—for someone who says they don't want to think about death all the time. It's fine for Sonny. It's his mission in the world, Beth told that to Jimmy-Jill Roman, and Jimmy-Jill said yes, he probably incorporated that sense of purpose into his personal grieving process. But Beth could say nothing of the sort for herself. She didn't know what her personal grieving process was. Or her purpose, for that matter.

This is the first time in her life Beth has left a job without giving two weeks' notice. She feels both guilty and thrilled, knowing that today is her last day at the funeral home. Monday is her first day at Lord, Himmelman & Schermer, an architectural firm on the thirty-third floor of an ultramodern office building downtown. There is an enormous window in the office Beth will share with her supervisor, and the tall ceilings seem to pull the light and air right in from the sky outside. Building instead of burying, she tells Jimmy-Jill, and Jimmy-Jill applauds the decision, in a noncommittal sort of way. In a way that says, "You go, girl! But don't blame me if you regret it."

Jimmy-Jill Roman has an airy halo of hair the color of an after-dinner mint. She wears the loveliest clothes. Goddesslike dresses that drape and flow to her ankle bones. She talks about Elisabeth Kübler-Ross and the five stages of grief. Denial. Anger. Bargaining. Depression. Acceptance. In the beginning, Beth didn't believe in any of that. She didn't see herself in any of those categories. She began attending the grieving group because she felt called to comfort others by sharing with them the grace and mercy of the Lord Jesus Christ. She told them how she found peace in forgiveness and faith. She thought they must envy her very much. She hoped they would find her to be an inspiration. What a load of crap that was, she thinks now, and she even smiles a little.

Jimmy-Jill Roman is an inspiration, though she wears too much eyeliner. She lost her entire family in a house fire, which makes her a sort of grieving superstar. She carries a white binder that says GOOD GRIEF! on the cover with a picture of Charlie Brown and Lucy. Lucy is in her psychiatrist's booth.

Five cents, please, Beth used to think unkindly, but she's becoming more flexible about such things. Sonny says she's blossoming. Beth hopes he will continue to see it in that kind light as he interviews replacement bookkeepers.

Pia

Dr. Ackerman held Pia's hand when he told her he was going to France for a month.

"A month?" Pia echoed.

"It's taken some time, but I think we've made a lot of progress. Your meds are stabilized. You're sleeping well and working. You'll be fine," he said, firmly patting her wrist. "If you have any sort of emergency, Dr. Massoud will be taking my calls. She's very competent and very discreet."

"A *month*?"

"It'll be all right, Pia. Really."

Pia realized he was misunderstanding, thinking it was him she needed every Monday and Thursday afternoon. In fact, it was Dalphine Pia couldn't see herself without. She didn't know if the corridor would allow her to go to Dalphine's shop if she wasn't coming out of Dr. Ackerman's office, but the first week he was gone, Pia came into the city twice. Monday and Thursday. The second week, she came on Tuesday and Thursday. The third and fourth weeks, she came three and four times. The following week, he was scheduled to return to his office, and Pia came into the city every day. But not to see him. The little bit of freedom affected her like a third glass of wine, like an irresistible music. Inside her coat, inside her skin, part of her was dancing.

The corridor had shifted, expanded. Now Pia went from her front door to the train depot, train depot to taxi stand, stand to the street corner, street corner to Dalphine's door. She passed by the tinted window at Dr. Ackerman's office, knowing she could choose to go in—*or not!* It was more exhilarating than Pia could have imagined.

"You're becoming my little apprentice, aren't you?" Dalphine teased.

Instead of simply stopping in for late-afternoon coffee, Pia arrived shortly after the doors opened and spent long days dusting shelves and displays, rearranging furniture and Persian rugs, cropping and drying roses that arrived from men Dalphine met at auctions and theaters and jazz places, and listening as Dalphine spun out what she called her "small, sweet stories." Sometimes customers came, and Dalphine would woo them. It made Pia slightly uncomfortable when Dalphine served them coffee in her favorite corner by the front window. Hardly anyone left without buying a brown leather Morris chair or silk-tasseled pillows or private gift-wrapped items from the back of the store. Sometimes the phone would ring, and Dalphine would argue and flirt in animated French or Spanish or Italian.

Then there were days like this one, when they just sat quietly, Dalphine reading a book, Pia working away at a manuscript, which she brought with her in a shallow white box and spread out in piles on the low table. Pia was working her way through the last in the Christian romance series. The publisher had offered her a contract for another six books, and Pia gratefully accepted, having discovered great comfort in the gentle characters, the predictable story lines, the idea that passion can and does exist in quiet places.

Dalphine got up and pulled her red chair into a square of morning sun from the ivy-painted window.

"*As for me—and listen well! My ecstasy is in the exquisite; yes, for me glitter and sunlight and love are all one society.*"

Pia looked up, and Dalphine indicated the slender volume of poetry she was reading.

"Sappho?" she said, but Pia wasn't sure whether the upward inflection was asking if Pia was familiar with Sappho or offering the book for sale. In either case, Pia needed to say no. She smiled and shook her head. "She's the only woman poet we find in ancient Greek literature, the only woman whose work survived. In amongst all the battles and heroes and horses, Sappho speaks of love. Some called her the tenth muse. Others, of course, called her a whore. What else could they call someone whose life is devoted to the celebration of pleasure?"

Pia didn't know how to respond. When this sort of conversation started, she was never sure if she wanted to run out into the street or kneel down in front of the red chair and lay her head in Dalphine's lap. Dalphine seemed to pick up on this and even, Pia thought at times, delighted in her discomfort. She turned a few pages and read aloud again.

"*My tongue shatters and a fragile flame saturates my flesh; my eyes see not one thing; my ears hear only humming. The sweat trickles down, a shuddering takes over every part of me, and then, fading like the dry grass, I feel near to the moment of dying. My mind is in two. I know not—*"

"Goodness," Pia interrupted. "That's a little overwrought for me."

"Hmm." Dalphine set the book aside and took another cup of coffee from the samovar. "I'm not sure I understand your meaning."

"I like poetry that doesn't feel so disorganized. Where there's attention to form. 'I shot an arrow in the air. It fell to earth, I know not where.' That's a poem. It's clean. It's simple. All that shuddering and swooning and sweating is just a little over the top for me."

"Ah, but that's the glory of it!" Dalphine held the book to her nose and inhaled as if the paper were made of violets and roses. "Decadence! Sensuality! When I read Sappho, I feel lavished upon. I feel blessed, anointed. But then, I'm reading it in Portuguese. Perhaps it loses something in the translation. Or perhaps . . ." She snapped the book shut and leaned forward. "Perhaps you lose something in translation, Pia. Hmm?"

"What?" Pia hugged her shawl around her shoulders. "What do you mean?"

"I mean you are a beautiful, deeply textured being, yet you organize yourself with little rhymes and shroud yourself with your mono-chromo-less-is-more—what was it your pretentious interior decorator called it?"

"Austerity," said Pia self-consciously.

"Oh, *tsh*!" Dalphine seized her hand and led her through the maze of displays and furnishings. "We are going to create for you a place in which the colors are like words or wine or music or good food. You'll drink them and bite down on them and listen to them and lie in them. Look at these *suzani* textiles. Blessed! Anointed! *Austerity*? Please! I don't even know what that *means*, sweet. I thought it had something to do with nuns and priests."

Dalphine stood in the center of the store, considering, divining.

"We'll start upstairs. You have upstairs and downstairs—yes? Of course. Good. Very good. Upstairs, then. Because we don't want to throw him into a coronary when he opens the door. You'll lead him by the hand, and by the time he reaches the top of the stairs, he won't even be thinking about . . ."

"About what?" Pia said warily.

"About . . . the peacocks!"

"No. No peacocks."

"Yes! Yes, think about it!" Dalphine led her to a corner where they'd moved an elaborately embroidered fainting couch just the day before. "It's a perfect place to start. The azure background will be stunning against the white walls. And the peacocks pick up the green and gold in this wall hanging. Do you see it? Do you not love that stunning, stunning sofa? It's perfect!"

"So perfect nobody wants it!" Pia cried. "You told me yesterday you'd been trying to unload it for almost a year."

"And now I know why! It was waiting for you, sweet! It couldn't possibly have gone to any ordinary home. Not with its history."

Pia tried to focus on the garish birds and looping branches, hoping they would drown out the familiar tug she was already feeling. *Don't ask,* she told herself. *Don't ask. Don't.*

"What history is that?" Pia asked.

"It belonged to a woman who used to bring me things from Portugal when I very first opened my little shop. We kept in touch over the years. For a while I even shared my apartment with her. Until she took up with her screaming Italian."

"Screaming Italian?"

Pia sat down on a wooden chair, and Dalphine sank sideways onto the little fainting couch, crossing her legs over the end, resting her head on the curved arm.

"He always screamed her name in the last moments of ecstasy. *Justeeeen! Justeeeeen!* He was a very oral person. He lived for wine, for words, for food, cunnilingus, opera." Dalphine cupped her hand at the side of her mouth and whispered, "He loved to ejaculate in her mouth and then kiss her."

Pia tucked her feet beneath the chair. The peacocks preened over Dalphine's shoulder.

"He was a great chef," Dalphine said, tracing a bursting blossom of embroidery with her fingers. "To excite the senses, his own and others, this was his life. He owned a very successful restaurant where all the best people came and raved over what a brilliant artist he was. He loved that. And he loved the life it brought him—adulation, respect, but best of all, the opportunity to eat and eat and eat all day long. Flowered vegetables with béarnaise and fresh parsley and wine, thick roast beef, racks of lamb, pretty Cornish game hens with little white boots, more wine, strawberries and chocolate and beautifully presented desserts. Anything delicious—including Justine!" Dalphine laughed. "Of course, he was terribly obese, but it didn't bother her. She liked it that he wasn't the slightest bit afraid of excess. The way he loved food—that was the way he loved her. He *consumed* her, lapped her up from the whiskey on her tongue to the dessert between her legs. He always wanted to get on top of her, but she was a tiny thing. Tinier than you, even. So she'd climb on top of him. She said it was like riding a carousel dragon up and down. She loved it. She loved him. She bought an apartment. She bought a king-size bed. She bought this little couch. Oh, she had plans for this little couch, let me tell you! She planned to see him on his knees in front of it. She began to gather things for a home, because she thought she would marry him."

"Why didn't she?"

"He had a stroke and died while he was making love to someone else."

"Oh, no!"

"All that excess. He couldn't control his appetites. She'd known that from the start. And she suspected things. The hostesses and waitstaff at the restaurant were all very young and beautiful—women and men. Of course, my dear friend's heart was broken, but it must have been horrifying for the waiter, poor mouse. Justine's great chef collapsed on top of him with all his weight. He couldn't move, could barely breathe. In fact, two ribs were broken. Fortunately, there was a telephone on the night table, and he was able to call for help and—oh, I know I'm terrible for laughing! You can guess how horrifying it was!

I mean, there he lay, spread-eagled, facedown on the bed with a dead man's gigantic cudgel still inside him, a brigade of firemen beating down the door, and oh . . . oh," gasped Dalphine, "the worst of it was—two weeks later, one of the paramedics called and asked him out to dinner!"

Pia was laughing now, too, holding her hand in front of her face.

"Glitter and sunlight and love." Dalphine held her hands up and made a gesture of concession, laying two graceful fingers across her lips.

She left Pia sitting in the square of sun while she wandered behind the counter, brought back a box of effusively embroidered table runners, and set them on the table between their two chairs. They sat quietly for a while, folding them for display, tassels extended on either side.

"More is more?" Barret said skeptically when he saw one of the runners stretched down the center of the dining room table three nights later. When Pia heard him repeat the phrase in his attorney voice, it did sound profoundly silly.

"I just thought maybe we needed some color," she said. She moved toward the doorway, hoping to drag his gaze away from the new window treatment.

"But we agreed on the white. We agreed that was what we wanted."

"Yes, but now it feels so . . . arctic."

"What?"

"Never mind." She'd been about to say *clinical*, but that would have drawn the curtain she'd grown accustomed to seeing across his face whenever anything like that was mentioned. "So you're saying you hate it, then."

"Well . . ." He paused in order to pinpoint the exact term. "It's a bit excessive."

"Yes! That's why I like it," Pia said. "The dining room seems like a good place for excess. For feasting."

He looked at her curiously, as if he'd just noticed her in the room.

"An old friend of Dalphine's came to the shop the other day and bought several of these beautiful table runners." Pia stood close to Barret, but with her back to him, making him lean forward slightly to hear what she was saying. "This woman's husband was a great chef, and he lived for all sorts of excess. That's why Dalphine was so very attracted to him. He didn't accept moderation or temperance in anything. I think I mentioned him in my letter."

"I remember," said Barret.

Pia took his hand and led him toward the stairway, planning a path past the blue fainting couch in the upstairs hall. Barret was already pulling at her clothes when they reached the Moroccan wall hangings above the first landing.

"Stop there first," Dalphine had told her, "and use each other till you're of no further use. I promise, he won't even notice the bedroom rug."

Pia let Barret trap her against the wall, lifting her legs around his waist, pressing his ear close to her mouth.

"He was huge," she whispered. "Dalphine told me she could hardly accommodate him. She used to climb on top of him and ride him like a carousel dragon, up and down."

"Do you have any idea how difficult it is," Barret whispered, "to read your letters and not be with you?"

"Should I stop sending them?"

He answered her without being able to answer, and they lay on the landing for a long while afterward. It was dark when they made their way up the stairs, not caring about eating dinner or locking the front door or anything but each other. They slept late the next morning, and Barret spent the afternoon talking on the phone with clients. In the evening, they watched television with their feet propped up on the new coffee table with flying bird inlays of ebony and tulip wood.

Monday morning before dawn, Barret nudged Pia awake, saying he wanted to make love with her before he went to the airport, but Pia said she needed to go into the bathroom for a minute first. When she came out, he was sitting on the edge of the bed, staring at his bare feet on the hand-tied rug, whose elaborate theme was called "Tree of Life."

"Pia," he said quietly. "Please, tell me everything is all right."

"Everything is all right," Pia said, hearing herself how hollow it sounded.

She closed her eyes, stood beside him, and pushed against his hand. She dragged her fingers through his hair, turned his head, kissed his mouth. She knelt down in front of him on the Tree of Life rug, which incorporated all the colors of glitter and sunlight and love.

Lily

(1512 days)

Long talk with one of the Jesus Chicks today. Not all religeanity and crap. Just like a human being sitting there talking with another human being. Jesus would have been proud of her.

JESUS CHICK: So do you think about what you might do after you get out?

ME: Sister, I think of little else.

JC: Will you be able to resume the career you had before?

ME: Oh, geez, I hope not.

JC: There are some great opportunities for reeducation once you get moved over to minimum security. Big library. Arts and crafts room. Sister Bernine is teaching a class where you can get certified as a Braille translator. Sister Antoine is offering a course in tailoring and alterations.

ME: I want to start my own business. When you have your own business, you have freedom. And freedom—that's everything.

JC: Ah! I have just the thing.

(She goes and gets this book—What a Great Idea! Building Your Financial Freedom from Inside Your Head by F. Scott Fitzhugh. This schmaltzy self-helpy thing. I flip through the preface, and it's all "If you can see it, you can be it!" and "I'll show you how to form an action plan to transform your dreams into cash-in-hand reality!")

ME: This strikes me as a cruel item to put in a prison library.

JC: Not at all! I can't think of anyplace where a positive attitude is more important.

ME: Um, 'kay.

JC: The Buddha once said, "To hope for miraculous blessings yet cling to wrong ideas can only prolong one's bondage."

ME: You're allowed to quote Buddha?

JC: Jesus said essentially the same thing. "The truth shall set you free."

(1513 days)

Hate to admit this, but F. Scott just blew my mind. He's all about the way people are prisoners of fear and self-loathing and negative crap and how freedom is a thing of the mind, and stone walls do not a prison make, and all this. And he just quoted this Wordsworth thing I read about a thousand years ago. "In truth the prison unto which we doom ourselves, no prison is."

It's like one of those stupid seminars, but it's true that no matter how hard it is to control external circumstances, you can always control yourself. I mean, even if you're a friggin' paraplegic, you can still change your mind.

I'm going to keep a Brainstorm Journal like he says. Just write every idea down, even if it sounds goofy, because it might make you think of something else. And I'm going to set goals. My first goal is five ideas per day, every day, without fail.

(1514 days)

Revised my goal to three ideas per day. Or maybe just the best one if I have several good ones.

BRAINSTORM: "State of the Art" art gallery

HIGH CONCEPT: Art gallery where everything is shaped like states.

BANNER: "Make a bold STATEment with STATE of the Art!"

REASON FOR BEING: Art needs no reason, but as far as marketing—people like their own state usually. Or maybe they used to live in another state they liked better and might want some art shaped like that as memorabilia.

BOOTSTRAPS: (1) Enjoy being around art-type people. (2) Good artistic sensibilities—wouldn't have crap art in my gallery. (3) I know the basic shape of at least probably 30 states.

CHALLENGES: (1) Being in prison. (2) Finding investors with whole prison thing as an issue. (3) Pia might think it's stupid.

ACTION ITEMS: (1) Get out of prison. (2) Make list of states, alphabetical if possible. (3) Find investors. (4) Find artists to do art on consignment (keeps up-front costs low). (5) Locate store space. (6) Come up with jingle/commercials.

(1516 days)

BRAINSTORM: Memor-mobile-ia

HIGH CONCEPT: Mobile photo developing/framing.

BANNER: "Call Memor-mobile-ia and see what develops!"

REASON FOR BEING: People always have a million rolls of film or disposable cameras, which they never get around to taking to the drugstore, so the truck comes, develops the photos in the mobile dark room, and then offers frames/scrapbooks and etc. like those little sticky picture corners and stuff.

BOOTSTRAPS: (1) Know how to drive. (2) Enjoy making scrapbooks (sort of). (3) I know a lot of people who take pictures and need them developed.

CHALLENGES: (1) Being in prison. (2) Finding investors with whole prison thing as an issue. (3) Pia might think it's stupid.

ACTION ITEMS: (1) Get out of prison. (2) Find investors. (3) Get equipment. (4) Learn how to develop film. (5) Come up with jingle/commercials.

(1523 days)

BRAINSTORM: Celebri-cheez Snack Crackers

BANNER: "Your favorite celebrities, only cheesier!"

HIGH CONCEPT: Snack crackers shaped like celebrities.

REASON FOR BEING: People love crackers and celebs.

BOOTSTRAPS: (1) Already thought up some great names:

Don Cheedles
Elvis Pretzlies
Johnny Dipps
Chow Yun Fat-free
Dorita Morenos

CHALLENGES: (1) Probably need permission for celeb likeness and they might be put off by prison thing. (2) Pia would definitely think this was stupid.

ACTION ITEMS: None at this time.

(1537 days)

Heard someone use "vis-à-vis" today, and it just felt good for some reason. Sometimes I feel like I've lost about 80 IQ points since coming in here.

BRAINSTORM: Hunan Puppy Restaurant

BANNER: "Everyone's an Asian at Hunan Puppy!"

HIGH CONCEPT: Like Chuck E. Cheese's, only Oriental. The "mascot," I guess you'd call it, would be Hunan Puppy—friendly, happy dog costumed character brings egg-rolls/

whatever to kid whose birthday it is. Then there would be a more refined area for grown-ups to have sushi/sake/whatever while the party is going on in the kid area.

REASON FOR BEING: There must be 8 trillion little kids in this city who need a place for birthday parties.

BOOTSTRAPS: (1) Place would primarily appeal to Asian people, who are usually rich/smart. (2) I love sushi. (Oh, God! I miss sushi! Why did I have to go and think about that?) (3) Portions could be small—Asians aren't big fat pigs like Americans. This would keep costs down.

CHALLENGES: (1) With child-oriented biz, prison record may be issue (vis-à-vis being in prison for murder of child). (2) Those costumed characters creep me out. What sort of desperate soul inhabits that thing? (3) Lack of familiarity with Asian birthday customs. Do Asians even have birthdays?

ACTION ITEMS: None at this time.

(1539 days)

BRAINSTORM: Passion of Jesus Christ Pop-up Book

BANNER: "Hey, kids! Christ suffered and died just for you!"

HIGH CONCEPT: Pop-up book illustrating Fourteen Stations of the Cross.

REASON FOR BEING: Fun way to educate children on suffering and death of Savior.

BOOTSTRAPS: (1) Catholics love that gory shit. (2) Bro former priest. This might be something we could talk about if we ever see each other again.

CHALLENGES: (1) Prison thing could hamper promotions/marketing. (2) Catholic-related stuff very depressing vis-à-vis Hell, death, blood, torture, etc. (3) Finding out stations of cross problematic vis-à-vis I am not allowed to make calls for 90 days.

ACTION ITEMS: (1) ~~Write to Sonny and get list of stations.~~ None at this time.

(1542 days)

Pia called. First good talk we've had in a long time. She's redecorating her house, and it sounds far out. Surprisingly cool, for Pia. Haven't heard her sound excited or even interested in anything in such a long time. Told her some of my biz ideas. Lot of noncommittal "Oh, that's interesting!" response. She couldn't remember stations of cross either, but got on Internet while we were talking. (Oh, God, I miss the Internet!)

Stations of cross:

1. Christ condemned to death
2. The cross is laid upon him*
3. His first fall
4. He meets His Blessed Mother*
5. Simon of Scyrenia (sp?) is made to bear the cross*
6. Christ's face is wiped by Veronica (Where was Betty? Ha!)
7. His second fall
8. He meets the women of Jerusalem (not a great way to meet women!)
9. His third fall
10. He is stripped of His garments
11. His crucifixion***

12. His death on the cross
13. His body is taken down from the cross
14. He is laid in the tomb

*Especially suitable for pop-up format.

(1545 days)

BRAINSTORM: Kama Sutra Pop-up Book

BANNER: "Holy Krishna! Look what just popped up!"

HIGH CONCEPT: Pop-up book of sexual positions.

REASON FOR BEING: Educational and entertaining.

BOOTSTRAPS: (1) As marketable as porn, only classier. (2) I used to have sex a lot. (Oh, God, I miss sex!) (3) Many sexual positions lend themselves to pop-up format.

CHALLENGES: (1) Finding publisher. (2) Having to think about sex that much would be kind of depressing/frustrating vis-à-vis being in prison, etc.

ACTION ITEMS: ~~1) Make list of King's~~ None at this time.

(1557 days)

Played cards with Kay and Danitra. Had an idea earlier—about surgery camp. Like space camp, only for kids who want to be surgeons. Got interrupted by fight before I could fully flesh it out. Cogetatus interruptus.

(1563 days)

BRAINSTORM: Fabric Resurrection Center

BANNER: "Hey! Don't throw that out! We might be able to use it at the Fabric Resurrection Center!" or "Bringing dead fabric back to life!"

HIGH CONCEPT: Take all the crappy clothes that people donate but are so crappy they can't even sell them at the Goodwill store, cut them up, and use the fabric to make funky items, car seat covers, lampshades—pretty much anything you'd weave or braid from strips of cloth or make with heavy/fibrous paper like we made in art class that one summer.

REASON FOR BEING: Ecology and/or funkiness—both worthwhile.

BOOTSTRAPS: (1) Fabric work could be done in prison. (2) Recently read article about making extra-nice paper from old fabric. (3) Many other ideas of what to do with fabric (braid rugs, weave potholders—like on those little plastic looms you can get). (4) Goodwill would probably give their old crap at little or no charge.

CHALLENGES: (1) Being in prison limits clothing pickup capabilities. (2) Use of scissors, seam rippers, razor blades may be discouraged by prison authorities. (3) Pia might think this is not a very classy occupation. (4) It's probably a stupid idea.

ACTION ITEMS: None at this time.

Pia

"Pia, come in!" Dalphine called. "You're in perfect time. I was just about to call next door for sushi. But as long as you're here—oh, be sweet and watch the store for me? I'm going to run up the street and buy some flowers, then we'll have lunch."

She gave Pia a quick squeeze about the shoulders and plucked a black and red mantilla from a shelf.

"Here's the menu," she said, thrusting a laminated bamboo-patterned paper into Pia's hands. "Why don't you call in the order—anything you like. My treat, I insist. If they deliver before I get back, be a dear and cover it, won't you? I'll reimburse you—or better yet! We'll barter for something lovely. Oh, and be sure to ask for a liter of sake. And extra ginger. They're always stingy with it. And miso soup? Or hot and sour? No, miso. I have some perfect little sushi settings over by the Edinburgh things, but feel free to look around and take down whatever you like for the table. And when I get back, we'll feast!"

Pia's lips were slightly parted, but they were dry and didn't move.

"Thank you, sweet." Dalphine breezed past, kissed Pia

on the cheek, and tossed the mantilla around her shoulders. "You're a treasure!"

The door chimed closed behind her. The store sat silent against a backdrop of muffled street noises. Pia stood between a marble-topped ebony buffet and a pair of brown leather bergeres, terrified, elated, confused, clutching the bamboo-patterned menu. She made a conscious attempt to organize her thoughts, to plan what she would do or say if someone came in, but the idea of that happening made her feel dizzy. She stood there for what seemed like a long time. People hurried by on the street, but no one opened the door or even glanced at the ivy-painted window.

Pia thought about a day when she was nine years old. She'd come home from school to find a hastily scribbled note saying that the elderly neighbor woman had fallen and needed to be taken to the hospital. Pia's mother, who'd been there every day of Pia's life, was gone. Sonny and baby Lily had disappeared into thin air. Pia was alone in the vast quiet of the afternoon house. The thrill was tangible enough to make her scurry for the bathroom, but instead of running to the one off the kitchen, she ran up the stairs to her parents' bedroom. She danced back and forth in the hallway, and then she saw her hand on the glass knob of the bedroom door, and then she was opening it, and then she was inside.

She crept into the bathroom. The master bathroom, her mother called it. Pia sat with her eyes closed and inhaled the lingering scent of her mother's perfume. She washed her hands in her mother's sink with a tiny, fragrant soap that was shaped like a cherub. She dabbed her cheeks with lotion from a spiraling pink glass bottle. She went to her mother's dresser and inched open a drawer. It was filled with silk, lace, and secrets. Things weren't crisply folded like they were in all the other drawers. They were tumbled and chaotic, like a basket of linens fresh from the dryer. Pia stirred her hand through the soft pool of private satin items and paused when she touched something solid beneath the silk. Something flat, rectangular. A box? No, a book.

And then she heard her mother downstairs in the hall.

For all of Pia's life, whatever mysteries were dispelled for her in the girls' locker room after field hockey, whatever fables lost their charm during tipsy late-night conversations at the sorority house, whatever she learned on her wedding night about the private world of adults, she was left with a tickle of insatiable curiosity about that solid object amid her mother's softest things. There always lingered an unarticulated longing, a *left-out-ness*, tinged with a mosquito sting of fear that some secret, unnamed element lurked deep inside her, because she was, after all, her mother's child.

Pia crept over to Dalphine's red chair and sat, curling her legs underneath herself. She discovered that if she held perfectly still, she could smell Dalphine's perfume.

The phone rang, and Pia leaped to her feet. Her stomach felt each jangle of the old-fashioned ringer. She wasn't sure she should answer it, but it didn't seem to be tripping any type of voice mail device, and the caller didn't seem ready to give up. Pia hurried to the back of the store. The phone sat on a little trestle table just beyond the display case, and though there was nothing between her and the table but the beaded curtain, for some reason Pia was afraid to step past it. The corridor. This was the perimeter. She pressed her hand against her heart, waiting for the sharks to start swimming inside. They would smell the red cloud of fear, and then—the churning. The feeding frenzy.

But the telephone didn't stop ringing. Pia finally reached one hand through the doorway, as if she were reaching through a hole in the ice, extending her arm into the murky lake beneath. Taking care not to cross the imaginary line below the lintel, she picked up the receiver and stretched the cord long enough to extend into the store where she stood.

She didn't know what to say.

"Dalphine!" said the voice on the other end. "*C'est toi?*"

"Hello—no. I'm sorry, she's um . . . hello?"

"Dalphine!"

"She stepped out for a moment. May I take a message?"

"*Quoi? Quoi? Parlez-vous Français?*"

"*Oui, je parle un peu*," Pia responded without thinking. The awakening of that foreign tongue in her own mouth startled her, and the elated, frightened feeling intensified.

"*Je voudrais parler avec Dalphine, s'il vous plaît?*" the caller said.

"*Non, je regret*. She's not here. Um . . . *Elle n'est pas ici.*"

"*Et vous êtes . . .*"

"A friend—*une amie. Je suis une amie d'elle, mais elle n'est pas ici.*"

"*Ah, mais non!*"

"I'm sorry. *Je suis desolée. Voulez-vous* . . . oh, damn . . . um . . . *rappeler plus tard* . . . call back? *Telephone encore* . . . oh—I'm trying to think how to say 'later' or um . . . *demain! Elle sera ici demain matin!* Tomorrow morning, *s'il vous plaît.*"

"*Demain? Non, non!*" the caller said, and then rattled on in a quickly pattering monologue, tumbling words and phrases, something about Tuesday afternoon or Wednesday morning. Pia caught the French words for box, glass, and store and "FedEx" and *ordinateur*, which she knew meant "computer."

"*Excuse-moi*," she interrupted. "*Je regret, mais je ne comprend pas. S'il vous plaît* . . . ah . . . if you could . . . *si vous parlez* . . . *plus lentement* . . . yes?" She wanted to ask him to speak slowly, but as she was trying to express that, the caller said, "*Mardi!* Tuesday!" thanked her, and hung up, leaving Pia with the phone pressed to her cheek and her mind grasping at forgotten French vocabulary. She reached through the curtain and gingerly replaced the receiver.

Pia had been to the back of the store before, but never behind the glass cabinet. The wooden doors on the back were closed, but a ring of keys lay on top, some silvery new, some tarnished brown, all attached to a brass griffin. Picking them up, Pia counted and traced each one with her finger, wondering which one opened the front door, which one unlocked the sliding door of the glass cabinet, which one turned the dead bolt on Dalphine's storage room beyond the beaded curtain, which one opened the door to the apartment where her whole mysterious life was kept.

Pia went to the front window and leaned forward, touching her hand to the painted ivy. Dalphine was up the block and across the street talking to an old man at the newsstand. She laughed and gave him a quick hug, then waved her hand and walked away, up the street toward the produce market where the flowers stood in large buckets on risers out front.

When Dalphine had disappeared inside the market, Pia went back to the glass case and took the griffin in her hand. Kneeling down beside the wooden doors, feeling for the lock and reading its Braille face in the quarter-light, she sorted the keys between her fingers. The first key was too small. The second could only be inserted halfway. The third went all the way in but wouldn't turn.

Pia glanced toward the window and slid the fourth key into the aperture. The lock gave way with a solid shift of the tumbler, and the door slid easily to the side. The first three shelves were made of glass and windowed toward the store. Necklaces, bracelets, and cuffs, silver and turquoise earrings, gold chains arranged by weight and design. The bottom shelves were inside the dark wooden base of the cabinet. Again by Braille, her fingers found velvet-lined trays laid with smooth dowel shapes, spheres, circles. She traced undulating curves, rigid ripples and rings, small-nubbed surfaces, long, smooth lengths, leather straps, silk laces, brass buckles and studs.

Pia glanced again toward the window, then over her shoulder at the corner lamp. She reached up for the chain and tassel, but her wrist bumped the green glass shade. Pia tried to grab it, but it tipped, dropped, and shattered on the floor. The concussion seemed to split open the dusky quiet. Immediately on the heels of the echoing smash of glass on wood came the jangling of door chimes, which carried in all the chaos of the street.

Pia crouched low behind the cabinet. Broken glass glittered around her knees. The brass griffin dangled from the trespassed lock. The feeding frenzy started. Sharks wheeled and thrashed inside her chest. Her lungs felt crushed, unable to take air, her heart felt choked and frozen against its own twisting. It was the desperate, dying feeling of being strangled and drowned at the same time. Soon the black vise would clamp across her forehead and slide down over her eyes. She needed her purse. She needed her medicine, but Dalphine's musician was standing in the open doorway. All she could do was focus on trying to breathe without whimpering.

"Dalphine?" he called.

He stood for a long moment, swore softly, called out to her again, then stepped back, allowing the door to drift close, muting the traffic and street noises.

Pia seized the griffin and dragged the cabinet closed. She stayed crouched behind it long enough to make herself breathe, then made her way to the coat tree, where she'd left her purse. She sank into her customary spot on the little sofa. Her hands were shaking. This was why she carried the pills in a small tin instead of the childproof bottle from the pharmacy. Swallowing it without water made her gag her a little, so she chewed and swallowed an Altoid after it. Then she waited until she felt steady enough to take her hands away from her face, to look at them and know them for her own hands, to turn them over and know *palm, thumb, ring—these things are real—I am not dying—I can breathe—my breath is real.*

The bamboo-colored menu lay on the coffee table. Pia picked it up and fanned herself with it. The breeze was cool against her damp forehead.

When Pia opened her eyes, she couldn't tell if she'd dozed off for five minutes or for an hour. Either way, Dalphine wasn't back yet, Pia was relieved to discover. At the back of the store, she swept the glass shards into a heap against the wall, then slid the menu under the pile and carried it carefully to a garbage basket beneath the cash register. With trembling hands, she reached through the beaded curtain and took the telephone again, leaning in just far enough to dial the number at the bottom of the menu.

A woman answered in a sharp, cricketlike dialect.

Pia haltingly explained that she was a friend of Dalphine's, flushing warm when she heard herself repeat that lie in her own language. Anyone who knew Dalphine would know Pia was merely an acquaintance, a customer, a trespasser.

"Yes? Yes?" The woman's voice chipped and cracked like the green glass bits as they slid into the metal basket. "Does she want her usual today?"

"Yes," said Pia. "That would be fine."

"For two or three?"

"Two, I guess."

"Miso soup with that? Or hot and sour?"

"Um . . . why don't you give us one of each," said Pia. That seemed on the safe side.

After she placed the order, Pia sat perfectly still on a side chair, holding her purse in her lap. Forty minutes passed. The door chimes rang the delivery in from the street. Pia paid for the sushi, returned to the chair, and waited another half hour for Dalphine.

"Pia?" she sang out as she breezed in. "What have you been up to? Did you find a book or have you been shopping?"

"Someone called for you," Pia said, trying not to sound unnerved or angry.

"Oh? Who was it?"

"I'm sorry. My French is very rusty, and he was talking too fast. But I know he said something about a shipment. A computer or maybe something you ordered online? Or a box, maybe. And he said it would arrive from Morocco Tuesday or Wednesday, I think."

"Hmm." Dalphine looked perplexed for a moment, then shrugged. "If it's such an important thing, he'll call back."

"And then . . . your musician came."

Dalphine looked up with raised eyebrows but didn't say anything.

"He didn't leave a message," Pia said.

"No, I suppose not."

"I'm sorry. I guess I wasn't a very good shopkeeper."

"*Tsh*." Dalphine waved that aside. "Everyone I deal with in Morocco speaks English. That was intolerably rude of him. As for the young man, he comes around here too often. He's starting to be troublesome. And as for you, *pattampoochi*"—she reached over and touched Pia on the cheek—"you are a perfectly lovely shopkeeper. A blessing! There's no one else I trust, so I'm forever chained to this place. It was a luxury, you can guess, to be able to walk down the street a bit."

The cool feel of Dalphine's fingers on her cheek met a warm surge from inside. But still, the sharks. These days, Pia's whole existence was engineered around avoiding them, and Dalphine had abandoned her to their swirling appetite.

"What is it, butterfly? You seem flustered."

"Well, it's just—I had no idea if—I didn't expect you to be gone so long."

"Oh, sweet." Dalphine looked abashed. "I'm so sorry. It seemed like just a few minutes. But"—she pressed her cool palms to Pia's flushed cheeks for a fleeting, unbearably pleasant moment—"fortunately, you did beautifully!"

"No, actually, I didn't," Pia said wretchedly. "I broke a lamp."

"Oh, dear."

"Your lamp. Not one that was for sale."

"Everything is for sale," Dalphine corrected her drily, glancing around the shop and quickly detecting the missing element. "Ah, that? A reproduction. Nothing terribly special."

"Are you sure? Because, of course, I'll pay for it."

"Oh, *tsh.*" Dalphine waved her aside again.

"No, really. I insist."

"Well, sweet, if it's that important to you." Dalphine smiled. "But honestly, I couldn't accept more than one-fifty for it." She squeezed Pia's hand. "Now don't you give it another thought. I'll just ring it up, while you prepare our feast."

Pia nodded, feeling a little stunned. She took her pocketbook from her purse and handed Dalphine a credit card. As Dalphine stood by the register waiting for the code to come back to her, she examined the naked bulb and dangling chain. She picked up a small piece of colored glass behind the cabinet.

"Hmm. Now how could that have happened," she wondered. "Were you looking for something?"

"No! No, I was just looking in the—in the case . . . at the lovely . . . um . . ."

Struggling to keep her voice even, to hold back the warmth she felt spreading upward into her neck and face, Pia searched the glass case for an alibi. Her eyes automatically settled on the largest item, a heavy peridot baguette and diamond necklace with matching cuff bracelet and earrings.

"Those," she pointed. "I was just looking at those."

"Oh! Yes, of course! These are perfect for you," Dalphine pronounced, bringing out the tray that held them. "I can't believe I didn't think of it, but yes, your instincts are quite correct. Did you have them in mind for a particular occasion?"

"No, no," Pia said. "I was just looking."

"Here. Put them on right now. They're perfect with the black cashmere. Wear them for the rest of the afternoon. You'll never want to take them off again." Dalphine stepped around to the front of the counter, took Pia by her shoulders, and turned her toward the window. "Here we are," she soothed, reaching around Pia's neck to fasten the necklace.

She took Pia's hands and slid the cuff onto her wrist, clipped the earrings in place, then stepped back to view her like an artist assessing her handiwork.

"Yes. Yes, I think so. Because your features are so delicate. You need the counterpoint."

Pia was conscious of the weight and color that lay against her chest. It made her feel aware of the presence of her body inside her blouse. She wondered what it would feel like to wear the peridot with a lower neckline, with her silk nightgown or one of the evening dresses she'd put into storage along with Lily's books and clothes and bric-a-brac.

The credit card receipt printed out from the little box by the cash register, but Dalphine took it and tore it in half.

"Let's not worry about that ridiculous little lamp. But *these*—these you must have." She rang the purchase and swiped the card along the slot again. "Yes. You absolutely must take those home today. You absolutely have to."

"Well, wait. How much are they?" Pia asked.

"Oh, *psh*, sweet," Dalphine said dismissively. "Take them home. You know you can always return them. Really, it's no trouble at all. I promise you won't be taking advantage. And please don't give the two hundred for the lamp another thought."

She handed Pia the receipt and a pen, and Pia's breath caught in her throat when she saw the price. Her hand went to her chest, where the necklace lay heavy and the cuff clanked painfully against her breastbone. She glanced toward Dalphine, who was busy sorting a stack of mail she'd brought in with her.

Pia knew she could not keep these. She knew she shouldn't sign for them in the first place, but as she did sign, she felt the diamonds and silverwork connecting to her chest, laying into her skin. Surely it wouldn't hurt to wear them just for today. Pia would show them to Barret and explain about the lamp and then return them. Right away next week, she told herself sternly, they would be back in the display case for someone else to buy. But even knowing that, Pia felt a wave of pleasure as she put her pocketbook away. They belonged to her right now, if only for a little while. They were hers. Never had she owned or thought of owning any such thing. When she looked into the mirror behind the counter, they seemed to lengthen and define a neckline she'd never seen before.

Dalphine removed some clocks from a low round table, shook out a lace tablecloth, and tossed two large pillows on the floor while Pia took dishes from the sideboard. Square pink plates, soft aqua saucers, little white sake cups, and black porcelain chopsticks.

"Now. Let's see," Dalphine said, opening a large, flat box between them. "A very nice assortment. You did a wonderful job. Oh, but look how stingy with the ginger. Here, you take it, sweet."

She scooped the ginger onto the corner of a square plate and handed it to Pia along with chopsticks and a shallow bowl for soy sauce.

"Low sodium," Dalphine said, holding up the bottle. "I always have my own. We don't want to retain water tomorrow, do we?"

Pia shook her head.

"Sake?"

Pia nodded, and Dalphine poured hot rice wine into the tiny cups.

"Oh, and of course the edamame is cold as a stone! I don't know why I keep going there." Dalphine tapped one chopstick against the table. "She hates me. I introduced a customer of mine to her son, who owns the place, and they ended up having a terribly sordid affair. His wife left him, and for that she blames me! The ridiculous old bitch. Pardon my language," she added when Pia tensed at the harsh sound of it.

Dalphine lifted a wooden tray from the box and placed it between them, perusing the artfully laid garden of sashimi, sushi, and condiments.

"Ah, look at this! Lovely. That's why I keep going, I suppose."

"Presentation is everything," Pia said softly.

Dalphine glanced up in surprise, then rewarded her with a long, generous peal of genuine laughter.

"Well done, Pia! I was wondering. I truly was beginning to wonder if there wasn't a little more going on with you than meets the eye. But I did suspect, and I'm never wrong."

Pia wasn't sure what that meant, but it made her feel foolishly pleased, like a little child whose teacher has rewarded her with a stick-on star. She took two ebi and a California roll and placed them on her square plate. Dalphine hovered her chopsticks over the tray, selecting several pieces of tuna, salmon, and eel, then putting back two of the tuna and taking three futomaki instead.

"He's half Japanese, half American," she said. "Not terribly handsome, but very sensual. And his body is perfect. Very long and graceful without being skinny or mean. He used to go every day to the club a few blocks from here. She saw him through the window, running on the treadmill. Fifteen miles he ran. Every day. Never getting anywhere, but admiring himself in the mirror all the way." She laughed and made long running legs with her chopsticks. "This customer—a dear, dear friend. What was her name?" She considered it as she selected a spider roll, then shrugged. "Well, anyway. I don't recall. But she was very tall, very beautiful. Distinctive. Though she always wore dark blue. Dark blue dresses, hats, shoes, everything. All the time. I wish I'd had the heart to tell her, 'Sweet! A little vermilion, a splash of tangerine, anything! Please!' But of course, that wouldn't have been my place. Or do you think I should have?" she asked Pia.

"I don't know. It's probably better not to get involved."

"Yes! Yes, you are so right. And you can guess, I wish now I hadn't, but I took her to lunch there one day and introduced them, and she was immediately taken with him. She knew the apartment behind the store was empty, so could she rent it, she asked me. She told me all about what she had planned for him, and I said, 'Darling, I cherish you, but I don't even want to know!' I just gave her the key and left. Well, the next day she told me—he wasn't a wonderful lover, she said, but he was long and had a pleasant curve and seemed willing to learn, so can she please rent the apartment from me for another month, she asks. Yes, I suppose, I tell her. So every day, closing time—there he is. Never says a word to me. Just smiles, nods, goes to the back, where she's waiting for him. Not my business! I'm not involved!"

Pia sipped her sake, saying nothing, but listening with a physical kind of listening that was more than just hearing. She could feel it in the back of her neck and shoulders.

"And so it goes for three or four months. Then one day—here's his wife. Right here in this very spot, weeping into her teacup. He'd told her all about the blue lady and the apartment and *details details details* and so on. God knows why! Ego. Cruelty. Not conscience, certainly. I don't think he was feeling at all guilty about it. Nothing like that. It was just *unkind*. You see, his wife had tried over the years to please him, but he wanted things she couldn't imagine herself doing, so he told her it was her fault he had to go to another woman. So you can guess. She wanted to kill herself. *But* he also told her she was the love of his life and the wife of his heart, and the woman in the apartment was a whore and not even particularly beautiful. Of course, I felt an obligation to share that with my dear friend, though I certainly took no pleasure in repeating such hurtful comments."

Dalphine clicked her chopsticks over the tray.

"Mmm. What to choose," she said. "I think . . . ebi ami."

She took two ebi and a California roll, while Pia waited, silently stirring at her tiny saucer. Dalphine dipped the California roll and ate it. She took a little more wasabi and stirred it into her little saucer. She looked up at Pia and smiled.

"This is nice, isn't it, sweet?"

"Yes." Pia nodded and smiled back. "But what happened with . . . with your friend? What did she do?"

"Oh, well—if you really have to know," Dalphine said, "it was a disaster. The next day, she bought some lovely silk scarves—oh, remind me to show you these lovely silk scarves I've just gotten in. They're lovely. And when he arrived, she pretended everything was fine. Said she wanted to play a little game. She blindfolded him and led him to this lovely old four-poster she'd *stolen* from me for thirty-eight hundred dollars. Late Victorian. Walnut. Pineapple finials. Posts fully eight feet tall. Pristine condition. Just thirty-eight hundred. Can you imagine? Including having it moved to the apartment and reassembled. And the coverlet—I don't even recall charging her for the coverlet. Yes, I think . . . I think the coverlet was a gift. Or maybe she paid a token one or two hundred dollars for it, maybe fifty a piece for the pillow shams, but I coordinated the entire ensemble. Honestly, I did everything but tuck her in."

Pia did her best to balance the chopsticks in her hand. The sake was doing a bleary little dance with the meds in her bloodstream.

"What sort of bed do you sleep in?" Dalphine asked.

"It's one of those with the . . . the what-do-you-call-it. A sleigh bed."

"Ah, lovely! The lines. So flowing, so graceful. Is it an antique?"

Pia nodded, not wanting to inquire further about the story, but reluctant to follow this tangent too far from it.

"Did you buy it here in the city?"

"My first husband and I bought it in eastern Pennsylvania," Pia said, trying to adjust herself to the new conversation. "At an estate auction. It was silly, really. The bids kept going higher and higher." She had to laugh, remembering the determined set of Edgar's jaw. "We ended up paying twice what it's worth. But he knew how much I wanted it."

"Ah. And now you sleep in it with your new husband."

"He's hardly new. We've been married for almost four years."

"Hmm. Nonetheless. It seems worth noting."

"Does it?"

Dalphine shrugged, selected a cucumber roll from the tray and ate it, then set her chopsticks across the tiny bowl.

"Because I don't think it does," said Pia, a crisping of irritation clearly present on the edge of her voice. "In fact—"

"Oh, don't get me off on a tangent!" Dalphine interrupted. "I'm just coming to the most hilarious part. So Miss Very Very Blue. She took two more scarves, tied his wrists, knotted them tight and secured them to the iron ring—you know, where the canopy drapes through? Only I didn't do the usual chintz or lace with it. I used this wonderfully unusual fabric I found in Nepal. That gave it a very different sort of drape. There was something about that—the liquid look of the fabric flowing through the iron rings—I've always loved that sort of paradox in terms of texture. But—wayward sushi husband. Back to him. He stood there, getting used to that feeling. Trying to decide if he enjoyed it. Deciding he did, as was evidenced by that lovely curve curving out from his body. She used her mouth on it—just enough to prop it up—then she took the blindfold off, and who do you suppose our blue lady has by the hand? Yes, that's right. His pretty little wife, and oh—the look on his face! She said his mouth fell open. You could have dropped a sea bass into it, she said. He sputtered and swore for a bit. But then he just stood there, and you can imagine what happened next."

"What?" Pia hated herself for asking, but she couldn't imagine. Not in a million years.

"Well, our Miss Azure To Be Sure began to berate him for insulting her and treating his wife so shabbily. You don't deserve either one of us, she said. She said, Look at this perfectly sweet wife you have. You don't even see her beautiful skin, these soft, sweet little breasts—and how many women have such a smooth, flat stomach after four children? But you don't see her. Don't even hear the sound of her voice anymore. She bent down and took the leather belt out of his own hastily discarded pants. Well, again the sputtering and swearing—oh, don't you even think about it and so on. And Miss True Blue said oh, I wasn't. And she handed the strap to his wife, who was a little unsteady because she and Miss Too Much Blue had been smoking hash together earlier and—oh! I'm out of ginger."

Dalphine leaned forward, her chopsticks poised above the ginger on Pia's plate.

"May I?"

"Of course. Go ahead." Pia nodded, purposefully sorting over the sashimi instead of meeting Dalphine's eyes.

"Thank you, sweet. I don't know why they have to be so stingy with it."

"So . . . did the wife . . ."

"Oh, she was too timid to do more than lay in a tepid lash or two, but I suppose it stung a bit. Or perhaps it just made him nervous. Anyway, he began to threaten and berate her, telling her if she was any kind of wife he wouldn't have to go out associating with whores. And how she was no better to lie down with than a wooden stool. He'd told her many times there was something wrong with her, and I suspect this was the first time she decided not to believe it. And that's when she truly began to flog him with a passion."

Dalphine poured sake in both their cups, and Pia took a sip from hers.

"She didn't stop until he was raging angry and stinging red, and then she sank down on her knees and just cried. Because despite everything, she really did love the man. And Miss Deeply Blue—she was a compassionate soul, after all—she knelt down and set the wife's cool hands over her husband's buttocks and turned him toward her. She showed her she didn't have to gag the whole thing down. That she could get by with the simplest tricks, just using her lips on the parts that were darkest in color, for example. Or doing what the Kama Sutra calls 'bite of the butterfly.' She instructed her on manipulation of the perineum.

Demonstrated how sensitive it is to the slightest flick of the tongue. She showed her how to apply the belt and explained the dynamics of corporal discipline. The word itself means 'to win over in discipleship.' So the purpose is not to dominate or punish. No, no—quite the opposite. She showed her the proper technique: apply the lash, tongue broad strokes across the affected area, then softly blow on the dampened skin. Discomfort, solace, evaporation. The purpose is to create an unexpected array of sensation to intensify the pleasure. It's not the feeble demonstration of physical power, she told the wife, it's the power to impart that intensified pleasure that bends the man to your will.

"Well, you can guess that was it for him. He was in absolute chaos. Begging his wife, cursing the whore, cursing the wife, begging the whore. Instead of seeing to his satisfaction, however, our Blue Lady settled the wife on the edge of the bed, positioned the wife so the husband could see everything. You may not appreciate it now, she told him, but I am giving you a great gift. She opened the wife's legs, like a ballerina's *plié*, and this Indigo Godmother, very gently, very patiently worked with just two fingers and her tongue, occasionally speaking to the restaurateur over her shoulder, explaining the physiology of his little wife's response as she was stimulated beyond all inhibition.

"Curiously enough, that seemed to have a greater effect on him than anything. Seeing his timid wife in her ecstasy. She'd never in all their years together climaxed this way. And all the while, he kept telling her that it was something wrong with her female organs. Have you ever heard anything so ludicrous? So *unkind*? But now! Oh, this was a very different situation. He promised to do better, begged her to whip him again, saying oh yes, he was cruel and bad and deserved a *damn good thrashing*! When my dear blue friend told me this, we laughed until our sides ached."

Dalphine placed her palms flat on the table.

"So. You can plainly see—none of this was my fault. But the wife left him and took the old lady's grandchildren, so the old lady hates me. Honestly, it's ridiculous. We're practically neighbors. And I spend a fortune there. Always ordering for groups and parties, and I recommend them to all my clients. Does she spend a dime in this place? Never. I happen to know they recently redid sixty seat cushions without even inviting me to submit a bid on the fabric!"

Pia couldn't think of anything to say. She hoped her expression wasn't anything too similar to that of the man in the story.

"And, anyway, he should thank me!" Dalphine pressed her hand to her chest in a gesture of innocence. "He should! And certainly, his wife should thank me. It was all her fault from the beginning."

"*Her* fault?" Pia blurted. "How so?"

"She should have taught him how to please her in the first place. That was her responsibility. To educate him. To insist. She should have *demanded*. But she wanted to be the one whose hands were tied, the one without responsibility, nothing more than paper is to the wind. And that's possible between people. Sometimes. If the balance is right. But after that day, he wasn't strong enough to take her and have her. *Ravish* her. After that day, he kept begging her to tie him and thrash him. He wasn't the lord and master of her any longer, so she left. Not because he made love to another woman, but because she no longer had any respect for him."

"I don't believe any woman wants her husband to be her lord and master," Pia said. "Not even a Japanese woman."

"Why do you assume she was Japanese?" Dalphine asked over her sake cup. "She was as American as Abe Lincoln. A dishwater blonde with hazel eyes. You can't ascribe any specific ancestry to that."

"Well, I just thought . . . not as a racial thing . . . in terms of race, but in terms of . . . of cultural . . . culture." Embarrassed at being caught in an assumption so politically incorrect, Pia stammered and searched. “You see, my husband often does business with Japanese men, and their wives are very . . . oh, I don’t know. At dinner, for example, when the husbands finish eating, the wives can’t eat any more.”

“Can’t or don’t? Perhaps they simply choose not to.”

“Whatever. Whether they’ve finished or not, they send their plates away.”

“Oh, Pia, think about it. American men and women are no different. And American women are such hypocrites about it! In Japan, the wife sends her plate away in deference to her husband. In America, the woman starves herself in an effort to be smaller than a man and consequently more pleasing to him. In Somalia, a little girl’s clitoris is cut off to prevent her from becoming a slave to her own pleasure. In America, a little girl is indoctrinated with such shame at the experience of pleasure, she may as well amputate the very possibility from her body. In Guatemala, a man says, ‘To clean the toilet is woman’s work. I won’t do it!’ In America, such a thing could never be said. But has your husband ever cleaned the toilet?”

“Well, no, but—but it’s not the same at all!” Pia struggled to put her argument into words. Her forehead was beginning to feel shiny and thick. “To say that women are oppressed is not to say they *want* to be oppressed.”

“Oppressed? Someone who submits by choice is not being oppressed. The power is within you, and keeping it there doesn’t diminish it. Your mother taught you to keep your sex like a sword in a sheath, didn’t she? She taught you that it cuts deepest when you keep it close to your side. When you take a lover, you lay your weapons at his feet. If you don’t, the blade turns inward to stab you in the heart. The woman who allows herself to be bound, whether by ropes or silk or tradition, is free of fear, and that’s what makes her powerful. Powerful enough to be chained. To be cherished.”

“No. No, that doesn’t make any sense,” Pia said.

“You want to be treated as an equal?”

"Yes."

"Then you want another woman."

"No! An equal partnership, I mean."

"Is that what you have?"

Dalphine waited for Pia's answer, knowing she didn't have one.

"Have you read *Story of O*?"

"In college," Pia said. "It's disgusting. It's vile."

"Such a feminist dilemma!" Dalphine laughed. "In demanding respect for ourselves and our desires, can we disrespect the desires of another? If you're free to decide that bondage is vile, why isn't she free to decide she likes it? The need to control rises out of insecurity, a feeling of powerlessness. To relinquish control is a courageous and confident act. Trust is bravery, acquiescence the ultimate triumph, bondage the ultimate freedom. It demonstrates a total lack of fear that can only come from the full knowledge of one's own power."

Pia settled back in her chair and yawned, feeling too languid and sleepy to even try to understand.

"It's good for women to stand equal to men in matters of business," said Dalphine. "Money. Negotiations. But supply and demand get so tiresome. Admit it. Women would rather be taken. Used. Bound and stolen. Whipped like a horse. Cleaved like a diamond."

"You can't mean that." Pia shook her head.

"Of course I can. Why shouldn't you want to calm the fears of your lover? Are you afraid to lay your weapons at his feet?"

Pia didn't answer.

"Women have all the power, though most like to pretend otherwise," Dalphine went on. "Because we have the ability to conceal our desire. To hide it in a pretty little box. A man—poor duckling! He wears his most vulnerable aspect out in the open for anyone to take hold of. His exigency is easily inflamed and impossible to obscure. It literally points out the direction he is compelled to follow."

Pia stared at the corner of the table, trying to determine if it was perfectly square or slightly skewed.

"Were you a virgin when you first married?" Dalphine asked.

"Yes."

"You kept yourself from him?"

"I *saved* myself *for* him," Pia corrected her. Somehow the semantics of it mattered to her now. "It was a mutual decision. I felt strongly about it, and Edgar respected that."

"Oh, of course!" Dalphine smiled skeptically. "So he never tried to persuade you?"

"No. Maybe a little. Not really . . . until the night before the wedding."

"Ah, but those few hours made all the difference in the world." Dalphine leaned in, resting her arms on the table. "The difference between a bona fide virgin bride and a whore in white satin. The difference between a legitimate transaction and outright theft." She waited without moving. "Didn't it, *farfalla*?"

Pia held the chopsticks carefully. They were a straight line while her thoughts were suddenly disjointed and out of sync with what, until this moment, she had clearly remembered.

"How old were you?" Dalphine asked.

"Twenty-one."

"Where were you married?"

"At a church near his parents' summer home."

"And what happened the night before?"

"The rehearsal dinner. And then we walked and walked. Just talking. I've never talked with anyone as much as I talked with Edgar. Always. Right up until the night he died. We never ran out of things to say. We just kept walking and talking until we came to the prayer garden behind the church. There was a pavilion. It was covered with jasmine, and you could hear the honeybees in the vines. I told Edgar, I wish we could be married out here instead of inside the church, and Edgar said we could be if we wanted. He said, 'We could be married right here, right now,' and he kissed me and kissed me and pulled me down on the ground . . . and I remember breathing that jasmine-scented air and listening to the crickets and the bees in the dark."

Pia stopped, and the quiet settled around them.

"And he was very persistent?" Dalphine gently prodded.

"More like . . . persuasive. Saying how he wanted to please me."

"Clever boy!" Dalphine tapped her temple with the tip of her finger. "A less sensitive man would have used flattery and begged for his own pleasure."

"I suppose."

"He lay on top of you?" Dalphine whispered. "Held you down with his body?"

"Yes."

"He could have forced himself on you."

"Edgar would never have done that."

"So you forced yourself on him."

"What? I certainly did not."

"Oh, but you did, Pia! You forced your virginity on him. You set him in a struggle against his own honor. Propriety on one side, lust on the other, struggling like gladiators for your entertainment. Every pleasure you kept from him ensured your place of dominance."

"No. That's not—I did not *keep pleasure from him*. I was very good at—well, let's just say I *pleasured* him. Plenty. Even though I never allowed him to give me the same satisfaction."

"Further demonstrating your power to control." Dalphine shrugged. "Though you're certainly entitled to pretend it was unselfishness."

Pia realized it was true. That night and for the eighteen years that followed. Everything except his death had been according to her agenda.

"Tell me about your wedding," said Dalphine. "Was it lovely?"

"It was different from what I thought it would be. I was different."

"How so?"

"I'm not sure. But you can see it in the wedding pictures."

Pia's lips felt flat and smooth. She wasn't sure suddenly if she was speaking English or the forgotten French that had come back to her, but she heard herself telling Dalphine how the photographer followed a few steps behind the long train of her gown, which was whiter than perfect blindness. She and Edgar stood like mannequins, repeated the vows as dictated by the priest. So much ceremony. It seemed to last forever. The dress seemed to be getting heavier, and Pia hungrier, thirstier every minute. She'd gotten so little sleep the night before, her legs quaked with fatigue. And then Barret lifted the veil from her face. No, *Edgar*. Edgar did. And she tasted the act of being kissed. And then she was different. And yes, the pictures showed this. The pictures she kept in a large white photo album with ornate gold lettering. OUR WEDDING DAY. Where was it? Pia felt a stab of panic. Did she still have it? She would have to go home and find it, because Dalphine was saying oh yes, do, I'd like to see it.

There was endless posing at the church, a conscious effort to create a history. Family of the bride, family of the groom, wedding party, bride alone, bride with the flower girl, flower girl with the ring bearer. At the reception, she and Edgar held magnums of champagne, smiling for the photographer. Kissing for the photographer. Feeding each other cake for the photographer. It amazed Pia when she realized how much of a wedding day is staged portraiture instead of life genuinely lived.

The photographer was a wiry, wizened little Romanian man hired by Edgar's father. His glasses were perched on his thin, oily nose and kept clicking against his camera. He clenched a cigarillo between his angled, yellow teeth. And he never took it out of his mouth while he was giving orders, commanding everyone in the wedding party to turn this way, touch hands like so, smile toward the ice sculpture. Smile. Press closer in. Don't blink.

Dalphine poured more sake, and Pia drank hers in one sharp swallow.

"Everyone was talking and laughing and glasses were raised and dinner was served. But the whole time Edgar was . . . he was methodically inching my skirt and the undersilk up under the table. And then he moved his hand between my thighs."

"Ah, like a cat through a silk curtain." Dalphine smiled, creating the gesture with her hand beneath the corner of the tablecloth.

Pia had to laugh. "It wasn't quite that poetic. It was . . . youthful. Edgar was always puppying. It was nothing obscene or anything. Everyone from the head table had sort of gone off to dance or whatever. We sat there together. The table and the flowers and the billows of the dress were hiding my lap. My aunt came over, all happy and weepy and powdery in this awful lavender chiffon dress, saying how we'd be starting a family soon, and what a lovely couple, and then she asked me if I was feeling all right, and I said oh yes, fine. And she said a little too much champagne, maybe? And I said yes, too much champagne. And as she walked away, Edgar . . . with just one finger . . ."

"Ah," said Dalphine, "but undoubtedly the best one."

"And I made this *noise*—it was—oh, Lord, it was like a *hiccup* or something!"

"Oh no!" Dalphine's long laughter shimmered against the exposed beams overhead.

"He laughed and laughed. And he gave me a sip of his champagne and pushed a little piece of cake between my lips with his finger, and I tasted myself mixed with champagne and sugar. And I asked him, do you think it's acceptable for us to leave? But he said of course not. We haven't danced."

"And so you danced?"

"Yes."

"And it was an exquisite form of torture."

"Yes." Pia closed her eyes, accepting the loss of balance. "And finally the car came. A long white limo with flowers and ribbons and cans dragging on strings. I went up and put on my white suit for traveling. And to surprise him . . . I wasn't wearing any . . . anything. Underneath. So I came down the stairs with my legs as close together as possible, my flowers and hat in front of me. And that's when the pictures were taken."

"The ones where you're different," Dalphine said.

"Yes."

"So the Romanian, he saw your secret?"

"I don't know how he could have, but . . . yes. He was leering at me. And I noticed that, um—not that I was looking! I wasn't! But it was very noticeable. He was obviously . . ."

"Enchanted?" Dalphine sweetly suggested.

Pia nodded. "Very much so. I couldn't imagine what might have affected him that way. Until I saw the pictures."

"He witnessed your awakening. *Documented* it," Dalphine said with genuine awe. "What an extraordinary thing to have done."

"Yes."

"And so . . ."

"And so . . . there was birdseed instead of rice, of course."

"Of course."

"And I threw the bouquet and all the girls leaped for it. And I got a little annoyed because Edgar—well, I thought he was looking at my sister Lily. She's quite well endowed, and the bridesmaid dresses were fairly low cut. Fitted, not ruffled. Lily absolutely refused to wear anything she called 'poofy' or 'chiffonny' or 'Snow Whitey.' Edgar said they looked like jazz singers instead of bridesmaids. They wore these sea-green satin, split-up-the-side gowns. I know it sounds tacky, but really, they looked beautiful. Lily especially."

"You didn't worry that she was more beautiful than you?"

"She is. But not in any way Edgar cared about. I was just being silly. Nervous, I guess. When we got to the curb, Edgar looked at me, and he inhaled this great big breath and smiled this enormous, grateful, completely *in love* smile and pulled me into the car, and the moment the door closed, he was kissing me, telling me how wonderful and lucky and happy he felt. And he moved his hands down over my body and up under my skirt."

"And surprise!"

"Yes," Pia laughed. "He was very surprised."

"But very glad?"

"Oh, very. Yes. He pushed my legs apart and pulled my hips to the edge of the seat. He covered my lap with his coat and got under it like a tent, and—oh, I had no idea it was going to feel like that. Like being *consumed*. And after a few minutes, as I'm feeling these intense waves of . . . of . . . just wave on wave of *intensity*—I started laughing, because—you know that mirror that comes up between the driver and the long cabin of the limo? Well, the reflection—it was actually sort of comical." Pia giggled in a girlish way. "There's me grasping at the upholstery and Edgar's head sort of bobbing away under this tent."

"Bobbing for cherries," Dalphine interjected, but the classical shape of her dialect and the reverent tone of her voice made it a gentle metaphor instead of the crude joke Pia would have cringed at had anyone else in the world said those same words.

"I threw his coat aside and worked my jacket off my shoulders, and I tried to pull the silk top up, but he stopped me. He tried to push my legs together, and when I asked why, he said—he said it was because of that mirror. It looks like a mirror, but it's just tinted glass. You can't see through it, but the driver can. For safety reasons. For liability or whatever. He knew this, because his friend—the best man—he owned the limo service. And his friend was driving us. As a wedding gift. So this was someone in our life. Not some stranger we would never see again. Edgar knew I would be humiliated later, when I realized that. So he told me to stop."

"He sounds like a good man, your Edgar. A decent man."

"*Yes*. Oh, he was, wasn't he? And I loved him so much for that," Pia said, still feeling it. "I loved him so much that . . . I didn't stop. I wrenched his trousers open and down like . . . like when they do that trick, you know? That sleight of hand where they whisk away the tablecloth and leave the wine bottle standing."

Pia and Dalphine both laughed at the analogy.

"I had touched him before," Pia said. "Obviously, I had seen him and touched him. But I guess I was always focused on not feeling, because I never felt how . . . I can't even think of words for it. Incredibly smooth skin over living, bone-hard muscle. I took it in my mouth in its *entirety*—I mean—just *took* it . . . and Edgar didn't hold my head down, but he tangled his fingers in my hair." Pia's hand went to the nape of her neck, feeling the loss of that tangled touch and of Edgar and of their life with a new keenness. "I was on my knees. With my back toward that window. I pulled my skirt up around my waist. It was a feeling entirely different from and far beyond nakedness. To feel his friend seeing me as . . . as I was . . ."

"Claimed?" Dalphine said.

"Yes!" Pia agreed emphatically. "That's it exactly! *Claimed*. I mean, isn't that what a wedding is? This public *claiming* of each other? And by waiting, we made it be that. Honestly, I don't think the intensity would have been there if we'd been having sex all along."

"True." Dalphine nodded and poured a bit more sake.

"Oh, I wish I had a picture of that in my wedding book." Pia took her cup between her palms, trying to feel some echo of warmth through the porcelain. "I wish I could see what Edgar was seeing in that mirror. What his friend was seeing through the window. Edgar took hold of my arms, thrusting his hips, pushing against my soft palate. And I could taste . . . you know those first early drops you can always taste?"

"Salty, milky. Sometimes the slightest hint of whiskey."

"Yes. Yes, exactly. And then you know there's going to be this amazing burst of . . . of energy and power and future and . . . *something*. Everything. Life. I wanted to drink it all in, but before he—before that happened, Edgar pulled me up onto his lap. He took off my shoes. Set my feet on either side of him. And then very, very tenderly—being so careful not to hurt me—he held my hips and let me—"

The phone jangled at the back of the store.

"*Oh God!*" Pia's hands startled up from her lap, knocking her cup onto the rug. She covered her mouth with one hand and dabbed at the spilled sake with the other. "*Oh, my God!*"

"It's all right, *chitta*, it's all right." Dalphine quickly knelt beside her, rushing to reassure her, trying to take the napkin from her hands. "Honestly, sweet. Don't mind that. It's nothing."

The phone continued jangling.

"Ignore it. We're not here!" Dalphine sang out a little too larklike. "I'm sorry, whoever you are, we simply don't exist this afternoon!"

There was an ineffective tussle of napkins and dishes and hands between them.

"Ah, *shatisse*! That must be our incredibly rude caller again," Dalphine said when the phone refused to be ignored. "With the worst possible timing. Pia, *fertito*! Stay right there."

"No, please—go ahead and answer," said Pia. It was as if the telephone were ringing directly against the back of her skull. Inside her chest, the sharks were rising. "I have to go. I shouldn't be here. I have to go."

"Pia, don't be silly. For heaven's sake!"

Dalphine scrambled to her feet and started toward the back of the store.

"Stay!" she called over her shoulder. "I'll be right back."

Pia struggled to breathe. She stumbled to the coat tree and dragged her scarf from the snarled brass limb. The sake and Paxil tangled around her brain stem. She just needed to be in her quiet house—in the calm, in the whiteness—but then she realized that place no longer existed.

"Pia!" Dalphine called, caught between the jangling phone and the jangling bells on the front door. But the corridor was closing, narrowing. Pia knew she had only a few minutes to get to the train.

Pia was sleeping when Barret got home, and a heavy amber headache was waiting when she opened her eyes.

"Hey, beautiful dreamer," Barret said.

Pia sat up, and the ache moved from the front of her skull to the base of her neck. She tried to smile at him.

"This is different," he said, fingering the peridot necklace, which had left deep red impressions on the side of her neck. "What happened to your pearls?"

"They're in my purse, I think."

"You think?"

"I was just trying these for today. I thought I'd try something a little more . . ."

Pia could see by Barret's expression that whatever she was trying for, she'd failed. She thought that maybe with a black dress they'd look a little less out of place, but Barret studied them all during dinner with a look that shifted between perplexed and almost amused.

"Would you stop looking at— *What!* Do you want me to take them off?" Pia finally asked in annoyance. "For God's sake."

"I'm sorry," Barret said. "Do you really think they suit you?"

"Don't you?"

"Well, your style is more classically tailored, and these—well, not to put too fine a point on it: they're gaudy, Pia. They look gaudy and cheap." He laughed out loud. "It's not as if I haven't given you the real thing! You've got enough expensive jewelry that you don't need to wear cheap costume—"

"Oh, they're not!" Pia rushed to reassure him. "I have the appraisal with the receipt, Barret. They're absolutely genuine. The diamonds and peridots are perfectly cut and the setting is in exquisite condition for something from this era. They valued the ensemble at six to nine—"

Pia caught herself, but not soon enough.

"Please, tell me you were about to say the word *hundred*," said Barret.

Pia felt her eyes growing round and dry.

"*Six to nine thousand?* Pia, good God!" Barret coughed. "What did you pay for them?"

"Well, not . . . not nine." Pia put her hand to her neck as if to protect their fading value. "She made me an excellent price on them. Well within the range of the appraised value."

"Oh, honey. Oh, my God. I'm stunned. I'm . . . I'm *flabbergasted*. And I have never once in my life used that word."

Pia struggled to recover some of the weight and color she'd felt when Dalphine first fastened the silver clasp behind her neck.

"Barret, I can return them if—"

"Well, I would hope to Christ!"

Pia flinched, and hearing himself bark, Barret took her hand and apologized.

"I'm sorry. I didn't mean to bite your head off." He brought his hand to her cheek and stroked the side of her face with his fingertips. "All right? I'm sorry. But Pia, be reasonable."

"I'll take them back on Monday," Pia promised. "I was planning to return them, Barret. I never intended to keep them."

"All right. Well, you go ahead and do that, and then next time I come home, we'll go together and pick out something that's a little more realistic price-wise and a little better suited to the image you want to present."

Pia nodded and smiled. She went upstairs and put the necklace and cuffs in an abalone box Dalphine had sent along to store them in on days when the weight and color were too much for Pia to carry. Like now.

"Did Dalphine put the necklace on you?" Barret whispered in her ear later that night.

"Yes."

"Did you like that? When she touched your neck?"

"Yes." She turned toward Barret, her lips very close to his. "In the back of Dalphine's shop," she whispered, "there's an apartment with a beautiful antique bed. She and her lover bought it at an estate auction. And during the bidding, he was touching her. Very discreetly, of course. He was a very decent man. He would never have embarrassed her in public. But even his fingertips on the back of her neck . . . on the soft skin of her forearm . . . he drew a pattern on the palm of her hand that made her think of all the incredibly intimate things they would do together in that bed. The bidding went higher and higher, but he didn't care. She wanted the bed, and he wanted to please her. He wanted that very intimate place to be perfect for her. He was willing to give anything, spend everything he had, if necessary, just to have her in that bed. And that made her feel so precious. So cherished. She let go of all her pride and fear. She let him tie her hands. She let him take . . . everything. She wanted to be stolen and used. Whipped like a horse and cleaved like a diamond. She wanted sensation. She wanted evaporation."

Lily

(1604 days)

So they came and got me for a visitor this morning, and I run like an idiot, 'cause I'm so excited. Nobody has visited me since Schickler brought the divorce papers like a thousand years ago. I'm thinking, "Sonny! It's gotta be Sonny! You big old dear old bro!" because Pia promised to never set foot in this place. And then I think no, it's gotta be King! He still loves me. I'm his shenanigan girl, right? So I'm skipping up the stairs like a friggin' pixie. I'm giggling like a goddamn crack monkey. I get up there and—what the fuck? It's ASS CLOWN!

ME: What the fuck?

AC: (through the glass) Pick up the phone.

ME: (picking up) What the FUCK!

AC: I know. I know, OK? But at least I'm somebody, right? You were always saying how you never got a visit, so just, you know, sit down and enjoy the visit, OK?

ME: What the fuck are you doing here?

AC: I need to talk to you, Lily. Please, sit down for a minute and let me talk to you.

ME: (not sitting) I don't know what kind of "Women in Chains" B-movie delusions you've been beating off to, but you can fucking forget it!

AC: Please stop saying "fuck" so much. Geez.

ME: Fuck you! What the fuck do you think those women are going to fucking do to me if they fucking see you in here, you garden tool?

AC: Nobody will even notice if you stop yelling! Just sit down and pretend I'm your boyfriend or something.

ME: Oh, there it is! Let's play Baby Doll Prisoner and Biff the Boyfriend. Let's play Bikini Girl and Mr. Lifeguard. Let's pretend I'm the surly Serving Wench and you're Master of the Joust!

AC: Would you please keep your voice down? Geez! Just sit. Please. The guard keeps looking over here, and if you don't sit down—

ME: (sitting) Whatthefuckever, pal.

(About ten years of awkward silence.)

AC: Maybe the conversation would go better if we, um . . . talk?

ME: About what?

AC: (with big stupid grin) Whatthefuckever.

ME: I thought you moved off somewhere to teach comp lit.

AC: I did. Well, I moved, that is. I'm in this Big Tex Burger franchise with two of my brothers. In Dallas. I do teach part-time, though. As a volunteer at a community college. ESL. English as a second language.

ME: Hey, hey. Way to put those grand McPrinciples into action.

AC: Yeah. So. I just wanted to see how you're doing.

ME: I'm doing fine. Mission accomplished. B'bye now!

AC: Lily, c'mon. I mean, OK. Fine. It's weird that I came. I'll concede that. But I just . . . I always liked you. You're not like the other women in here.

ME: Yes, I am. I am exactly like them. Why do you think they need numbers to tell us apart?

AC: You're smart and funny and educated. You don't belong in here.

ME: Danitra is smart. Rachel is funny. Kay worked on Wall Street. Do they belong in here?

AC: Well, Kay probably does.

ME: I'm not laughing.

AC: Yes, you are. You're laughing on the inside.

ME: (not laughing) I killed someone. A little girl.

AC: I know.

ME: Then you know I belong in here.

AC: That's what you did, Lily. It's not who you are.

ME: Who I am is a murderer. Even after I get out of here, this is exactly where I will always belong.

AC: May I tell you something, Lily?

ME: Like I have a choice? I'm in prison, pinhead.

AC: When I was thirteen years old—thirteen plus two days, actually—my dad took my brothers and me on this deer-hunting trip. Because of my birthday, right? And so . . . we got to Minnesota. And we're all pretty excited. Me and my brothers. And . . . so . . . ah, God. This is hard.

ME: Don't tell me. You killed Bambi.

AC: No. I um . . . I killed my brother.

ME: Oh, screw you. I do not want to hear this.

AC: I shot my little brother in the head, and he died.

ME: I said I don't want to hear it!

AC: He was facedown on the ground, but the um . . . the exit wound . . . it was pretty significant, and when my dad—

ME: Shut up, Ass Clown! I mean it! Just SHUT. UP!

AC: My family was destroyed, Lily. I was totally isolated by the blackest, ugliest brand of guilt. My whole life I was alone with that. I had resigned myself to it, Lily. I had accepted that I was going to spend my entire life guilty and angry and alone in the dark, because no one else could ever know what it is to be imprisoned by sheer, unrelenting remorse. And then a couple years ago, I escorted you to your parole hearing. And when I heard you tell what happened, I was like . . . oh, geez, I was like Finally! Finally, there's one other human being on the planet who knows what this is! Lily, you think you're all alone. You're not! I know how you—

ME: Oh, don't even! Don't you dare say you know how I feel, because I don't feel a goddamn thing. All that parole hearing stuff is just me trying to get the hell out of here. And don't say I know how you feel, because I don't give a crap.

(He sits there looking at me with this stupid twitchy expression.)

ME: Oh, for the love of—what! What do you expect me to say here? I'm sorry for your brother, OK? That is a horrible tragedy. I'm sorry for you. Really. But if you're looking for someone to tell you it's not your fault—

AC: I'm not.

(He just sits there giving me this watery-eyed kicked puppy face.)

ME: Look, my time is almost up.

AC: OK.

ME: So . . . I'm sorry and . . . thanks for stopping by and . . . I'm very sorry.

AC: Lily, wait.

ME: I have to go.

AC: Would it be okay if I write to you?

ME: No. No, that is not a good idea.

AC: You don't have to write back, but I would like it very much if you did. And I won't use up your phone calls if you don't want me to, but if it's OK, I would like to come see you again.

ME: Hello? Earth to Ass Clown! You don't come back and date people you used to strip-search.

AC: Hey, I never strip-searched you! I never even looked!

ME: You chained me to my bus seat!

AC: You threw Anna Karenina at my head! Tolstoy, man! That hurt!

ME: You sprayed me with a fire hose! You confiscated my tampons!

AC: Oh, go ahead. Dredge up every little thing, but I'm over it. And I'm better than nobody, right? Better than sitting in your room.

ME: My room? My ROOM?

AC: Your cell. Your cubicle. You know what I mean. I'm not pretending it's anything but what it is. I know what it is, Lily, and if you—

ME: Stop calling me Lily! You do not say my name.

AC: (so soft in the stupid phone thing) Lily. You hear me? Lily, and Lily again, and Lily until you believe me.

ME: Stop it.

AC: Lily of the Valley . . . Lily of the Field . . . Water Lily . . . Whisper Lily . . .

ME: (coming undone because it's been so long and I can't stand it and I'm scared) Please don't do this. I can't do this. Not in here.

AC: Tiger Lily . . . Day Lily . . .

ME: (crying and hating him because his hand is on the glass and my hand is on the glass and the glass is thick with guilt and hard time and I am untouchable) Fuck you fuck you fuck you . . .

AC: They're telling me to go, Lily.

ME: Fuck you, Ass Clown!

AC: My name is Cabot Wray Armstrong. Look for letters from Cabot Wray Armstrong.

So now I'm wrecked. Wrecked, racked, rocked, rolled over. And I was doing so well lately. I was doing fine.

Pia

They had dinner out. With *friends*, Pia told herself sternly. Jenna was just a friend now, not her boss. And Jenna's husband, Fakar, was just an acquaintance, not someone they'd all seen humiliated by Barret on cross-examination on three separate occasions. Pia focused on recasting the evening this way as they drove to the restaurant. She was dressed in her most pleasant self, purposely not wondering why Jenna had been so persistent about getting together, not thinking about how Jenna's husband must have reacted to himself and Barret being included.

Barret was not bothered by any of it. Eclipsing any discomfort he may have felt was his unabashed thrill at the idea of Pia being willing to go out at all. She hadn't quite realized how it must have been for him, trapped in the corridor with her all this time. Not until those seemingly rigid boundaries had begun to soften lately. One evening a few months earlier, she had taken a walk with him. To the park. She'd gone with him to a movie the following week. Then a play. She struggled to stay awake through the opera another night, but the medication eventually won out, and she awoke at the end of the third act with her head on Barret's shoulder, Violetta dead on the stage floor, and the rest of the audience on their feet shouting. So now she was going out to dinner. She was out. And with only a moderate amount of turbulence.

"Pia, we haven't had a chance to catch up in so long," Jenna said after they ordered drinks and appetizers. "Tell me what you're working on."

"I'm doing copy editing," Pia said.

"What sort of projects are you involved in? Technical? Legal?"

"Fiction, actually."

"Really?"

"Romance novels," Barret volunteered.

Jenna didn't even try to disguise what she thought of that.

"Pia!" she coughed. "*Really?*"

"Yes. And I enjoy it. So—tell me about Ethan and the girls," Pia said. "Missy graduates this year, doesn't she?"

Jenna said yes and asked about the boys, and Pia tried to make it sound like she knew them, like she spoke to them more than twice a month. Shortly after the calamari arrived, cutting through the small talk with a surgical precision she was famous for, Jenna reached across the table and took Pia's hand.

"Okay," said Jenna. "Here it is. We need you back, Pia. We need your energy. We need your brains. We need that indefatigable, eagle-eyed, God-is-in-the-details thoroughness. We need your dedication and determination. We need your steadying influence."

Pia absorbed this with a distant sort of wonder that she really had been all those things once upon a time.

"We've got some important work to do right now," Jenna told her earnestly, "and we're ready to do whatever it takes to convince you to join this task force."

Pia pulled her hand into her lap and sat staring at her plate.

"Now, I know you've been going through some changes in

the last few years," Jenna continued. "I don't even pretend to get what's been going on with you. But if you sit out any longer, you're not going to have many options open to you, Pia. I'm going to be brutally candid here. Frankly, I doubt you have a lot of options now. Certainly, you're not going to have anyone else inviting you to write your own ticket, and that's what I'm inviting you to do."

There was a weighty silence around the table. The first one who speaks loses, Pia told herself.

"This wouldn't happen to be related to Chilton Energy, would it?" Barret asked.

"As a matter of fact, it is," Jenna said flatly. "Is that something you're going to be involved in?"

Barret laughed. "Well, apparently there's been some talk about it."

"I don't know what you mean."

"Suddenly, after all this time, Pia is the only possible candidate to head this task force of yours? But of course, this has nothing to do with my possible involvement in the matter. A matter that involves potentially—oh, I'd say roughly seventy-two million dollars. What do you think, Fakar? Coincidence?"

"Look, Barret," Fakar reluctantly volunteered in the soft Nehru accent Pia knew Barret would be making fun of on the way home, "this isn't the first case we've tried to get Pia on board with in the last five years. One would hope that you'd have enough respect for your wife's abilities to recognize what she's given up. And one would hope you'd support her in getting her career back on track."

Surprisingly, Barret seemed to back down. He looked at Pia for a long moment, then reached toward her lap and took her hand.

"It's up to you, Pia," he said quietly. "If this is something you want to do, I'll support you however I can."

Pia felt cold. She started ransacking her mind for any excuse to leave the table, to say they had to leave, to go home, to shut the door, but before she could say anything, Barret cleared his throat and turned back to Jenna.

"The truth is, Pia and I were planning to be in Europe for several months this year. In fact"—he smiled confidentially at his familiar adversaries—"I already told the other partners I wouldn't be able to do anything beyond a few initial briefs for the Chilton case. The Iberia Petrotech matter is my main concern right now, so I've decided to make the Paris office my base of operations this year. And I'm selfishly thinking it would be a lot more enjoyable for me to have Pia there with me. Paris the first six months. Then four weeks each in London, Salzburg, and Bern. Then a month in Spain and another three months in Paris. And when we get back, I'm going to need Pia's help on my congressional campaign."

"Well, that's *wonderful*! I mean, it's disappointing for us," Jenna said, "but *wonderful* for you, Pia. Really . . . wonderful."

Pia nodded and agreed vaguely.

"I'm really glad for you," Jenna said, moving on to the calamari. "It's about time you finally saw Europe. You always talked about going, and Edgar was such a homebody, it seemed like it might never happen."

Pia was still fuming about that remark late that night as she and Barret lay in the dark.

"Edgar never prevented me from going anywhere. And you're not going to force me to go anywhere," she added, "no matter how *wonderful* Jenna thinks it would be."

"Well, it would be, Pia," Barret said to her. "We'd finally be living together."

"We wouldn't know how! We'd probably end up divorced."

Barret didn't say anything.

"I'm sorry, Barret. I like being home. I need to be in familiar surroundings."

"What's familiar around here anymore?" He rolled onto his back and crossed his arms on his chest. "Every time I walk in the door, you've changed something. And it's all this profuse, peacocky, scrolling, flowering—whatever it is. I can't tell if I'm in my own home or some Muslim temple in Uzbekistan."

Mosque, Pia thought, but didn't say it. To correct him—that would be unlike her.

"And that damn ottoman. Every time I try to walk to the bathroom at night, it manages to find its way over to bark my shins, just to remind me how obscenely expensive it was."

There was a silence between them then, a tangible break as cold to the touch as the iron gate outside.

"Dalphine has an ottoman similar to that one in her apartment."

Pia spoke only very softly, but she felt Barret pause beside her, not wanting to let go of the argument but unable to pretend he didn't want her to go on.

"And she has a drawer full of secrets and lace, and in it she has a selection of ivory toys."

Barret rolled onto his side, facing Pia without touching her.

"Sometimes she stands in front of the mirrored closet doors, and her skin is so pale, it's almost blue in the moonlight. She has a pair of black shoes that lift her heels to just the right height so that her legs are just the right angle when she sits on the ottoman. At first she sits with her legs together, swaying her hips, letting herself feel the textured upholstery on the back of her thighs. Then she opens her legs and faces the mirror, and she watches herself, watches her own hand. She takes one of her toys . . . gliding it in and out of her mouth."

Pia paused, listening to Barret breathing. She waited until she felt his hand on her abdomen.

"And when it's wet and ready and she's wet and ready, she eases it inside herself a little at a time. The room is all white and blue and moonlight and it's all there again in the mirror, only distant and unreal, and she watches herself in that unreal world."

"What if . . . what if someone else was watching?"

"He would stay in the shadows."

"Yes," Barret whispered. "I'd stay in the shadows. Watching her . . . getting more and more . . . involved."

Beneath the blankets, Barret took Pia's hand and set it between his thighs, and the bed rocked back and forth slightly with the motion he orchestrated.

"Does she know?" he asked against her neck. "Does she see me watching?"

"No."

"I want her to."

"If she saw you, she would stop."

"No," Barret whispered, seizing Pia's hand, pushing himself into her palm. "No, she won't stop. She won't stop until . . . I'm ready for her. I'm ready for her *now*," Barret groaned, taking Pia by the shoulders, pushing her downward, telling her with no small urgency what he wanted her to do. She tasted the first milky sweet taste and, after a minute or two, the full burst of life. She wiped the side of her mouth on the sheet and let it lie tangled between them. After a little while, Barret leaned over and kissed her cheek, and without saying anything more, he turned his back and went to sleep.

"Your name came up in conversation yesterday," Dalphine said, dropping two sharp-edged sugar cubes in her cup. "A customer said she used to work with you in Washington."

"Oh?"

Dalphine mentioned Jenna's name. The way she said it, you could hear the hyphenation, the whole story of the name, the shadow of context.

"We had such a lovely talk," Dalphine said, and Pia felt a little sick inside when she heard it. "You were sweet to send her to me. She stayed all morning and left with a full set of dinnerware—the Dutch ceramics—and that mahogany display case. The one with the lions."

"Ah." Pia nodded. "Well. I'm glad. That's . . ." She trailed off and just nodded again. There was something bitter at the back of her throat.

She hadn't wanted to mention the store, but Barret had invited Jenna and her husband to come in for coffee, and Jenna gushed over every little item in the dining room, insisting she simply had to know where she could get some of that gorgeous blue-and-white ceramicware. There was nothing Pia could say but where she'd gotten it. She tried saying she couldn't remember the address, but Barret deftly volunteered to go look it up on a credit card statement, and Pia certainly didn't want that.

"Is she a close friend?" Dalphine asked.

"We worked together for about twelve years," Pia said, and then realized it didn't really answer the question in her mind either. "She was my boss, actually. We also knew each other in college. We were involved in a lot of the same things."

"She said the two of you had made plans to go to Europe, but it didn't work out."

"We made plans, yes," Pia said, hating that she was being forced to explain herself twenty-four years later. "The summer after graduation. We thought we'd go. But Edgar didn't want to wait to get married so . . ."

"And you see each other often?"

"No. Barret's firm oversaw a hostile takeover of her first husband's company about ten years ago, so ever since he and I were married . . . it's a little strange."

"How sad. To lose a friend that way."

"She wasn't a friend, really. A business acquaintance."

"Still."

"It wasn't Barret's fault. It was just business. And anyway, she's married to someone else now. A man from her office."

"I'm not one for many girlfriends," Dalphine said, and Pia resisted remarking on that. "It always ends up wrong. And then I have to feel guilty, and I hate that. Really. What a waste of time. To sit there hating yourself for something that's done and over and probably for the best anyway."

Not sure what else needed to be said now, Pia sat on the floor and spread a manuscript in front of her on the coffee table. Dalphine stretched out sideways in her red chair.

"I do love this chair," she said. "It's one of my favorite things. Do you love this chair as much as I do?"

"It's lovely." Pia nodded without looking up.

"I think you should have it. If you love it, yes, you absolutely should have it."

"Oh, no. I wouldn't want to take your favorite chair. And I really don't have room."

"*Tsh!* There's always room for something lovely. It would go beautifully with—"

"Dalphine," Pia said, keeping her eyes anchored to the neatly spaced lines on the page in front of her. "No."

"Ah. Whatever makes you happy, butterfly." Dalphine relaxed back into the chair and crossed her ankles over the curved arm. She let one high-heeled pump drop to the floor, then the other. "Such a busy, busy bee these days. I love to watch you work. Really, we are quite the same, aren't we? I take a piece of fabric, a lamp, a vase, or a chair—I'm not the craftsman who created these things, but I know how to make them seem like something valuable. You do the same thing with words." Dalphine nodded toward the manuscript on the low table. "They're your cups and saucers and gravy boats."

Pia lowered her eyes to the manuscript again, feeling a ridiculous, childlike blush of pleasure, a lifting moment of pride.

"So much red ink," Dalphine commented, nudging Pia's knee with her bare foot. "You must be very precise in your work."

"Yes."

"Everything exactly so."

"Yes," Pia said, wondering what it was in that remark that

gave the blush a slightly bitter aftertaste. "It's the proper way to do it. There's nothing wrong with that."

"Absolutely nothing," Dalphine said. "My point exactly. Why shouldn't it be as perfect as . . . blindness?"

"What? I don't know what you mean by that," said Pia, "but making corrections is what I get paid for, so that's what I do."

She turned over another page. She circled something on the first line and put a question mark above it.

"What's wrong with that?" Dalphine asked, reading over her shoulder.

"In the first chapter, she said the character was twenty-eight. Then here in chapter ten, she says twenty-six."

"Oh, but that would be lovely! If we could start out here—in chapter ten—and grow younger. Think of that. Being as wise as we are now, as beautiful as we were then. Oh, Pia! You should leave that alone. Let her have that."

"I'm not saying I disagree." Pia smiled and turned another page. "But the author can't just have people defying the laws of time and physics."

"Why not?" Dalphine cried. "If an artist can't, who can?"

"Well, she has to be reasonably true to life. It's not science fiction."

They were quiet for a while. Pia turned a few more pages, making red marks here and there.

"Do they always have happy endings? These romance novels?"

"Yes."

"And you think this is true to life?"

"It's part of the formula. They all end with the man and woman getting married."

"So the book is all about how they find each other?"

"Essentially," Pia said. "They meet. There's some kind of conflict that causes them to not like each other, but underneath, there's this irresistible chemical attraction. They're thrown together in some situation where he kisses her. Around page thirty-five or so. Then the conflict gets more complicated. Angry words are exchanged. By page sixty, they're no longer speaking. Then something comes up where she's at the mercy of the elements or a mechanical problem with the elevator or her car or a wild boar or something, and he shows himself to be good and true, but pride gets in the way until someone elderly dies or there's a plane crash and one thinks the other is killed or whatever. She swallows her pride, they confess their feelings, kiss again. And it all works out just the way the dead elderly person knew it would. The end."

"The end?" Dalphine repeated. "But when do they make love?"

"They don't. They kiss. Some imprints allow him to touch her breast, but only after they decide to get married."

"Oh, the poor things!" Dalphine frowned. "You leave them there frozen for eternity all brimming with nothing to be done about it."

"I suppose." Pia made a shorthand squiggle and flipped another page.

"Well, honestly, I had no idea you could be so cruel."

"It's not up to me."

"You know how it should end?"

"Hmm," Pia said absently, making another mark and a notation off to the side.

"She doesn't swallow her pride. She swallows him! They could still hate each other, but have wild, uncontrollable sex anyway. Cheap, unflattering sex in which nothing matters except the basest sort of gratification. Then she could cast him off and make a dramatic exit. Though she would walk differently for a half hour or so, because there was anal penetration, ensuring he would never forget her. Or—I know! They're in the elevator. She has him up against the wall, and she penetrates *his* anus with a toy from her purse. He ejaculates just as the doors open, and there stands *his wife*! What better ending could there be? I defy you. There is no better ending possible."

"That's not exactly what they mean by *romance*," said Pia.

"Oh! Here we are! They should be lovers from somewhere around, oh, say chapter two. In fact, they should leap right in. Chapter one! *Page* one! We don't even need to know their names. They're just two fools rushing in where angels fear to tread. Then by the time chapter ten rolls around, they've done everything you could imagine in florid detail. And then one night—it's summertime and it's raining a little—he takes her out for a drive, and somewhere along the quiet rural road, he pulls off to the side and takes her in his arms and they kiss and kiss and touch each other's skin and pull at each other's clothing. He opens the door and steps out into the light rain. She turns the radio up a little and climbs out with him, and they dance to the music and the rain until her hair is wet and clinging to her neck and her dress is wet and clinging to her body, and then he lifts her hips onto the back of the car, working her dress up around her waist, and she reaches down to discover he's raging with passion. She locks her legs around his waist, and like a bolt into a lock he is. But then she looks over his shoulder, off down the road—headlights! *Faster, faster*, she's urging him. Closer, closer come the headlights. It's an enormous truck—an eighteen-wheeler transporting petrol and explosives and cases of kitchen matches! It loses control, careens toward them. And just as her lover jettisons inside her, filling her with the nectar of his passion, she lifts her face to the rain, lost in wrenching waves of fulfillment—and at that precise moment, they are crushed beneath a tangle of flaming, twisted metal, and so gripping is her climax, so intense their embrace—the two charred bodies cannot be disentangled, but crumble to ash in the hands of the weeping rescue personnel." Dalphine sat back in the red chair and nodded. "*The end!*"

"Hmm." Pia bit the end of her red pen. "Definitely not allowed."

"No, I suppose not," Dalphine sighed. "I suppose if you want to be true to life, she gains forty pounds because she's having trouble with her thyroid, so he fantasizes about the au pair while he's playing golf, and she sees him looking at the nanny's breasts, but she doesn't care, because she knows nothing will ever happen due to his erectile dysfunction, and they both go on antidepressants."

"Oh, yes," Pia said drily. "Wouldn't that be great fun to read?"

"Then my story is better! Admit it. If I was the alchemist making your magic formula—conflict or not—he would take hold of her and she would seize him in her arms and the story would end with both of them lost in mind-rending bliss."

"Well." Pia shuffled her pages together in a stack, realizing that some of them had gotten out of order. "Of course, there's a market for that, and there are other romance novels that are full of—well, you name it! But this is a Christian romance series. The women in this demographic are *nice*."

"I'm sure they are."

Something about the way she said it stiffened Pia's neck and shoulders.

"Not everyone is constantly obsessing about sex," she said.

"Oh, Pia!" Dalphine laughed. "Of course they are! Sex is the essence of everything. Male and female, supply and demand, debt and salvation, the richness of reward and the enticement of opportunity. Sex is symbolic of the balance of the universe. What is it Alexandra Firestein says? 'Life itself is a series of erections and resurrections.'"

"Well, that's fine for you and Alexandra, but these are educated, churchgoing, family-oriented women who've never even thought about anything like that."

"Oh, sweet. Don't be naive. No one loves pornography more than puritans. Because sex is so much easier to be scandalized about than anything else that may be going on in the world. The larger issues of morality leave them so conflicted, they find comfort in prurient matters, which feed the dual need for public righteousness and private smoldering."

"They aren't *smoldering*. They don't have time to smolder! They're doing charity work, taking care of their children. Most of them have jobs. And anyway"—Pia put her hands on the table in a finite gesture she hoped would end the discussion—"I told you it's not up to me. That's the formula."

"Piss on the formula! Courage, Pia! It's the role of the artist to fly in the face of formula, whether it's prescribed by her publisher or politics or the bloody damn pope!"

"I never said I was an artist."

"Then why dabble in it? Do you think you're contributing something to the world of literature with your ridiculous . . . plastic . . ." For once, Dalphine seemed unable to find the right word. "Why not choose a profession better suited to cowards?"

Pia sat perfectly still for a long moment before she answered.

"Actually, Dalphine, this profession is perfectly suited to cowards. That's why I'm doing it. I don't expect you to care about anything beyond my available credit or what sick little fetishist stories you can extract from me, but it so happens I used to be a very brave woman in a very brave profession. I fought other people's battles and stood up to Goliaths, and that work left me with memories of an entire life lived over the phone, a dead husband, and two sons who neither know me nor care to know me. Everything went around the Ferris wheel and came back to me. I used to leave people behind, now I'm the one being left. I used to be afraid to live in my house, now I'm afraid to leave it. And not just afraid like a child is afraid of the dark. I am profoundly, clinically *terrified*. My whole life is structured around the avoidance and circumvention of the thousand things that cause me terror. *That* is my real occupation. This . . ." Pia picked up the raft of papers and flung them against the back of the sofa. "This is just a little something to make me look busy while I'm waiting."

"Waiting for what?" Dalphine actually laughed. "Waiting

for your old husband to stop haunting you? Or your new husband to come home for five minutes? Waiting for someone to tell you that you are a beautiful, wealthy woman who is richly blessed and ought to stop her self-centered whining? You sacrificed your freedom for a false sense of security. Now you find that your cozy little world is a prison cell. You have no one to blame but yourself."

Pia inhaled sharply, and her hand went to her breast. Beneath her palm, her chest felt tensed and cold. The sharks. They were still there, still hungry. Pia pressed her hand against her chest, physically pushed them back to their dark habitat.

"And what are you waiting for, Dalphine?" Pia started tentatively but gained strength as she went forward. "Your next cart of fake Iznik pottery? Another young musician to exploit? Another sweet, dear customer to bleed dry?"

"Pia, my sweet little dear," she said without expression. "I have no agenda. While you analyze and overanalyze and struggle to find a formula for life, I simply live."

"Do you?"

"Yes!"

"Or do you just talk about living?"

"*Ha!*" Dalphine made a short, clipped sound. She sat back and looked at Pia, nonplussed. "I don't know what has gotten into you today. I really cannot guess."

Pia held her hand against her heartbeat, willing it to be constant, regulated, a string of pearls.

"Did you tell Jenna what I told you?"

"I have no idea what you're referring to."

"About Edgar?"

Dalphine shook her head and shrugged.

"Edgar," Pia said, her jaw clenched so hard it ached. "The limo driver. His friend. Dalphine, I know you know what I'm talking about!"

"So that's what this is about." Dalphine smiled. "Your little secret was like your virginity, and now you feel cheap for having shared it with me. Pia, I'm wounded! I wouldn't speak a word! Why on earth would I? And if you're so worried about protecting your little secret, why did you confide in me in the first place?"

"I don't know," said Pia. "I really can't imagine. I mean, I've been lying awake the last several nights, trying to understand why—*why* would I tell you something like that?" She found the courage to meet Dalphine's eyes. "How do you make people tell you such things?"

"What things?" Dalphine asked innocently.

"Private things. Intensely personal, private things."

"Sweet dear, I can't *make* anyone do anything. People have an innate need to confess, and I'm willing to listen, should they choose to unburden themselves. Perhaps they feel free to speak openly about intimate things because I speak openly about intimate things."

"No, you don't. You don't say anything intimate at all. You talk about other people. About their personal lives. You never say anything private about yourself."

"Well, that's just not so."

"It is!" Pia asserted. "In all this time, I can't think of one thing you've told me about your own life. You collect the experiences and private thoughts and intimate details of other people just like you collect your Islamic antiquities and your batiks from Jakarta, and you sell them for money."

"That's ridiculous! These are just sweet, small stories. They can't be used to cast a spell over a person."

"Oh!" Pia laughed out loud when she thought of Barret's bare feet on the Tree of Life rug. "Now, that I *know* to be untrue."

"Pia, honestly. It's not witchcraft, it's just innocent conversation."

"Then *honestly*, Dalphine, why is the innocent conversation never about you?"

"Fine!" Dalphine threw her arms out in exaggerated surrender, then sat up straight in her chair, directly facing Pia, and folded her hands in her lap. "What is it you would like to know? Go right ahead. Ask me anything."

Sitting in the uncomfortable spotlight of Dalphine's direct gaze, Pia felt sheepish and silly. Any question she could ask now would feel like stirring her hand through the dresser drawer of fragrant secrets with her mother standing over her shoulder.

"Hmm?" Dalphine prompted impatiently.

"Do you—I mean, have you . . ." Pia tried to sound defiant but ended up faltering. "Have you ever been married?"

"Yes."

"Was he tall?"

"Yes."

"With dark hair?"

"Yes."

Dalphine looked at her expectantly, one eyebrow arched in irritation, and it was suddenly clear to Pia how hopelessly outmatched she'd been from the very beginning. She couldn't understand how she could have failed to see the strategy whereby her thoughts and her time and her money had been extracted from her. She was like a little child trying to play chess with a master. Pia stood and started to gather her things, shuffling the manuscript into itself and into its box, setting her cup and saucer on the tray, reaching under the table for her purse. She'd kicked off her shoes when she first came in. She stepped into them, retrieved her coat from the hall tree.

"He liked it that my skin was darker than his," Dalphine said.

Pia paused, then picked up her gloves and took a few steps toward the door.

"He liked it that my eyes weren't round like his own. He thought I was exotic. And I probably was. Back then."

Standing in the middle of Dalphine's treasures, Pia hesitated. She held the manuscript box against her chest and breathed short, shallow breaths.

"He liked it that I didn't grow up in America, though my parents were both American citizens. Naturalized. My mother always made a point of mentioning that. They live in a nursing home now. In Chicago. I worry they won't be treated well because they're Muslim. So much ignorance and hatred these days, you know. Their home is on the North Shore. I haven't been able to sell it, but it's all closed up and quiet and what little furniture is still there is all swathed in sheets. Like the women in the country where I did grow up."

Dalphine leaned back in her chair and kept her hands folded in her lap.

"Or at least I grew up in a house in that country. There was a separate school for the children of English and American businessmen and a few very lucky families who associated with them. My parents made sure I was part of that world. My contact with their culture was limited to these huge, tangled-looking art pieces in the dining room. And a small scar. Just a little scar left by the nanny they employed when I was newborn and kept until we left there when I was . . . oh, I suppose I was nine or ten. She did it out of love for me. When I was six or seven years old. To protect me from impure thoughts. To show reverence for the beautiful woman I would be someday. It was an accepted practice in her culture—there was no abusive intent associated with it. No more than there is with male circumcision in the Judeo-Christian culture. To her, the clitoris was a protruding, ugly thing that makes a girl susceptible to whoring and unattractive to men of good position. Especially a girl of questionable family. So she snipped it away with a pair of little scissors. Of course, I had no understanding. I recall being hurt, frightened. There was blood. I don't recall telling my mother. If she knew about it, she never mentioned it."

Without saying anything, without looking at Dalphine's face, Pia let herself sit on the arm of an easy chair.

"When I married, all that haunting, twisted artwork came to hang in my dining room. My husband was an alcoholic. I suppose I knew that when I married him, but I was very young and very much in love. I didn't know that the charming drunk you fall in love with rapidly becomes the wretched drunk you can't depend on when the rigors of the long term set in. Housekeeping, obligations, taxes, and what not. Eventually everything becomes a task. Eating dinner becomes a task. Sex becomes a task. The beginning of each day becomes a dragging, miserable task. And instead of being the adventurous, unfettered lover, you are the bitching, earthbound taskmaster. You're not free or beautiful or spontaneous anymore. You're one of those women you never liked. The kind whose husbands you used to sleep with. You're someone you yourself despise, so it's no shock that you're someone he no longer loves. And he is very aware of this lack of love. Oh, yes. He knows this in the front of his mind. Even when he's too fucked up to know the way down his own driveway, he knows that he doesn't love you anymore.

"The situation became very complicated. It was a bad time for a man of Middle Eastern descent to be in any sort of trouble. He was arrested for beating a prostitute. His beating me was apparently not as offensive to them. There were the endless legalities. Expenses. I tried to help him, but in the end he divorced me and they deported him. He left me with less than nothing. Credit cards. Debts. Things I had no idea about.

"When I opened this little shop of delights, most of the merchandise was from my own home. And my parents' home. They have no idea their house is virtually empty. All these things with which I'd grown up, things I'd received as wedding gifts, things I'd carefully considered and bought for myself, things I'd been given by lovers and by my husband. By other women's husbands. But . . ." Dalphine shrugged, laughed a little, made a gesture with her hands like freeing a bird from a cage. "*Tsh!* I sold them. I felt no sentimental attachment. All these things I thought I loved at one time or another. Every single item had a story attached to it, but now I just wanted the money. That's the way, isn't it? Honestly, it's not rich people who are obsessed with money—it's people who don't have it! In fact, I think it's that way with . . . oh, many things. Money, love, sex, freedom, self-respect. Everything. You don't know the true power of a thing until you're left wanting it. But eventually, you discover it's not the thing itself. Obsession is never about an object or a person. It's about the power of that *wanting*. The way we have of focusing on those things that have been withheld from us. That's what makes a person think of killing herself. Recognizing that whatever she might have in her life, she'll still be missing the object of her obsession, because she is in fact addicted to desire, and that renders all things meaningless. Wealth without worth."

Pia felt a familiar ache in her chest, a void that went deeper than medication.

"We always want what we can't have. Isn't that what they say, sweet? And whatever we're most lavishly blessed with, well, that's the thing we tend to grow weary of. We grow to feel contempt for the most doting lover. We grow to feel imprisoned in the home we've so carefully constructed, trapped in the careers for which we sacrifice our lives. We grow so tired of our own existence, even the lovely things start to sicken us."

Pia tried not to make a sound, but a small sound escaped her. She leaned forward and crossed her wrists over her head, weeping.

"Oh! Poor sweet!" said Dalphine. "This isn't at all what you wanted to hear, is it? Of course, you didn't want to hear about all my little scars."

"I wanted to hear the truth," Pia said without lifting her face from her lap.

"*Truth*?" Dalphine smiled sweetly. "The air is filled with little stories that terrify and titillate us. We embrace whatever fable makes us feel secure and righteous, and we call that truth. But the *genuine* truth—well, that's almost always suicide on some level. To know the truth is to awaken from a dream. We're required to embrace the end of the world as we know it. Is it any wonder we prefer our peaceful little slumber?"

Dalphine set her own cup and saucer on the tray beside Pia's. She stood close to Pia's side, stroking the back of Pia's neck with her cool fingertips and exquisitely sculptured nails.

"You wanted a lovely story about all the luscious cocks and perfect bodies I've labored over and lain under, didn't you? You wanted me to tell you how I'm free to do everything you can't. And then you wouldn't have to feel blessed and anointed by your life. You could cherish all your little scars and stay home with them, keeping them as long as you want, never having to face the simple fact that life goes on. The story doesn't end with the coming of a lover or the leaving of a spouse. It isn't a happy or sad anecdote or an erotic episode, so very nicely contained in itself. It goes on. Glorious. Devastating. Immaculate. Corrupt. An endless series of little deaths and resurrections. There's always more of what you love. More of what you hate. More of . . . whatever it is you're afraid of."

Pia felt Dalphine's breath close to her temple. A tear slid down her cheek, and the trail evaporated, leaving an intensely light sensation on her skin. She was painfully aware that if she were to turn her head ever so slightly, her mouth would be very near Dalphine's.

"Don't cry, butterfly," Dalphine whispered. "We must be like Sappho. 'My ecstasy is in the exquisite . . . I refuse to disappear, to die in the dark. I shall go on living with you, my lover, my beloved.'"

Pia inhaled a jagged breath as Dalphine took the tray and disappeared behind the beaded curtain.

Lily

Dear Cabot Wray Ass Clown:

You haven't worn me down with your campaign of driveling correspondence. This letter does NOT count as writing back. Please don't imagine I am in any way participating in your fucked-up universe. (And where do you get off telling me I say "fuck" too much, by the way? Fuck you if you don't like it.) I just wanted you to know that, even though I was raised to write thank-you notes, I have no intention of groveling with appreciation for the oatmeal cookies you sent. I recognized the Jesus Chicks' recipe with the little currants and walnuts. Obviously, they got it straight from God. First time I ate one of those cookies, I knew it was as close as any murderer can get to heaven. That was years ago. I don't suppose I'm even the same person. But I still love those cookies. So thanks, I guess. But seriously, dude—bug off. For your own sake as well as mine.

With the courage of my convictions,
Prisoner #77373-3219
Cubicle D24***
Partridge Unit***

***Please note the change of address! (For cookies only.)

(1662 days)

Cabot Wray Ass Clown called this afternoon. Should have hung up in his stupid face, but I didn't want to waste my call.

ME: Look, Chucklenuts, I'm sorry you can't find a girlfriend out there in Freeworld, but I don't get contact visits, and you're obviously a friggin' pervert. So I really don't think this is gonna work out to be a love connection, OK?

AC: That's cool. I just want us to stay connected in whatever way feels comfortable to you. Even if that's just me baking your favorite cookies once in a while.

ME: You are one sick puppy, aren't you?

AC: What—because I'm a nice guy?

ME: I am more afraid of you than you are of me, and I'm the one in jail for murder. Do you not find that just a little strange?

AC: It's actually an interesting spin on building a relationship. I mean, people get physical way too soon these days. They don't take time to really know each other before they hop in the sack.

ME: Sack? There is no sack. No hopping. No sacking.

AC: Right! That's what's so perfect about it. Hey, did you get the notebook?

ME: Yes.

AC: Cool. All right. I hope you enjoy it.

ME: I'm sure I will. Thank you.

AC: It's to celebrate your transfer to minimum. Now you can have spiral-bound.

ME: Who but a prison guard with an English degree would get the significance of that?

AC: Happy "You're No Longer Considered a Danger to Yourself and Others" Day!

Dear Cabot Wray Armstrong:

I'm sorry to hear about the death of your dad. I do not have any desire to know you, and I do not in any way care about you, but I do feel bad for your loss. That's harsh circumstances, even when you know it's coming.

It's good you can find things to laugh about when you think of him. I have to admit I was laughing and also feeling kind of choked up when I read your letter. It made me think of my own dad, who was the stereotypical clueless never there kind of dad, but I really loved him. It killed me when he died. I was very close to my mom, too, so I know exactly what you mean when you say you couldn't breathe at night. It's weird how the air doesn't seem adequate to feed your lungs when you cry that hard. When my parents died, it sort of sucked all the oxygen out of my entire world for about eight months. I guess I was pretty much out of control. And that's when ~~the accident happened~~ ~~my niece died~~ I killed my brother's daughter. It wasn't a good stretch for my family.

You know what, Cabot Wray Armstrong? I've been in here 1800 days today. Days with zeroes are bad. Days with two zeroes are worse. Last time I had a three-zero day, I cried all afternoon and threw up all night. And that was almost a thousand days ago. If my hearing doesn't go well next month, and I have to face day 2000 in here—well, they might want to think about rescinding my spiral-bound privileges. There's no telling what I might do.

Really, most of the time I'm OK with it, because I'm guilty and I deserve this. But then other times I get insanely frustrated because—c'mon! What is the ever-lovin' point? Is it to make me feel guilty and remorseful? I do! Is it to make me reflect on what I did? I have done nothing but reflect on it for five years, and I have no doubt I'll continue to reflect on it every day until I'm rendered for fertilizer. Is it so my sister-in-law gets some satisfaction that I've been adequately punished? She never will! There's not enough years or prisons or chains or cavity searches or rancid food or loneliness or getting beat up or hating myself or working laundry or general all-purpose suffering in the universe for me to pay her back. It just ends up being a waste of my life and of her life and now yours.

Anyhoo, this got off track. I just wanted to say sorry about your dad. And I kind of do enjoy the letters about your brothers and sisters and their kids and everything. It's like The Waltons, only instead of the Depression, they've got Milwaukee. I guess if you continue writing, I might write back occasionally. So thanks for the stationery and stamps. Gotta be honest with you—I sold a few of the stamps. Most of them, in fact. All but three, actually. I really needed a few personal essentials, and postage is like platinum in here. I'll pay you back, though. I'm going to be starting a business, so I'm good for it.

Yours in carceration,
Lily

Dear Cab,

Thanks for the King Kong movie poster. I love it. And that's too funny how you got your name. I put the poster on the bottom of Kay's bunk so I can look at it when I'm lying in bed. The first thing I see when I wake up is "Bruce CABOT . . . Fay WRAY . . . Robert ARMSTRONG" and then, of course, a huge ape leering down at me. Good morning, Partridge Unit!

Don't know about you, but I couldn't help noticing the strategic placement of King's middle finger. Interesting. Also interesting: my husband's name is King. Ex-husband. And there were times when he sort of reminded me of a giant gorilla. In a good way. He was basically a good guy. Anyway, I'm telling you—look at it. Kong's second finger is tucked right between her legs. And her toes are pointed, which I think indicates orgasm.

But enough on that. We agreed as one of our ground rules there would be absolutely no talk about sex, and this may overstep that boundary a bit. Down boy.

Stay frosty,
Lily

Hey Cab,

It was so good to see you yesterday. I'm glad you came. Hope the Big Tex brothers managed to keep the burger joint jumping in your absence.

I know I've started my last ten letters with this, but thanks for the stamps. You sure know how to make a girl feel special. Postage! Seriously, that's my connection to the free world. It means more to me than you can know. All my friends pretty much went the way of the wind when I got into this trouble, but I like to drop them a postcard now and then, just to remind them what shit-heels they are.

How do you like these note cards? My William Penn's Fruits of Solitude series. I've read that book about a hundred times since you sent it. Would you believe I made this paper? Don't think this is gross, but I made it out of underwear. (And don't get some creepy thrill out of that either.) I got new ones donated by the missionary women, and the old ones were kind of silky and washed a lot, so easy to shred just right. The fibers are superfine. The binding solution is my own weird little recipe, which I cooked up in the arts and crafts room, which is where I work now, instead of that friggin' laundry. (God, I love minimum!)

Anyway—the missionary chicks saw my Rossetti poem cards and asked me to make some with Bible verses. They gave me a Bible, which is actually a lot more interesting than I remembered from Catholic school, plus this calligraphy book that shows how to do cool letters and ornamental squiggly-doos and stuff like that. They want to sell the cards at this craft-fair thing they have every year to raise money for orphans or homeless people and all kinds of Jesusy-type endeavors.

I'm serious about starting a business when I get out of here, you know. People actually might pay good money for environmentally responsible, artistically funky little cards such as these. And nobody has to know they're made of recycled murderer panties.

Okay, now I know you're fondling the note card, Cabot Wray.

And now you're blushing.

Still life with Plexiglas,
Lily

Dear Cab,

Sorry I couldn't come to the phone tonight. Got involved in a scuffle yesterday and lost 30 days' good time, 10 days' privileges. I shouldn't complain. Kay lost 60 days, and the others are awaiting transport back to medium security.

I didn't used to mind solitary. You can't take phone calls, but if nobody's calling, you may as well be in isolation where people can't mess with you. Nowadays I'm so pathetic—I really live for those three phone calls per week, Cab. You have reminded me that there's goodness and kindness and love outside this place. So it means a lot to me that you call and visit and everything, but I'm concerned that you're investing a lot of money and time and care in this ~~relationship~~ situation, and I'm afraid that might be kind of warped. The last thing I wanted was for someone good and true to be stuck in prison with me. I already had Beth and Sonny and Pia and King on my conscience. Now you.

Also I'm scared about losing my toughness. It's a lot easier in here when you don't feel anything. If you unhinge even the slightest bit, the pecking order kicks in, and the predators emerge, and you wind up in solitary with your cheekbone throbbing, and your lip swelled up, and a hematoma the size of a golf ball on the back of your head. I've worked hard to shut off anything that might disrupt this thick scar tissue I've developed. It was pretty crushing for me when King dumped me, and you can't imagine how much I miss Pia since she withdrew into whatever her world is now. But once I got used to the idea, it sort of helped. The less connection I had out there, the easier it was to be in here. As soon as you start to feel something, King Kong crashes through the wall. He can crush you or eat you whole or rip you in half if he wants to. All you can do is hang there, hoping he has honorable intentions.

I'm not saying I love you. It's not possible to apply "I love you" or any other conventional language to this thing. But you are making me feel something, Cab, and I'm scared it's going to undo me. I want out so bad, my teeth hurt. I dream about peeling my own skin off just to get free. I lie there at night with my hands on the wall, counting pores in the cinder blocks, forcing myself to not know what it would be like if you could actually touch me.

Cab, if things don't go my way at the hearing next week, I don't want you coming here anymore. I don't want you to call or write or think about me. If they decide not to let me go, I just need to hang on to the good time I've accrued and serve out my time. But in order to do that, I need my toughness. And for that, you will have to go away.

Tired and retired,
Lily

Beth

This is not a good day for Beth.

She hates this place. Hates entering and exiting. Hates the reason. Hates Lily.

No one else comes anymore. There used to be the police officer who smelled the alcohol and made the arrest, but he has most likely forgotten about Lily, even if the broken sight of Easter is forever etched in his bad dreams. There used to be the lawyer Pia and Edgar paid for, but his interest in Lily ran out with the retainer. King lasted only a time or two. Now there's just the parole board people looking weary, and Lily looking stricken, and—someone else. Beth doesn't know this man. She thinks at first he might be a new lawyer, but he's not sharply creased like a lawyer would be. He looks rumpled and nervous.

Lily comes in with a guard on each side of her. Beth hates it that they make such a fanfare over it. Lily's hardly a dangerous criminal. She's a faded party girl. A withered orange hibiscus, two days past its bloom. She never deserved the dramatic title of murderess, because what she did to Easter was so much worse than any crime of passion or calculation or insanity. It was the casual dismissal of Easter's value. The eye rolling. The lack of effort. The unwillingness to expend even enough care to bring her home in one piece. The utterly unrepented waste of Easter's life until it meant the waste of her own.

The man Beth doesn't know sits forward in his chair. When Lily sees him, her eyes fill with tears, and his eyes fill with tears, and Beth comes to the sickening realization that this is some sort of boyfriend she's attached herself to. The heat in her throat. This is the feeling Beth hates most. Anger, sorrow, and vomit boiling just beneath her thyroid gland.

The man is Cabot Wray Armstrong. He spells his name and gives his address for the record. He has traveled a long way to be here, and he travels that distance every week, he testifies, because Lily is worth it. He testifies that he is a former corrections officer, who knows Lily to be fully rehabilitated: free of alcohol and drugs, filled with remorse, eager to become a solid citizen. He says he will take responsibility for her, should they decide to be fair and recognize the time she's already served is more than the average sentence for the same crime. He doesn't use the word *crime,* though. Or *murder* or *manslaughter*. He says in *the same situation*.

"She's been in here five years now," he says. "Five hard years. And that's more than most anybody is even sentenced to in the same situation."

Words like that annoy Beth. Just say it. Don't hide behind euphemisms.

Beth's turn is next. She says what she has always said. She says that although she will never recover from the loss of her daughter, she takes comfort in knowing Easter is in the arms of the Lord, and through the grace and mercy of Jesus Christ, she has come to forgive Lily. As she says these things, she looks at the parole board people one by one. She looks at Cabot Wray Armstrong, whom she suspects to be unchurched. She does not want her words to be a stumbling block in the embryo faith of Cabot Wray Armstrong. She wants her example of unconditional forgiveness to reveal the Holy Spirit to him and to the members of the parole board and even the guards who stand with shackles in hand, ready to return Lily to the underworld. She wants her grief to be an evangelism to others. She doesn't look at Lily. Lily is beyond evangelism. Beyond grace. Lily was lost long before today.

Beth sits down, and Lily sits in the wooden chair, and at first she speaks the familiar words. She starts by saying how terribly sorry she is, continues with her hopes and prayers—*prayers*, she says!—for Sonny and Beth, and then they ask her to describe the events of that day, and she starts to speak of the dotted Swiss dress Easter was wearing, how Lily bought it for her just that morning, carefully wording everything to reflect the fact she accepts total responsibility for her actions. But something is different. Lily stops talking. She is looking at Cabot Wray Armstrong, shaking her head.

"I'm sorry, Cab," she says. "I'm so sorry you had to come all this way. I can already see it's gonna be pointless. Because every year, I come in here and I tell this story, and what difference does it make? Look at her sitting there. We could keep doing this for the next however many years, and she'll still sit there just like that. I'm a piece of shit, and she's a saint, because people are so stupid! They think tragedy automatically makes you a goddamn saint."

A gentleman sitting at the parole board table sharply tells her to watch her language.

"You wanna know what happened that day, Cabot?" Lily says. "Because I don't give a crap about these chuckleheads, but you need to know."

The gentleman issues another warning. He threatens to write her up.

"I got sucked into babysitting, and God knows I tried to get out of it, because Easter—oh geez. She was a holy terror. She was a hateful little yeti, I kid you not."

"*Lily, don't!*" says Cabot Wray Armstrong, but Lily goes on.

"God's honest truth? She was the brattiest little shit I've ever had the misfortune of sitting next to in a restaurant. Because *you*"—and she points her finger at Beth—"*you*—Mrs. Nicest Mommy in the World—holy Saint Beth over here, let her run wild. She and Sonny let her have anything, do anything, say anything she wanted, and nobody could speak a word about it because—*oh, poor Easter!*" Lily's voice turns high and mocking. "Easter has a learning disability. Easter is allergic to everything on the planet. Don't blame poor little Easter for smashing Mom's antique cookie jar—she has ADHD and she can't take her meds when she's on antibiotics for strep throat, and she can't cover her slobbery mouth when she coughs, because she forgets! King and me—we were so sick of that crap! He could hardly stand to go to Mom's house anymore, because that little horror flick in her frilly little Polly Flinders descended like a rabid spider monkey, with her hands in the birthday cake and her runny nose dripping in the salad and her incessant whining and tantrums over every little thing. *Aunt Lily won't let me have a frosting flower! My milk isn't cold! Grandma's in my chair!* Would you believe Beth asked my mother—*my mother* as she is *dying* of emphysema!—to give up her chair because Little Miss Bad Seed on Acid wanted to sit there? She was a tyrant! And nobody did anything to control her. You couldn't say boo to this kid without Saint Beth coming down all over you like—like ugly on an ape, Cab! Ugly on an ape!"

Lily laughs loud and harsh, but Cabot Wray Armstrong is sitting with his eyes focused on his hands.

"So I tried to make the day go by as quickly as possible. I took her to the mall, bought her whatever she wanted, which was pretty much everything she laid eyes on. I got her that dress! That dress was just—oh, my God!—she looked like a Polish sausage in it. But she wanted it! So I got it for her. And then I took her to the arcade. I stuffed her fat little face with ice cream and candy and friggin' pretzels from *Pretzel Time! Pretzel Time! Pretzel Time!* Because *it's not the same* if it's not from *Pretzel Time*! I tried to take her to the movies, but the people around us practically lynched me, she drove them so crazy. So we had to leave, and then she had a bird about that, so I told her, 'That's okay, Easter! Don't cry! We'll rent movies.' And we go back to my house, and King is pissed, because he truly cannot abide her in the house. He knows she's going to leave a ten-foot wake of destruction, which she does. She breaks the TV remote, she tips over a plant, she tries to flush a bar of soap down the toilet and overflows it. And *why*? Why, Beth, would she try to flush a whole bar of soap, for Christ's sake? And King leaves. He goes. He can't stand it. So I call out for pizza, because she's just gotta have pizza for supper, and not just any pizza—it's gotta be *Domino's* pizza, because *it's not the same* if it's not *Domino's* pizza! And while we're waiting—listen up now! Here it is! *God forgive me!*—while we're waiting, I have myself a boilermaker. I go, 'Hey Easter, watch this!' And I drop a shot glass of whiskey in a big old mug of beer and try to drink it down before it fizzes all over. And she laughs like crazy, so I do it again, and—honest to God, Beth—it was all I could do to refrain from giving her one, just to settle her down, and how many nights—*how many nights, Beth*, have I lain there wishing I had?"

Lily sits forward on the wooden chair. She presses her hands flat against her thighs, rocking forward and back just slightly.

"So then—a while later, I have a glass of wine while we're waiting and waiting, and then I have another glass, because the pizza's not getting here and it's already been an hour and she's pitching a holy fit, and so I call and say, 'Where the hell is her pizza? You're killing me here!' And they tell me they're backed up, and I can come and get it or I can wait another hour. And so . . . so . . . I'm like, 'Fine!' because I didn't feel—anything. I mean, I didn't even think about how incredibly stupid and dangerous and irresponsible and . . . and . . . So we're gonna go get the pizza. And I sit her in the back of the car and I tell her—I tell her, 'Buckle your seat belt, Easter.' And she says, '*No!*' She says her mommy—her mommy—*her mommy!*—doesn't make her have it on if she has a tummy ache, and she has a tummy ache now, because she's *soooo* hungry."

Lily's breath is coming in shallow gulps now. She doesn't seem to know what to do with her hands.

"But I buckle it on her. Oh, yeah. I tell her, 'Yes, Easter! You have to have it buckled,' and she says, 'Why?' And I say, 'Because I can't stand you bouncing around the car like a friggin' marmot.' And so we're driving to get the pizza, and she's screaming and crying because she doesn't want to be buckled, and she sees—she sees a dime. There's a goddamn *dime* on the dashboard, and she decides she wants it. And I tell her—Beth, I tell her she can have it as soon as we get to Domino's. 'You can have it,' I tell her! '*You can have it when we get there!*' But she wants it now! '*Now! Now! Now!*' she's screaming, and I'm screaming, '*Get back in that backseat and sit your ass down and buckle that goddamn seat belt*' and she's screaming, '*My mommy says I don't have to obey you! My mommy says you have a foul mouth! My mommy says you don't know Jesus!*' And—oh, Christ! I hate that little shit, and I tell her she is never coming to my house again—I go, 'I am *never, never ever* babysitting you again!' And she slaps me! She hauls off and plants one right upside of my face! And I slap her back and she starts—she's just—it's like having a friggin' wasp in the car! And I'm screaming at her to get back in that backseat. I'm like, '*Sit down and buckle that goddamn seat belt, Easter!*' I'm screaming at her to do it, Beth! And she's slapping me, and I'm slapping her, and—and I didn't see that they stopped, because the light turned yellow, but—but they did stop—and so all of a sudden *they were stopped!* And when I hit, the air bags went like . . . like . . . everything just . . . *exploded* and . . . and she stopped screaming and she was just . . . down there . . . and she wasn't . . . up . . . and I tried to see if she was breathing and she wasn't . . . and I tried to . . . to see and . . . and I tried to call like *somebody help me* and somebody came and then they said no, and I didn't know what . . . what that thing was, and I kept saying '*Easter, Easter, wake up!*' but they went . . . they just went like that and . . . and I said . . . I said about my brother, but because I was crying, I couldn't . . . I couldn't say Pia's cell phone number and . . . I told them to call Edgar, not my brother Sonny . . . Father Sonny . . . my brother . . . I go, '*No, no, please, don't call him,*' because I couldn't tell him she was dead. I couldn't tell him . . . I killed her."

Lily rocks back and forth with her arms tight around herself like a straitjacket.

"So . . . that's all. I couldn't *stand* that bratty little pain in the ass, but I never wanted her to be dead. Of course—*of course*, I never meant to destroy my whole family and my marriage and throw my whole life in the toilet. But I did. That is mine. I carry that. But I am not going to carry it alone. Not one more step. I know you didn't mean to harm her, Beth. But you did. You did it to her as much as I did. As much as she did it to herself, that grabby little shit biscuit! She did it to herself, and she did it to me. *She did this to me!* And I might rot in hell for saying so, but it won't be heaven for me unless I can wrap my hands around her stumpy little neck and slap the snot out of her!"

Everyone stares. Beth tries to swallow, but her mouth and throat are coated with grit.

"So fine!" Lily says, angrily brushing the back of her hand across her streaky face. "This isn't what I'm supposed to say to make you guys let me out. And you know what? I don't want you to. *Fuck* you people. And *fuck you*, Beth! I'm gonna sit here and serve every goddamn day of my time. I am going to pay my debt to society so I can walk out of here knowing that I don't owe anybody a goddamn thing."

The gentleman behind the table is on his feet, shouting at Lily that this will cost her, that he's never heard anything so callous as blaming a grieving mother and even a little child for her own death, and obviously Lily is unwilling, even after five years, to face up to what she's done.

She gets up from the chair. The guards surround her.

Beth feels her face attached to the front of her skull like a plaster mask. Only one small muscle at the side of her left eye is able to respond, and that small muscle—too small for you to even know you have it until it flitters like a fly caught on the grille of the car—it twitches independent of Beth's will to be unmoved.

The guards are shouting at Lily, and Lily is shouting back. But Cabot Wray Armstrong sits there. And he looks . . . glad. Yes, he is beaming at Lily as if she just won a spelling bee.

"Tiger Lily," he says in an odd, choked voice. "*You're free!*"

Pia

Barret was disappointed when Pia stopped writing to him. He missed her letters, he said on the telephone. He made a point of telling her that he no longer allowed his secretary to screen his e-mail. Pia tried to write to him, but her hands felt heavy over the keyboard. She tried to use a pen and paper, but found herself staring at the lavender stationery. Across the expanse on which she hadn't yet written, fine threads of blue and red laced like capillaries.

"Did you see Dalphine this week?" he would ask her when they were in bed together on the weekends.

"No," Pia would say, "not this week. Maybe Tuesday."

She meant it. She knew she needed to go back. She had a list of things she needed to return, and another list of things she'd bought and paid for that had never been delivered, because there was no room for them at her house. When Pia stood alone in her living room at night, she couldn't look in any direction without seeing something for which she was going to have to pay. As she lay in bed, allowing herself to travel back over all those sweet, small stories, Pia realized that at the heart of each one was someone needing and never satisfied. They were more about disappointment than ecstasy, really, and when Pia saw this, she realized her own story was, too.

In her dreams, she kept returning to the moment Edgar lifted the veil and kissed her mouth. Only now, it felt like a curtain being drawn from her eyes. The preservation of her virginity was more than a pale scrim that separated them for the sake of propriety. It was the need necessary to fulfillment. She had wanted this thing—this marriage of her life and Edgar's—and now she had it. It was hers. Not stolen or given away, but bought and paid for. Rightfully hers, by a bargain struck between them. Half his life and self for half of her. And when she recognized that, Pia realized what was wrong between her and Barret. Theirs turned out to be such an unequal bargain. Pia wasn't the wife Barret thought he was getting, and trying to be that person had quickly depleted her scant resources. It left her feeling indebted and, after a time, impoverished.

Pia waited several weeks to go into the city again. When she finally went, she spent an hour sitting in the corner of the Japanese restaurant, then took a cab back to the train station. Barret was home when Pia unlocked the front door. She was startled to see him sitting on a chair in the entryway, but the relief of having someone else in the house lifted a heaviness that had settled into the middle of her back.

"Barret! What a wonderful surprise. I wasn't expecting you until tomorrow."

He looked up but didn't say anything.

"How was your flight? Have you had lunch?"

As she approached his chair, she saw an ashen quality in his face that made her stop with her keys still in her hand.

"Is everything all right?" she asked. She could feel a half-smile frozen across her mouth. Her voice sounded hollow to her own ear. As if she were hearing it through a plastic cup on a string. "Barret, you're scaring me. Is something wrong?"

He nodded but still didn't speak.

"Oh, God . . . are the boys all right?"

"The boys are fine," he said. "Yesterday, I tried to get their plane tickets for Christmas. For them to come home. But when I entered the credit card information, it was denied."

"Oh?" she said without any definable expression.

"It wouldn't go through, Pia, because it was maxed out. In fact, it was over the limit by several hundred dollars."

"Well . . . why didn't you just use—"

"I did. They're all maxed out, Pia. Three are well over the limit. So I thought there was obviously some mistake. Some kind of identity theft was all I could think of. Some kind of fraud. So I had the statements faxed to my office."

Avoiding his eyes, Pia put her keys into her purse, set it on the entry table, took off her coat, hung it carefully on the hall tree.

"Pia, what the hell were you thinking?"

"I got a few things for the house," she said carefully.

"A few things for the house? For this kind of money, we literally could have *bought* another house! Christ Almighty, do you have any idea—Pia, do you even realize how much money you've spent here?"

"Barret, it's an investment in—"

"Oh, please! *Please*, don't ever insult me with that again. We both know it isn't anything of the sort. We both know it's pure—it's absolutely—*bloody hell!* I don't even know what it is! I can't even speculate."

Pia sat on the edge of the sofa, her arms hugged tight across her chest.

"How could you have spent this much in less than a year?" Barret asked. "I've been looking at these statements and trying to imagine why you would—my God, Pia, how could you even think we could afford this? I mean, what in *hell* were you thinking?"

He wasn't used to struggling for words. He had to physically step back to reorganize his thoughts, and Pia stayed perfectly still while he paced them out.

"All right. First of all, let's clarify the whereabouts of all this merchandise. Where is all this stuff, Pia? A Chinese dining ensemble for twelve thousand dollars?" He held out his hands, looked around the room as if he expected to suddenly see it. "Three Indonesian carpets for almost four thousand each? And this . . . whatever it is—I don't even know what a *kaidan tansu* is, but I sure as hell haven't seen one around here. And anything this expensive ought to be pretty goddamn hard to miss."

"It's a Japanese staircase, and it was priced well within the appraised value," Pia said, but she was struggling to remember what the price was or what it looked like.

"Well, where is it? Did you resell things for cash? Were they gifts for somebody?"

"No! Some of it is in storage, and some of it—well, not everything has been delivered yet, because . . . because I was still in the process of planning the . . . the process of—"

"I thought we agreed that you were going to return these."

Barret held out the abalone box with the diamond and peridot necklace and cuffs. Pia's breath caught in her throat. She waited for him to produce the tortoiseshell case that had been tucked in the drawer beside it. He stood expectantly. Long moments ticked by beneath the swinging pendulum inside the hall clock. Pia's eyes finally dropped away from Barret's unwavering gaze.

"You had no right to go through my things," she murmured, and it felt like forfeiting everything she'd fought for since she came out of the hospital.

"We agreed," Barret said flatly. "You told me you would return them, and you didn't."

Though she'd turned her back to him, she could feel the force of his gray suit, the straight lines, the creases of it. It was his "power of attorney" suit, she used to tease him when they were first together, when Barret laughed more easily and hadn't yet turned that power on her.

"There's a courier coming from my office tomorrow to take some documents downtown for me," Barret said calmly. "Is there any valid reason why he can't return these to your friend's shop at the same time?" He gave Pia a long time to answer, then repeated, "Is there any valid reason?"

"No." The reasons she could think of would never pass that sort of test.

"Fine, then. That's something, at least. We'll start to deal with the other items tomorrow." He laid the box on the table next to a marbled gray courier package from his office, satisfied with that small concession. "Pia, what's wrong? This isn't like you."

Pia laughed out loud.

"That's your highest form of criticism, isn't it? To say that something is unlike me?" she said. "The thing I can't understand, though, is how I can be so unlike myself so much of the time. I mean, there must be a point where a changed person is no longer unlike her old self, but exactly like the new self she has changed into. I don't understand why you think unnaturally dogged consistency is some kind of virtue. When terrible things happen in your life—that changes you. It *should* change you. And pretending it hasn't changed you is just another form of suicide."

"What?" Barret squeezed his temple between his thumb and fingers. "What the hell are you talking about?"

"Forget it," said Pia. "Never mind."

"Forget it? That's your answer?"

"I'm sorry, Barret! I am terribly sorry! What else do you want?"

"I want to know what the hell is going on!" He threw the statements on the table beside her things. "I can see from these records that you were in the city, buying something at this store, several days a week for four months. I can tell you stopped seeing Dr. Ackerman long before we decided you were ready to discontinue treatment—a decision I sure as hell don't feel very confident about at the moment. Virtually every day I wasn't home, every day we talked on the phone and you told me you were here all day or at the movies or the library, you weren't. You were at this *place* with this woman. And . . . and my God, you must practically own the place by now! Is there anything left but bare walls?"

"I have my own money," Pia flared. "It's not like I'm taking bread out of your mouth."

"You don't have this kind of money, Pia. This money was a line of credit I have spent years carefully assembling. You have effectively destroyed the foundation of my campaign financing. And that's only part of the problem. I don't like being lied to. I don't like being deceived. I want to know what's going on, Pia. I want the truth. What kind of life do we have together if you don't tell me the truth?"

He couldn't understand why she laughed sharply at that.

"Oh, that's rich, Barret! That is rich. You want to know what's going on! That's why you manufacture excuses to be away from home five days a week. That's why I have to wear long sleeves and heavy bracelets. That's why we've not had one single conversation about the fact that I tried to *kill myself*, Barret! Yes, I did! Don't look away! *I tried to commit suicide.* If you're so keen on truth, why do you refer to it as an *accident* on those rare occasions when you can't altogether avoid acknowledging that it ever happened? You keep asking me to go with you here and there, even though you know I *can't* go. You've known all along that I was incapable of going, but it doesn't fit with your idea of the perfect congressman's wife. You want to be married to someone who looks nice in campaign ads, someone whose job history of tilting at windmills lends a whiff of political correctness to your job history of environmental rape and pillage. You don't want to be married to someone who's scarred and debilitated, so you gloss over it with your romantic invitations and your grandiose travel plans." Pia laughed out loud again, but it was a coarse, joyless sound. "You don't want the truth, Barret. There hasn't been a day since you met me that you didn't prefer fairy tales over truth."

Barret stood looking at her as if she were a stranger. The abalone box seemed to anchor them in the entryway, while every fiber of each of them wanted to be somewhere else. The pendulum dragged a long minute across the face of the clock.

"Barret, if we could . . ." Pia began, but he turned away as soon as he saw he'd won. The first one to speak loses. Pia knew this simple rule from years of negotiations, but she could never get around it with Barret.

"I'm going to have to ask you for your credit cards, Pia. And please—*please*—just give them to me. Don't make this any harder for either of us."

Pia opened her bag and took out the cards he knew about. Her fingertips brushed over the ones he didn't know about, and it gave her a vivid, distinctly sexual pleasure.

"The courier will be here in the morning," Barret said before he turned and went up the stairs, leaving Pia next to the landing, wondering what she was supposed to do now. Go to the kitchen and smash things? Follow him up to his office and beg his forgiveness? Or take him to the bedroom, tie him up, and whip him with his own belt? Pia made dinner later, but it sat untouched in the kitchen until she scraped the plates into the garbage. They spent the evening in separate corners of the silent house, but later, when Pia was just on the edge of sleeping, she felt him lie down beside her.

"Barret," she said into the dark. "I love you, and I am so sorry. About everything. From the very start. It was never fair to you. I shouldn't have married you, and I knew that."

"Pia, don't say that. We can work this out. It'll be a bit of a juggling act, but I'll get it taken care of."

"I'm not talking about the money."

"Shhhh . . ."

He leaned over her, kissed her cheek and her forehead, nuzzled her breasts, keeping the silk of her nightgown between her skin and his open mouth.

"Why don't we let it go until tomorrow?" he whispered.

Several reasons came to Pia's mind, but her voice stayed somewhere inside. Barret found the divide in the gown. When she didn't immediately open her legs, he went back to kissing her neck and shoulder, whispering with his lips against her skin. Pia lay still for a long while, listening to him.

"C'mon," he said, stroking lightly along her thigh. "Let's not have this thing between us."

"This isn't the thing between us, Barret."

Barret stopped stroking her, his body tense. Outside herself for a moment, Pia made a conscious choice to be the first one to speak. She wanted to forfeit. To be won. To speak, in any case, without being afraid of losing. But before she could assemble the words, she felt something smooth and elongated in Barret's hands. The object was no longer foreign to Pia, but when he laid it between her breasts, it felt more stark and obscene than it had the first day she saw it.

"I see you found one of the missing items," Pia said carefully, and held her breath until she heard a low rumble of laughter from Barret. "What do you think of it?"

"I think . . . I like it. And I had the idea that maybe . . . maybe Dalphine taught you how to use it." Barret paused, then resumed a shallow, strained breathing. "Did she?"

"Yes."

"And was she a very good teacher?"

"Yes."

"What did you learn?"

"Oh, a great many things, my love."

Barret laughed again, low and mellow. He teased the object along her jaw, across her neck, down the length of her arm and pressed it into her hand.

"Do you play with it when I'm not here?" he asked.

"Sometimes."

"Show me."

"No. I would rather not."

He got up and dragged the bedroom curtains aside, letting in a wash of blue-tinted moonlight mixed with halogen glow from the patio below.

"Show me," he said, and there was nothing playful in the tone of his voice.

Pia went to the closet and stepped into a pair of dark red pumps she particularly liked. She lay across the ottoman with the heels perched at one end and her head hanging back slightly over the other side. For some reason—Pia didn't understand the actual physiology—this position greatly increased sensation for her and enhanced the effect of the foreign object. But the familiar sensations never came. The effect was lost on her right now, with Barret standing over her like a National Guardsman at the airport, bearing her deceit and humiliation and all the weight of the day like an AK-47. Pia tried for a while, and then she just cried.

"Shhh. It's all right." Barret tugged her back to the bed, trying to salvage something of the moment. He pulled her shoes off and tossed them toward the closet door. "Don't be upset. Everything's going to be all right. Just like it was before."

And as much as she didn't want that, Pia let him cradle and kiss her until their bodies echoed each other in a practiced but genuine response.

"Tell me about Dalphine," Barret murmured against her shoulder. "Tell me Dalphine is here . . . right now . . . in this room . . . letting me kiss her . . . here . . ."

Barret shifted Pia closer to his side, fingering and palming her.

"And I take the toy," he said, "and slide it deep inside her. And I find her perfect little clitoris . . . and I suck her clit until it's swollen . . . and wet . . . and red as wine."

Pia's breath caught in her chest as she felt the ivory and the story and the entire little ritual being taken from her hands. She felt herself fading, slipping into the background, then disappearing altogether. She tried to lock her legs around her husband, but he rolled her onto her stomach and pushed a pillow under her hips.

"She wants me to get behind her," Barret said. "She wants me to take her from behind while she has the ivory cock inside her."

Pia made a small sound, which Barret mistook for pleasure, if he heard it at all.

"She likes it like this," he groaned. "She wants it deeper . . ."

"*Barret!*" Pia whimpered. "*You're hurting me.*"

"*Dalphine!*" he called out from somewhere that would have seemed very distant if not for his iron grip on her pelvis. Barret's pace was frenzied now, forcing a steady rhythm of creaks and groans from the sturdy headboard. Pia tried to brace herself, but she couldn't keep her head from banging against it. "*Dalphine! Ah! Ah! Dalpheeeeeeen!*"

As soon as Barret collapsed and relaxed his hold on her, Pia fought herself free of his weight. He caught her arm and pulled her back at the edge of the bed, but she turned on him and slapped his face as hard as she could.

"Pia, don't be—"

She slapped him again, and he grabbed her arm.

"*Pia!* What the hell is wrong with you?"

"I don't know what's wrong with me, Barret. Why don't you tell me? Why don't you explain it to me? Because I feel like I've been getting better. I think I'm better than I have been in a long, long time. Maybe there's something wrong with *you*."

"Pia, for Christ sake, don't do this. Don't *do* this!" Barret held her back against the headboard. "I love you, Pia, and I am trying my damnedest to make things right."

"By pretending I'm someone else? That's your version of *all right*? I am not Dalphine, and I am not the lobbyist you used to face in court, and I am not the perfect congressman's wife."

Pia yanked the bracelets from her hands and pushed her wrists roughly toward his face. "*This* is what I am, Barret. And nothing is ever going to be all right until you look at it."

Barret turned away and sat on the side of the bed, gathering his equilibrium for a moment.

"Barret, look at me."

He got up and quietly walked to the bathroom.

"Barret, don't walk away."

He turned the shower on hot and stood quietly until the steam began rising. He seemed startled to see Pia's reflection in the foggy mirror. She took a white hand towel from a basket on the shelf, soaked it under the tap, knelt down, and washed him gently, making a ritual of the waxy soap and warm water, kissing the clean skin, inhaling the lavender scent that lingered.

"I love this part of you, Barret. Your most vulnerable, most private part. I love to touch it and hold it in my mouth. You can't even *look* at the most vulnerable part of me," she said, standing in front of him, holding her hands out as if they were shackled. "I can't cover it up anymore. I can't devote all my energy to pretending it didn't happen. I need you to know this. I'm not going to lie about it anymore."

Barret pressed his fists against his forehead, fighting to breathe evenly.

"Here's what you don't understand, Pia. *You're* the most vulnerable part of me."

They stood without speaking, without sound for what seemed like a long time. But then Barret did take hold of her wrists, one and then the other, barely touching them at first, studying them for a long while before drawing Pia out of the harsh light of the bathroom. He sat down on the edge of the ottoman and pulled Pia toward him, holding her hands, kissing the fragile bones, tracing the blue veins with his tongue, then growing more aggressive, grazing the heel of her hand with his teeth, sucking and biting at the scars, mouthing her forearm with the appetite of a vampire, evoking a powerful feeling Pia instantly defined as ecstasy. The sheer intimacy of the moment brought tears to her eyes; it was a fleeting glimpse of his experience of her scars. Tenderness and concern, followed by revulsion, rage, betrayal, profound sadness, and finally fear—a vague, inexorable unease that stayed and scarred everything, even as there emerged a sense of future. He spoke her name, pulled her down onto his lap, pushed himself inside her. Pia kissed her husband's mouth, wanting to breathe his breath, wanting him to breathe hers, fully married.

"One more small story I have to tell you," Pia said, so close she touched the lobe of his ear with her bottom lip. "That day . . . I went to the doctor. I tried to tell him about the new meds . . . that I hated the way they made me feel. Wooden. Dry. I wanted to feel like I did when we first met. Do you remember that day on the airplane? All you did was hold my hand at first. All you did was kiss me right before we landed. You kissed my hands. You kissed my wrists. You kissed my mouth. You didn't even ask me if you could come to my house. We walked right past the driver who was standing there, holding a big card with your name on it. There were no questions or answers or doubts. Only this deeply immediate need to be together. And I told Dr. Heller—I said I needed to feel that again. But he told me I should be grateful to have a normal life. He said feeling is less important than functioning. But it wasn't true for me, Barret. I needed to feel my life happening, even if the price of that was to feel afraid. So I stopped taking the meds. I threw them away. I didn't know you can't do that. I didn't know that if you just stop the meds, all that crazy that's been pushed down under the surface—it comes rushing up to the top of your head. I didn't know what was happening to me. I was alone and terrified, and all I could see was this relentless progression of death through my family. Mother, Daddy, Easter, Edgar. I was convinced that if I didn't die, someone else—James or Jesse or Lily or my brother—I couldn't stand it if I lost one of them. I couldn't stand it if I lost you, Barret. I thought . . . to protect the people

I love . . . but I knew that was a wrong thought. So I took the razor, and I cut my hair . . . to start fresh . . . and to get that wrong thought out of my head. But it didn't get out."

"Pia, please," Barret said softly, "don't make me hear this."

"I didn't want to be alone. I wanted to feel you close to me. So I took your suit. Not a good one. Just that gray one. I didn't think you'd mind. And I put it on . . ."

"Please, don't say any more."

"I laid down towels to keep the mess off the floor. I turned on the water to wash away the blood. And I broke the bottle on the edge of the tub . . ."

"*Pia!*" Barret rasped. "*I'm begging you—*"

"You see, Barret? I wasn't crazy. At the time . . . it all made perfect sense."

He'd softened and slipped from inside her, so Pia moved her mouth to his nipples and down across his abdomen. She worked on him for a while with her lips and hands, then gently but firmly instructed him, just the way Dalphine had described it to her. How to position himself on the ottoman, when to breathe, where he should hold his knees—open toward the sides at kidney level, not straight up to the chest. She remembered how to pleasure the perineum with her tongue and at what angle to penetrate him, first with a finger, then with two, and finally the ivory object, always speaking softly, solicitous but persistent.

"Relax, my love. Here's a little more. All right? A little deeper now. A little rhythm."

Barret became bone hard. He was sweating, clutching his knees. He rolled his head to the side, clenching his teeth. Pia leaned forward and whispered in his ear.

"Say my name."

"*Pia!*" he groaned.

"Say what I am."

"*My wife.*"

"Say what happened, Barret. The truth."

"*Pia . . . my wife . . . tried to commit suicide.*"

Pia allowed him to lower his legs and brushed the tears and perspiration from his temple with the back of her hand. She straddled him, took him in, bracing herself to regulate the pace. With hunger, love, and great thankfulness, she descended on him. And then she let him sleep, while she sat quietly in the corner with a notebook and calculator, forming a plan to put things right.

Part III

The Prodigal Wife

Lily

(2190 days)

I have been in this place six years.
Eight days longer than Easter lived.

(2196 days)

slow cell days crawling
no books no ideas just
haiku and bad food

(2197 days)

HAIKU TO YOU, KAY:
read this book again, and I
rip your fat face off.

(2198 days)

Dreamed about Cab, and he called today. Good mail drop, too. Pia letter and my Lit Classic selection. Walt Whitman Collected Poems.

> I wander all night in my vision,
> Stepping with light feet, swiftly and noiselessly
> stepping and stopping . . .

(2222 days)

Cool the way the numbers line up. And it turns out twos are lucky. Cabot came, bearing oatmeal cookies and Gilgamesh.

CA: Let's move to Mexico when you get out. We'll be fish farmers.

ME: Too hot.

CA: We could get a burger franchise in Montana.

ME: Too cold.

CA: We'd keep warm.

ME: Ya think?

CA: I'm not pushing, but I believe it's important that we spend as much time together as possible when you get out. It'll ease the culture shock to be around someone familiar.

ME: You are so see-through. You are Opaque Man.

CA: You're right. I just want to play stern prison guard and unruly cell block bitch.

ME: OK. You be the bitch.

CA: (laughing, deliciously laughing his beautifully delicious laugh) I could be into that.

ME: (after long silence) You look pensive.

CA: I'm thinking about one time when I got angry and wrote you up, and you lost 90 days' good time over it. If I hadn't done that, you'd be out already. I'd be making love to you right now, instead of driving away from here with this ache at the foundation of my gut.

ME: I'm sorry, Cab. I probably made you do it.

CA: You did, you know! Geez. But at the time, boy, I thought I really got you good. Little did I know, I was actually screwing it to my future self.

ME: Karma, sweet cheeks. You do something to somebody, you do it to yourself. I did it to you, you did it to me, to you, to me, and out into the universe until it comes back to you and me again. Chain of fools.

CA: Sing it, girlfriend.

ME: This is all getting very Buddhist today, isn't it?

CA: Hey, let's be Buddhists when you get out. We'll go live in Hindustan.

ME: Aren't they Hindu in Hindustan?

CA: Montana, then.

ME: OK. Montana.

CA: We'll get a wood-burning stove. And a Scrabble board. Or we can play cribbage. Do you play cribbage? I keep forgetting to ask you what games you like to play.

ME: Bobbing for Nipples.

CA: (glancing here and there, but laughing) Lily . . . geez . . .

ME: Pin the Tongue on the—

CA: OK, stop right there! I mean it.

ME: (laughing, laughing feels so good) I love to make you blush. Man, you blush like a Kewpie Doll.

CA: Yeah, well, I'm going to have to stand up and walk away in a few minutes, and it's going to be embarrassing. And not because I look like a Kewpie Doll.

ME: Payback, dude.

(Moment of silence for payback.)

ME: Hey, Cab? I promise I won't be so harsh after I get out. I won't be so raunchy.

CA: You'll be you, Tiger Lily. Raunchy in all the right places.

ME: There's the time clock. I wish you didn't have to go.

CA: I wish you didn't have to stay.

ME: No sh— I mean . . . no kidding.

CA: Three more months, Tiger Lily.

ME: Three more, Cab.

CA: Stay tough.

ME: You, too.

CA: Just do what you have to do to accrue that good time. Don't lose anymore.

ME: I won't, Cab. I promise. Unless, of course, KAY KEEPS LOOKING IN THIS BOOK AND I AM COMPELLED TO CHOKE HER WHILE SHE'S SLEEPING. GET IT, KAY, YOU FAT FREAKY COKE-SNORTING WALL STREET WHORE?

Beth

This is a good day for Beth, though she doesn't know it yet.

Between the time Sonny gets up to shower and the moment Beth will open her eyes, she dreams she and Lily are shackled together, running across a field toward a high wall. They hear gunshots from above, dogs barking behind them. The wall is topped with a coil of razor wire, and in the dream, Beth feels Heaven on the other side. She falls, and Lily drags her. Lily falls, and Beth drags her. Sonny calls her name from the guard tower.

Beth . . . Beth . . . hey, Bethy?

She feels a warm breeze on her face, and realizes it's his mouth moving softly against her forehead.

"Beth, honey?"

"Hmm?"

"It's quarter after."

"Okay."

"I'm going. I'll see you there at noon, all right?"

"Okay."

Beth is awake now, but she thinks her hands may be bleeding from the razor wire. She's afraid to look and see that they are not.

"Coffee," she decides out loud. And that's a conscious choice between waking and sleeping. Beth gets up, and even though a vaguely unsettled feeling stays with her, she forgets the dream. She will not think about Lily again today.

Sonny is waiting for her at noon. As promised when Easter's grave was relocated, it is a lovely spot. And this is a lovely day. Easter's thirteenth birthday. Beth has brought a cake. No frosting, because they always break the cake up and feed it to the birds. Sonny has brought sandwiches from Subway, two Bartlett pears, and a bottle of wine.

There are two bright red cardinals on the lawn.

"Sonny," Beth says, leaning into him and tucking her knees up under her chin, "why don't we ever talk about Easter?"

She feels him tense against her back.

"I don't know if you really want me to answer that right now," he says.

"No, I do. Why is it?"

"Because, when you talk about Easter"—he proceeds with caution—"Bethy, I don't know who that is you're talking about. You always talk about this perfect little angel. It's as if you're remembering the child you wish you'd had instead of Easter. And I want to remember Easter. My daughter, who I loved—and still love. But I get the feeling you don't want to hear that."

The cardinals are tugging at something in the ground. A small root. A worm? A maggot, maybe. Beth purposely does not follow that thought any further than grass level.

"Would you say Easter was . . . was she a tyrant?" Beth asks. "Was she a horrible brat?"

Sonny breathes a deep sigh, and the scent of wine in it makes Beth want to kiss him again. If only to keep him from answering.

"Well," he says finally, "I wouldn't phrase it that way, but if we're being honest . . ." And then he starts to laugh, down low at first, from deep inside his thoracic cavity, but then it cascades up through his belly and chest and takes over his whole face. "Yeah. She was."

"Sonny," Beth says earnestly, "was she a grabby little shit biscuit?"

Sonny roars with laughter until his laughter is all spent, and then he sighs a great, relieved sigh.

"Oh, dear God. Beth, you know that she was."

Beth nods.

"But that was our fault, Bethy, not hers. We should have done better with her," Sonny says, and his eyes pool with tears. "The hardest thing for me about all this was accepting that I had failed her on so many fundamental but profound levels. Someday, I will have to hold myself accountable before God. I was not a good father. She was my baby, and I wanted to keep her that way. I tried to give her everything she wanted, but I didn't have the fortitude to give her what she needed. In the end—my only hope for redemption is that I loved her."

Beth reaches out to him, and Sonny grasps her hand, holding on to it for dear life.

"And you know, Bethy, she brought me joy. Still does. Sometimes I just have to laugh. I can't feel sorrowful when I think of her. Because she was so precious to me and so true to what human beings are at their very essence. Not being able to hide it—that was her disability. She was angry and selfish and brutally honest—but she was also immediately forgiving and unconditionally loving. And she was vivacious and funny and utterly open to anything and overflowing with this immense relish for all the pleasurable and blessing things about the world. Little things like a penny on the sidewalk—you remember, Bethy? How she always had to grab that penny on the sidewalk? And if it was a nickel or a dime, well, boy howdy, that was really spectacular. Because she was saving up for—"

"*A horse!*" Beth does remember suddenly. "She was going to buy a horse."

"And name it Sock Monkey for some reason," Sonny adds, and when they laugh together, that moment of Easter rises up like a miraculous little crocus out of the cold earth.

"All those things that made her so impossible as a little kid," Sonny says, "those are the things I was hoping would sustain her as a woman, you know? I mean—how many people can generate such a grandiose vision from a lousy dime on the sidewalk? How many people get that much happiness from such a small gift? How many people are that stubborn and tenacious about doing what they think is right? How many people are brave enough to stand up to someone five times their size?" Sonny's voice catches in his throat. He breathes very deeply and leans back against the tree. "I feel bad for anyone who didn't appreciate the amazingly wonderful aspects of who she was, because it made the rest so very worth it."

Beth breaks apart birthday cake for the cardinals. Sonny's hand rests warm between her shoulder blades, and she smiles, remembering a thousand small things she still loves about Easter.

"You know, I realize that whole thing with the flood and the relocation and all the delays and everything—I do know how hard that was for you," Sonny says, choosing the words wisely. "I'm not trying to say it wasn't an unthinkably awful thing to have happen. But I have to tell you . . . I like this place a lot better. You can't hear the traffic at all. And there's a lot more shade. Even the flowers seem to grow better here. In a way, I'm glad it happened."

"Hmm," says Beth, not ready to agree.

"I didn't feel like I could share this with you back then, but . . . that day we were in the office, and Carlos Amada was sweating bullets, and the whole place was this mud pit—I know this sounds crazy, but I got in my car that afternoon, and I couldn't stop laughing."

"Laughing?" Beth says.

"Yes! Think about it, Beth! Every night at nine o'clock, we'd try to put her in bed, and every time we tucked her in, she'd pop back up with some new issue. *That isn't my usual radio station. I don't have Captain Cat. I don't like this pillowcase. It's stripey.*"

"Oh . . . oh, you're *awful*!" She covers her mouth with her hand, but she's laughing now, too. "Oh, my gosh. You're right."

"By ten-thirty I was ready to pound my head against the wall," says Sonny. "And I'd be trying to sound all stern and gruff, like 'God bless America, Easter, you get your little patootie back in that bed!' And she'd be totally undaunted. Thirty seconds later, she's back downstairs. *You hurt my feelings, so now I can't sleep!*" Sonny laughs so hard, he has to hold his fist against his rib cage. "So I'm sitting there in that guy's office in the middle of this Stephen King scenario, and all I can think is, *My fan is squeaking! My nightgown has wrinkles! I need a drink of water!*"

"*Not that water, fizzy water!*" Beth chimes in.

This strikes them both as so blessedly funny, they literally collapse against each other, and for a while, all they can do is lie there, trying to catch their breath, resting their heads on the soft, grassy mound where Easter sleeps, if only for the moment.

Pia

The house sold quickly, and to Pia's great relief, much of the furniture sold with it.

"We were lucky to sell to a family so, ah, *culturally diverse*," the realtor said, picking through a politically correct vocabulary. "They're actually interested in purchasing some of your unusual decor elements."

The new town home was much smaller but very upscale. It was simpler, closer to the city for Pia's convenience, and to the airport for Barret's. It had a spacious living room with a vaulted ceiling, a sterile chrome-and-white kitchen, and a pleasant office with a bay window, where Pia could sit and work on her manuscripts. This was best, they decided, at least while they considered what to do next.

"I don't want to fail at another marriage," Barret kept telling her, as if their marriage were a case to win. He made an effort to be home more often, and every night that he was home, he made love to Pia, deliberately, purposefully, as if to prove that nothing had to change. And nothing did overtly change, which made Pia happy on the only level that mattered to her at the moment.

Pia had her own aversion to the idea of divorce. She was no longer a practicing Catholic, but a belief system that deeply ingrained doesn't simply evaporate. An ambient Catholicism clung to her, along with an odd little memory of the only divorced person she'd known as a child, a woman who cleaned their house. Pia had gone with her mother to deliver a casserole to the woman, who had been in the hospital for some reason. She lived in a mobile home park, and for a long time, Pia thought that's what divorced meant. That you were banished to a strange little village, so that others would not be infected with your disease, and you lived in a house on wheels, ready to move on to your next marriage at a moment's notice.

Pia resumed her twice-weekly appointments with Dr. Ackerman and allowed him to think he was helping her as she forcibly expanded the corridor, step by step, according to the plan she'd made in her notebook.

"It's mainly just airplanes now," she told him. "And curbs."

"I understand the airplane issue," he said, "but exactly what are you afraid will happen if you step off a curb?"

"I don't know. The same thing you'd think if you were stepping off a cliff," Pia tried to explain. "It's the end of the world and you're alone."

"I see," said Ackerman, though he obviously didn't. This didn't bother Pia, since things were going well, for the most part. She was functioning again in a way that seemed normal, and Pia recognized now that normal is a perception, not a reality. So if you seem normal, you are.

There were the credit cards, however. The ones Barret knew about, he paid off, partly with what little remained of her savings, the rest with the sale of the house. But the ones he didn't know about—these weighted her purse like stones. Pia remembered a documentary she'd seen long ago. About the sinking of a paddle wheeler. The hoopskirts and bustles and corsets on the drowning women. This is how Pia felt about the payments she struggled to make each month. She took on more manuscripts—a baby-naming book, a biography of Lady Bird Johnson, a guide to gardening using the principles of feng shui—but she was still unable to do more than make the minimum payments, as late charges and overlimit fees drove the balances higher.

Pia thought of all the pieces she had in storage and, worse, the things she'd never even brought home. To continue to pay for all those items still in the store was ridiculous. To drown in debt because she was afraid to face Dalphine—Pia knew this was beyond foolish. And yet six months went by before she set foot in the store again.

It was early when Pia took Barret to the airport that day. Just after five in the morning. He tried to insist she stay home in bed, because he had to arrive well before the departure time in order to allow for the searching of his luggage and other inconveniences that always accompanied international flights. But she insisted on driving him. She'd finally started driving again, and she wanted to show him how sure of herself she could be. He'd been acting very strange all weekend, nervous and impatient. Pia had to remind him to kiss her when he got out of the car. She watched his straight gray suit disappear into the crowded terminal, and she stayed there, watching, until the skycap rapped on the car window and asked her if there was a problem.

"No," she told him. "I'm fine."

Pia heard herself say that, and she knew she could make it true. She could go to Dalphine and reach some sort of arrangement whereby the charges for all those items still in the store would be removed from the cards. She would offer to pay a 15 percent restocking fee; that was only right. She would make arrangements to sell everything she had in storage, if not to Dalphine, then to one of the other dealers in the area. Then she would purchase a plane ticket and take whatever medication was necessary to endure the journey to meet Barret in Paris. She would tell him she loved him, because she did, and she knew by the way he walked away from her that morning he wouldn't love her much longer unless she made everything right.

A slow autumn rain began falling as she pulled away from the terminal, and the drops turned the windshield to a beaded curtain. Waiting for them to search the car and wave her into short-term parking, Pia gripped the steering wheel, feeling the movement, the rolling motion of the pistons and wheels and gears around her. It still felt new, like it was when she was sixteen and her father sat beside her, barking instructions and warnings, but it didn't stir the shark pool the way it did when she first resumed driving. She hadn't exactly noticed that feeling fading away, but it had. It had left her during the same gradual transition through which the scars on her wrists became part of her own body and the foreign colors from Dalphine's shop integrated themselves into her bedroom and living room and closet. She was shedding the wax layer of skin and fear and bewilderment. The being that emerged felt raw and shivering naked, but also new and clean and very strong. She was different, but she was whole.

It wasn't like her, she mused. But it was her.

Pia took the shuttle to the main terminal and bought the last seat on the evening flight to Paris. On her way to the car, she stopped at the duty-free shop and bought a French-English dictionary, in order to brush up on her vocabulary during the flight. She wouldn't bother going home to pack a bag, she decided. She would buy everything there so it was new and different and foreign to her skin. And she wouldn't wear panties. Because who wore panties in Paris?

She would create a new formula, she decided. The man meets his wife at the airport in chapter eleven and somehow they erase everything that happened between chapters six and ten, and his tongue slides magically into her mouth for the first time, though she's tasted it ten thousand times before, and suddenly it's chapter two again. Like the reader who compulsively flips to the back page first, she knows he's going to love her in the end, because it's taken her ten chapters to become her chapter-one self again. Her body is perfect, unscarred, never harmed by herself or the world. She walks down the jetway, lays her weapons at his feet, and it all ends in mind-rending bliss.

When Pia pulled up outside the shop door, the pewter closed sign was still hanging on its silver chain. Pia knocked. She wasn't entirely surprised when there was no answer. It was not quite nine. Dalphine might still be sleeping. Pia sat down on one of the little wrought-iron chairs in front of the window to wait for Dalphine to open the door. But nine o'clock came, and Dalphine didn't appear.

Nine-thirty, ten.

A sickening unease began in Pia's stomach. She walked up and down the block, passing the store over and over. At one point, she thought she saw a shadow inside and ran over to pound on the door.

"Dalphine? *Dalphine!*"

No answer.

Pia walked to the end of the block and sat on a bench until noontime.

"Excuse me, could I speak to the owner?" she asked a slender young woman behind the reservations podium just inside the door of the Japanese restaurant.

The woman smiled. "I'm the owner."

"Well, no, I meant . . . the older lady?"

"I'm the owner," the woman repeated. "She's just been working here the last few months."

"Oh—of course!" Pia laughed out loud, remembering that while she'd sat absorbed in small, sweet stories, there was an actual real world going on across the street.

"May I help you?"

"I'm looking for a friend," Pia began. She looked over the woman's shoulder and saw Dalphine's boy musician sitting at the sushi bar. "Excuse me. I see him," she said, stepping past the podium.

He looked startled when she touched his shoulder.

"Hello. I don't know if you remember me."

"Oh . . . sure. Of course," he said, but Pia could tell he really didn't. "How are you?"

"I'm a friend of Dalphine," she prompted when he still stared blankly. "You came to my house. In Artevita. You delivered an ottoman. From Dalphine's store."

"Oh. Right."

Something in his expression shadowed. Pia smiled when she saw it, the way his mouth turned down when he heard Dalphine's name. He loved her, she realized. Pia could easily imagine him writing songs about her with the blind, bound devotion of someone very much enthralled.

"I'm looking for Dalphine," Pia said gently.

"She hasn't opened this morning?" he asked.

"No, and I really need to see her." Pia wasn't sure what she was seeing in his eyes. "Is something wrong?"

"I don't know," he said, but with that same shadowed expression. "She just—she called me to come over and move some stuff a couple days ago, and she seemed . . . off. Like she was making arrangements. Taking care of paperwork and stuff. I thought maybe she was thinking about leaving the country."

"Oh, no. Oh, my God." Pia covered her face with her hands.

"Are you all right?" he asked, and put his hand on her elbow. "Would you like some wine?"

"But she . . . she can't be closing the store. I mean—oh, God. That isn't possible." Pia never thought of herself as the handwringing type, but she felt herself twining her fingers and fists and realized that must be what they mean by that. Wringing your hands. Struggling like Lady Macbeth to undo what's been done. Done irrevocably. Done to death.

"Look, maybe she's just sleeping in."

"She's not usually one to miss business hours." The young musician poured some sake into a tiny cup and handed it to Pia, pulling out a chair and guiding her into it.

"Well, maybe she had a late night."

"Stranger things have happened," he said drily.

"Right," Pia agreed desperately. "Right. That's probably all it is."

"Or she could have left town for a few days," he said. "Who knows? It's just the way she is. But I have a key to the shop if that helps."

"Yes! Please, um . . . I'm sorry, I don't recall your name."

"Ben."

"Ben," Pia nodded. "I'm Pia."

"Nice to meet you. Again," he said, and raised his cup toward hers.

"Ben, do you suppose . . ." She looked at him and bit her lip.

"Do you want me to go with you?"

She nodded, and he smiled, tipped the last of the sake into his mouth, and followed her to the door. A bamboo curtain had been lowered inside the front window, and the shop's displays, tableaux, and curios took on a dusty, tired look in the filtered quarter-light. An amber wall sconce had been left lit in a back corner near the glass cabinet, and Pia found her way to it through the maze of antique valets, kneelers, and side tables.

She hesitated at the beaded curtain, but Ben pushed past her to the door of Dalphine's apartment. He knocked, waited, knocked again, then unlocked the door and turned on a light in the narrow hallway, calling her name softly.

The walls were a dark rose color, textured with a faux treatment that made them look soft and thick. Womblike. The hall opened into a single large room, where a delicately appointed kitchenette occupied one corner and a canopy bed and armoire the corner opposite. A conversation area facing the fireplace was equipped with a long, low sofa and two wingback chairs, a coffee table, footstools. Against the walls there were leaning mirrors, framed paintings, and a secretary's desk. Pia took it all in with a breath of Dalphine's sandalwood and lavender scent.

"Dalphine?" Ben called softly.

At the far end of the room, the bathroom door stood open to reveal a white-tiled floor and pedestal sink, toiletries in baskets, a tall mirror. Pia could only see the foot of the bathtub, but on a window ledge above it, candles had burned themselves down to hollow wax shells. Ben stepped across the tile and picked up a red silk kimono from the floor, and when he thought Pia wasn't looking, he buried his face in it, breathing deep.

In the narrow hallway, there was a plain gray suitcase. The kind that fits neatly in the overhead bin, with a handle that extends and little wheels on the bottom. A matching carry-on leaned against it. They were surprisingly ordinary, Pia thought. Plain gray bags. For Dalphine.

Pia went to the secretary's desk and sat down with her arms folded tight in front of her. There was a jumble of stamps and receipts in a fancy tin. A painted cup of pens and highlighters. Mailing labels. Sharpies. FedEx forms. A hastily scribbled note beside the phone. It was like seeing someone you know from one place—seeing them entirely out of context someplace they don't belong—and not being able to put your finger on who they are. Recognition traveled slowly from Pia's eyes to the back of her mind and then seeped through to actual realization. It was Barret's secretary's handwriting. She had a distinctive, almost square penmanship. Pia picked up the note and slowly unfolded it.

Hotel d'Angleterre Champs-Elysees, 91 rue de la Boétie.

If Mr. Mayor is unable to meet you at the airport, a car will be arranged.

Placing her hands flat on the desk to steady herself, Pia let her eyes play over the stacks of mail, the stationery and envelopes. Beneath a manila folder was a marbled gray courier's bag from Barret's office. Inside there was a bank envelope with a crisp layer of cash, a key, paperwork for an e-ticket from New York to Paris. Pia recognized the evening flight number.

She heard herself breathing hard, half sobbing. It sounded like the soft, high mewing of a kitten. She heard herself say Barret's name, heard Barret say Dalphine's. The vacuum in her chest expanded to encompass her head and neck and fingertips and feet. She stumbled out into the store and sank down onto a small wooden piano stool in the back corner behind a large cabinet of linens. Pia hugged herself, rocking, her hand clamped tightly over her mouth.

"Um . . . are you okay?"

She looked up to find Ben staring at her, bewildered. His eyes were large, full of curiosity and compassion, but he obviously had no idea what to say. Instead of saying anything, he took Pia's hand, led her from behind the cabinet, and put his arms around her. She gave herself to the uncomplicated comfort of the embrace, and they stood that way for what seemed like a long time. When she opened her eyes, she saw they were standing in the one small square of sunlight on the floor, a rhombus of colored light that filtered through a pane of stained glass above the door, and she was amazed that something as small as that could make her feel so blessed and anointed.

"Well. What's this?"

They both startled at the sound of Dalphine's voice, though she didn't sound angry or even particularly surprised. Amused, maybe. Or curious. But then she realized it was Pia, and her expression hardened to a smooth mask.

"Pia!" She strode forward and opened her arms. "How wonderful to see you!"

Pia tried to allow the embrace without going rigid.

"And this one!" Dalphine reached up and cupped her hand at the side of Ben's face. "You found your way back, I see."

"Yeah." He nodded, then shrugged and said he had to be leaving.

Dalphine waved and blew a kiss as he ambled toward the front door, then she linked arms with Pia and guided her to the conversation area where they'd spent so many hours.

"Well, Pia!" she said in a breathless sort of way that might have been happy or exasperated. "Pia, Pia, Pia. What a wonderful, delightful surprise. But your timing, butterfly! This is such a shame. I have very little time today. Everything's going mad, and I'm about to leave for a few weeks."

"Oh?" said Pia. "Where are you going?"

"A little buying trip. To Portugal, actually. An estate sale. An extraordinary opportunity for me to bring back some astonishing pieces for very little investment. You know this business. I'm always searching, searching, searching—off on my little treasure hunts. I hate to leave the store closed while I'm gone, but I really don't have anyone I trust."

"What a shame," Pia said.

"I'm guessing you're here to collect some of your things."

Pia nodded and forced a smile.

"Well. Sweet, that's fine, of course. The only thing being—well, as I said, everything's gone mad today. I have a thousand errands and . . ." She trailed off with a helpless shrug, a small giggle. "Honestly! It's such a coincidence, your visiting today of all days!"

"Yes." Pia smiled. "I'm so lucky I caught you. Before you left. So . . . why don't you go do your errands. I'll watch the store, and while you're gone, I'll figure out what I can take with me today, and when you get back, we'll discuss arrangements for the rest."

"You're so sweet, but I couldn't impose."

"Oh, I insist!" Pia cried. "It's no trouble at all. Honestly."

"Ah. Well." Dalphine glanced toward the door, then at Pia. "All right. Yes, that would be perfect, wouldn't it?"

After Dalphine left, Pia went to the back of the store and set Dalphine's plain gray bag on the counter. Thinking of her mother's secret drawer, she drew the zipper around one corner and then the other. It had been carefully packed, the contents neatly organized. The scent of Dalphine's perfume wafted up when Pia unzipped the various inner compartments.

From the largest compartment, Pia drew black lace stockings and some other unbearably delicate underthings, along with a bag of toiletries, a green silk kimono, and some matching slippers. Pia tucked the stockings in her purse, then pushed the undergarments into the trash basket, carefully arranging some wadded tissue paper over them. After all, Dalphine wouldn't be needing those in Paris, would she? Pia extracted a white blouse and black skirt, a pair of blue jeans, and a sweater, but she left the rest—a cream-colored skirt suit and two scoop-necked T-shirts—in a neat layer.

The griffin key chain was on its hook beside the cabinet. Pia took it down and tried the various keys until the dark bottom of the case slid open. She brought out the tray, removed the largest of the ivory brothers—the genuine article in all its illegal splendor—and set it in the suitcase. Then, using Dalphine's clothes and some bubble wrap from behind the counter, she packed a variety of other treasures from the cave. A huge black dildo, a red leather harness with two large protrusions opposing each other in the front and a smaller one bucking inward at the back, a pair of handcuffs with a long chain, some rings and balls of some sort, a leather riding crop with a phallus grip, a tightly wound whip with a spray of knotted silk cords, a nubby palm hummer, a thick vibrating shaft, an anal stimulation wand, a prettily painted wooden spanking paddle. Pia changed her mind and took the lace stockings from her purse. She tied them in a frilled bow around a battery-powered device that reminded her of a two-headed dragon and zipped the bag shut. When Dalphine returned from her errands, it was back on the floor as if it had never been moved.

"Did you decide?" Dalphine asked.

"I think so," said Pia.

Looking around the shop, she had to laugh. *You must own*

the whole place by now, Barret had said, and it was true. Pia wondered how she could have spent so many days here without noticing how many items in the store carried the little yellow SOLD tag. Even after the garage attic and Lily's storage unit were all full of furniture, batiks, tasseled pillows, and potbellied Buddhas, and there was no conceivable way she could actually *have* a fraction of these things she supposedly owned, Pia kept buying more. Dalphine simply put a little yellow SOLD tag on it somewhere, and that tag gave Pia as much pleasure as seeing the item when she opened her eyes in the morning. There was no love for those things, no emotional attachment. But the buying of them had been so sweet. The real thrill shivered from the getting, not the having.

Pia would tell Barret that, she decided. Someday when they could talk about all this. She suspected he would soon understand what that meant.

"Actually," Pia said, "I think I'm going to leave things here for now. Maybe you could call me when you get back?"

"Of course, sweet. I'll call you in a few weeks. Then we'll have all day for talking. Just like old times."

Dalphine leaned forward and pressed her cheek against Pia's, and they said good-bye.

When Dalphine came out of the store an hour later, pulling the gray suitcase on its little wheels, Pia was watching from a little table outside the coffee shop up the block. Dalphine hailed a cab, tucking the marbled gray pouch into her purse. After the cab disappeared, Pia walked down the block, drew the griffin key chain from her pocket, and unlocked the door. She walked through the silent maze of artifacts, collecting the yellow tags, snipping the strings with a pair of nail scissors, and dropping them in her pocket.

A few customers came and went. Pia sold an embroidered settee, a bent wood rocker, and a pane of stained glass. She served coffee to a woman who complimented her on the diamond and peridot baguette necklace and cuff she was wearing.

"They're not for sale by any chance, are they?" the customer asked.

"Everything's for sale," said Pia. "Except for these. They're mine."

Between visitors, Pia dusted the display shelves, allowing all the obvious questions to trickle through her mind. Was this their first meeting? Had they been seeing each other all along? No, when Barret found out about the credit cards, he still didn't know what Dalphine looked like. He thought she was white. Big-breasted. Pieces of the puzzle filtered through and fell into place, forming a story that was neither terrifying nor even terribly sad.

He must have brought the necklace and cuffs himself, instead of sending the courier. He must have come, thinking he would force her to take back certain items and refund some quantity of money to the credit cards. But of course, that wasn't going to happen. Because, without meaning to, Pia had set a trap for him, constructed a paper dragoness who, without having to say one word, had all his weapons at her feet.

Pia took the plane ticket from her bag, turned it over in her hands, and tore it in half. The stiff paper ripped with the satisfying feel of fairness. This was the least she owed him. The freedom to take whatever pleasures were his to take and to make whatever choices were his to make.

As late afternoon pulled shadows across the tall windows, Pia sat in the red side chair, waiting for rush hour, drinking coffee and humming a little. She thought carefully about the pros and cons of stepping into the traffic as opposed to stepping in front of a train. She could wait for the right moment. To make sure this time. To eliminate the possibility of waking up in the hospital again, because Pia didn't want to leave her sons some Madame Bovary–type mess to sort through.

At five-fifteen, she lowered the bamboo shade, set the lock on the door, and went out, carefully turning the pewter sign to CLOSED. It felt like turning a page that said THE END.

What better ending could there be? He would be up against the wall soon, Dalphine's body weight against him, the solid flat of a strange place at his back. Pia thought maybe she would feel it through some kind of emotional telegraph, but whether the connection was with her husband or with Dalphine, she couldn't say and didn't spend too much time wondering.

"Lady? You want the taxi?" the driver called in an accent that sounded like far pavilions.

He didn't understand why Pia was standing so close to the curb. He assumed she was hailing a cab.

"No, thank you."

She stepped off the edge, out of the corridor and into space. And she didn't even feel it, really—the cold and the pavement, the thrushing of the traffic. The top of her head felt open to the air. Partly because she was unaccustomed to being outdoors without a hat, but more so because of the light that seemed to pour down, reflecting off the glass and steel of the city, raining down in particles or waves or whatever it is in which light rains down.

Pia reached the other side, elated to be alive. All this time, it had never occurred to her that if she stepped off the curb into the traffic, all the people on the street would step off the edge with her, and the traffic would flow around them. She looked back at the pewter sign swinging from a chain that linked a day to a night to another day, another night. More of what she loved. More of what she hated. More of what she was afraid of, until the day love would win out, and she would no longer be afraid of anything.

Tilting her face up into the drizzle, Pia felt herself watered like a garden. She felt herself growing and being grown, loving and being loved, forgiving and being forgiven, mourning and being mourned. She smiled at the thought of Dalphine on the crowded concourse at the airport, searching and being searched.

Lily

(Day 1)

CA: Somebody call a Cab?

ME: (feeling this big moment and not quite knowing what to do)

CA: Time to go home, Tiger Lily.

ME: (just making sort of an awful, sobbing, yippish sound)

CA: (coming to me and nothing but air between us) Day Lily . . . Water Lily . . . Whisper Lily . . .

ME: (so crying I can't even walk until he takes me into his whole human comfort, hard beating heart, true man body, deep good kisses, full wingspan hug)

CA: Lily of the Valley . . . Lily of the Field . . .

Beth

This is a good day for Beth.

Lord, Himmelman & Schermer has just won an important bid. They will be designing a major annex, educational wing, and underground parking complex for the city's Grand Opera facility. There will be a reception to celebrate after tonight's performance of *Tristan and Isolde*, and at the party it will be announced that Regina, the firm's financial manager, is retiring, and Beth is to replace her. Sonny has rented a tux for the occasion. Beth is going to wear an olive lace dress she bought from the Spiegel catalog just before Christmas.

Looking through the mail, she finds a card from Pia—the kind that folds into itself, secured by a gold seal. Beth has always liked cards that fold like that. They make so much sense, the way they fit together. This one is made from an unusual sort of paper. Heavy and fibrous. It feels textured and warm in her hand. Embossed on the back is a lily-shaped logo with the words *Easter Women, Inc. Recycling & Resurrection* in a circle around it. Her heart expands a little when she opens the card and a soft gardenia scent breathes from it. Inside, a Bible passage flows between the folds in carefully made calligraphy.

I will make a way through the wilderness
and streams in the dry land.

Beth lays the card beside a pitcher of zinnias from her cutting garden. She centers the flowers on a fresh white tablecloth in the middle of a large square of sunlight that counterframes the kitchen table at the heart of her home.

This is a good day for Beth. Because every once in a while, it just is.

Acknowledgments

This book (not to mention my life and career) would not have been possible without the generosity and support of the following: Bookish women Jas Lonnquist, Dr. Wendy S. Harpham, Denine Rood, and Elizabeth Ostrow Smith, who read early versions of the manuscript and offered insightful feedback. Lara Owen, who corrected my appalling French grammar. The staff at the Harris County District Attorney's Office, who educated me on legal issues. My amazing agent, David Hale Smith, who has the mind of a capitalist, the soul of a Buddhist, and the energy of a roadrunner. All the production and PR folk at HarperCollins, who take a manuscript and make it act like a book. Jerusha, a thoroughly good cookie; Malachi, my own personal *Daily Show*; and Gary, my Rock of Gibraltar. I'm especially grateful to Marjorie Braman, my editor, mentor, and friend. In addition to the unyielding and perceptive tenderness with which she shepherded this story, she has provided me with direction, comfort, and advice—exactly what I needed, exactly when I needed it—including a lovely Japanese fan for use during hot flashes. Shalom, many thanks, and love to you all.

Insights,
Interviews
& More . . .

About the author

About the book

Read on

Meet Joni Rodgers

© 2006 by Tré Ridings

"I spent and misspent my youth on odd jobs—disc jockey, vagabond player, bull semen dispatcher, singing clown, and forest fire lookout."

I WAS BORN into a family of bluegrass musicians, the youngest of four sisters bookended by two brothers, and grew up on stage, opening for sequin-spangled Country Western stars of the 1960s and 1970s. When I was four, my sister Diana decided I should learn to read. She started me on her *Betty and Veronica* comic books, and soon I was consuming books like a wood chipper. My first professional writing gig was in junior high: torrid *True Confessions*–type short stories, tailor-made to feature the purchaser and her current crush, two wide-ruled pages for a dollar. I spent and misspent my youth on odd jobs—disc jockey, vagabond player, bull semen dispatcher, singing clown, and forest fire lookout—then settled down with my second First Great Love, Gary Rodgers. While our two children were tiny, I taught theater, did radio shows, and lent my mellifluous alto shrill to over 3,500 radio and television commercial voiceovers. Like many voracious readers, I dabbled at writing, perpetually "working on a novel."

The day before Thanksgiving 1994, I was diagnosed with non-Hodgkin's lymphoma and given slim odds of long-term survival. Chemo kept me isolated in a crappy little apartment in Houston, where we'd just relocated. Bald, wretched, and without an immune system, I was pretty much a sucking black hole of sorrow, panic, and need. My single purpose was survival, and my survival mechanism of choice was writing. Alone inside my head, I stopped dabbling and gave myself over to the story voices, insulating my heart and mind from the crushing reality of what I was going through. By the time my ponytail grew back, my first two novels had been published to good reviews.

In 2001 HarperCollins published my memoir, *Bald in the Land of Big Hair*, in which I was able to set the cancer experience in the context of life, reflecting on cancer's far-reaching spiritual and emotional impacts. The book was a healing journey for me and launched a speaking career that brought me full circle—back to the stage. Writing *Bald*, I'd learned to laugh at this thing that terrified me, so my shtick is often the "spoonful of sugar that makes the medicine go down" at oncology conferences and fundraisers.

During ten years of solid remission, I've written several books, a syndicated newspaper column, many magazine articles, a blog, an advice column, some bombastic op-ed rants, rafts of terribly witty e-mails, and piles of false starts that will hopefully never see the light of day. I also serve as a memoir guru (nice idiom for "ghostwriter"), helping clients—some famous, some merely fascinating—find their voices and tell their stories. But my ▶

> "I spend most days in voluntary isolation now, attempting to fold my inner clowns and forest fires into stories that mean something."

Meet Joni Rodgers ***(continued)***

first love is fiction, so I spend most days in voluntary isolation now, attempting to fold my inner clowns and forest fires into stories that mean something. My ambition is to transport, provoke, and entertain, but my mission is still survival. Of my hard-fighting little band of "chemo buds," I am the only one left alive—a fact that leaves me feeling hideously lucky, guilty, blessed, and beholden. All I can do in the face of it is hold tight to my purpose and *type faster.* Having shoplifted a second chance from the Five & Dime of Death, I feel compelled to live, which means (for me) to examine life, advocate love, purvey shalom, and speak gently but firmly about things that matter.

Readers and book clubs often ask about my kids, who are frozen in time in the pages of *Bald* as an unruly second grade boy and a precocious kindergarten girl. In real time—which has flown by much too quickly for my taste—they've evolved into bright, witty college students. Malachi is a film major and history buff with a hilariously cynical ear for political satire. Jerusha, who attended most of my chemo sessions with me and became fascinated by all things cellular biology, is a premed fashionista on track to become (what else?) an oncologist. They are both profoundly embarrassed by me, which I think is healthy. After twenty-three years, my spouse in shining armor has given up any hope of leading a normal life. He makes wine in the hall closet, fixes jet planes, and takes me spelunking in France. I am deeply loved and well published. I have two good dogs and six fertile pecan trees. My life is an embarrassment of riches.

"After twenty-three years, my spouse in shining armor has given up any hope of leading a normal life. He makes wine in the hall closet, fixes jet planes, and takes me spelunking in France."

The Empowering Story Behind *The Secret Sisters*

IN THE SPRING OF 1999 my husband went on a fishing trip to Cabo San Lucas, and I tucked an erotic novella in his suitcase just as a sexy little surprise. *Dalphine* was a diverting trifle about an unscrupulous antiques dealer who uses lurid little stories to seduce and bleed dry an emotionally fragile customer. And because I love it when things come full circle, it ended with a suitcase into which a wife tucks a sexy little surprise. It was never intended for publication, and I had no plans to expand it to a novel, but over the next several months, the characters stayed with me.

The story itself didn't quite have the legs for a book, but it did open the door for an engrossing backstory. My focus cross-faded from Dalphine, the con artist, to her client, Pia, and the necessary questions begged at the back of my head: What could have rendered this strong woman so fragile? Why would an intelligent person be so willingly taken in? I thought about the fear and fragility that overwhelmed me during and after chemo; how I had recoiled from the noise of life, retreating into a world of made-up stories. Ultimately, I had decided—yes, it was a conscious decision—to participate in the world again, to live in joy instead of terror, despite the uncertainty that shadowed my life. I didn't want to write about cancer, so I struck Pia an even more paralyzing blow—the death of her husband. Her story began to unfold in jarring bits and pieces, leading me into ▸

The Empowering Story Behind
***The Secret Sisters** (continued)*

some fascinating research on agoraphobia and panic disorders. I titled the new working manuscript *The Widowed Sister.*

A few months later, my sister Linda's husband suddenly sat up in bed and told her, "You are the dearest person in the world. I love you so much." Then he collapsed against her and died. He was forty-nine. Stunned and devastated, Linda descended into a valley of grief, and I guiltily set aside my manuscript. The plot device cut too close to the bone now. I didn't want Linda (or anyone else) to think I was writing about her, so I moved on to other projects, but again Pia stayed with me. I dreamed about her from time to time, sitting patiently on a chair in a waiting room.

One evening, at a book club discussion of my novel *Sugar Land*, someone asked, "Who's the least sympathetic character you can imagine as a writer?"

"Good question," I said. "Who's the least sympathetic character you can imagine as a reader?"

"A drunk driver," said someone with an obvious backstory of her own.

"A drunk driver who *kills* someone," said someone else.

"A drunk driver who kills a *child*," was the final consensus.

We went on to wine, cheesecake, and conversation (as the best book club discussions do), but the bad seed was planted. This irredeemable character took root, charging me with the task of her redemption. As I drove home from the meeting, Pia's cussing smart-ass sister, Lily, stumbled onto the scene, causing the destruction of her and

> "My sister Linda's husband suddenly sat up in bed and told her, 'You are the dearest person in the world. I love you so much.' Then he collapsed against her and died. He was forty-nine."

Pia's family by causing the death of their niece, Easter. And the moment I felt Easter die, my mothering heart went out to Easter's mother. Beth emerged, closely guarded, unwilling to say much, but refusing to budge or be ignored.

Over the next year or so, I was haunted by Pia and her sisters. They appeared in my dreams, acting out scenes and dialogue, which I dutifully recorded upon waking and kept in a folder under a new title, *The Prodigal Wife.* I didn't have the first clue what this story meant or what the people in it were trying to tell me, but I thought if I waited and listened and remained open to their voices, I would find out.

"I didn't have the first clue what this story meant or what the people in it were trying to tell me, but I thought if I waited and listened and remained open to their voices, I would find out."

September 11, 2001, invaded the story, as it had to invade any story set during that time, beginning with the rewriting of any scene taking place in an airport. The mechanics of travel were different now on a more than superficial level. In those reeling months that came in the wake of the terrorist attacks, I watched the panicked people around me with a *through the looking glass* sort of curiosity. Afraid to get on airplanes or put off by intrusive security procedures, many public speakers baled on scheduled events, leaving conference planners stranded. The Dalphine in me saw an excellent business opportunity. My book *Bald in the Land of Big Hair* had been released earlier that year, and I was eager to get out and talk about it. I had my agent put out the word that I was willing go anywhere to fill in for anyone, no matter how short the notice, and I was rapidly booked solid through 2002.

Because my husband works in the airline industry, we knew that much of the ▸

The Empowering Story Behind
The Secret Sisters ***(continued)***

heightened security was theater. There were those who stood to benefit from keeping people fearful, and they operated brilliantly. I had not the slightest qualms about traveling to those engagements—or anywhere else. (To the horror of our family and friends, Gary and I took our kids to Morocco on New Year's Eve 2002, despite FBI warnings about travel to that country.) Cancer had long ago acquainted me with the choice that so many now were facing: abide in fear or abide in joy. I (with the help of an excellent shrink) had chosen joy. He helped me see that my posttraumatic depression was about more than the cancer that invaded and terrorized me, and I could rise above it only if I stopped seeing myself as a victim.

"Accountability doesn't mean you blame yourself," he said, "but it would be to your detriment to pretend that you didn't set the stage for both your health problems and your unhappiness."

I was empowered, not shamed, by that accountability. It opened my eyes and spurred me to change my life in positive ways. Perhaps with strong, wise leadership, we would have done the same thing as a nation. Face our fear, hold ourselves accountable for our own sins, and rise above. Instead, we were told that the best thing we could do in response to the terrorist attacks was "go shopping." Not a terribly difficult mandate to follow. Consumption is momentarily comforting. Anyone who's ever eaten a quart of ice cream in the wake of a bad breakup knows that. Fragile, fearful, desperate to be distracted, willingly misled, *We the People* allowed our national resources (including our integrity

"To the horror of our family and friends, Gary and I took our kids to Morocco on New Years Eve 2002, despite FBI warnings about travel to that country."

and the good will of the world) to be squandered while oppressive financial and moral debts were incurred. We pretended we could shut out the world with duct tape and plastic, distracting ourselves with media that pandered to our prurient side. I saw Pia's story play out before me in macrocosm and finally understood its meaning.

The Secret Sisters is a parable about how easily manipulated we are when we embrace fear as a lifestyle. It's about the soothing art of seduction, the blissful but dangerous state of denial, and the emotional prisons we construct for ourselves—isolating and unforgiving as an ironclad cell. But Pia and her sisters also tell a story of empowerment, accountability, and the transformations that take place when tragedy is cross-pollinated by grace. I believe in God and in an inner core of goodness and strength—the Buddha nature—in all people. I believe we can find the courage to open our eyes, step off the curb, and cross over to our better selves. What we're going through now as a nation is what any individual goes through when dealt a stunning blow—the death of a loved one, the death of a dream, the loss of the foundation of one's security. Survival is a painful but possible process. Grief and cleansing anger are necessary steps in that terrible journey.

Watching my sister reclaim her new self and rebuild her new life has been affirming, even *thrilling*, for me and everyone else who knows her. Having been a home-schooling mother of four, she put her vast knowledge of children's literature to work at an independent bookstore in order to pay her way through ▸

“What we're going through now as a nation is what any individual goes through when dealt a stunning blow.”

The Empowering Story Behind
The Secret Sisters ***(continued)***

nursing school. She graduated at age fifty-one and volunteered her newfound strength and skill at a hospital in AIDS-stricken Swaziland. She made the conscious decision to live beyond her personal tragedy and became the lioness she might never have been without that trial by fire.

The overarching theme of this novel is not fear or grief. It's resurrection.

The title *The Secret Sisters* comes from the Easter account in the Gospel of Luke. The second morning after Jesus was crucified, the Secret Sisters—Mary, Joanna, and Magdalene—went to his tomb, stricken, terrified, and bereft. There they were confronted by angels, who asked them a question that still resonates: "Why do you seek the living among the dead?"

We are the living, dear reader, and the past is dead. Fear, denial, guilt, ancient dogmas, glorified tragedies, and antiquated hate will imprison us there, until we make the conscious decision to embrace joy and rise again.

Meet My Sisters

LINDA IS THE CRUSADER, Diana the adventurer, Jas the procedural genius. My sisters are the authors of me in more ways than they will ever know. When I was little, I toddled after them, longing to be included in the secret, fabulous lives I was convinced they must live while I was sleeping, and that hasn't really changed. Their style, grace, wit, and creative genius with everything from computers to Campbell's Cream of Mushroom soup still intimidates and inspires me. The books they've shared with me have influenced me as both a reader and a writer, so I wanted to share a few of their favorites.

A problem solver by nature, Linda loves a good mystery. She cut her teeth on Trixie Belden books and graduated to Agatha Christie. A strongly conservative Christian, she says the Bible is the book that has most influenced her, of course, specifically the writings of Paul. She loves the boldness of his stories and identifies with his driven nature. Having home-schooled her four children and worked in a children's bookstore for several years, Linda has an encyclopedic knowledge of children's lit. Her current favorite: *When Pigs Fly* by Valerie Coulman, illustrated by Roge Girard. "It's about a cow named Ralph, who wants a bike. When everyone tells him cows don't ride bikes, he says, 'Well, not yet.' His father tells him that he can ride a bike 'when pigs fly.' So Ralph figures out how to make that happen."

I asked Linda if any one book on grieving or loss that had been especially helpful to her after the death of her husband, and she said ▸

“My sisters are the authors of me in more ways than they will ever know.”

she would recommend *Will I Ever Be Whole Again?: Living Through the Death of Someone You Love* by Sandra Aldrich. "It's a spiritual yet extremely practical guide to widowhood that tells you what you need to know instead of trying to tell you how to feel." A book I loved and recommended to Linda is *The Year of Magical Thinking* by Joan Didion, which is not about widowhood so much as it is about the stories we tell ourselves in the falling silence of loss.

Diana's taste in books always ran to the classics. She particularly loves Charlotte Brontë's *Jane Eyre* for its "marvelous dialogue and beautifully articulated sentiments with a feminist story line" and *The Good Earth* by Pearl S. Buck, because "there are foreign countries, and then there are *really* foreign countries. Buck's stories of China open this country up to westerners." Having spent three transformative years in the Peace Corps in Gabon, Diana says *The Poisonwood Bible* by Barbara Kingsolver is "the best depiction of Africa I've ever seen. Usually people think of sweeping vistas and loping, exotic animals. This book talks about the smell of rotting wood, the trees fighting for the sun, and the real price of the diamonds and cotton people wear so casually."

"Having spent three transformative years in the Peace Corps in Gabon, Diana says *The Poisonwood Bible* by Barbara Kingsolver is 'the best depiction of Africa I've ever seen.'"

I asked Diana, "What's your favorite book about sisters?" and she surprised me by saying, "*Gone with the Wind* by Margaret Mitchell. It's really about Scarlet's relationship with her sister-in-law, Melanie. Then there's the animosity between her and Ashley's sister, India. And Scarlet even marries her own sister's beau. You really don't get the fullness of that from the movie. You have to read the book." If you asked her about the best book I've sent her way recently, she would say *The Time Traveler's Wife* by Audrey Niffenegger. "This book creates its own reality—like any good science fiction—and then weaves a wonderful story into it." Or she might mention *The Remains of the Day* by Kazuo Ishiguro, which takes you inside the orderly world of an English butler and examines the compelling question: What constitutes a wasted life?

Since Jas started writing seriously a few years before I did, she blazed a trail for me and provided me with some valuable resources, including my first copy of that essential sledgehammer in any writer's tool shed: *Writer's Market*, a comprehensive listing of American book and magazine publishers, along with helpful articles on breaking into print. "Don't be cheap," she told me. "Buy a new one every year." And I repeat that advice to every aspiring writer I meet. Jas also turned me on to *Writing Down the Bones* by Natalie Goldberg ("Handwriting is more connected to the movement of the heart. Yet, when I tell stories, I go straight to the typewriter") and Anne Lamott's *Bird by Bird: Some Instructions on Writing and Life* ("We are a species that needs and wants to understand who we are. Sheep lice do not seem to share this longing, which is one reason they write so very little"). Both authors are passionate about the art of writing, diligent about the craft, and savvy about the business. The same can be said about my sister.

"Jas . . . provided me with . . . my first copy of that essential sledgehammer in any writer's tool shed: *Writer's Market* . . . 'Don't be cheap,' she told me. 'Buy a new one every year.'"

Ten Good Books About Sisters (and "Sisters Under the Skin")

- *Little House on the Prairie* and others in the series by Laura Ingalls Wilder
- *Little Women* by Louisa May Alcott
- *The Color Purple* by Alice Walker
- *One Heart* by Jane McCafferty
- *The Joy Luck* Club by Amy Tan
- *Fried Green Tomatoes at the Whistle Stop Café* by Fannie Flagg
- *What We Keep* by Elizabeth Berg
- *Till We Have Faces* by C. S. Lewis
- *My Sister's Keeper* by Jodi Picoult
- *The Virgin Suicides* by Jeffrey Eugenides

Learn More About Panic Disorders

- *An End to Panic: Breakthrough Techniques for Overcoming Panic Disorder* by Elke Zuercher-White (New Harbinger Publications, 1998)
- *The Anxiety and Phobia Workbook* by Edmund J. Bourne (New Harbinger Publications, 4th edition 2005)
- *An Unquiet Mind: A Memoir of Moods and Madness* by Kay Redfield Jamison (Vintage, 1997)
- National Institute of Mental Health (www.nimh.nih.gov)
- National Center for Post-Traumatic Stress Disorder (www.ncptsd.va.gov)
- American Psychiatric Association (www.psych.org)
- National Alliance on Mental Illness (www.nami.org)
- Society for Women's Health Research (www.womenshealthresearch.org)

Have You Read?
More by Joni Rodgers

BALD IN THE LAND OF BIG HAIR

More than a survivor's saga, the story of Joni's chemotherapy and recovery from non-Hodgkin's lymphoma is an affecting tale of self-discovery and unremitting perseverance that will appeal to all readers.

While there's nothing funny about having cancer, Rodgers proves there's plenty funny about dealing with it. Through her hilarious and poignant takes on matters such as life, death, sex, parenting, body image, humiliation, God, and doctors, her touching story delivers a powerful message of hope, humor, and inspiration. Rodgers brings the gifts of wisdom and compassion to her work, and shows us the hidden rewards of surviving life's difficulties.

Like Betty Rollin's huge bestseller *First, You Cry*, *Bald in the Land of Big Hair* is ultimately a moving celebration of the true meaning of human triumph and courage, the importance of community, and the imperative of living every day with joy.

"Impressive. . . . She describes in ways others may find helpful how cancer has affected her sexuality, her faith, [and] her family."
—Janet Maslin, *New York Times*

"A mix of Molly Ivins's blowsy wit and Anna Quindlen's suburban logic, [*Bald in the Land of Big Hair*] manages [a] literary feat."
—*Entertainment Weekly*